OUR SUMMER

ASHLEY LAUREN

Cover Design by Graicee Gibby / By Studio June

First Edition September 2025

Paperback ISBN: 979-8-9991958-0-7
Hardcover ISBN: 979-8-9991958-1-4
Ebook ISBN: 979-8-9991958-2-1

Library of Congress Control Number: 2025942091

To anyone who has the
audacity to believe they can.

You will.

CHAPTER ONE

I'M JET LAGGED FROM THE PLANE RIDE, MY DAD IS tapping his fingers on the steering wheel to the beat of the music, and my phone won't stop buzzing with texts from people back in Colorado. It's overwhelming, and though a nap *should* be my first priority after barely sleeping last night, I know there's a beach nearby. I've never been to the beach, and it's the only part of this dilemma I'm excited about. It may not cure my heartache, but it sure as hell won't make it worse.

My phone lights up with another text. Anger courses through my veins like molten lava, but it doesn't surprise me. It was just last night that I decided to spend the summer on the opposite side of the country with my dad, whom I haven't spoken to in four years. Less than twenty four hours later, I'm in the passenger seat of the same beat-up black Honda Pilot I grew up riding around in, driving toward what will either be the best summer ever or my worst decision yet.

Ignoring the notifications, I roll the car window down and get the first whiff of the ocean. I think I might be in love from the smell alone. Salty sea breeze hits my face and blows blonde strands of my hair all over, and for the first time in my life, I don't have to pretend to be the girl in the movie who got her heart broken.

My dad turns the radio up so we can hear the music over the wind. His love for classic rock still hasn't changed. "Highway to Hell" by AC/DC is playing, and I don't fight the small upturn of my lips at the irony. Maybe it's a sign telling me this summer will be a disaster after all.

We pass a wooden sign welcoming us to New Haven, South Carolina, and I wonder for the billionth time if coming here for the summer was the right choice. It was Deadbeat Dad over Scumbag Ex-Boyfriend, so it's not like my options were that great to begin with. I just hope I chose the lesser of two evils.

New Haven is a small tourist town on the beach, and it's exactly what I expected it to be. "Downtown" is a couple blocks of old, colorful buildings—a town hall, a fire station, a church, and other essential businesses. There's also a variety of restaurants serving mostly seafood and department-store-like tourist traps with everything a family could possibly need for the beach. I get a glimpse of the boardwalk once we're out of downtown, a row of shops with a million windows looking out on the water, and then my dad pulls into the neighborhood right down the road from all of it.

I don't expect him to pull onto a cement driveway leading to a small two-story house, the beach right out the backyard. The faded turquoise siding is one of the many colors lining the neighborhood streets, and I struggle to get past the shock of *this* being my dad's house. I imagined a trailer dumpyard and me sleeping on the dirty sofa for the summer, so this place is a major upgrade.

The white garage door rolls open at the push of a button, and he pulls the Honda into the left stall. The back walls are lined with shelves holding construction tools. The open right side of the garage has a large tool bench and random pieces of furniture littered around in a variety of states. He must have acquired a new hobby of refurbishing after he left Colorado.

The music cuts off as he takes the keys out of the ignition. I head around to the trunk to grab my suitcase and backpack, but my dad beats me to it.

"I can get it," I snap. I don't want his help. It's bad enough his place is the only option I have to get out of Colorado for the summer, and therefore the only reason I made any contact with him in the first place.

"I know," he responds, but he doesn't hand my bags over. He swings my backpack over a shoulder, pulls the handle of the suitcase out, and rolls it along behind him toward the door. I huff out a breath, cross my arms across my chest, and follow him.

There are two steps up to the door. My dad skips the first one with ease. I repeat his actions, forgetting until now it's a trait I picked up from him. I'm always taking the stairs two at a time to Andy and I's apartment and, more often than not, moving too fast to stop myself from slipping at least once.

Once inside, there's a blur of black and brown in my face before I can even take my shoes off.

It's a dog.

A German Shepard, to be exact.

My dad has a dog.

I begged for a dog for years, and he always told me no.

Of *course* he got one after he left.

There's a red collar around his or her neck. I search for the attached tag so I don't have to ask him what the name is.

Groot.

A quick check under the belly confirms Groot is a he.

His eager kisses and wagging tail distract me for a moment. I scratch between his ears, and his tail wags faster. I'm already in love with him, but an equally strong wave of loneliness washes over me. Groot is the only friend I have now.

I stand up and shake off the realization, taking note of the house. Before my dad up and left Denver, he was leaving one mess after another in our apartment. Whether it was takeout containers stacked on the kitchen counter, a pile of overdue bills on the coffee table, or a collection of empty bottles on his night stand, he had no idea what clean meant.

So, needless to say, I don't expect the cleanliness. The house is an open concept; the living room takes up the front half of the house, and the kitchen takes up the back half. Almost all of the walls are light blue with the exception of the dark blue behind the white kitchen cabinets. The floors are all a light hardwood, and the mix-and-match furniture looks like my dad's redone it all himself.

I feel more at home than I want to. Than I should. Maybe it's the family pictures of Andy and I when we were younger hanging on the walls, an AA 1 Year Sober medallion hanging next to one of them, or the fucking sunflowers in a vase on the kitchen table.

Or maybe it's the fact that my dad is standing beside me and no matter how much I've said I hate him in the last four years, I've missed him more than I could ever hate him.

I still hate him, though.

"Where's my room?" I ask. The sound of waves hitting the shore has been in the distance since I stepped out of the car, rushing through the open windows, and I'm itching to find the way to the beach. To finally see it in person.

"Up the stairs," he says, pointing straight ahead. There's disappointment in his voice, but I ignore it. He might have been expecting a forgive and forget, but he won't get one. That's not what I came here for.

I wordlessly take my bags from my dad. The ascent to my room is awkward, the bottom of my suitcase hitting the edge of each step. Groot follows me up, his toenails clicking on the wood.

At the top, there's a small landing with two doors. I peek my head in the first and find a nautical-themed bathroom. It has the same light blue walls and wood flooring as downstairs, and a navy blue shower curtain with little white anchors hangs over the bathtub. I didn't think my dad could design an *anything*-themed bathroom.

The second door leads to my new room, and I don't hesitate to close the door behind me and Groot. I've never had hardwood floors in my bedroom, but it's a nice change to the old, stained carpet from the apartment. The walls are light pink, a small comfort— I've loved the color since the day I came out of the womb.

I ignore the fact that my dad remembers this about me.

A giant window takes up the backside of the room, opaque white curtains hanging down on either side, and a smaller window with matching curtains sits above the bed. It looks like most of the furniture has been refurbished; the bed frame, nightstands, dresser, and desk are all white, but the slight variation in styles gives it away.

There's no way my dad put this room together in the time since I texted him last night asking for a ride from the airport. This room has been waiting like this for a while, bare of decorations except for a small beige lamp with a wicker-like base on the nightstand and a white mirror hanging next to the closet.

This room has been waiting for me, and I once again feel more at home than I want to.

Not that *home* feels like home anymore. The only person left there is Andy, but even my big brother isn't enough to cure the loneliness creeping through me again. Groot jumps onto the bed, circles around himself on the white and beige patchwork quilt, and plops down.

I lift my luggage onto the bed next to Groot and turn to the giant window across from my bed, the ocean visible in the distance. Then I notice the white railing. A closer look confirms the giant window is actually a set of double doors, and I forget about unpacking.

The balcony juts out over a back patio, and the view I have of the ocean is unbeatable. The sound of crashing waves is clearest from up here, and I *need* to feel the sand between my toes.

Back inside, I unzip my suitcase and throw stuff on the bed until I find what I'm looking for. My favorite red swimsuit looks good against my pale skin, and it'll look even better when I'm tan. Plus, narcissistic tendencies aside, looking this good makes the pit of heartbreak and loneliness feel a little less deep.

I tie my hair up in a messy bun, pull on a white sundress, and dig some cheap flip flops out from the bottom of my suitcase. Armed with my phone, sunglasses, and the Airpods gifted to me by The Scumbag for my last birthday, I leave the safety of my room. In the bathroom cabinet, I find a yellow and white striped beach towel.

At the top of the staircase, I pause when I hear male voices. In addition to my dad, there's one, maybe two others. Groot is on my tail as I slowly descend the stairs, not wanting to make a commotion in front of the company. I'll just let my dad know I'm going to the beach and slip out the back door. Groot doesn't make a quiet descent possible, though, and he bolts down the stairs, skidding across the wood at the bottom.

I still approach quietly, a minimal "hello" and "goodbye" still possible. But when I turn the corner to the kitchen, I meet the most gorgeous eyes I've ever seen, and I freeze.

CHAPTER TWO

My gaze snaps away from the beautiful stranger to my dad, a weak attempt to make myself look less like a creep for staring. "Oh, perfect timing," my dad says, clearly not realizing my predicament. "This is Aliyah. Aliyah, this is Dave King and his son, Easton. They live next door. Dave works with me at the construction firm."

So the gorgeous specimen has a name. *Easton*. It suits him.

I look at Dave first, then Easton. The two of them have almost identical features. Dirty blonde hair, though Dave's is peppered with gray. Sharp jawline. Slender nose. Full lips. The only difference is their eyes. Dave's are a deep green, and Easton's are the darkest eyes I've ever seen. He's wearing black swim trunks and a white T-shirt with a pink breast cancer awareness sign on the upper right side. The shirt looks worn and a little too small, like he outgrew it years ago but refuses to get rid of it.

"Hi," I say, forcing what I hope is a small smile on my face.

Easton stares at me with no concern as to whether I realize he's staring or not, like he's trying to peer into my soul. My cheeks heat up under the intensity of his gaze, and I turn my own gaze back to my dad. I still feel a set of dark eyes not leaving me as I say, "I'm going to the beach."

He nods, "Do you know how to get there?"

I shrug, walking around the three men towards the back door. "There's gotta be a path or something, right?"

Before he has a chance to answer, Easton says, "I can show her, Mr. Redding. I was about to head down there anyway."

You've got to be kidding me.

"Perfect. Is that okay with you, Aliyah?"

It's not like I'm going to say no. I'm not a *total* bitch.

Usually.

"Yeah," I force out through gritted teeth. The three of them either don't hear it or pretend not to.

"Follow me," Easton says. He grabs a dirty white baseball cap from the kitchen counter and throws it on backwards, his dirty blonde locks barely peeking out around the edges. I didn't know I was a sucker for backwards caps until this moment.

I mutter goodbye to my dad and Dave and follow Easton out to the back patio.

We set off on the worn grassy path. Easton walks with a certain pep in his step, like a little kid going to the beach on the first day of vacation instead of a teenager who has probably lived here his whole life. It's not long at all before my hopes for a silent walk are cut short. "So, what brings you to New Haven, Aliyah Redding?" he asks, and I almost groan, despite my name sounding like my favorite song coming from his lips.

He's one of *those* boys. A small town boy with an ego too big for this town, strutting around like he owns the place and not realizing the problems other people have going on in their lives. His upbeat tone makes it seem like he's assuming I've got nothing better to do this summer than hang out at the beach. *Joke's on you, buddy.*

"I wanted to be at the beach this summer."

"Well, of course. Who wouldn't?" he says, and I think the

conversation's over. He pauses for only a couple seconds before asking, "But what's the *real* reason?"

And maybe I had him all wrong. *Maybe he really was looking into my soul back in the kitchen.* A small town boy who thinks with his ego would believe me at face value. I don't know how Easton saw through my bullshit, but it catches me off guard.

It's why I take a deep breath and say, "My boyfriend of three years cheated on me over spring break when he was in Mexico with one of my friends. Everyone knew and no one told me." Speaking the words into existence makes it hard to swallow as I fight back tears. Now that I've said it aloud, there's no pretending it didn't happen.

"Oh," Easton mumbles, his dark eyes widening.

"Not what you were expecting?" I snap, defaulting to anger to hide the need to cry. I'm being cruel, but it's better than the alternative. I've always burned hot, and I'm too heartbroken to care about controlling it right now.

"I was expecting something more to do with your dad, I guess," Easton shrugs, and I go quiet. I don't know how much he knows about the situation with my dad, but it's not a can of worms I'm opening with him.

Ex-boyfriend? Sure.

Daddy issues? Not a chance.

The path opens up to sand, and there are people everywhere. Tanning, building sandcastles, splashing in the water. I see a group of teenagers throwing a football around. They resemble something I was once a part of, and I ache to have it all back. For everything to go back to the way it used to be so I don't have to deal with this stupid, incurable loneliness.

It's not going to happen, though, so there's no point in wishing for it. So, I wave and start walking away in the opposite direction.

"Wait," Easton says, and I look over my shoulder. "Do you

want to come hang out with us?" he asks, gesturing to the group of teenagers. I pretend to contemplate it.

"I'll pass. Maybe next time," I say, with no intent for there to be a next time. I walk away for real this time and reach a patch of open sand. Three girls around my age sit not far from me, giggling at whatever they're looking at on their phones. I turn away from them as I lay down on my towel.

My phone buzzes again. With a sigh, I finally look at it. I have twenty two new messages since I last looked in the car. All of them are from friends wondering where the hell I am and why I decided to up and leave for the summer. Over half of the texts are from my best friend, Ellie.

Ex-best friend. She got demoted real fast for knowing what happened and not saying a word to me about it.

The only reason people even know I left is because of the farewell picture I posted at the airport on my Instagram story with a petty *Have fun in Colorado, bitches*. Not my most mature move, but nothing will ever be worse than what they did to me. They should be grateful I didn't egg all their houses or key all their cars.

Over a hundred messages have added up since I posted this morning, but I don't bother reading any of them. Instead, I delete all of the private threads and group chats with people I've known since kindergarten. There are glimpses of "sorry" and "WTF" and "what happened?", but it does nothing to cure the betrayal simmering under the surface. The betrayal that starts boiling at the audacity some of them have.

Asking me what happened like they didn't all have a front row seat to the show? *Oh, please.* Save the sympathetic bullshit for someone who will actually fall for it.

I take the extra step and block all but one of the numbers. My finger hovers on the last person, a magnet at odds with the same pole, but I can't bring myself to do it.

When the messages are gone, the rage hardly contained, I'm only left with two from Andy. The first one is from this morning after he dropped me off at the airport, and the second asks if I landed safely. I call him instead of responding, needing a sense of familiarity. He picks up on the first ring.

"I take it you landed safely?" he asks in lieu of a greeting.

"I'm still alive, so it must have landed safely."

"So the flight was good?"

"Again—I made it, didn't I?"

"Everything still intact?" I roll my eyes at his double and triple checking. He's always been the over protective brother, but I can't blame him with the life we've had.

"I think so."

"I already miss you, Ali. The apartment is empty without you."

"Yeah, you don't have enough attitude to fill the space," I say, and it makes us both laugh. Hearing his voice brings me immediate relief, all my muscles releasing pent up tension. "I miss you too."

"How's New Haven?"

Silence follows, filled by the unasked question: *And dad?* I stare out at the sea, the vastness of it something I wish I could escape in. No heartbreak, no daddy issues, no betrayal.

"Dad's been good so far. He has a nice place. Right on the beach. Even has a dog."

"That's good. That's really good."

"Yeah. I have my own room on the second floor. The balcony faces the ocean."

"How's the ocean?"

"I already love it."

More silence. For as long as I can remember, there has never been an awkward silence between Andy and I. Until now. It's a moment of weakness, and I'm opening my mouth to spill everything when he speaks again.

"Ali?"

"Yeah?" I whisper. I start picking at a frayed yellow thread on my towel.

"What really happened?"

My moment of weakness is over no matter how much I want to tell Andy. I wanted to tell him last night when screenshots of conversations I was *not* supposed to see were posted on TikTok by none other than the girl Nate cheated on me with so she could join in on a trend. I kept my tears to myself for both of our sakes. He's my big brother, and this will hurt him just as much as it's hurting me. Plus, it's humiliating.

"Andy," I say, my voice cracking. A few moments pass, and he lets out the breath he was holding.

"Nate came by today."

I panic, the simmer of rage heating up to a boil once more. Did Nate already tell him? "Why?" I gasp, my heart rate speeding up as the anger takes control. That son of a bitch and the audacity to—

"He was wondering where you were. He said you haven't responded to him since last night. That you haven't responded to anyone."

My forehead lands on the beach towel, relief coursing through me. I exhale, closing my eyes and wishing this would all go away.

"Did something happen with you and Nate? I thought you guys were doing great."

"I thought we were, too," I whisper. Tears threaten to break past my defenses, the cold exterior I've mastered wavering for the first time in its existence. I've tried to pretend this situation isn't affecting me, but who am I kidding? I lost my boyfriend and all my friends because of a fucking one night stand in Mexico.

I'd like to think if I was able to afford to go on the trip, this wouldn't have happened. If I had been in Mexico with everyone else, Nate wouldn't have even thought about kissing, much less sleeping with, another girl. The two of us would have enjoyed our spring break with our friends, just as in love as ever.

But it happened, and if it didn't happen then, it was bound to happen eventually.

Once a cheater, always a cheater.

"Aliyah," Andy murmurs.

"I don't want to talk about it," I snap at Andy, the words coming out harsher than I mean them to.

He sighs in frustration, but it doesn't change my mind.

Eventually, he says, "It's going to be weird not having you around this summer. I don't know what I'm going to do with the apartment all to myself. Who's going to play Monopoly with me?"

"You can finally bring your secret girlfriend home," I tease, bringing up one of our favorite inside jokes to lighten the mood. When our dad walked out on us, Andy had no choice but to up his hours to full time at the restaurant he bartends and serves at. I make fun of him and say he's always out with his secret girlfriend when he gets home from late shifts or doubles.

"Maybe I will," Andy chuckles. "I start work in twenty, so I've gotta go. I'll call you tomorrow, okay?"

"Have fun. Make lots of money," I grin.

"You know I will. And Ali?" His voice turns serious.

"Yeah?"

"Don't be too hard on Dad."

CHAPTER THREE

MY SCANDINAVIAN BLOOD IS NOT MADE TO SIT IN THE sun for extended periods of time. Three hours and a sunburned back later, I gather my things in my arms and head back to my dad's house. I don't bother putting my flip flops on, letting them dangle from my hand instead.

Inside, the air conditioning feels amazing against my sweaty and sunburned skin. I'll need to find a store around here within walking distance I can get some aloe from. The boardwalk is a short walk away, so maybe I'll venture over there after I have dinner.

My dad is reading a book in the living room, and Groot is laying down at his feet. They both look up when I step inside and close the door. I only nod at him before turning away so he won't try and start a conversation with me. He would be stupid to try, anyway, since I still have my Airpods in. I drop my sandy flip flops in the corner where there's already a pair of his sandals, and I head around the kitchen corner to the hallway.

I take the stairs two at a time, not shocked at all as I trip and barely make the last step, grasping the railing for support. I close the door to my bedroom and drop the rest of my belongings onto the bed, finally pausing the breakup playlist I was listening to. My phone is battling for its life at two percent, so I dig through my backpack and pull out my charger. After plugging it in, I fall back onto the pillows, careful not to disturb my roasted back. The discomfort is inevitable, and I grimace.

The pillows are firm, like they're fresh out of the package and unused. In fact, the entire bed feels like it hasn't been broken in, another reminder this room was set up for me without ever knowing if I would be here to use it. The smallest, teensiest bit of gratitude leaks into the place in my mind reserved for my dad. It's full of nothing but negative emotions, but that little bit of gratitude makes room for itself no matter how hard I try to push it away.

My stomach grumbles, and I debate my options. Do I leave to get my aloe and find somewhere to eat, or do I face being in close proximity to my dad while I make myself something to eat in the kitchen? I don't even know what kind of food he has. What if the only options are beer and microwave meals? It wouldn't be the first time.

I check the status of my bank account, and when I see the total balance of nine dollars and eight cents, my hope of eating out goes down the drain. I blew most of my money on the last minute plane ticket, which was *not* cheap, and I need to have some money for my aloe. And for the rest of the summer.

Like nine dollars and eight cents will get me very far. *Fuck*. I'm going to need to find a job, and soon.

With finding something to eat out of the question, I'll have to suck it up and be around my dad. Hopefully he has a box of mac and cheese or a frozen pizza I can whip up.

I pull myself off my bed, wishing I could take my phone to listen to music but knowing it will die immediately. There's no point. I open my door and see Groot sitting patiently in front of it, waiting for me to let him in. "You gotta let me know you're out here, dude. Next time paw the door or bark or something, 'kay?" I scratch his head and smile as he follows me downstairs. He might be the only good thing about my summer.

My dad is still in the living room reading his book. I head straight for the kitchen, realizing I have no idea where anything is. I could open cabinets until I find an acceptable dinner, which would probably have him asking if I need any help, or I can save myself some time and just ask.

If only there was an option where I didn't need to talk to him at all.

The stubborn independence wins. I turn to the living room and ask, "What kind of food do you have?"

My dad turns to me so fast with raised eyebrows and a hopeful smile, I almost feel bad I'm doing my best to talk to him as little as possible.

Almost.

"Are you getting hungry?" he asks, like I'm seven years old again and he's confirming whether he should start making dinner for me or not.

I nod, deciding not to tell him I haven't eaten anything since last night. The thought of eating anything until now, even the little bag of pretzels the flight attendant gave me on the plane, made me want to puke.

"I was thinking we could order pizza. Do you still like pizza?"

The words, *It's pizza. Of course I still like it* are on the tip of my tongue. I don't say them, though. Just bob my head again.

"Toppings?" my dad asks, setting his book on the coffee table and lifting himself from the couch to join me in the kitchen. He sits down at the table and pulls his phone out of his pocket, waiting for me to answer. I want to escape to my room until the pizza gets here, but I remember Andy's words from earlier: *Don't be too hard on Dad.*

I sigh in defeat and sit down across from him. I ease against the back of the chair to avoid irritating the skin on my back. "Anything's fine," I mutter. He nods, holding up his phone as he waits for the pizza place to answer.

"Hi, yes, can I please get a large pizza with extra cheese, pepperoni, sausage, peppers, and black olives?"

I think it's shock I'm feeling that my dad remembers my favorite pizza combo. All along I thought he was too hazed out and drunk whenever we got pizza to know, much less remember, my favorite, but here he is rattling the order off without hesitation. The gratitude for him grows.

This gratitude thing needs to stop. I didn't come to New Haven for the summer to make amends with my dad. I came to get away from my douchebag ex-boyfriend and my shady-ass lying group of friends. There's no room in that equation for my dad.

But Andy told me not to be too hard on him, and I already opened the door by sitting down. I can't turn around and slam that door in his face.

When he hangs up, he looks hesitant to say anything to me, his blue eyes looking back and forth between me and the table. It's beyond an awkward silence, and I find myself scrounging for something to say to break it.

"Is there a store on the boardwalk I can get aloe from?" I ask.

The tension in my dad's face relaxes, and he nods, settling his gaze on me. "You can probably find it at any of them. Were you going to head over there?"

"Yeah, my back is a little burnt." I almost snort at my own words. *A little burnt, my ass.*

"Feel free to take the bike from the garage if you want."

"I'm okay with walking," I say, forcing a smile. It's tight and feels weird on my face. Groot sets his head in my lap. "I can take Groot with me."

My dad nods, and another silence falls over us. I scratch Groot's head for something to do with my hands.

"I work until four tomorrow, so I won't be around for most of the day," he says. I nod. I know he's been working at a construction firm since he got back on his feet, and unless I'm interested in the projects they're working on (which I'm not), there's not much I can say.

He sets his gaze out the back door, and it hits me how different the man sitting in front of me is from the one who left Andy and I four years ago. His skin is tan from working outside so much, a stark contrast from the paleness I remember. His graying auburn hair is cropped short, the greasy strings that used to hang around his face no more. And his beer belly is long gone, replaced by a flat stomach. I don't care to know if my dad has abs or not because that's disgusting to even think about, but there's no denying his construction job has been a blessing for him in more ways than one. He's cleaned up his looks, and he must have cleaned up his act if he's managed to keep his job.

Despite all of this, nothing changes for me. He walked out on Andy and I when we needed him most, and I'll be damned if I ever forget what that did to us.

The minimal conversation is painful until the pizza arrives twenty minutes later, and I'm so relieved I'm not even bothered by Groot barking when the delivery man rings the doorbell.

I scarf down two pieces of pizza, anxious or eager (or both) to get out of this situation. As soon as I swallow my last bite, I ask my dad where Groot's leash is. I'm clipping it to his collar when he says, "Aliyah." His voice is small, and I slowly turn to face him with Groot's leash in my hand, ready to make a break for it.

When he sees he has my attention, he averts his gaze and continues, "I know, um, I'm not your favorite person. But, if you ever need...or want...to talk. I'm here to listen." My eyes narrow at his words, ignoring the uncertainty in his voice. Why would he *ever* think I would talk to him about my problems when he's the most consistent one I have?

I turn and walk out the back door with Groot. I may not have anyone to talk to, but I'm not desperate enough to open up to *him*. I'd sooner combust from holding everything in.

The crowded beach is starting to clear out in the distance, the sky above the sea starting to darken as the sun begins its descent. I take a deep breath, the ocean air swooping into my lungs, and it starts to cure all the tension from the last thirty minutes. Groot trots along without a care in the world, looking back at me with his tongue hanging out the side of his mouth, and it brings the smallest of smiles to my face.

CHAPTER FOUR

THE BOARDWALK IS CRAWLING WITH PEOPLE, AND IT'S easy to pick out who's a townie and who's a tourist. I try not to pay much attention to the photos being taken everywhere, parents rounding up their young children, and the obnoxious teenagers born and raised here. With all the commotion, I'm surprised Groot is as well behaved as he is. He's sniffing all over the place and wagging his tail at everyone who passes, tugging on the leash but returning to my side once he feels it go taut. He hasn't barked once.

My dad was right when he said I could probably find aloe in any of these stores. The little convenience store, souvenir shop, or boutique all have the necessary beach essentials for the "Best Summer Ever," as the souvenir shop sign indicates. How cheesy.

Now would also be a good time to fill out some job applications to fix the nine dollars and eight cents (soon to be less) in my bank account. The sooner I get hired, the better, and I can't think of a more appropriate place than the boardwalk. The five minute walk means avoiding asking for a ride, and I'd get the view of the ocean all summer

I look for any hiring signs in store windows as I walk down

the weathered wooden planks. The coffee shop, *Bean Hut*, is hiring, but waking up at five in the morning doesn't sound at all appealing. I like my sleep too much.

The souvenir shop next door isn't hiring, but I see the aloe I need. The door is propped open, and there's a few customers lingering around. I kneel to tie Groot's leash around a bike rack right outside. He starts licking my face.

"I love you too, boy," I smile, scratching between his ears. "Be on your best behavior. I'll be right back."

I head inside and grab the biggest bottle of aloe they have; my sunburn-prone skin will surely need it. This bottle of aloe and I will become well acquainted this summer. Maybe it will be my new best friend. The position's open, after all.

There's an older couple checking out at the register, and I wait in line behind them, glancing over all the souvenir items. Magnets, postcards, shot glasses, keychains. They all say something about beach life, New Haven, summer, or a combination of the three. I'll have to buy a magnet to put on the fridge back in Colorado.

When the older couple leaves with their brand new matching coffee mugs and a keychain for each of their grandkids, I step up to the register and set the aloe down. The cashier is a girl around my age. Her hair is platinum blonde and chopped to her neck, and the tips are dyed a dark blue. Her eyeliner matches the ends of her hair, bringing out the navy color of her eyes. A silver hoop in her nose glints in the sunlight.

"I like your hair," I say as she scans the aloe. She's wearing stacks of friendship bracelets on both wrists.

She smiles more than she already was, and her energetic response matches it perfectly. "Thanks! I just dyed it last night. My mother almost buried me alive, but I think it was worth it."

"Definitely worth it," I agree, tapping my card. She puts the bottle in a plastic bag and asks me if I want my receipt. I shake my head.

She tells me to have a good night and I wave in response. I exit the store five dollars and thirty two cents poorer. Now it's job time.

Groot is sitting down right where I left him, his tongue hanging out as he sniffs at the people who walk past him. When he sees me, he stands up and wags his tail. "Who's a good boy?" I say, in the voice people reserve for their dogs and their dogs only. I unhook him from the bike rack and walk further down the boardwalk, keeping an eye on the windows.

The boutique isn't hiring, the convenience store isn't hiring, and the arcade isn't hiring. The restaurant has a *Now Hiring* sign in the bottom corner of one of their windows, but I've heard Andy complain about chaotic rushes enough to know I want no part in it. I would take the coffee shop over that in a heartbeat.

I pass a few more stores, Groot leading the way, and see a hiring sign in front of the ice cream shop, *Scoops at the Beach*.

Now *that's* a possible contender. Scooping ice cream for the summer doesn't sound so bad. There are a few families eating their ice cream on the white patio furniture outside the shop. The hours posted are eleven to nine, seven days a week. Not too early, not too late. I tie Groot up on another bike rack and ask one of the mothers eating ice cream if she wouldn't mind keeping an eye on him. She happily complies, and as soon as I give permission, her two children are all over Groot.

I push open the door, a little bell jingling above. I'm blasted with A/C, something I didn't know I needed until I had it.

The shop is, to no shock, beach themed. The floors are light wood, a close match to the floors at my house. I immediately figure out why the owners chose the shade: it hides the sand people track in from the beach. A closer look is all it takes to see the grains all over the floor.

The walls are (surprise!) light blue, and there's a beach mural painted on the one stretching all the way to the back of the dining area. There are a few more families enjoying their ice cream with the A/C inside, and there are two people behind the counter. An older man and woman are stocking ingredients and supplies.

I approach the counter, and the older man turns to look my way. There are wrinkles in the corners of his dark eyes and mouth, and I take that as a good sign. "Hi," I say, suddenly nervous. I've never had to pursue a job like this before. My job back home was at Target, and my (now ex) best friend's mom was the general manager. The job was a given when I turned sixteen.

"What can I get started for you?" the man smiles. He doesn't speak any louder than he needs to, but his voice fills the entire shop like a security blanket. The comforting voice and corner eye crinkles from years of laughing are both green flags. His name tag reads "Fred."

I like Fred already.

"Actually, I saw the hiring sign you have outside. I was hoping I could fill out an application," I reply, trying on a smile. I may be a moody teenager, but Fred and the woman behind him don't need to know.

The woman turns around at the mention of the hiring sign. She has the same wrinkles as Fred. "I'll grab an application from the back," she says, her voice soft. In its own way, it's another security blanket in the shop. I don't get a chance to read her name tag before she turns away, disappearing behind the swinging door.

"What can I get you?" Fred asks, grabbing a medium sized bowl and a scoop.

"Oh, I'm okay, thank you though," I rush out with a wave of my hand, knowing the three dollars and seventy six cents in my account now is not enough for even a small bowl.

"On the house," Fred insists, waving it away with his hand. I feel bad, but I don't want to argue with my (hopefully) future boss, and who am I to turn down free ice cream?

"In that case," I grin, scanning the flavors before settling on my all-time favorite: vanilla. "Can I get the French Vanilla Bean? No toppings."

"Great choice," Fred says. The smile hasn't left his face since I walked in. "All of our ice cream is made in-house, and I'm particularly proud of this one." He dishes my ice cream into the bowl as the woman comes back with the application. Her name tag says "Mandy."

Mandy hands the paper to me with a pen and says, "I hope he wasn't tormenting you too much." She's smiling the entire time, and it doesn't take a genius to figure out the two of them are married.

I like them even more. What's not to like about an older couple who own an ice cream shop on the beach?

"Just a little," I respond, holding up my thumb and pointer finger with a centimeter of space between them, and Fred chuckles. Mandy jokingly swats his arm.

As if I already have the job, she says, "You'll get used to it in no time. Lord knows I have in the last fifty years."

"Fifty-two, darling."

I grin at their banter and smile as Fred hands me my ice cream. "If you have any questions, you let us know," he tells me.

"I will, and thank you for the ice cream. I appreciate it," I reply. I head outside to sit beside Groot and thank the family for keeping an eye on him when I was inside. I set my bag with the aloe on the chair next to me.

The first bite of the ice cream is creamy like French Vanilla, but it has the same flavor as vanilla bean. It's absolutely delicious. I mean, all ice cream is delicious, but there's something about this specific vanilla flavor that has my taste buds wanting *moremoremore*. The crossover of the two vanillas is something I've never thought of, but I love it.

I start filling out the application, eating my ice cream and sharing some of it with Groot. The sun begins to set, turning the sky into a painting with different hues of pinks and oranges. Tourists start to pack up their belongings and head back to their rentals or find somewhere to eat for a late dinner, but I stay seated. Groot waits impatiently between each spoonful of ice cream I feed him, putting a paw on my lap to let me know he wants more.

We finish off the ice cream, and I pull out my phone to scribble down some references on my application. A manager from Target (NOT the general manager, for obvious reasons), the couple across the hall from Andy and I who I pet sit for, and our landlord's number. Sometimes I help her out with organizing mail for a little extra cash.

"Okay boy, you be good while I bring this back," I tell Groot. I leave the table and throw the empty bowl into the garbage. The overhead bell jingles again when I step inside the shop. It's almost eight, and Mandy and Fred are starting to clean up. She's sweeping pounds of sand off the floor, and he's stocking ingredients for tomorrow. Mandy looks up when I walk in, a twinkle in her green eyes as she smiles.

"You can set it on the counter. I'll take a look over it tomorrow and give you a call," she tells me, gesturing to the paper in my hands with the broom.

"Sounds good, thank you," I say, setting the paper on the counter.

"What did you think of the vanilla?" Fred asks me, pausing in the middle of dumping a bag of mini M&Ms into a container.

"It was delicious. The name explains the crossover perfectly," I reply, the corners of my lips turning up.

"You're hired," he grins, moving down the counter to pick up my application. "Anyone who knows and tastes the difference between the two is perfect for the job. Right, Mandy?" He winks at her.

"You are correct, sweetheart," she says, sounding exasperated in the most romantic way possible. When she glances over at him, her eyes light up with an even brighter twinkle. My eyes used to twinkle like that when I looked at Nate.

I think that twinkle would turn to knives if I saw him now.

Mandy turns to me and says, "Looking over your application is a formality. You'll fit in just fine here! I'll call you tomorrow, and we can discuss hours and pay."

"Oh, thank you!" I say, not hiding my surprise well at the job offer. Mandy and Fred both chuckle.

"Redding. You wouldn't happen to be related to Trevor Redding, would you?" Fred asks, moving his eyes away from the paper in his hands.

My smile drops at the mention of my dad. Did I just get a job at a place I won't be able to escape him? I try to save face by plastering on the fakest smile I've ever worn and hope Mandy and Fred don't notice. "Yeah. I'm his daughter."

"He works with our son at the construction firm. The two of them actually redid our flooring two summers ago," Fred says, gesturing to the now almost-free-of-sand floors. It's still packed into the nooks and crannies between the floorboards. Those grains are never being swept away.

"It looks great," I say truthfully, but I want the conversation to move away from anything involving my dad.

"Best decision we ever made," Mandy laughs. "It conceals most of the sand until the last hour or two when tourists come in for dessert. Then it's a lost cause."

I'm not faking my smile anymore, but it remains small. "I should probably get going. It was nice meeting both of you, and thank you again!"

"It was nice meeting you too, Aliyah. I'll call you tomorrow," Mandy says, and her and Fred wave goodbye as I exit the shop, the bell above the door jingling as I leave.

"Guess who got a job, boy," I say to Groot as I untie him from the bike rack and grab my aloe. He looks like he has a smile on his face as we head toward the house. The boardwalk is much less crowded now, but the New Haven nightlife is starting to come out. More teenagers are replacing the families of tourists. Though the boardwalk isn't as crowded, they seem to be everywhere. The beach, the arcade, the restaurant.

Another wave of loneliness hits, this one bigger than all the other ones so far. Everyone around me is with their friends and ready for the night to begin, and I'm going back home alone to find something to watch on Netflix. I used to be just like them, gathering with my group once we were all off work to make the most of our summer, and I can't help but feel an empty void from the joy it always gave me. A void New Haven has no chance of filling.

New Haven got me away from Nate, though, and once I'm reminded of that, the void seems a little less heavy.

CHAPTER FIVE

THE CURTAINS NEVER GOT CLOSED BEFORE I WENT TO bed last night, so when the sun rises at precisely five thirteen, I wake up. Since the balcony doors of my bedroom directly face the ocean, the sun has a clear path into my room the second it's above the horizon. My eyes are blurry from the abrupt wake up. *When was the last time I was up this early?*

I sit up, my back screaming in agony. Every move I make stretches the burnt skin, and when my T-shirt grazes the skin, I can't help but flinch. The pain snaps me out of my grogginess enough to stumble over to the doors and close the curtains.

I don't think I've ever been this sunburnt in my entire life.

Crawling back into bed is a slow process, and I situate myself on my back, the pain subsiding after a few seconds. With minimal tossing and turning so as not to disturb the sunburn, I try to fall back asleep, but it doesn't find me. I give up after only a few minutes and sit up.

Despite not being able to go back to bed, sleep still clouds my eyes, and I rub them with the heels of my hands. My eyelids feel heavier than my backpack during finals week, and I despise myself for not thinking about closing the curtains before falling asleep at two in the morning. My laptop is folded shut on the bed beside me, holding on to its last one percent of life after a season two binge of *New Girl*. I was too lazy to dig for the charger in my backpack when the low battery notification popped up, so I fell asleep instead.

I throw back the quilt and swing my legs over the side of the bed, bare feet touching the wood floor. The cool surface will take some getting used to after stepping onto carpet for my entire life, but I like it. Maybe I'll strip and lay down on it to soothe my back later.

After not-so-easily applying a thick layer of aloe to my skin, I grab my phone and shuffle out of my room, trying not to make a sound. Groot hops down from the bed to join me, his nails clicking along the wood floor. *So much for trying not to make a sound.* My T-shirt sticks to my back from the aloe, but it feels better than the alternative.

My first priority is coffee. As soon as I have some more money in my account, I'll have to venture out to the coffee shop on the boardwalk. Until then, homemade will have to do. I saw a coffee pot in the kitchen during dinner yesterday. Not that I plan on ever telling him, but I'm glad my dad chose a classic coffee pot over a Keurig. My coffee always tasted watered down when I would make it at Nate's.

I creep toward the stairs, but Groot doesn't seem to know the definition of silent. I'm worried about waking my dad up, but once I'm at the top of the stairs and see the lights on, I know it won't be an issue. I freeze, one foot on the first step.

The temptation to turn around and retreat to my room is at the tips of my fingers, but Groot is already trotting down the stairs. It would look suspicious if he shows up alone.

Plus, I want my coffee.

Now.

"Morning, buddy," my dad says to the dog, and I imagine him leaning over to pet him. I take another step down the stairs, taking my sweet, sweet time in prolonging the inevitable awkward conversation.

When I round the corner to the kitchen, he looks up from the newspaper he's holding at the dining table and says, "Morning. How'd you sleep?"

"Fine," I shrug, tunnel visioning to the coffee pot. There's already some brewed.

"Where are the mugs?" I mumble. I glance over my shoulder, meeting his blue eyed gaze. The blue eyes I got from him.

"Upper cabinet next to the fridge," he replies, pointing in that direction with a pen. I open the cabinet and see different shapes and colors and sizes. I grab a lavender one with white butterflies on it (why does my dad have such a girly mug?), setting it down on the counter with a soft clink. I pour the coffee until my mug is a little over three fourths full, leaving room for cream.

Except he doesn't have any creamer in the fridge. I look around and move some things to the side, and there's nothing. The only dairy item is skim milk. I hate plain black coffee, so it's going to have to do.

"Are you looking for something?" my dad asks as I grab the jug, his voice cautious.

"Creamer. This'll do," I say, holding up the milk. I pour it into my mug, watching the white swirl into the black. It's one of my favorite things.

"I can add it to the grocery list. Is there a certain kind you like?"

I'm surprised at the immediate offer. He never used to get things Andy and I wanted. If we asked for something that wasn't a "need," the answer was no unless it benefitted him.

"Any vanilla is fine. I'm not picky," I shrug, putting the milk back in the fridge and turning to my dad. The newspaper is lying on the table now, open to the crossword page, and he scribbles on a blue piece of paper next to it. It must be the grocery list.

"Is there anything else you want me to add to the list?"

I shake my head.

"If you think of anything, text me. I'm going to the store when I get off work tonight."

"Okay." I won't.

I debate going back to my room with my coffee or sitting with my dad before he leaves for work. Andy's words ring in my ear once again, and I begrudgingly make the decision to sit down at the kitchen table across from him. He looks as shocked as I am reluctant, unable to hide his eyebrows raising higher than the sky. I relax my back against the chair, the pain diminishing as I get used to the feel. The same tense silence from last night settles in.

I take a sip, staring at the newspaper splayed out so I don't have to look at him. The crossword is half done, but I can't read any of the clues or words. My drink isn't as sweet as it usually is, but I know my vanilla creamer will fix all of that tomorrow morning.

The silence hangs in the air between us as we sit across from each other. He resumes the crossword, and I sip from my mug every few seconds. Sitting quietly in the morning while drinking coffee and reading the newspaper is usually a time when silence is peaceful, but the tension in the air breaks that stereotype. The awkwardness grows thicker and thicker, suffocating me under the weight. I scramble for something to say and blurt out the first thing that is relevant.

"I got a job."

My dad looks up from the paper, eyebrows once again raised, no doubt at the sound of my voice. A twinge of guilt pinches my heart.

I remind myself of the childhood he created for me. Drinking away his paychecks, stumbling through the door at two in the morning, and up and leaving the second Andy could legally take care of me. I shouldn't feel guilty for keeping our conversations to the bare minimum.

"Where at?" he asks, caution lacing his voice like a little kid trying not to get in trouble.

"The ice cream shop on the boardwalk. I filled out the application last night and got hired on the spot."

"That'll be a fun place to work. Stays pretty busy in the summers. I redid the floors there a few years ago."

"That's what they said when they recognized the last name."

"Do you know when your first day is?"

I shake my head, taking another sip of my coffee and staring at Groot. He's situated himself on the floor beside me, his head resting on his paws and hind legs tucked under his body.

The conversation is over, and I realize with a surge of irritation it wasn't that bad. Talking to my dad about something as simple as me getting a job felt normal, like we have simple conversations every morning over our coffees. I hate it.

He gets up and rinses his empty mug in the sink before putting it in the dishwasher. Groot lifts his head at the movement, deems it insignificant, and lays his head back on his paws. I take another sip, zoning out on a little scratch in the wood table.

Despite my crispy back, I want to go back to the beach as soon as it warms up, but I still have a few hours to kill until then. The big question is: what do I feel like watching on Netflix?

"Anything you want for dinner?" my dad asks as he slips his work boots on and double knots the laces.

A memory flashes through my mind of Andy teaching me how to tie my shoes when I was four and he was eight. We shouldn't have been left home alone at those ages, but that didn't stop him. Andy and I became the modern day versions of Matilda, learning how to provide for ourselves. I cried a lot, and Andy was always trying to distract me with different things. One day, it was learning how to tie my shoes. It stopped the crying for a month as I focused on perfecting the bow on each foot.

"Whatever's fine," I mutter, not meeting his eyes as I take another sip of my coffee. It's almost gone, and the temperature has cooled to the weird lukewarm that makes it feel like you're drinking coffee flavored bath water.

"I'll get stuff for spaghetti. I'll be home around five or six."

He heads out the garage door, leaving Groot and I and the awkward leftover tension to ourselves.

I finish my coffee flavored bath water and rinse my mug, putting it in the dishwasher next to my dad's. I'm already starting to feel the caffeine doing its thing.

With Groot on my heels, I head back to my room. After applying another layer of aloe to my back, I brush my teeth to get rid of the coffee breath and throw my hair into a careless messy bun. I stay in the oversized T-shirt and cotton shorts I wore to bed —there's no point in changing when I'm putting a swimsuit on in a few hours.

Back in my room, my laptop is officially dead. I dig the charger out of my backpack and settle into bed to watch *The Notebook* for the millionth time, foolishly hoping a happy ending will put my heart back together.

CHAPTER SIX

I'M BAWLING AS I WATCH THE END OF THE MOVIE, JUST
like every other time I've watched *The Notebook*. Every time I
think I might be able to make it to the end without a single tear,
Old Noah goes into Old Allie's room, and I lose it.

It's even worse this time, because seeing a love as powerful as
Noah and Allie's is too much for my shattered heart to handle.

I'm closing my laptop and sitting up when Groot barks and
flies off the bed. I jolt back into my pillows, a wave of sunburn-
induced pain washing over my back. He paws at my bedroom
door to be let out, looking back and forth between me and the
door with his ears perked up.

Sniffling, heart pounding, and wiping snot away from my
nose, I slip off the side of my bed and open the door. Groot bolts
out and skids around the corner on the wood. I follow him, not
sure why he's acting like he's on crack at eight in the morning.
Did someone ring the doorbell and I didn't hear it over my
crying?

Rounding the corner of the kitchen, I freeze as I come face to
face with none other than Easton. His darker-than-dark eyes land
on me and widen. My stomach shrivels and drops off the face of

the earth as his lips curve into a grin, an attractive sight with the dirty blonde hair curling around the edges of his backwards hat.

I look like I got run over by a truck, thrown into a dumpster, and attacked by rabies-infected squirrels. Or raccoons. Or both. With my oversized T-shirt, ratty bun hanging on the side of my head, and tear stained, snotty face, this might be the most embarrassing moment of my life. Nate and I were together for three years, and not even he ever saw me in a state like this.

It's easy to see Easton is seconds away from losing his shit. My cheeks feel hotter than my back does, and I wish I could have five seconds to at least splash some cold water on my splotchy face.

When I snap out of the initial shock of seeing this boy petting my dog in my kitchen at eight in the morning, I wonder why he's in the kitchen at all, and I cross my arms across my body.

"What the hell are you doing here?" My voice is much harsher than I mean it to be, but with my defenses on high alert, the bite in my voice is uncontrollable. Easton is unable to contain himself any longer, and he bursts out laughing.

I want to be mad. I want to scream at him and ask him what the fuck he finds so funny. I want to feel that flare of impulsive, uncontrollable anger in my chest I'm so familiar with—the rapid-heart-beat, chill-in-my-spine, gravity-defying anger.

Anger is not possible with the sound of Easton's laugh. The sound is like being wrapped in my softest blanket when it's fresh-out-of-the-dryer warm. In any other situation, I would go as far as to say his laugh is contagious. The most addictive kind of drug out there.

I opt for being annoyed instead, something that *is* possible. I stare at his hunched over figure, keeping my arms crossed tightly over my chest as I wait for him to respond. Easton continues to tremble, hands braced against his thighs for support. I start tapping my bare foot after a few more seconds.

Finally, he straightens up, laughter still trickling out of his mouth. "Oh man, I'm sorry. Not very nice of me at all."

"No, it wasn't." My defenses are still up, but the bite in my voice is gone. *That's a first.*

"You look like you're surviving an epic hangover right now," he tells me, grinning like this is all some funny joke. I hate his smile, how I can't look away.

"And that's supposed to make it better?"

His smile drops when he notices I'm not laughing with him. "No," he frowns, the humor in his voice gone. "I'm sorry, I didn't mean to upset you. I shouldn't have laughed."

The apology is appreciated, but I don't comment on it. I change the subject so Easton doesn't have time to ask me why I look like I'm, as he *so* kindly put it, "surviving an epic hangover". I ask him the same question I asked first, albeit without the initial attitude. "What are you doing here?"

He doesn't miss a beat, "I normally take Groot with me on my morning runs. He likes the exercise and your dad doesn't mind if I let myself in."

"Okay? You couldn't have knocked on the door or something?" I ask, the attitude back.

My dad and Dave must be pretty close, therefore making Easton a regular visitor over here. And, if he's taking Groot on runs most mornings, he's been letting himself into the house to do it. Why would me suddenly being here change that?

"I didn't think you'd be up. Most people our age are still sleeping at this hour," Easton shrugs. I hate that he's right. If I hadn't left the curtains in my room open, I'd still be passed out on my bed, dead to the world.

"Fair enough," I huff. It's the end of the conversation, but Easton makes no move to take the leash from the hook on the wall. I shift my weight from my left to my right foot, waiting for him to actually do what he came here to do. The corners of his lips turn upward at my squirming, and then he's laughing again.

I still can't find it in me to be angry at him for laughing, but it hurts a lot more the second time around. Once upon a time, I would have channeled that hurt by snapping at him to knock it off. Instead, I can't find the words as I set my glare on him, not able to stop the single tear that falls down my cheek.

Easton sees it and sobers up immediately. I see the pity flash in his beautiful eyes, but I don't want it. I turn on my heel as I wipe it away in haste, stalking toward the stairs with the biggest strides I can take.

Safe in my room, I slide down the door until my butt hits the floor. Sliding my back down the wood is the biggest mistake of the century, and the angry skin erupts in flames. I arch my back away from the door to give the skin some relief, and the pain fades. I pull my knees into my chest and rest my chin on my arms, staring at the dark room in front of me.

What an ass. What an absolute ass—

There's a tap on my bedroom door. His voice is muffled through the wood, but he speaks loudly to make up for it. "Aliyah." When I don't say anything, he continues, "I'm really sorry. I feel awful." The apology is short and to the point, but the genuinity carries through the door loud and clear.

I still think he's an asshole.

Another tear falls as I ignore Easton's apology, and I hear soft footsteps retreating a few moments later. Feeling more alone than ever, the darkness in the room leaves space for unwanted thoughts of Nate and Ellie and Sierra, their faces taunting me with the secret that is no more. I picture Nate and Sierra—

No.

I can't go down that rabbit hole. Not now, and not ever.

The stabbing pain of betrayal in my chest hits hard and heavy.

This is just one more round of shitty cards I've been dealt, and I was foolish enough to believe I had the jackpot in the palm of my hand. God, how could I have been so *stupid*.

Memories of the last three years flash through my mind. Prom. Sleepovers. The toilet paper fort Ellie and I secretly built at work. The ski trips I took every year with Nate and his family.

The fact that spending the summer with my dad is the better option says it all. The dad who walked out on me, who I hate with every bone in my body. *He* was the better option than the people who have always had my back. Who were always supposed to have my back.

I don't know how much time has passed when I lift my head from my elbow. I take a deep breath, then two, then five.

Pulling myself off the ground isn't easy, the weight of what's in my mind weighing me down. Once I'm standing, I reach for my phone on the bed and check the time. It's just past eight thirty. I might as well get dressed to go to the beach and make myself something to eat. Pancakes are sounding like the perfect comfort food, and by the time I'm done making them, it'll be the perfect time to go tan.

Moving past the mirror, I finally catch sight of what I look like.

I can't help but laugh.

Easton was right. I *do* look like I'm surviving an epic hangover right now. My bun is even more lopsided than it was when I put it up, hanging above my left ear. There are a few strands poking out in random directions, and a huge chunk behind my right ear never made it up in the first place. My face is splotchy, my eyes tired and puffy.

If I had been in his shoes, I wouldn't have been able to hold it together, either.

I remember how mean I was to him for laughing, and a sledgehammer of regret hits my chest. Easton didn't deserve me snapping at him just because everything is dogshit in my life.

Something needs to be done with my hair, but the band holding it hostage is tangled in the strands. I yank and wince until it comes undone, a good-sized chunk of my hair coming out with it. I run my fingers through the rat's nest to the best of my abilities, trying to separate the strands knotted together. Not wanting to risk another disaster on top of my head, I opt for braiding it down my back instead, and I pull some pieces out to frame my face. My back screams the entire time.

My T-shirt is added to my pile of dirty clothes from yesterday. I need to get a hamper as soon as I get my first paycheck to avoid them ending up all over my room. The space is too cute to become a disaster.

Since my red swimsuit probably smells like B.O. from how much I was sweating in the humidity yesterday, I opt for a black bikini top and matching bottoms. I slip into a baby blue floral patterned sundress, taking a peek in the mirror. The dress makes my eyes stand out, and I muster up a smile at my reflection.

"You'll be okay," I whisper, her mouth moving with mine.

I turn away from the mirror and contemplate putting on some makeup. The decision is a fast *no*, which comes as a surprise to me. I hardly ever leave the house without a thick layer of mascara and some concealer at the bare minimum. It's pointless in the humid heat, though.

I grab my phone from the bed, my sunglasses and Airpods from the dresser, and another beach towel from the bathroom (this one dark blue with white polka dots). I find a bottle of sunscreen in the cabinet with the towels. There's no hesitation in snatching it from the shelf and adding it to my collection. My flip flops are by the back door, so I head downstairs with bare feet and a refreshed feeling.

CHAPTER SEVEN

EASTON SITS AT THE KITCHEN TABLE, HIS HAND resting in the handle of a navy blue mug. His eyes snap to me as soon as I'm visible, white baseball cap sitting on the table beside his mug, and my jaw drops. From the intensity of his gaze or the sight of him in my kitchen yet again, I do not know.

"What are you still doing here?" I ask.

"I wanted to make sure you were okay."

His voice is soft, and I turn to face him. "It wasn't you. You... really didn't do anything wrong." God, those eyes are hard to look away from. I don't like the way they peer into my soul and send a shiver down my spine. I set my beach supplies on the counter and start hunting for pancake mix.

"I was laughing and you started crying."

"Barely. Anyways, I would have started laughing, too," I say.

"Promise?" Easton asks, taking a sip of his coffee before standing up and stretching his arms above his head. His shirt rides up a little bit and shows off his lower stomach, and I get a flash of smooth, tan, muscular skin. I look away, but the image is already ingrained in my mind.

"Swear on my life," I respond, continuing our conversation as if I'm unphased at seeing his abs, which is totally not the case. I find a yellow box of Bisquick in the wall length cabinet. I make note the cabinet is used as a pantry and I'll find most of the dry goods in there for future use. Maybe I'll take some time today to snoop around the kitchen so I don't have to keep asking my dad where things are.

My answer seems to satisfy Easton, and he sits his hat once again on his head. When he sees the box in my hands, he pulls out a frying pan from a lower cabinet. "I still shouldn't have laughed."

"Easton, it wasn't you," I sigh, his name coming off my lips for the first time since meeting him. Red warning signs flash in my mind; I should not like saying his name and the way it feels on my lips as much as I do. *God, what is wrong with me?*

I pull eggs and milk out from the fridge, skirting around his body as he grabs a mixing bowl from one of the upper cabinets. In a voice not much louder than a whisper and refusing to meet his eyes, I say, "I told you yesterday what was going on. I'm not exactly feeling stable right now."

"I know," he responds. I risk a glance at him, but he's not looking at me as he grabs a whisk from the pitcher of utensils near the stove. "But laughing at you was the last straw. I feel awful."

"Don't. If I tell you I laughed once I saw myself, would that make you feel better?"

"Infinitely."

"Well, I did. Better now?"

"Much."

I crack an egg on the edge of the mixing bowl, whatever's left of my anger transferring into the task. The shell shatters into the bowl. "Perfect," I mutter. It's a mild inconvenience that feels like the end of the world, but Easton doesn't miss a beat. He's already grabbing a spoon from the silverware drawer and spooning out the floating shells before I think of the next step.

"Would a terrible picture of me in the making of an actual epic hangover make you feel better?" he asks while he's fishing for shells.

"Maybe," I shrug, a small smile gracing my lips. He finishes fishing out the shells and pulls his phone out of one of his pockets, and after a few taps and swipes, he's turning his screen in my direction. I lean in to get a better look.

The picture is the epitome of the birth of an epic hangover if I've ever seen one. Easton's laying on the edge of a bathtub, his blonde hair a mess and puke smeared down his chin. His eyes are almost closed, open just enough for him to see what were surely his blurry surroundings.

I lose it. I grip the edge of the counter as laughter tumbles out of me, the first true sign of anything happy from me in the last two days. I've witnessed enough nights end like that (and unfortunately experienced one myself), but this is by far the funniest one. "Just...why the bathtub? Was the toilet occupied?" I manage to ask.

"Who knows?" Easton grins. "That was the first time I ever drank, and my buddy didn't tell me the jungle juice had an extra handle of Everclear in it."

"Not the Everclear!" I gasp, another fit of giggles taking over.

"I don't like to assume, but it does seem like this has helped you feel better."

"Tremendously," I say as my laughter trickles away. "I hope you learned your lesson about Everclear after that night."

Easton chuckles. "Never again have I disgraced myself." He holds up a hand as if he were swearing into Scouts, and I roll my eyes as I turn back to the task at hand. The laughter was nice, but I don't like how easy we fell into conversation. Conversation leads to being friends.

The two of us work in silence as we resume making the pancakes, and Groot lays on the ground by the fridge, clearly waiting for something to fall. I don't want to break it to his puppy eyes that pancake batter doesn't taste good, even to a dog.

While I cook the pancakes on the stove, blueberries sizzling from the heat, Easton sits down at the kitchen table. Groot gets up to plop down at his feet. The sound of his nails clicking against the wood floor reminds me why Easton was here this morning to begin with.

"How was your run?" I ask, but then question if he even went. There's no sign he's broken a sweat, so he's either Captain America's long lost son or he didn't go.

"I didn't go," he confirms, the corner of his lips just barely turning up.

"Sorry," I mumble, focusing on the pancake.

Easton's laugh fills the room once again, and I do wonder what's so funny this time. This boy really needs to get a grasp on when it's socially appropriate to laugh.

"Why are you laughing? Again?" I accuse as I remove the first pancake from the stove and slide it onto a plate. The blueberries leave purple streaks on the white surface.

Easton, unbothered by my tone, says, "Because I'm the one in the wrong and you think you have to apologize for that." I pour more batter into the frying pan and sprinkle it with blueberries.

"Your point?" I ask, leaning back against the counter so I can see him at the table. I cross my arms across my chest, the action only adding to the attitude I'm portraying.

Once again, when he realizes I'm not following, his laughter cuts off. "I don't have a point," he says, his tone matching my seriousness. "I just don't think you have anything to apologize for."

"Well, I think I do."

"Okay. Humor me. What do you think you have to apologize for?" His grin returns, and I'm glad he's across the room so he can't see the goosebumps that appear on my arms at the sight of it.

"Ruining your morning plans."

He sighs through his grin. "Aliyah," he starts, and I know he sees and chooses to ignore the shiver that runs down my spine at the sound of him saying my name. "I could have left you here and gone on my run if I really wanted to go that badly. If anyone should be apologizing, it should be me. So *I'm sorry.*"

"You already said that."

"And I'll say it again. I'm sorry for making you cry."

"I wasn't crying."

"I saw a tear."

I huff. We're clearly not going to see eye to eye on this, which I should have known with the foot of height between us. Instead, I finish making the pancakes in silence, divide them evenly between two plates, and set one down in front of Easton. He opens his mouth to protest.

"No," I say, pointing my finger at him before he gets a sentence out. I sit down across from him. "We can agree to disagree. Take this as a peace offering."

He closes his mouth and nods, picking up the fork on his plate and digging in. In contrast to his massive bite through all five pancakes, I delicately rip a smaller chunk off the top and eat it.

"These are good," Easton says once he swallows.

"Thanks," I murmur, tearing off another chunk. Groot moves from Easton's feet to mine, sitting up and tilting his head to the side. I realize he hasn't gotten breakfast yet. I'll fill his bowls when I'm done eating, but until then, I can't say no to the wide eyed gaze and perked up ears. I rip a larger chunk off of my pancake and hold it out for him. He grabs it and swallows it in a single bite.

Easton devours his entire plate in a similar manner to Groot before I even finish my first pancake, and now it's my turn to want to laugh. I don't, because it's really not that funny; it's just been a really fucking weird morning. Easton gets up from the kitchen table and rinses his plate in the sink, putting it on the bottom rack of the dishwasher.

"You got any plans for the day?" he asks as he rejoins me at the table. He leans back against the chair and folds his arms across his chest. I'd be a liar if I said I haven't noticed the muscles before now, but crossing his arms defines each ridge and line. He must really work hard to stay in such pristine shape.

"More of the beach," I shrug, transferring my gaze to my plate and hoping he didn't notice me ogling his arms. I don't think I was looking at them for long, but who knows?

"You should come hang out with us," he invites again, and I remember the laughter I heard from his group yesterday. The longing and hatred for it.

"Why?" I mutter, glancing at him.

"Because you're new and, I swear, I mean this in the least offensive way possible—"

"If you have to say that, it's probably offensive."

He gives me a pointed look, and I shrug again.

"I just mean you don't know anyone here, therefore you don't really have anyone to hang out with, so you should come hang out with us. Everyone's really chill."

Chill or not, my decision doesn't waver. "Maybe another day."

Easton seems to accept this answer, and then he stands up. "Alright Groot, you ready to go?" he says, clasping his hands together above his head and extending his arms upward. He bends back to stretch, a few bones making a satisfying *crack*. His T-shirt rides up a few inches over his stomach, and I'm for sure ogling this time. How could I not? I notice a small white scar about three inches long on his left hip, right above the waistline of his shorts. I open my mouth to ask about it, but asking him about it would give away the fact that I've been checking him out. *Yeah, not happening.*

At the mention of his name, Groot stands up and wags his tail, staring at Easton. Easton walks to the back door and grabs the leash from the hook, clipping it to Groot's collar with the ease of someone who's done it a million times before.

When he slides the glass door open and steps out, I call out, "Don't puke." I glance up when I don't hear the door close, and Easton's staring at me with his head ever so slightly cocked to the side. What seems to be his signature grin plays on his lips, and his obsidian eyes have a twinkle in them.

"You are something else, Aliyah Redding."

CHAPTER EIGHT

My phone rings on my way down to the beach, cutting off the random summer playlist I was listening to. It's an unknown number with an area code I don't recognize, but I have a feeling it's my new boss. I shift everything I'm holding into one arm and answer, "Hello?" I hope she can't hear the little bundle of nerves I suddenly feel in my chest.

"Hi Aliyah, it's Mandy, from Scoops," she says, her grandmotherly tone clear even over the phone.

"Hi Mandy! How are you?" I step onto the sand, kicking up pebbles with every step in my flip flops. I set my eyes on a spot near the water and head that way.

"I'm great! Like I said last night, I'm calling to set up hours and pay with you. We'd like to get you started as soon as possible since the tourist season is pretty much here, and the more hands we have, the smoother things will run. What's your availability like?"

"Availability is wide open. I don't have anything else going on this summer, so I can work whenever you need me too."

There's a smile in Mandy's voice as she says, "That's amazing to hear. Do you know how many hours you'd like to work a week?" I hear the clicking of a keyboard in the background. "And how does twelve dollars an hour sound?"

I weave through groups already at the beach and reach my spot. "I can work as much as you need me to. And twelve sounds perfect." It's less than the hourly rate I made in Colorado, but I'd rather take a pay cut than spend any time there this summer.

"You're going to be a life saver, I can tell," Mandy jokes, and I laugh. "I do my best to split hours evenly between our employees, but some of them do need a week off here or there for other commitments. If at any point you feel like you're working too much or need some time off, you let us know, okay?"

"Absolutely," I agree, setting my stuff down in the sand.

"I mean it," Mandy warns in the most unthreatening way possible. "Our staff's wellbeing is the most important thing to us, a business to run be damned."

A laugh trickles out of my mouth at her words, though they mean a lot. "That's really good to know. Thank you."

"Of course," Mandy says softly. "Would you want to start today or tomorrow? I can put you on the schedule pretty much whenever you want."

I don't think much before answering, "I can start tonight." I have nothing better to do. At least starting work will stop me from spending all night in my room watching Netflix. Might as well make some money.

"Perfect! How does five to close sound?"

"Sounds like a plan," I say, nerves jumping back into my voice as the conversation wraps up. I blame it on the whole talking-on-the-phone-with-my-new-boss thing.

"Fred and I won't be here, but our grandson is the one closing. He can start training you in. He's about your age, so I'm sure you guys will get along great."

"Awesome," I say again, though working with a boy my age doesn't sound awesome at all.

"Perfect," she says slowly, like she's also marking it in the schedule on her end. "Do you want to work tomorrow at all? I'll be in and we can finish up your paperwork then, too."

I must have applied at the perfect time to already be getting hours, but I'm not complaining. "Yeah, any time works!"

"I'll put you down for eleven to three. Sound good?"

The perfect shift to come and enjoy the sun afterwards. "That sounds perfect! Thank you again, Mandy."

"Of course, sweetie. Do you have any questions for me?"

"Not at the moment. I'll let you know if any come to mind."

"You can text me if you have any. I think that's everything I needed to talk to you about, so I'll see you tomorrow!"

We say our good-byes and I hang up the phone, my music starting up again. It's a popular song that came out a few weeks ago, a tune on its way to being a song-of-the-summer. It helps keep my spirits up as I lay out my towel and ease onto my back.

I WALK INTO SCOOPS ON THE BEACH RIGHT BEFORE five, and the sight of Easton handing a little boy a giant ice cream cone from behind the counter has me stopping in my tracks. You've *got* to be kidding me.

The family with the little boy starts heading toward the door, and I move out of their way without taking my gaze off my neighbor. Easton sees me standing there, a wide grin breaking out onto his face. "Aliyah, come on back," he motions with his hand. I place one foot in front of the other, pieces falling into place as I walk behind the counter and follow Easton into the back room.

Mandy and Fred said my dad and their son replaced their floors a few years ago, and they worked together at the construction firm. Dave is their son, which makes Easton their grandson, and their grandson is closing tonight.

Why oh why, of all the places on the boardwalk, did I end up getting a job at the place my annoyingly handsome neighbor works at?

Is it too late to apply at the Bean Hut?

Easton shows me where the aprons are, gives me two T-shirts, a black one and a light blue one, with the Scoops on the Beach logo in the upper right corner, and shows me where I would normally clock in. He explains since I haven't filled out paperwork with Mandy yet, I won't be able to clock in properly and she'll manually put in my hours for this shift once my account is up and running.

"How was your day at the beach?" he asks me as I pull the white apron over my head and tie it behind my back. The Scoops on the Beach logo is centered across my chest.

"Hot," I mutter, following him through the swinging door.

"I noticed you didn't come to hang out with us at all."

"I didn't feel like it."

"Well, when you do start to feel like it, let me know."

Yeah, right.

I don't respond, and Easton moves on to show me where bowls and cones and toppings are, even though everything is clearly right in front of me. "Also," he says, spinning around and grabbing two colorful sample spoons from the bin beside the freezer and handing one to me, "Feel free to sample any flavors when you want or make a bowl for yourself."

Easton digs his little spoon into the cotton candy ice cream and scoops out a big bite. He leans back against the counter with his sample, making himself comfy. I scoop the spoon he handed me into the vanilla. It's cold and creamy and puts a smile on my face.

"Vanilla?" Easton says, raising an eyebrow in question at my choice. "Out of all twenty choices?"

"Are you going to laugh at me again," I challenge, tilting my head to the side. I realize only after I say the words I'm joking, slipping back into my usual antics without a thought. It only further proves my decision to stay away from him is the right choice. *This wasn't part of the plan.*

He doesn't realize I'm joking. He shakes his head a little too fast, like he's worried I'm actually mad at him again. It's my turn to be the one to laugh first. Easton relaxes the moment the sound leaves my mouth, his frown turning into a grin.

"You really had me there for a second."

"That was the point."

"I'm having a very hard time figuring you out," Easton says. He crosses his arms and raises an eyebrow, like he's trying to dig into my soul and find my deepest, darkest secrets. His dark eyes are boring into me, and the shiver that runs down my back has nothing to do with the cooler of ice cream behind me.

I open my mouth to ask him what he means, but the little bell above the door goes off as a family of five walks in. A little boy no older than four bolts for the glass separating him from the ice cream.

"Time to see if you're up for the job," Easton mutters with a grin, approaching the cash register with ease. "Hey y'all, welcome to Scoops!"

The mother smiles, a one or two year old girl perched on her hip. Another young boy, around six or seven, stands beside the dad, seeming to already know exactly what he wants to get. He's not looking at the flavors excitedly like his younger brother.

The dad urges the boy forward with a gentle nudge, and the boy says to Easton, "Can I please have a small cup with vanilla ice cream and Oreo cookies on top?"

"You got it, little man," Easton says, his demeanor not much different from how he's been with me or anyone else I've seen him with. Granted, I've only seen him interact with my dad and Dave, but still. He doesn't put on the fake customer service voice most people have.

"See, vanilla's not that bad," I say quietly to Easton as he grabs a bowl and starts scooping, a small, triumphant smile on my face.

"He's getting cookies on it, though. He's basically getting cookies n' cream."

"Touché."

"Miss, can I please try some of that one?" the four year old boy asks, pointing to one of the flavors through the glass. I don't know exactly which one he's pointing to, and Easton senses the hesitation before I ask the little boy *which* one.

"Sure can, little dude." And then, in a much quieter voice, "He's talking about Rocky Road."

I take a sample spoon and scoop some of the Rocky Road onto it, making sure to get a good chunk of the marshmallow before straining my arm over the glass to hand it down to the little boy. His eyes light up at the giant marshmallow, and I take it as a small win.

Easton finishes scooping the vanilla into the bowl and tops it with the Oreo crumbles at the topping case. I watch his movements to see if there are any tricks he might have. It's hard to tell if there are any tricks because Easton is so relaxed doing it, like he's done it a million times before.

"Yum!" the little boy I helped says loudly. "I really like that one. Can I please get it?"

"In a small, please," the mother jumps in, and I smile at her before turning and grabbing a bowl.

Scooping the ice cream is *not* as easy as Easton made it look. The cold ice cream seems to fight back against the metal scoop like a toddler who doesn't want to leave the toy aisle. I wrestle for every bit of ice cream I can get, incapable of getting a decent sized scoop; the bowl of Rocky Road ends up having multiple little scoops shoved together instead of a solid two scoops like Easton's bowl.

I hand the bowl over to the little boy and get a loud thank you in return. "Matthew, inside voice, please," his dad says, and Matthew nods before taking a big bite of his ice cream. The chocolate smears all over his mouth as he joins his older brother at one of the tables inside.

"Anything else for y'all tonight?" Easton asks, ringing up the two ice creams they have so far on the register.

"A two scoop vanilla in a waffle cone, and that's it," the mother says, and since Easton's ringing it up, it's up to me to scoop it. It takes me more time than it should. The dad has handed over his credit card and Easton has handed it back, and I'm still not done.

I pass the cone over the freezer in a rush with an overly peppy "have a good night" before they leave, the boys trailing their parents out to the boardwalk. Easton's leaning against the counter again, arms crossed over his chest and a single brow raised. The exact same look and stance he had before the family came in.

"*You* have a customer service voice?" he accuses, like he didn't expect me, of all people, to have the infuriating facade reserved for customers.

I nod. "If I didn't have a customer service voice, the amount of reviews we'd get for having a server with an attitude problem would be through the roof."

"I'm beginning to realize that."

"Also," I say in a happy voice, "They got plain vanilla with no toppings. It's clearly a more popular choice than you think."

"I'm more concerned with your scooping skills than how popular vanilla is." I know he's teasing because his grin only widens. I'm beginning to realize if Easton has a grin on his face, his words are not meant to be hurtful or taken seriously. In another life, before my heart was broken and betrayed, Easton and I would be two peas in a pod.

"It's a lot harder than it looks," I defend.

Easton's grin turns into a smirk as he says, "Not to worry. You'll have bad boys like these by the end of the summer." He uncrosses his arms and flexes them so his muscles are on full display. I don't want to stare, but I can't help it. His muscles are beautiful: they're visible and anyone can tell he works out regularly, but not so much where his body seems to be proportioned incorrectly.

To stop myself from staring even longer than I already have, which is sure to become a problem since I'm working with him all summer (damn Easton and his gorgeous face and body), I switch the subject to something else.

I swallow, "What did you mean when you said you were having a hard time figuring me out?"

Easton drops his arms and braces them back against the counter as he shrugs. "Normally, I'm pretty good at reading people. You're not so easy. One second you seem like you've given up on everything and everybody. The next, you're completely on defense and ready to attack at any sign of bullshit. Or now, you're goofing around and are more relaxed than I've ever seen you, like you don't have a care in the world."

"Oh."

I don't really know what else to say. He said he's having a hard time figuring me out, but he could write a book called "The Emotions of Aliyah Redding" after twenty four hours of knowing me.

"I mean that all in the nicest way possible, of course. It's just... usually I know how to act around people. You're different. I don't know if I should be joking or serious or worried. You keep surprising me."

You keep surprising me.

There isn't anything special about those words, but the way they sound coming out of Easton's mouth makes them sound like my survival is dependent on whether or not I can keep him on his toes.

"Is that a good thing?" I ask, already knowing what my answer is. Keeping someone on their toes is never a bad thing in my books, and I *pride* myself on being able to do it so easily.

One point for Aliyah.

"It's definitely a good thing." The smile he gives me is so different from the grin he normally has plastered on his face, and I realize maybe, just maybe, his customer facade isn't just reserved for customers.

Maybe working with Easton this summer won't be such a bad thing after all.

CHAPTER NINE

Tossing and turning, I finally give up on trying to fall back asleep and throw the bedding off me, disrupting Groot. Everytime I close my eyes, the only thing I see is Nate. He's an asshole and he cheated on me, but I *miss* him. I miss watching movies in the dark and going on walks in the middle of the night and when he would bring me coffee during long shifts at work.

And I'm mad at myself for missing him.

I'm mad at myself for thinking about him at all.

The wood floor is chilled against the bottoms of my feet as I pad across my room to the bedroom door. A glass of water sounds nice, and maybe it will help me fall asleep. Groot, already back in a comfortable spot, barely looks my way as I open the door and step into the hall.

I'm shocked to see a faint glow coming from downstairs, illuminating the steps enough for me to see without turning the light on. I take the steps slowly, and when I'm on the main level and round the corner, I'm even more shocked to see my dad sitting in the armchair with the lamp on, a book open in his lap.

Why is he up in the middle of the night?

He looks up at my appearance, eyebrows raised in surprise.

He's probably just as shocked to see me as I am to see him. I don't want to talk to him, so I nod my head once at him before turning to the kitchen and keeping my back to him.

The silence is beyond awkward as I pull a cup down from the cupboard and fill it up from the fridge. I wonder again why he's awake. Is this a normal thing? Can he not sleep or does he choose to be awake in the middle of the night?

I feel my dad's gaze burning holes into my back as if he wants to say something, but I don't give him the chance. Instead of leaning against the counter and drinking my water slowly like I had planned, I mutter a "goodnight" to him and bolt back upstairs. A little bit of water sloshes over the rim in my haste.

Groot has not moved from his spot, and one ear perks up at my return. I sit down on the side of my bed, set the water on my nightstand, and take a deep, deep breath.

This sucks.

I pick up my water cup and chug it. It does nothing to help, and when I crawl back under the quilt and curl up next to Groot, I'm haunted by an image of Nate holding my hand as he walked me through the botanical gardens on our first date.

It's going to be a long night.

———

I FALL INTO A ROUTINE CONSISTING OF THREE THINGS over the next week: the beach, work, and Netflix with Groot. Four, if you count rewatching *The Notebook* an ungodly amount of times. The routine starts to feel normal, and other than the fourth activity, it keeps my mind off of other things I'd rather not think about.

On Monday morning, I hear the rain before I move to get out of bed. It's hitting the roof and walls of the house softly, and I know going down to the beach to tan is out of the cards for today. I'll have to find something else to do. I could continue my *New*

Girl marathon, start rewatching *The Office* again, or maybe find some movies to watch that won't put me in tears every time. My dad works until four, so I could watch it on the flat screen in the living room instead of my laptop screen in bed.

A change of scenery does sound nice.

With that thought in mind, I pull myself out of bed. I'm assuming Easton didn't go on his run today with the rain, because Groot is still laying on my bed. When I leave my room with my phone and Bluetooth speaker in hand, the dog hops down and trots after me, keeping on my heels as I head downstairs. I pull my hair into a high ponytail with an elastic from my wrist.

The kitchen is Easton-free when I round the corner, and I almost find myself missing his presence.

Not Easton, specifically. Just the way he fills the space around him. Having him around keeps the loneliness at bay and puts me at ease, and without him in the kitchen this morning, the loneliness latches on stronger than usual.

I brew a fresh pot of coffee and pull out a mug (a light green one from The Bean Hut), setting it on the counter to wait for the coffee to be done. I open the fridge to find something for breakfast, deciding on an omelet. I pull out the carton of eggs, shredded cheese, and deli ham my dad makes his sandwiches with each morning.

Before cracking any eggs, I shuffle the summer playlist on my phone I put together this weekend. The curated summer playlist I was listening to was great, but I wanted to add my own songs, too. I turn the volume on my speaker all the way up.

As the music fills the room, I start dancing around and shaking my hips. I feed Groot and fill his water bowl, and he goes to town like he hasn't eaten anything in three days.

I crack two eggs in a bowl, whisk them with salt and pepper, and pour the mixture into a frying pan for my omelet. I sprinkle cheese and torn pieces of ham into the pan while performing my wicked dance moves, and when I turn to grab a plate, I see Easton standing stiffly by the door with a stupid smile on his stupid face, his clothes spotted with rain drops and his hair a mess on top of his head.

The almost-healed skin on my back protests for a second as I yelp and back into the cupboards behind me, my heart rate skyrocketing into next year. My hip explodes in pain as I hit the handle of a drawer. I grab my phone from the counter and turn the music down until it's playing softly in the background. When I look back at Easton, clutching my hip in pain, there's a dangerous twinkle in his eyes.

"Permission to laugh?"

"Go ahead," I mutter, my cheeks flaring as the sound fills the room. It's better than any song I could listen to. Shivers start in my sternum and spread out in five directions. The hairs on my neck stand up, tingles reaching to the very tips of my fingers and toes. I'm angry at the reaction.

I turn my back and finish my omelet, avoiding looking at Easton as he laughs. I don't like how much I like the sound of it. My movements are robotic as I pretend to be void of any emotions. My coffee finishes brewing, and I pour it into the Bean Hut mug and mix in my vanilla creamer. I transfer my omelet from the frying pan to a plate and sit down at the kitchen table.

Easton sits down across from me, leaning back with his hands behind his head and doing the man spread with his legs. He's grinning, and I have no idea what he's going to say.

I take a bite of my omelet.

"So that's what you like to do when you're alone," he states with his usual teasing tone.

"Sometimes. I usually don't expect people to sneak up on me." There's no playfulness in my voice. Despite Easton's good mood already lifting my mediocre one, I'm embarrassed he saw me having a dance party for one. "Why do you always come over here in the mornings? Don't you have your own kitchen?"

"Woah. Someone's extra snappy today." His grin only widens.

I don't play into it. Instead, I take a sip of my coffee. The creamer has cooled it down just enough to be the perfect temperature to drink without burning my tongue.

When Easton realizes he's not getting a rise out of me, he shrugs his shoulders and answers, "It's more fun being over here than alone at home." I don't respond, and a few moments later, Easton says, "So, I have a question." I raise an eyebrow as I meet Easton's dark eyes, waiting for him to go on. "Why are you so intent on not making any friends here?"

"What makes you think I don't want to make any friends here?"

He raises an eyebrow, and his grin turns into an *are you kidding me?* smirk. "Why are you so defensive?"

I take another sip of coffee while formulating my answer. "I used to think my friends would do anything for me, but they let me down. Every single one of them. I don't want to deal with that again. I don't want anything tying me down here. I'm here for the summer and then I'm gone. I don't plan on coming back."

"Why don't you want to come back? I mean, your dad is here. Wouldn't you want to come see him?"

"No."

Easton's dark eyes widen at the cruel look in my blue ones, and his arms fall to his sides. I hold his gaze, and he doesn't back down. I don't plan on elaborating, but Easton clearly has no problem being patient until I do. I hate it.

I also can't ignore the fluttering bullshit happening in my stomach right now.

I'm used to everyone knowing about my dad, knowing it's a touchy subject, and knowing I am the only one allowed to bring it up. I've never had someone ask me about him and give me their undivided attention while they wait for my answer.

I hate that Easton does just that. It makes me want to tell him everything simply because he cares. He cares enough to ask, and he cares enough to listen.

"Can I say something?"

Easton's voice brings me out of my thoughts, and I take another bite of my omelet.

I nod.

"This isn't my place, especially because I've only known your dad for a few years and you've known him your whole life. I don't know exactly what happened before he left, but I know what's happened since then. He talks about you and your brother constantly. As soon as he moved in, he was already putting together plans with my dad to add on the second floor so you and Andy would each get your own room if you ever decided to visit. He wanted to reach out, but he knew if he was going to have any kind of relationship with y'all, he would have to wait for y'all to come to him. When you called last week and told him you were coming for the summer, I don't think I've ever seen him so happy."

"What's your point?" I ask harshly.

For once, Easton looks pained. "My point," he says softly, the complete opposite of my tone, "Is your dad loves you *so* much. He knows he fucked up, and he's done everything in his power to make himself into a better man so he could finally be the father he should have been all along."

I don't want to hear anymore, nor do I want Easton to see the tears welling in my eyes. I stand up with so much force, the chair I was sitting in falls back and hits the wood floor with a *thud*. Groot jumps away from where he was resting on the floor at our feet. I grab my phone from the table and turn my back on Easton, heading towards the stairs.

"Aliyah—"

It sets me overboard. I turn around so quickly, the end of my ponytail whips me in the face.

"Don't you *dare*," I drawl, my voice a deadly calm as I try to push back the tears. A few of them push their way forward and start to slowly fall down my cheeks. I wipe them away with the back of my hand. "My father left my brother and I the *second* Andy turned eighteen. Andy had to sacrifice *everything* so he could provide for me. While all of his friends were going off to college and having the time of their lives, he had to work over forty hours a week just to keep us in our apartment and have some food on the table." I take a deep, trembling breath. "I don't care what the hell my dad has done to fix his mistakes, or that you seem to think you know all about our situation. It doesn't change the fact that he made them in the first place."

This boy in front of me knows nothing about the pain I feel every fucking day of my life. I may not know what shit he's had to deal with in his life, but there's no way he would be saying these things to me if he's ever felt the same anger I do. It's not the kind of anger one can forgive and forget.

I turn on my heel and storm up the stairs. Once in my room, I slam the door behind me and pace the floor. Angry tears rush down my cheeks, and I let out a frustrated sigh at how uncontrollable my emotions are. I almost never have breakdowns like this.

Why did Easton have to stick his nose in my business? He doesn't know the first thing about what my dad's done. How dare he act like it's something I can forgive.

It was an asshole move on his part, and I'm furious.

Who the hell does he think he is?

CHAPTER TEN

I TAKE A WARM SHOWER AND SLIP INTO A GRAY
sweatshirt and black athletic shorts. I want to keep the hood of
the sweatshirt up simply for the comfort it brings, but my wet hair
sticking to my back is the equivalent of hearing nails on a chalk-
board, so I pull the hood down and pull my hair out.

When I'm downstairs, I don't turn toward the kitchen where
I know Easton will be. Instead, I head for the living room and curl
up in the corner of the couch with a blanket. I know Easton will
come and sit down before he does. He makes himself comfy on
the other end of the couch, patting the space next to him for
Groot to hop up. The dog settles right at my feet, staring at me
with his big eyes. Despite everything, I smile and scratch between
his ears.

I wasn't planning to apologize, but those dark eyes turn me
into a puddle as soon as I see them. "You don't need to say you're
sorry," I say quietly, not meeting Easton's gaze. "You were trying
to help, and I flipped. I'm the only one who's allowed to be
sorry."

"I am sorry, though," he insists, his voice just as soft as mine,
and I look up. "I knew I was overstepping, and I still said those

things anyway. I—I have a habit of doing that." Faint color rises in his cheeks, and I fight the gravitational pull for my jaw to drop. *Easton is blushing?*

I shake my head to stop myself from staring.

We settle into a few minutes of peaceful silence. I'm too mentally exhausted to fight the calm that blankets me when I'm around Easton.

Maybe, ever-so-slightly maybe, a little bit of calm in my life wouldn't be so bad.

"My dad really built the second floor for me?"

"Yeah," Easton nods, and I look up to meet his gaze again. His eyes are too tempting. The rare smile he wore at work last week makes another appearance, and I commit it to memory. The dimples, the way one corner of his lips is slightly higher than the other. His eyes light up with a realness when the smile meets them, a rare genuinity most people are incapable of showing.

Easton's confirmation unwillingly expands the part of my brain where my dad lives rent-free. It's the smallest expansion, not enough to change the anger I feel, but enough to keep the smile on my face.

"I know you said you didn't want to make any friends this summer, but I'm overruling that decision. You and I are going to be friends."

I sigh, "Why are you so desperate to be friends with me?" My smile remains on my face despite the defeat I feel; I can't be angry at him for forcing his way into my life when he already has done that. Running into him in the kitchen or throwing insults back and forth at work have become part of my routine.

Easton grins at his success, "Because you really need a friend right now, and since you're trying so hard to *not* have any friends, I'm going to try even harder to be your friend. I'm not taking no for an answer."

"Okay."

Easton's eyebrows shoot up to the ceiling, and his jaw drops to the floor. I laugh.

"Cool," he says, getting over his shock and reaching for the remote on the coffee table. He switches the TV on. "What do you want to watch?" he asks, sinking into the couch like this is our normal routine.

"I'm not picky. Ideally something that won't make me cry."

He puts on an episode of *New Girl*.

Like I've said before: two peas in a pod.

I settle into the couch and train my eyes on the TV, watching as all the guys try to hook up with girls at the bar while Jess hangs out at home by herself. It's one of my favorite episodes, mostly because Nick and Jess have their first kiss at the very end.

"I've always wanted to play True American," Easton says when the characters on the screen start playing.

"It's really fun at first, but once people start getting super drunk, it's pure chaos. I don't think I've ever truly finished a game," I reply, trying not to think about the handful of times I've played it or the people I've played it with.

Easton turns his gaze to me and asks, "Will you teach me? It's half the reason I've never played. No one can ever agree on one set of rules. It's pure chaos before the game even starts."

His words make me laugh, and I say, "Yeah, pull out your phone. I'll explain it as best as I can." Easton does just that, and I start from the beginning.

That's how we spend the rest of our day. Easton orders a pizza from Dominos for lunch, and I feel bad about not being able to help pay until he tells me he has enough points for a free one. We do an extra cheese, pepperoni, sausage, half with bacon, the other half black olives and green peppers. The rain doesn't let up, so we remain on the couch binging *New Girl* and figuring out the best course of action for playing True American with his friend group.

My dad gets home right after four, and Groot hops down

from the couch to greet him. Easton turns towards the door and says, "Hey, Mr. Redding. How was work?"

"Hey, Easton, hey Ali." At the mention of my name, I turn to him. Our eyes meet, and I quickly look away as he bends down to untie the laces on his work boots. "We were putting up the roof at the house we're building, which was not a fun task with this rain. What have you two been up to?"

"Just watching TV, nothing special. There wasn't much more we could do," Easton grins, getting up from the couch. "I should probably get home, though. My grandparents are coming for dinner."

"What about the shop?" I ask. I haven't worked with anyone else, so I assumed the four of us were all they had.

"My cousin Jackie and her friend Naomi are closing. They were both at soccer camp last week. You'll meet them soon enough," Easton smiles, looking in my direction as he heads to the back door and slips his feet into his sandals. Groot trots over, and Easton scratches the dog's head in parting. "See y'all later," he calls as he slips out the back door and takes off in the direction of his house.

"How's work been?" my dad asks as he heads into the kitchen. I remember everything Easton told me earlier, but facing him now, nothing has changed. Anger builds up in my chest, fire itching to come up my throat.

I'm so fucking back and forth about how I feel, and I wish my mind and body would make up their own minds so I could make up mine.

I turn the TV off and stand up from the couch. "It's fine," I say, already making a break for my room with my phone in my hand. Groot follows me, slipping between me and the stair railing to race me to my room. He's already made himself comfortable on the bed when I walk through the door. I close the door behind me and fall onto my back beside him.

"Now what?" I ask him, turning my head so my nose is lined up with his. The tip of it is wet, and he opens his mouth to give me some kisses in response to my question. I put my hand in front of my face so he can lick that instead.

My phone starts ringing, and I turn away from Groot to see who's calling. It's a random number I know by heart and have been unable to block.

I stare at the two circles at the bottom of my screen. I want to hit decline, just like I've been doing for the last week, because I never want to hear his voice or see his face ever again in my life. I sit up and hit the green button, the smarter version of me floating two feet above in horror. I hold the phone up to my ear and say, "Hello?"

Nate exhales, and it sounds like he's been holding that breath in for a week. "It's so good to hear your voice." I almost tell him the same thing. He speaks again before I get the chance, and I realize the mistake I've made. "Your brother said you went to your dad's. When are you coming home?"

Anger surges through my veins at the laid back tone he uses. *The absolute nerve of this shitty excuse of a human to act like he has any right—*

"Why does it matter to you?" I snarl, a sound so backed with rage, I don't think I've ever made it before.

"Ali..." His voice sounds like I stabbed him right where it hurts most. *Good.* "I miss you. You didn't even say goodbye."

Did he always sound like this? Like he did nothing wrong and the other person is the one at fault? Like it's *my* fault we're in this position for leaving and not saying goodbye? Can he not take ownership for his own shitty actions?

His words trigger the bomb, cutting the wrong wire instead of disarming the explosive like he probably intended.

"Why the *hell* would I say goodbye to the person who created this mess in the first place?"

"So that's it? You're going to give up on us without even trying to work through it?"

Excuse me?

"Fuck off, Nate."

I hang up, something I shouldn't have to do in the first place. The audacity of him—

How could anyone be so fucking delusional—

Trying to put the blame on me for *not trying*—

I can't keep up with the angry thoughts streaming through my mind. I'm burning hotter and hotter, unable to get myself under control. The urge to scream, to yell, to do *anything*—

My phone flies out of my hand and hits the wall, but the roaring in my mind doesn't withdraw. The device clatters to the floor, and I watch as it settles face down on the wood. I stare at my phone, at all the issues it's caused, and a numbness settles in as the roaring subsides.

Was Nate always so manipulative and unwilling to take any accountability? Moments flash through my mind of him complaining about how much I worked and how we didn't get to spend enough time together and sometimes convincing me to request off more time than I could really afford. He knew I helped out Andy with the bills, that I didn't get the choice to live like every other teenager, but that never stopped him from making me feel guilty.

I believe the saying "love is blind", but I always thought I was smart enough to not be one of the blinded. How wrong I was, and my phone laying across the room is proof of this.

Part of me doesn't give a shit at how broken my phone surely is. A broken phone would erase a whole lot of problems in my life.

I also realize I have no money to pay for a new phone or a screen repair. I hop off the bed and cross the room to pick my phone up. It lights up through a shattered screen. I sigh. Not completely broken, but definitely not good.

It wasn't even cracked this bad when I dropped it off a thirty foot cliff last summer.

Great.

Just. Fucking. Great.

CHAPTER ELEVEN

When I go down for dinner and set my phone on the table next to me, my dad's eyes don't miss the shattered screen. He doesn't seem surprised, though, as if he heard the *thump-thunk* when I threw it. His lips pinch in a frown, like he wants to ask what happened but thinks better of it. I'm still heated from the conversation with Nate, and it shows.

Dinner is perfectly seasoned chicken and Spanish rice, and I hate that it tastes so good. Amongst many other hobbies, he must have also learned how to cook in the four years since he left, and I don't want to give him credit where credit is due.

I remember Easton's words from this morning about my dad being happier than ever when I called to tell him I was coming for the summer. Do I at least owe him an explanation for why I came? He had his hopes up we would be able to start over, and that's not even on my to-do list.

As much as I want to ignore him and go about my day like he doesn't exist, he deserves to know why I came running to him if it's not actually for him.

When my plate is cleared, every last grain of rice eaten, I speak up. "I need to tell you something." My voice cracks after not talking for a while, and I clear my throat before continuing. His blue eyes are laced with curiosity and concern, and I know I'm about to destroy the ghost of a smile on his face. "I didn't come to New Haven to make amends with you. My boyfriend and I broke up, and I had a falling out with all of my friends because of it. That's why I'm here."

Simple and straight to the point. No more than what he absolutely needs to know.

My dad's face falls at my words, ghost smile no more. A horrible, awkward silence fills the air around us. Despite the itch to escape the room as soon as possible, my butt is glued to the chair and my body refuses to move. I look away from his blue eyes so I don't start to feel worse than I already do.

Stupid fucking uncontrollable emotions.

"I figured when I picked you up from the airport there was something else going on," he says quietly. "I'm sorry for what happened with your boyfriend and friends. If there's anything I can do to at least cheer you up and help you enjoy your summer here, let me know." The unsureness from when he said similar words on my first day is still present in his tone, but it doesn't stop the rise of anger I feel toward him for once again thinking he would be of any help.

"I know you're trying to be all caring and help me through my shit, but I didn't come here for a parent. You are a roof over my head this summer, and that's it."

In my anger, the glue holding me to my chair melts away. I stand up so fast the chair falls back with a *thud* that has Groot jumping away from the table. My dad's face is stricken and pale, and I see my words replaying over and over again in his mind. I don't want to sit here and feel the second-hand pain I caused, so I grab my cracked phone and bolt upstairs.

I CAN'T HELP BUT GLARE AT THE SHINING SUN AS I scarf down some peanut butter toast before work. I'm scheduled eleven to five today, which means I'm missing the entire window to sit on the beach and work on my tan. All the glaring hurts my eyes, though, so I grab my phone out of habit, not sure what to do to pass the time now since I deleted all my social media apps.

No more scrolling through Instagram, no more skipping through people's Snap stories, and no more laughing at my favorite TikToks.

I set my phone down on the counter and pick up the black and white chevron mug, taking a sip of my coffee as I relax against the counter. There was a freshly brewed pot when I came downstairs earlier, an obvious gift from Easton I must remember to thank him for.

Speaking of, a shirtless Easton slides the door open as I'm shoving the last of my peanut butter toast into my mouth, and I yelp at the sudden noise. Groot bolts directly to his water bowl, and Easton grins at my scare, throwing his shirt onto the back of one of the chairs. "Morning, Li."

I stare at his bare, glistening chest for a few seconds before I realize I am, in fact, staring, and Easton has, in fact, noticed. I divert my attention to my coffee so he doesn't see me blush, only now registering the nickname.

"Li?" I question, already forgetting about my blush. I look up and directly into his eyes, raising an eyebrow. I ignore the fact that his tan, muscular, and, most importantly, bare chest is only a few inches below where I am looking.

It's not an easy task, and I'm horrified with myself.

"Yeah," he nods, helping himself to a glass of ice water. He knows my dad's kitchen better than I do and has no problem making himself right at home.

"Any particular reason for the nickname?" I ask, my snarky attitude making its first appearance of the day.

Easton finishes chugging the entire cup of water before

saying, "Well, it's not like I can call you Ali. You despise every person who calls you that."

"Not Andy."

"That's different. He's your brother." I roll my eyes as Easton sits down across from me at the table, and the subject changes. "So, if we're going to be friends, I need your phone number."

"Why?" I ask.

"Because friends have each other's phone numbers. I found the perfect meme to send you last night but had no way to send it to you!" Easton grins, pulling his phone out of the pocket of his shorts. He taps a few things and then looks up at me expectantly. A small sigh passes between my lips. It's not worth it to fight it.

And plus, he's right. I agreed we could be friends, and friends *do* have each other's phone numbers. Even if it's not just for memes.

I tell him my number, and a few moments later, my phone lights up on the table with a text from him. The meme, to be precise. Easton glances at my phone and does a double take. "Damn!" he gasps. "When did that happen?"

"Last night," I murmur, my phone call with Nate replaying in my head. I feel myself shutting down, retreating behind the wall I've built around myself.

Easton sees all of it. His voice is soft when he asks, "Do you want to talk about it?"

'No' is the first word that comes to mind. I open my mouth to say it without a second thought, but I hesitate. It's hard to say no to Easton's awaiting dark eyes.

I want him to know about my conversation with Nate last night, and realizing that surprises me enough to stop the rise of anger in my chest. My wall gives way, and I swallow my attitude.

"Nate called again last night. I was stupid and answered. I hung up on him and chucked my phone at the wall."

"Nate's your ex?" Easton confirms, and I nod. He's silent for a few moments before saying, "Well, if it's any consolation, I don't think you're stupid for answering." His voice is so far from the easy going tone it normally carries.

"How am I not stupid for answering? I knew answering would only piss me off more than I already am."

"You're not stupid for answering because you needed to hear his voice. Despite what he did, you were still in love with him for three years. You needed to face him, and now you can check that off your list. It's part of moving on."

I'm shocked Easton remembers how long Nate and I were together.

"I still shouldn't haven't answered," I say stubbornly.

Easton rolls his eyes, clearly knowing my mood has turned a small corner and it's okay to joke. "Do you want to talk about the actual conversation?"

Again, the 'no' comes to mind, but I swallow it and nod instead. "He said he missed me and I didn't even say goodbye, and then he said I was the one giving up on us and not wanting to work through this."

"What did you say?"

"I told him to fuck off, and then that happened," I say, pointing at my phone.

Easton grins, "Thatta girl." It makes me smile.

"Would you expect anything less?" I challenge, raising an eyebrow as I finish my toast. My mood lifts quickly, something I can only credit to the grinning boy in front of me.

"Never."

I finish my coffee and stand up to do my dishes. With my back to Easton, I ask, "What about you? Any horrible past relationships?"

"Nothing worth bringing up," Easton replies. "Are you coming to hang out today?"

I glance at him over my shoulder at the abrupt conversation change and say, "No. I work until five."

"Bummer. It's a perfect beach day."

"Don't remind me. And even if I did have the day off, I still wouldn't hang out with you guys," I say, emphasizing that work is not the reason I won't be joining him and his friends.

Easton huffs dramatically and shakes his head as I rinse my plate and mug. "Li, one day this summer, I will get you to hang out with us. I guarantee it."

"Bet," I chuckle, now determined to stick by my word. I set my clean dishes next to my dad's to dry.

"It's on."

I dry my hands on a towel and hold one out for him to shake. He takes it and makes a big shaking gesture, but I'm more concerned with the full-body tingles I feel from his hand simply coming into contact with mine.

Noooooope.

Nope nope nope.

NOPE.

N-O-P-E!

I yank my hand away, mumbling, "I have to finish getting ready for work."

"Work is boring. Come hang with us."

"Easton," I say, giving him a pointed look as I continue, "I can't just not show up for work. Your grandparents would hate me. They've already called me a life saver more times than I can count on my fingers and toes. I'm not risking that reputation." I leave the kitchen and head toward the stairs, and Easton doesn't hesitate in following me. Groot is on his heels.

"Not yet, you can't. Keep making your good impression and then you can do whatever the hell you want."

"Yeah, right. Your grandparents would love that," I snort, heading into the bathroom to brush my teeth. Easton sits down on the floor in the hallway and pets Groot, who clearly doesn't know he's a little too big to be a lap dog.

Since I'm already wearing my work clothes and my hair and makeup are done, I'm ready to go with a couple minutes to spare after I brush my teeth. Easton and I head back downstairs, and I make myself a ham and cheese sandwich to eat on my break. I let Groot out to go potty, and then Easton and I set off. When we step off the back porch, he asks, "What's your favorite memory from your childhood?"

I turn back to look at him, slowing for a brief moment so he can catch up to walk beside me. "That's a random question."

"I know," he shrugs, his usual smirk in place. "I'm trying to get to know more about you. Remember, we're friends now." He nudges my shoulder with his own.

"How could I forget?" I roll my eyes.

"So are you going to answer it?"

"What if I don't want to?"

"Do you not want to?"

"I don't know." And I really don't. I don't even know what my favorite childhood memory is. A montage flashes in my mind of my dad stumbling home only to crash on the couch with another beer or losing yet another job. Not exactly a favorite.

"If you don't want to answer it, you don't have to," Easton says, some of the softness from earlier returning.

"What's your favorite memory from your childhood?" I shoot back, adding a smirk so he knows I'm just being difficult.

Easton laughs, "Nice try. You first."

I roll my eyes and think for a couple of seconds.

One does jump out at me, and I smile as I replay it for Easton. "I was seven or eight, I think. In a brief week of sobriety, my dad took Andy and I to the mountains for a weekend so we could finally go skiing. It was always an empty promise he had made until then. One Friday, he came home and told us to pack a bag, and we left within the hour. We spent the entire next day skiing." I remember the hills we went down, fresh with powdery white snow that made the inevitable falls soft and cushiony. He taught us all the basic moves, waiting for us as we figured out how to stay upright on our skis without slipping or falling. It was the most patient I've ever seen him.

It was also the last time I had hope things would change.

"Your favorite childhood memory involves your dad," Easton observes, his tone weary, and rightfully so.

The snippy remark comes out before I can stop it. "Your point?"

"Woah, Li, I didn't mean to upset you," Easton rushes, dark eyes widening in guilt.

"Yeah, well, you said you're good at reading people. You should know any mention of my dad pisses me off," I say, the words bitter as they come out of my mouth.

We reach the boardwalk and he stops walking, tentatively touching my arm at the elbow as I step onto the first step. His touch is a superpower all on its own, and the anger I felt only moments before disappears. I turn to look at him.

"Li," he says softly. He doesn't say anything else until I relent my stubbornness and meet his dark eyes. They're filled with worry, an endless black hole sucking me in. He repeats, "I didn't mean to upset you."

"You didn't upset me." Lie.

He raises his eyebrows as if to say *really?* I pull my arm away from his touch, not able to collect my thoughts with the unwanted tingles.

"I have to go to work," I say quietly, taking another step up the boardwalk now that I'm out of Easton's hold. His lips fall into a frown as I take another step away, and I know exactly why.

Easton is a people pleaser, and he's much too good of a person to have any kind of association with me and my attitude. I want to puke at the prospect of leaving him standing there when he knows I'm upset. Ellie was a people pleaser, and if she knew anything she did upset someone, she couldn't focus on anything until it was made right.

I would hate to be her right now. Not an ounce of sympathy can be found for her in any of the atoms that make up my body.

But every atom is desperate to make sure Easton doesn't spend his day worrying about me. I need to say something so he knows I'll be okay and this bout of anger will pass. As strong as it can be, it always does.

So, walking backwards and hoping I don't trip or accidentally walk into someone, I grin and point to him. "You owe me a memory."

I know I've said the right thing when his real, true, kid-on-Christmas-morning smile breaks his face. Butterflies roar in my stomach at the look, and it takes everything in me to turn away before I start walking back toward him.

CHAPTER TWELVE

I DON'T KNOW WHAT I WAS EXPECTING TO COME downstairs to on Friday morning, but Easton standing at the stove making pancakes in black and white swim trunks and a white T-shirt was definitely not it. I can't help but grin and say, "Good morning."

"Morning Li," he says, looking up at me. He turns his body and leans back against the counter, his dark eyes watching me as I set my beach stuff down by the door and join him in the kitchen to make my coffee. He crosses his arms, his bicep muscles on full display and filling the sleeves of his shirt. I see a flash of the pink breast cancer awareness sign on his right chest.

The same shirt he was wearing the day we met.

Stop staring, you moron.

"Is there a reason you're making pancakes at my house instead of yours?"

"Yes, actually. Groot's here to keep me company," he teases, waving his spatula in the direction of the living room, where Groot lays on the couch. He perks his head up when he hears his name.

"I'm sure he's been doing an amazing job at that."

"We've been bonding. Right, dude?" Groot continues to look at Easton with his big eyes without a clue.

"He's not answering. I don't think he wants to hurt your feelings," I whisper, holding up my hand to shield my mouth from Groot.

Easton chuckles, turning back to the stove to flip the pancake as he says, "I've hardly seen you this week, so I've made the executive decision that Friday mornings are for pancakes."

I smirk, "What if I want waffles?"

"Smartass." He smirks back at me, not missing a beat as he corrects his words, "Friday mornings are *breakfast* mornings."

"Sounds good to me," I shrug. "Coffee?" I ask, gesturing to the pot almost done brewing.

"Yes," Easton nods, and I pull two mugs out of the cupboard. "Also, now that we actually have time to hang out, I still owe you a memory."

"That's right. You do," I muse, pulling the creamer out of the fridge as Easton flips the pancake. "So, East, what's your favorite childhood memory?" I grin. His nickname comes out of my mouth naturally, like I've been calling him that since I could talk.

"Hmm," he says, tapping his chin as he thinks about the question. I pour coffee into both of our mugs, leaving room for creamer in both (one with significantly more room than the other).

I almost miss it: in a split second, the easygoing look I've associated with Easton disappears. I turn all my attention on him, forgetting the coffee.

"When I was younger, my mom and I would always make chocolate chip cookies together. She has this famous family recipe, and they were the best cookies I've ever had. She would always sit me down on the counter beside the mixer so I could put all the ingredients in the bowl and watch them all mix together. She would play her favorite music from the eighties and nineties and dance with me around the kitchen while the cookies were in the oven."

I can't help but wonder what happened with his mom as Easton goes silent, whether she's still around or not. I've never seen her, but that doesn't mean she hasn't been living next door this entire time. Easton's quiet tone is a dead giveaway she probably isn't around, though, so I take a step forward and place a comforting hand on his forearm. "She sounds like she's an amazing mother," I say softly, still using the present tense because I don't want to assume. Easton's eyes snap to meet mine, and my heart breaks at the pain in them.

"Was."

"Huh?"

"She *was* an amazing mother," he says quietly, and without me having to ask or say anything else, he explains. "Breast cancer. I was fourteen. It was her second time around, and it all happened pretty quickly. One day she was screaming her heart out at my games, and the next she could barely open her eyes in the hospital bed." He looks away from me, gaze falling on the back doors.

And I was right about one thing: his customer facade isn't just reserved for customers. He puts on a massive smile for everyone in his life. Easton has taken the words "fake it till you make it" to heart, and he has perfected exactly what they mean.

"I'm so, so sorry," I whisper, slipping my hand into his. I lace our fingers together and squeeze, because this is not the moment where I should go on a rant about how his mother's in a better place and blah blah blah. He's not faking a good mood right now, and I feel honored he's okay with me seeing this side of him.

I refuse to mess that up.

Our hands mold together, and being near the stove has made his warm to the touch. I let him hold my hand for as long as he wants, ignoring the shocks of electricity sending my entire arm into a frenzy. Whatever they mean isn't important right now.

But they do mean something.

A few seconds or minutes later (I can't concentrate with the constant tingles running up and down my arm), Easton meets my eyes once again and smiles, though there's no sign of a sparkle in his eyes. "Thank you," he murmurs, and the low tone does things to my stomach I don't want to acknowledge. I nod, pulling my hand out of his. After losing his touch, I crave the feel of his calloused palm against mine.

"Is that what your shirt is for?" I ask, glancing down at his shirt. The pink lettering below the breast cancer symbol spells out *Team Michelle*.

Easton nods, glancing down at his shirt. "The school district did a fundraiser when she got diagnosed the second time to help us pay for treatment. It's my favorite shirt."

"That's sweet," I murmur.

"What about you? You never mention your mom," Easton remarks, his tone soft as he changes the subject. It catches me a little off guard that he doesn't know about my mom with how much he seems to know about my dad's situation.

"I never met her," I shrug, turning away from Easton's piercing gaze. "She had a high risk pregnancy with me and passed away right after she gave birth." I pour creamer into each of our mugs.

Easton places a gentle hand on my shoulder and offers me a smile. A *real* smile. The one he hardly shows. My favorite one. "I can't imagine what that must have been like. My mom and I had our differences, especially as I got older, but I'd rather that than never getting to meet her at all."

I shrug again, leaning back against the counter. Easton's hand falls from my shoulder as I grab my coffee and take a sip. "I didn't even know what a mom was until I started preschool. Everyone came in with both of their parents, smiling and happy. My dad dropped me off and practically sprinted out of there. My now ex-best friend came up to me when I started crying and said she would share her mommy with me. She had to explain to me what a mommy was, but we were inseparable after that." Talking about my dad and Ellie starts a rise of anger in my stomach, and I'm not even sure why I opened up about how Ellie and I became friends. I close my eyes and take a deep breath to reset whatever caused the rambling.

A burning smell starts to fill my nose, tearing my mind away from what we were talking about, and I quickly turn my attention to the pancake. Steam is rising up and around the perfectly golden side, but I see the crispier edges of the bottom. "Dude!" I exclaim, the vulnerable moment over for both of us.

"Shit!" Easton laughs as he abruptly turns to face the stove, sliding the spatula under the pancake and slipping it onto the small pile he has started on the plate. I flip it over quickly, the pancake hot against my fingertip. It's black, and I make a sound of disgust.

"That one's yours. I'm not touching it," I say immediately, taking a step away as I shake my head. I take another sip of my coffee as I sit down at the kitchen table.

"Perfect. Hockey Puck is my favorite flavor," Easton jokes, starting on another pancake.

"It's a match made in heaven, then," I say, and then, "You should have your grandpa make an ice cream flavor called 'Hockey Puck' just for you."

"It would be the hit of the season, for sure."

"A new tourist attraction for New Haven."

"Why come for the beach when you could come for Hockey Puck Ice Cream?" Easton says, his voice matching every generic video advertisement.

It has me losing my cool, and when I devolve into a fit of giggles, Easton does, too.

CHAPTER THIRTEEN

THE SUNNY DAY WE WERE HAVING TURNS INTO A wicked thunder storm while Easton and I are at work. When we close up the shop for the night, it's pouring rain and the wind pulls at the palm trees. I dread walking back through the wet sand to my dad's house, and the fact that I'll be soaked to the core before even stepping off the boardwalk only makes matters worse.

The lights of the shop are off, the floor is swept, the alarm is set, and Easton has his key ready in his hand to lock up. We're just inside the door, knowing the second we step foot out there, it's game over.

Easton sighs. His dark eyes reveal the same defeat I feel. "Now or never. Ready?" He looks down at me, and I glance up at him before nodding. "The second the door is locked, we run."

"Oh no," I laugh in disbelief, shaking my head. "I'm not waiting with you. The second I step foot through the door, I'm gone."

"You're not gonna wait for me?"

"You can run significantly faster than I can. Even with my head start, you'll probably still make it back before me."

"Wanna make it a race?" he grins, a devious glint in his eyes.

"What do I get when I win?" I ask immediately, the promise of a challenge too addicting to pass up. His grin widens.

"The winner gets to pick the movie tonight."

"I wasn't aware we *were* watching a movie tonight."

"Well, there's not much else to do in this kind of weather," Easton chuckles, gesturing his head in the direction of the door.

I want to tell him my words were more along the lines of "I didn't know we were hanging out at all," but he's so sure of these plans like we made them weeks ago that I can't think of a way to say no without sounding like a complete bitch.

Also, I don't want to say no.

So instead, I say, "Deal," push the door open, and take off into the rain. I need as much of a head start as I can get, and the element of surprise will buy me another second or two. Not only is Easton faster than me, he's used to walking and running in the uneven sand.

No one's on the boardwalk as I tear down it. The rain drops are warm and soak through my clothes immediately, the wet cotton clinging to my skin. It's windier than I thought it was, wet strands of my ponytail whipping behind me, and the waves are crashing onto the empty beach with a terrifying strength.

"THAT WAS UNFAIR, LI!" Easton roars from behind me, but the sound only puts a grin on my face and motivates me to run faster. I don't slow down as I near the end of the boardwalk, hoping the transition from wood to sand won't end poorly.

With the first step on the unsolid ground, I almost trip and face plant—exactly what I had hoped wouldn't happen. I struggle to regain my balance, but I'm moving forward the whole time trying not to eat the sand, and that's all I care about. The rain helps the sand pack together, making it easier than usual to run on. With every step, the sand I'm kicking up hits the back of my bare legs.

It's impossible to hear how close Easton is with the rain and wind in my ears. It's not worth the risk of eating shit if I turn my head back to check, so I don't worry about how close he could be. I just focus on how fast I'm running. The faster I run, the higher my chances of winning are.

And I do win, but barely. My hand touches the door handle right as Easton slams his foot down on the porch step. "Damn, girl! You can run," he gasps, following me through the door and quickly shutting it so the rain doesn't blow into the house. Both of our shirts are completely soaked through, and my hair drips down my back and onto the wood floor.

The two of us catch our breath as we slip out of our shoes and are greeted by Groot. I take my socks off, hating the soaked feel of them as they cling to my feet like a second skin.

"I'm gonna go change. I have some of my brother's old T-shirts that would probably fit if you want," I offer, slowly heading in the direction of the stairs as I wait for Easton to respond.

"That would be great," Easton nods from his spot on the ground. Groot is eating up all the attention from him, and I smile as I turn my back to go to my room.

I strip out of my wet clothes and slip into leggings and an oversized T-shirt. After hanging my sopping wet clothes over the shower rod in the bathroom to dry, I grab an extra T-shirt for Easton and my hairbrush.

Back downstairs, Easton still waits by the door, but he's on his feet now. "Here," I say, tossing Andy's old shirt to him from across the room. He easily catches it, and he has no shame as he strips out of his current T-shirt to change. My eyes snap to the scar above his hip. "What happened?" I ask, pointing to it.

He glances down at the scar and then meets my eyes. "Shark attack."

I blink once, then twice. Easton cracks a smile when I blink a third time. "Damn it. I was hoping I would get you."

Shaking my head back and forth, I laugh, "I'm not stupid. What really happened?"

"I, um...I fell down the stairs when I was eleven. Sliced it clean open with the scissors I was holding."

I fight back the urge to laugh at first. "You cut your hip open because you fell down the stairs?" Reluctantly, Easton nods, and for once, I'm the one who bursts out laughing at him.

"Yeah, yeah," he grumbles. There's only a second between his words and when his dripping wet shirt lands on my head. My laugh turns into a shriek as I quickly remove it, glaring at Easton before trudging down the hall to the laundry room.

With Easton's beautiful laugh filling the main level, I toss his shirt into the dryer and, because he threw it at me, set the temperature on low. He can have a dry shirt, but he sure as hell is not getting a warm one.

Back in the kitchen, Easton digs through the pantry and pulls out a box of popcorn. I pull my hair out of my ponytail and start brushing through it, watching as he unwraps a bag and puts it in the microwave. "How bad did it hurt?" I ask.

"It was terrible. There was blood everywhere and my friend Gabe thought I was going to die. I didn't want him to think I was a baby so I refused to cry until my dad and I were in the truck."

"Oh, you poor thing," I tease. My annoyance from the wet shirt disappears quickly, and I don't try to hold onto it.

I do come back to the thought of Easton somehow making plans for us without actually ever discussing them. It's a summer Friday night and he's here making popcorn with me instead of hanging out with his who-knows-how-many friends, this Gabe dude included.

"East, why are you hanging out with me on a Friday night instead of your friends?"

His answer doesn't miss a beat. "Because if I'm with them, then you're spending your Friday night alone, and that's just sad."

"Yeah, but I'd be choosing to be alone."

"Doesn't mean I have to let you be alone. Anyway, it's my

dad's turn to host poker tonight, so I'd be going home to a bunch of rowdy men."

"Is my dad there?" I ask, my good mood dropping as I think about what poker nights usually mean. Too many beer cans to count sprawled out, a paycheck gambled away, and an angry father until his next one comes in. I thought he had truly stopped that kind of lifestyle, but—

"Yes, but it's sober poker nights. Your dad said it was fine for them to keep drinking, but they weren't having any of that."

I don't know how, but Easton seems to be following exactly where my thoughts are going. *Damn him and those dark eyes that can see into my soul.*

Holding Easton's gaze, I take a deep breath, "You're sure?"

"Positively sure. Plus, they all put in a set amount, so nobody is gambling their life away."

Another deep breath. "Okay."

"Okay," Easton nods. Smiles. He gives me a moment, then asks, "So, what movie are we watching tonight?"

And just like that, I'm not worried about my dad falling back into old habits. I trust Easton, and if he says my dad is okay, then my dad is okay.

I pretend to think about it, like I didn't already know the second I won our race. "Hmmm. I think I want to watch *The Notebook*." I have a theory Easton might let a tear or two slip at the end, and I need to test that theory and figure out if I'm correct.

"Never seen it," Easton says, opening the microwave right as the timer starts to go off. He pulls out the popcorn, finds a plastic bowl in one of the cabinets, and empties the contents of the popcorn bag into the bowl. I'm still amazed with how well he knows my kitchen.

I gasp at his words. "How have you never seen *The Notebook*? That is unacceptable! Our friendship is on pause until you do!"

"Damn, Li. You'd cut me off for a movie?" Easton grins, leading the way into the living room. We sit down in the same spots we sat in when we binge watched *New Girl* earlier this week. Groot sits impatiently in front of Easton, eyeing the popcorn like his life depends on it.

"This is not just *any* movie," I defend, grabbing the remote from the coffee table and pulling a blanket over my body. "This movie is iconic. You need to see it."

"Ugh," he groans, shoving a handful of popcorn into his mouth. A piece falls onto the couch beside him, and Groot snatches it up right away. *Little stinker.*

"Hey! I don't want any grumbling or complaining until after the movie's over. That is, if you still want to grumble and complain."

"Fine," Easton grumbles, and I grin as he crosses his arms and tucks his chin into his chest like a pouting child. He man-spreads his corner of the couch, staring at the TV and waiting for me to start the movie.

"This movie was part of the reason I looked like—how did you put it? 'Like I was surviving an epic hangover?'" I tell him as I go into Netflix.

"*That's* why you looked like that?"

I laugh, "I mean, that and the fact that my ex-boyfriend is a cheating, lying scumbag." A surge of anger appears in my stomach, trying to claw its way into control.

"Huh. Who would have known?" I'm laughing again as I navigate to the movie, anger retreating. "So, how can a movie be good if it wrecks you that much?"

"You'll see," I grin, hitting play.

CHAPTER FOURTEEN

No surprise, I'm bawling toward the end of the movie. Easton's staring passively at the screen, but he's leaning forward with his elbows on his knees, hands clasped together, his legs bouncing beneath him. His face may not be showing much emotion right now, but his body language is all the evidence I need to know how invested he is in this movie.

Now I just need to wait for a tear. A single tear is all I need to prove my theory correct. Even through my bawling for Noah and Allie, I'm equally invested in watching Easton.

And then I see it. One lone tear leaks out of the corner of his eye as Noah goes to lay in bed with Allie and she remembers who he is. "Ha!" I say, abruptly standing up from the couch and pointing at Easton. The blanket drops to the ground and Groot jumps up at the sudden sound of my voice. Easton looks at me, quickly wiping away that tear. I don't bother trying to hide all of mine. Nothing could conceal my tear-stained face.

"I don't know what you're talking about," Easton says, but his voice sounds tight, and his typical grin is so transparent even Groot could tell it's fake.

"Admit it. You loved it," I say through my sniffles. I remain standing, waiting in a defensive position with my feet wide and grounded until Easton admits what we both already know.

He remains silent for a few seconds as the ending credit scene rolls around. His lips are set in the teeniest pout of defiance, and I catch myself staring for a few seconds.

No, Aliyah.

I force myself to look into his dark eyes, raising an eyebrow and turning my lips upwards in a smirk. A grin pokes through on his face, and my smirk widens at his next words. "Fine. It was much better than I was expecting. Happy?"

"Very," I say smugly, picking up the blanket and sitting back down on the couch. I grab my phone and check the time. It's just past eleven thirty. "How late do poker nights usually go?" I ask Easton as he stands up, stretching his arms above his head and yawning. My eyes land on his scar once again, and I imagine an eleven year old Easton tumbling down a flight of stairs.

"Midnight at the earliest. Your dad won't be back for a while," he responds through his yawn, grabbing another blanket before sitting back down. "I'll probably hang out here until it's over."

I grab the remote from the coffee table and toss it to him. "Since I'm so nice, you can pick next." I'm growing tired, but I'm not ready to go to sleep yet. I hope Easton picks something noncommittal to watch.

"Thanks. It would be my honor," Easton snorts, catching the remote with ease. He puts on *New Girl*, picking up where we left off.

I make it through the first episode before I can't keep my eyes open, and I pass out on the couch with my head on the arm and feet curled up against Groot.

———

I WAKE UP EARLIER THAN USUAL THE NEXT MORNING, the sun streaming in through the back door and lighting up the main level of the house. I groan as I sit up, stretching out my neck to try and get rid of the weird kink from the awkward position I slept in. I blink a few times, yawn, and feel my bladder about to explode.

I throw my legs over the couch and try to stand up, falling right back onto the couch since my feet are trying to stand on something that is definitely not the ground.

"Oof," the something says as I fall back, and I lean forward to see Easton clutching his stomach, his head resting on a pillow and body covered with a blanket.

A million jumbled thoughts run through my mind at the sight of him on the floor of my living room on a Saturday morning, and the first one I'm able to form into words is, "Did you sleep here?"

I want to facepalm at the question with an obvious answer. It's early, though. Excuse me for being surprised there is a boy on the floor below me.

"Yeah," he says, his voice raspy. It's a beautiful sound, just like his laugh, and I want to hear it more. He sits up and yawns, looking at me with tired eyes. The sun glints off their dark color, adding a gold tint. A small, half smile forms on his lips. It's his real smile, despite being small. "Thanks for the wake up."

I grin in response, unable to tear my eyes away from his until I'm reminded I have to pee when my bladder tries to empty itself. I put my feet on the ground, making sure I won't step on Easton this time. "I'll be right back," I say, and I head to the bathroom down the hall.

After doing my business and washing my hands, I rejoin Easton in the main area. "What are we feeling for breakfast?" I ask, filling the coffee pot with water.

"We had pancakes yesterday. Eggs and bacon?"

"Sounds delicious," I say, pulling the ingredients out of the fridge. Easton joins me, and we work silently side by side. I crack the eggs into a bowl and stir while he gets a frying pan out for the bacon. I pull out some more ingredients to mix with our eggs and he starts scrambling them in another frying pan. I put together two mugs of coffee and he divides our breakfast between two plates.

When we're sitting down at the table to eat, my dad appears from the hallway with Groot on his trail. So that's where the traitor ended up.

"Morning, you two," he says, helping himself to a cup of coffee. I feel bad we didn't make enough breakfast for him, but he wastes no time in taking out a few more eggs to make himself some.

Wait. I should not be feeling bad for him.

"Morning, Mr. Redding," Easton says, and I hear the change in his voice. It's small, something most people probably wouldn't pick up on. There's a little more pep in the tone, a sure way to put anyone around him in a good mood. I'm pretty sure the only reason I'm able to hear the difference is because I'm still thinking about the raspiness his voice held when I stepped on him.

I don't say anything. I do shovel a very large forkful of eggs into my mouth, though. Easton did a great job with them.

"How'd you sleep on the floor?" my dad asks Easton, taking down a mug and pouring himself some coffee.

"Wasn't the most comfortable, but I made do," Easton shrugs, his signature grin pulling at his lips. "Thanks for letting me stay."

"You two were out cold when I got back. I would have felt bad waking you," he responds, taking a sip of his coffee. "Any plans today?"

I open the shop with Mandy, but I have no desire to take part in this conversation. Thankfully, Easton has no issues filling in the gaps.

"Probably meeting up with some friends at the beach," he says. "The usual." My dad nods, remaining in the kitchen instead of joining us at the table. I'm sure it has something to do with giving me some space. I appreciate it.

Since I've spent the last two minutes shoveling food in my mouth so I don't have to contribute to this conversation, I finish my plate in record time. With my dad and Easton immersed in a conversation about the high school football team, I put my dishes in the sink and hurry upstairs.

I get dressed for work, braid my hair down my back, and brush my teeth in the bathroom. Back downstairs, my dad is cleaning up the kitchen, and Easton is nowhere to be found. I ignore the small ache of not saying goodbye to him.

When my dad sees me, he says cautiously, "Hey. I was scrolling through Facebook Marketplace this morning and found a chair that would look good in your bedroom if you like it. It needs a little bit of work, but it's nothing I couldn't do."

It's the last thing I ever thought I'd be having a conversation with him about, and I find myself saying, "Can I see it?"

He nods, wiping his hands on a towel before pulling his phone out of his pocket. I meet him in the kitchen, and he turns his phone screen toward me. It's an egg shaped chair hanging from a wooden base, the egg made of a wicker-style material and a cream cushion sitting inside it. The chair does need a little bit of work, touch ups on the scuffs and some of the wicker rethreaded, but it's not bad at all.

I'm shocked my dad picked out something I love so much. "I like it," I say, offering the most awkward of smiles. I head toward the back door to pull my Converse on.

"I'll see if I can pick it up today," he responds, offering me the same awkward smile in return.

"Thank you," I say, and I don't know how I'm still breathing with the most awkward tension in the air I've ever felt. "I gotta get to work," I say, gesturing toward the door.

"Yeah—yeah, of course," he says, and I'm out the door in a flash.

It's a relief to breathe in the sea breeze as I make my way toward the boardwalk. People are already filling up the beach, and

I have a feeling it's going to be a busy day at the shop by the looks of it.

Mandy's already inside when I get to Scoops, and she left the door unlocked for me. At the sound of the bells above the door, she calls, "Good morning, Aliyah!" from somewhere in the back.

"Morning, Mandy," I call back in return, heading in the direction of her voice to clock in and put an apron on.

"Looks like you and Easton had a pretty busy night last night," she says from the office, her voice down to a usual tone.

I lean against the doorway as I respond, "Yeah, it seemed like the entire crowd from the beach came in, but once it started raining it cleared out."

Mandy laughs, "That sounds about right. Being located right on the beach does mean our business is dependent on the weather."

"I'm beginning to realize that," I chuckle. Mandy stands up from the desk and grabs the cash drawer, and I lead the way to the front to start pulling out ingredients for the day.

"How have you been picking up on everything?" she asks me, pulling her own apron over her head.

"Pretty good, I think," I say. "Scooping definitely tires my arm out more than I thought it would." This makes Mandy laugh again as she links up the drawer with the register.

"It takes time to build up those muscles, but I promise, by the end of the summer, you'll be able to do it in your sleep."

I start taking the lids off the ice cream cartons as I say, "Hopefully."

"And how has Easton been? He hasn't been too persistent about things, has he?"

I have a feeling she's not just talking about her grandson as my fellow coworker, but I'm not planning to open up to her about how *persistent* he was about being my friend. "Other than teasing me for my lack of muscles, he's been nothing but pleasant," I respond.

Mandy laughs again, "I wouldn't expect anything less. I know how he is, but he also means well." Her words are simple, but I'm quickly realizing, despite my initial impression of Easton, how true they are.

"I know," I say, and I don't miss the way Mandy's eyes soften.

"Good," she responds, and I have a feeling she knows I'm not just talking about at work.

CHAPTER FIFTEEN

I HAVE MONDAY OFF, AND I PLAN TO TAKE FULL advantage of it. Now that the three dollars and seventy six cents I had in my bank account has gone up to just over one hundred and fifty after my first paycheck from work, I've decided it's time to do some shopping to get some things for my bedroom.

Except when I map where the nearest Target is while eating my peanut butter toast, it's fifteen miles away. The bike in the garage won't cut it, which means I have to ask my dad if I can either borrow the car or if he can bring me. I really don't like the sound of either of those options, but he did say if there's anything he can do to help me feel at home this summer, he would do it.

He's probably going there for groceries, anyway, so it's not like I'd be asking him to go out of his way to go there. I'll just hitch a ride in the Honda and suffer through the twenty minute drive.

I can do that for the sake of my bedroom feeling more like mine.

I send my dad a quick text, asking him if he can pick me up before going to Target. Short, simple, and to the point.

After I finish my toast and coffee, I clean up my small mess and head upstairs to change into a swimsuit. Since my day plans of going to Target have turned into evening plans, I might as well head down to the beach to tan some more. Not only do I have a solid tan now, it's not disappearing after a few days like it usually does in Colorado. Consistency is key, I guess.

And being closer to the equator.

I tie my hair into a messy bun, grab my beach essentials (I add a small beach bag to my list of things to get tonight, right after a hamper), and head downstairs. I let Groot out to pee before I leave.

It's just past nine, and the beach isn't crowded yet. I claim a spot near the water, a place I rarely find due to it being a popular zone for tourists.

I lay out my towel and make myself comfortable, shimmying my body into the sand to mold it for maximum comfort. I push my Airpods into my ears and start playing my music, closing my eyes and basking in the morning sun. It's breezy today, but it feels good as the sun starts to warm up my body. Even with my music playing at a decent volume in my ears, I still hear a wave crash onto the shore if it's a particularly violent one.

I've flipped a few times, drank half of my water bottle, and had an unfortunately adorable golden retriever shake out his fur right next to me when a shadow suddenly stands over me and an earbud is pulled out of my ear.

"What—" I start to say, turning to the culprit and stopping in my tracks when I see a grinning Easton squatting down beside me.

A *shirtless* Easton. His golden chest gleams with sweat, and the muscles are perfectly sculpted with a softness I have an urge to trace my fingers over.

What the actual fuck, *Aliyah?*

"Hello there," he says obnoxiously, rocking back and plopping down in the sand. Some of it flies onto my towel, and the googly eyes I'm sure I have turn into a sharp glare.

"Can I help you?" I drawl.

Easton gathers my things in his arms, including my phone. The remaining earbud is pulled out of my ear, and without a single peep from me, he puts both into the case. "I told you I would get you to hang out with us one day this summer, and that day is today." He stands up and holds a hand out for me. I groan, dropping my head onto the towel.

Damn this beautiful boy.

"I really would prefer not to. One friend is enough," I say into the towel, my voice muffled.

Easton laughs, "I didn't really understand what you said, but I know you're grumbling about not wanting to hang out with us. I'm not taking no for an answer."

And I know he won't, which is the only reason I cave. I call it playing smarter, not harder.

I groan and look up at Easton, holding a hand up over my eyes to shield them from the sun. The smile on his face is the rare one I haven't seen him wear around anyone else. Maybe I'm not the only one who does get to see it, but no one can blame me for thinking I am with the evidence I have.

It's the combination of my "smarter not harder" motto and the real smile on Easton's face that has me smiling as I hold up my hand.

"Yes!" he says happily, fist pumping before grabbing my hand and pulling me to my feet. He's a little too excited with his movements and slams me right into his chest. I immediately push him away, but not without an embarrassingly large shiver running down my spine at the amount of direct contact.

It feels just as soft as I had imagined.

I scrunch my nose and say, "Ick. You're so sweaty. Be careful next time."

"Yes, ma'am," he jokes, saluting me at the stern tone in my voice. I don't mean to sound so defensive, but that shiver I still feel throws me off. Easton's teasing shakes off some of the mindlessness, and I roll my eyes as I take my belongings out of his hands and roll them up in my towel.

"Well, lead the way, tough guy," I say, gesturing my hands for him to go in front of me. He doesn't waste any time heading toward his friends, and I reluctantly give up my spot by the water.

Weaving through the crowded beach, Easton walks with ease in the sand, something I have not mastered yet despite our race from the other night. My goal is to be able to navigate the sand with the same ease he does by the end of the summer.

I don't try to run to catch up to him. It's not worth the inevitable face plant into the sand. I take my time, not worried about losing him because the group of teenagers isn't hard to find. They're the loudest group on the beach, though the families with squealing kids and speakers at full volume are a close second.

Easton doubles back to join me right before we reach the group so we arrive at the same time. One of them blasts music from a speaker, a summer playlist I'm sure is similar to my own. I pretend the nerves in my stomach don't exist. Not only have I never been introduced to a big group like this, I haven't had to make a new group of friends since elementary school.

Easton says, "Everyone, this is Aliyah." I lift my hand for a small wave, not missing the fact that he introduced me as Aliyah and not Li. "That's..." He points people out as he says their names, but they go in one ear and out the other.

I do take the time to look at each of them, holding a hand over my eyes so I'm not blinded by the sun. They all look super friendly, their tanned skin a permanent feature from their lifetime of living by the beach. Most of the girls have their hair up in messy buns, ponytails, or in braids down their backs. My own messy bun fits right in. I see the same girl from the souvenir shop my first night here, her nose ring glinting in the sunlight. Her short hair is in two stubby French braids, the faded blue strands poking out. When Easton points to her and says, "Evianna," it's one of the only names I remember. I also remember who Gabe is, a boy with brown skin, light brown eyes, and messy black hair who wears the same mischievous grin Easton usually does.

The inviting smiles from everyone are quickly washing away the anxiety I felt about meeting them, and the next wave that crashes onto the beach has me forgetting about my "no friends" rule for the time being.

When Easton finishes introducing the group, I say, "It's nice to meet all of you. I'm not good with names, especially with a group this big," I say, giving Easton a pointed look that has a few people chuckling. "So please don't be offended if I ask for your name again."

"No worries at all," Gabe grins, tossing the football he's holding into the air.

"What are the rules?" I ask, gesturing to the football as he catches it.

He winds his arm back to toss the ball to me, as he, Easton, and another guy start explaining the rules. It's a light toss, and I catch it with ease, grinning at the fact that he thinks he'll need to take it easy on me.

"You can be on my team. Then teams are even," Gabe finishes. He has an arm wrapped around one of the girls now, and it's clear from the way she's leaning into him they are together. Her auburn hair is pulled back into a braid, and her emerald eyes crinkle with laughter as he whispers something in her ear. I catch the look in his eyes as he watches her laugh, a look so familiar I have to turn away.

It's the same look Nate used to give me. Eyes shining, wide smile, high cheekbones.

The look of being in love.

The pain in my chest doesn't come on as strong, and I plaster a smile on my face so no one gets suspicious as a pit forms in my stomach. Easton sees right through my act, and he nudges my arm as everyone starts to organize teams again. "You okay?" he murmurs.

"I'm great," I say, my voice a smidgen too high. He raises an eyebrow, and I let my smile drop for only him to see. "I'll tell you later, okay. We've got a game to play." A small, feather light smile replaces the fake one I had moments ago.

"Okay."

My smile turns to a smirk. "Also, you're so going down, King."

"Not if I tackle you first, Redding."

I snort, "You wish."

———

IN EASTON'S KITCHEN AFTER DINNER THAT NIGHT, when we're cleaning up the pasta mess and our dads have gone out back to sit on the deck, he finally asks, "What happened earlier?" It takes me a few seconds to remember what he's talking about, and then the image of Gabe and the way he was looking at his girlfriend, Josie, pops into my mind. "Oh," I say, my cheeks heating up in embarrassment. "It was nothing." I turn back to scrubbing the dirty dishes.

Easton shakes his head with a soft frown, "It wasn't nothing. You looked like someone ran over your puppy."

I gasp and turn away from the sink to look directly at him. "Don't say it like that!"

"Then tell me what was wrong." A small, taunting grin grows on his face as he dries the saucepan in his hands, and that is the only reason I cave. That, and my inability to say no to those dark eyes.

I sigh, turning away from him and looking back at the dishes still remaining in the sink. "You can't judge me, okay?"

"Li," he says softly, his voice losing all teasing tones. I hear him move and take a few steps toward me, and then he's standing right beside me. He leans against the corner next to the sink, resting an elbow on the edge. "I would never judge you."

I glance at him, and the look on his face is patient and ready to listen to every word I'm going to say. I open my mouth, "For a split second, there was this shine I saw in Gabe's eye when he was looking at Josie. It reminded me of how Nate used to look at me, and for a few seconds, that thought of knowing I will never see Nate look at me like that again completely took over."

My voice cracks at my last words, and I turn away from Easton so he won't see me forcing away tears. He's smarter than that, though, and he wraps his arms around my shoulders to pull me in for a hug. He's tall enough to rest his chin on my head as I rest my cheek against his chest, relaxing into the feeling of his arms being around me. I ignore all the warning signs flashing in my mind about getting this close to someone in New Haven, because I haven't felt this content since before everything happened with Nate.

Being able to have this moment of nothing means absolutely everything.

I close my eyes, and all I can think about is the way Easton's arms wrap perfectly around my body. There's no awkwardness of his arms being too long or too short, and my body betrays me by molding into his touch. He smells faintly of sunscreen, like he's worn so much of it in his life that the coconut smell has permanently scented his skin. It's not a smell I ever thought of as comforting until now.

The sound of the back door sliding open wakes me out of the peaceful trance I was in, and I jump away from Easton and turn back to the sink. Our dads' voices fill the open space. They're discussing something about work for the week, so I have no problem zoning out and scrubbing a plate more times than necessary. The hug from Easton has my nerves doing quadruple backflips, the adrenaline something I want more of.

"Aliyah, you ready to head to Target?" my dad asks, my name breaking me out of the mind trap I was in. The reminder of going to the store and not being around Easton right now seems like the perfect plan after how nice that hug was. I don't like the feelings it's making me have.

Setting the plate I scrubbed too many times to count on the drying rack, I turn to him and say, "Yeah, I'm ready," a little too enthusiastically. I notice the uncomfortable smile on his face, and I'm sure mine isn't far off.

"You guys are going to Target? Mind if I tag along?"

Why?

"Um—"

"Not at all," my dad says cheerfully, the awkwardness of his smile melting away. I know right away it's because if Easton is in the car, he'll fill in the conversation just the right amount, and the tension between us won't exist because that's the kind of effect Easton has on people.

"Sweet," Easton grins, turning his obsidian eyes to me with a playful gleam. "Race you to the car. Winner gets shotgun."

He runs out of the kitchen and doesn't even stop at the front door to put on his shoes; he just swipes them up as he rushes by. I groan in defeat, knowing I'm not going to win this race he has an unfair advantage in. Instead of running to the front door like Easton did, I slump my shoulders and drag my feet on the wooden floor. I feel little sand grains against my bare feet, a second skin that has become impossible to get rid of.

Dave starts laughing at my sullen posture, and even though his laugh is directed toward me, I smile. My dad joins in on the laughing, and for a moment, everything feels normal. There's no years of tension between us, the wall I put up is broken down, and I'm smiling as I goof around with the neighbor I feel like I've known forever.

For one split second, everything feels right.

My smile falls as I push open the front screen door and descend the porch stairs, numbly walking across the yard toward a smug looking Easton. He's leaning against the back of my dad's car, arms crossed and smirk in place. When he sees me, he pushes off the car and drops his arms to his side. His smirk transforms into a worried frown. "You good, Li?"

I shrug. Between the reminder of Nate this afternoon and a second of my life feeling normal, conflicted feelings are warring in my mind and stomach.

"So you're not good," Easton declares, his voice soft as I reach him. His eyes bore into me, reading my mind and soul like no other. It makes my heart melt, and feelings I don't want to feel begin to form. "Is it Nate again, or something with your dad?"

The words are spilling out of me before I can stop them. I tell him how the laughing made everything feel normal and I don't understand why it felt that way. That everything I thought I wanted disappeared for a moment and suddenly it was easier to breathe. When I finish and take a deep breath, he analyzes me for a couple seconds. He opens his mouth to respond, but another voice says, "You two ready to get going?"

For the first time ever, I'm grateful my dad is present. He pulls the car keys out of his pocket and unlocks the Honda, and I swiftly skirt around Easton and snag the passenger seat. He realizes my motives a second too late, reaching for the door right as I close it.

"Li!" he gasps, grumbling as he slides into the back seat. He buckles himself into the middle seat so he can easily lean forward over the center console. "I won fair and—"

"Oh no you didn't," I cut him off, shaking my head and wagging my finger back and forth. I shift in the seat so I can look him directly in the eyes, ignoring the flutter that follows in my stomach. "Nothing about that was fair and square. You were out the front door before the race was even a thing."

My dad turns the key into the ignition of the car, and the first thing he does is roll down the windows.

"But—"

"—And, not to mention, there was no count down. You had an obvious advantage."

My dad chuckles at our antics as he backs out of the driveway and starts driving down the road. The classic rock station is already playing, and, ironically, "Highway to Hell" is once again the song of choice. I'm thrown back to my first day in New Haven when he was driving me to the unknown. In some aspects, maybe it was my highway to hell, but not everything has been bad.

Easton scoffs at my reasons and sets his gaze on my dad. His jawline looks phenomenal at this angle, and I want to reach out and trace it with my finger. "Mr. Redding, will you please tell Aliyah I was the clear winner of the race and I should have gotten shotgun?"

"Easton," he sighs, but I hear the laughter not far behind, "I hate to break it to you—actually, I don't—but Aliyah made some fair points." My dad having my back makes me happier than I thought it would.

"Not you too!" Easton says, but he's smiling as he turns back to me.

"Told ya," I smirk, holding his gaze and letting myself bask in this moment. He's staring directly back at me, the goofy smile still on his face. His eyes hold an excitement I don't recognize, but I like it. They're the matching puzzle piece to the smile he rarely wears.

My dad turns onto the interstate. As he picks up speed, the wind blows louder into the car, and our conversation ceases. We'd have to yell to be heard. The silence feels natural and, for once, not awkward at all.

Maybe letting him in wouldn't be such a bad thing.

CHAPTER SIXTEEN

IT'S PAST MIDNIGHT, AND EASTON AND I ARE LAYING ON opposite sides of the couch in the living room. I have my back resting against the arm so if I look forward, I'm staring directly at Easton. *New Girl* plays quietly on the TV screen, and Groot is asleep on top of my feet between the two of us.

"Where'd you learn to play football?" Easton murmurs, breaking the silence we've been in for over an hour.

I smirk, tearing my gaze from the TV to look at him. "What, did you think I would sign myself up for failure?"

"No, that's not your style. I guess I just wasn't expecting that from you."

I shrug, "Yeah, well—" I stop abruptly before saying I had a good teacher. I don't want to bring up Nate at all. I'm content right now.

Happy, even.

I glance at Easton, and he's got an eyebrow raised as he cocks his head to the side. The silence remains for a few moments, and I wait for him to ask me what I was about to say.

Instead, he surprises me by saying, "You should come hang out with us more often. I think everyone really liked you."

"How do you know they liked me?" I snort. "I was a bitch more than half the time."

"You weren't being a bitch," Easton grins. "You were just being yourself."

"Myself is a bitch."

Easton laughs, the noise filling the main level. With my dad's room right down the hall, I worry Easton will wake him up, so I grab the gray throw pillow under my head and launch it at him. The sudden movement disrupts Groot, whether it be from my feet moving or Easton trying and failing to catch the pillow. It falls to the floor behind him. I *tsk* and shake my head in mock disappointment.

"What are you shaking your head at?" he grins. His eyes hold a look of trouble, and I can't look away.

"Absolutely nothing," I shrug, and I make my next move before he makes his. I slip my feet out from under Groot so I don't launch him onto the floor when I get up from the couch. I have to run past Easton to make it to the stairs, and fortunately, he hasn't processed that I'm escaping in time to try to grab me.

I scurry up the stairs, Easton's footsteps hot on my tail and the click of Groot's toenails behind him. Easton laughs loudly again.

My bedroom is in sight, and I shoot through the open doorway. I'm too slow to close it, though. Easton manages to push it open, so I do the next best thing and attempt to run for the doors to the balcony.

Hands grab my hips and stop me from escaping, and then his fingers are tickling my sides and I'm laughing louder than he is. "Oh my gosh, Easton, stop!" I screech, falling to the floor in a heap. I move my body this way and that, squirming to try and get away from his revenge.

"Not until you say sorry."

"For...what?"

"For throwing a pillow at me and laughing!"

"Why...would I...say...sorry...for that?"

He starts tickling me harder.

"Easton!" I screech, trying a new tactic to get him to stop. Instead of trying to push him away from me, I grab his fingers and squeeze so he can't move them anymore. The tickling stops, but the feeling of my hands wrapped around Easton's and my back pushing against his chest sends an even more stimulating feeling through my veins. My brain can't focus on anything except the contact between me and Easton.

I quickly let go of his hands, and I'm able to move away from his grasp. The floor is cold against my hands and knees, and it throws me back into reality. "I hope we didn't wake up my dad," I whisper, turning around and sitting a few feet away from Easton. He shrugs at my words, and I can't help but grin at the goofy look he's giving me.

I wish I could see him give me that look everyday for the rest of my life.

Easton repositions himself so he's leaning back against his arms, his long legs out in front of him. He's facing the balcony, the moonlight streaming in through the open curtains. It's a crescent moon, so there's not much light, but there's enough for me to see how relaxed Easton looks. Between his posture and the smile on his face, he looks like he's having the most peaceful time of his life.

I relax to match his stance, laying on my back and using my arms as a pillow. I stare at the ceiling, and the stick on stars I got at Target earlier glow back at me. They're scattered across the ceiling in a perfect abstraction. There's no awkward empty spaces or one star too close to another. I worked very hard on it when we got back.

"This is the first time I've been in your room," Easton says, and I hear him shift. I tilt my head to watch as he lays down beside me, staring at the stars like I was only moments ago. I turn my head back and trace the Big Dipper I purposefully put up there.

It's my favorite constellation only because it's the only one I can find.

"What do you think of it?"

"It's kinda empty. It looks like a bedroom in a model home."

"I've only been here a few weeks, and I don't have a ton of money to decorate it. Plus, all of the things that would make it my bedroom are at home. Double plus, there would hardly be any pictures. You would only see me and Andy."

"We should take a picture." I turn my head to look at Easton, not sure if he's joking or not. He turns to look at me, sitting up and reaching for his toes. I'm surprised he can even graze them. He turns back to me and, seeing I haven't moved a muscle, says, "I'm serious."

"Why?" I smile.

"So when you do finally hang pictures in here, and when you go back to Colorado and never return, you'll have a picture to remember this summer." His words are soft, pulling at every single heartstring as they settle into my mind in a place I know I'll never forget them. It's dangerous, what he's starting to do to me. It's so hard to fight it when he's right in front of me, though.

"Okay." I sit up, pulling my knees into my chest. "How do we want to do this?"

"You're putting all the work onto me?"

"Well, it was your idea." And, though I would never admit this to him or anyone else, the idea of taking a picture with him feels intimate. Taking pictures with anyone for the first time feels intimate. It's like taking the next step in a relationship; it's acknowledging you have hit that point where you are close enough to take pictures.

"Touché."

A giggle slips through my lips, and Easton shakes his head back and forth as he gets to his feet.

"So," he starts, reaching out his hand for me to grab, "We can take a selfie, or we can set a timer and do something goofy. The decision is up to you."

A selfie means getting relatively close to Easton, so I opt for the self timer. After he pulls me up from the ground, Easton sets his phone up on my dresser as I stand there awkwardly, my right arm hugging my left elbow to my body as I scour ideas on how we can be goofy without this being uncomfortable.

Once his phone is propped up against the wall behind my dresser, Easton turns back to me. "So, what are we going to do?"

"Oh no," I shake my head, "It's your turn to make a decision. I made the last one."

"Ugh," he throws his head back. "You've never been this bad at making decisions before."

I gasp, dropping my chin as I head over to the bed to grab a pillow. Turning back to Easton with a white one in my hands, he's shaking his head at me but holding out his hands in preparedness. "You take that back."

"No," he taunts, and I see him take a step closer to me. Not wanting to be in an easy line of fire, I crawl onto the bed and stand up. I tower over him as he approaches the bed, realizing there's no way to grab me easily without one of us most likely getting hurt.

Or so I thought. I move to the middle of the bed, but Easton's arms are long enough to reach me. I'm not expecting him to reach for my ankles and pull them out from under me. My back hits the mattress and the pillow falls out of my hands beside me. "Rude!" I laugh.

"At least you weren't able to throw it at me this time," he points out through his laughter.

"You act like that's a good thing," I say as I sit up. With me sitting on the bed now and him standing beside it, he's taller than me. The way he's looking at me in the dark gives me goosebumps up and down my arms, and I turn away.

"Isn't it?" he responds.

I roll my eyes, standing back up so his dark eyes can't continue to look at me like they are right now. On my way back to my feet, I get an idea for a picture, and I say, "Turn around." He raises an eyebrow but does so without question, and I don't give him any preparation. I loop my arms around his neck and legs around his stomach.

So much for not getting close to him.

"Woah!" he laughs, stumbling forward a couple steps before regaining his balance and grabbing my thighs to hold me in my place.

I really didn't think this through. If I had, I wouldn't have willingly put myself in a position where I am wrapped around Easton like a sloth and his hands are on my bare skin. His hands are warm and calloused against my thighs, and I do my best to remain in the present with the pink walls around me and stars on the ceiling.

Easton's hands are on my thighs.

Easton walks across the room to the camera and presses the red button, backing up so we're centered on the screen. It starts counting down from ten, and Easton asks, "Serious picture or goofy? And don't say it's my turn to pick."

"Technically, it is, since I chose the pose," I grin, an idea already forming in my mind. I keep my eye on the clock.

"Both, then."

"Okay."

Right as the timer hits one, I move one of my hands away from Easton's neck and bring it right into his armpit. The flash goes off right as Easton almost drops me, both of our faces lighting up with shock and amusement. I fall to the floor with a thud, but I'm laughing hard enough to ignore the pain spreading through my tailbone. Easton bends over laughing, resting his hands on top of his knees to keep himself on his feet. I fall onto my back and let the laughter escape freely.

"If my dad wasn't already awake, he for sure is now," I manage to say.

"He's gonna hate me!"

Easton's words keep me laughing, but when I finally settle down and think about the picture of us now on his phone, I say, "That was perfect. I want to see how it turned out."

Still laughing, Easton stumbles over to his phone and collapses onto the ground beside me with it in his hand. I sit up and lean over my knees as I wait, our faces only centimeters apart. He exits the camera and pulls up his photos, clicking on the one we took.

The flash illuminates both of us in the dark room. We're blurry with the sudden movement of me tickling Easton, but it only adds to the candidness of the photo. You can see the pure happiness in both of our faces, the wide grins and high cheeks and raised eyebrows giving it all away. I didn't think it would be possible for me to be happy this summer at all, but I guess anything is possible when Easton is involved.

I laugh even harder when I see my left leg and arm flailing as Easton's left arm lets go of me, pointing to the screen so he'll know what I'm laughing about. I fall onto my back and return my gaze to the stars, letting myself soak in every ounce of happiness in this moment.

CHAPTER SEVENTEEN

IT RAINS FOR MOST OF THE WEEK, VIOLENT thunderstorms shaking the palm trees and large waves crashing onto the empty shoreline. Most nights, I sit in front of the balcony doors and watch the lightning strike and light up the sky, listening for the clap of thunder soon to follow.

Easton gives me a ride to work in his truck when needed so I don't have to make a break for it in the rain like we did a couple weeks ago. We fall into a routine of spending the days in either of our living rooms, marathoning the Marvel movies and playing countless board games. Groot is always with us, curled up on the couch or at our feet. Again, I wonder why Easton isn't hanging out with his big group of friends. I don't question him about it, despite the ongoing war I have with myself about how attached I'm getting.

Friday morning, the sun is out and there's not a cloud in sight. It shines through the balcony doors, the curtains intentionally left wide open. I'm the furthest from a morning person, but something about seeing the sun after days of endless rain and clouds is enough to put a big smile on my face and get me out of bed. I change into a swimsuit and grab my new beach bag by my bedroom door, and I head downstairs to get something to eat.

I'm not surprised to find Easton in the kitchen making bacon and French toast, despite it barely being after seven. Friday morning breakfast has turned into every morning, and on the rare mornings Easton's not downstairs when I wake up, I miss him and the hurricane of butterflies more than I want to admit.

I also fight myself for feeling that at all.

"Woah," he grins, taking his eyes off the stove to look over at me. I meet his gaze with the same smile I've been wearing since I woke up. "Who are you and what the fuck have you done with Li? Did you bury her in bed?"

I laugh, swiping a piece of bacon from the plate between the stove and coffee pot. Easton tries to smack my hand away with the spatula, but I'm too quick for him. My smile widens, the corners of my eyes crinkling as I stare into his dark ones. Standing with my back tucked into the corner of the cabinets, I jump up and sit on the counter without breaking our gaze.

Easton grins back, the smile meeting his eyes and sending a twinkle of some kind of emotion through them. "Really, though," he says, turning half his attention back to the stove, "What's got you in such a good mood today?"

"Have you not looked outside?" I gasp.

Easton makes a big deal of leaving his spot in front of the stove and looking out the window above the sink right next to me. He pretends like he's trying to find something specific, moving his head this way and that with his hands braced on either side of the sink. His left wrist presses against my bare thigh, and though we're both acting like it's no big deal, I can't ignore the tingles shooting through my leg.

He turns his head back to me, removing his wrist from my skin. I fight the frown, but I don't need to fight it for long. He turns and leans back with his forearms now supporting his weight against the counter, his right arm directly lined up with my thigh.

Woah.

"What am I supposed to be looking for outside?" he grins, a playful glint in his eyes. It takes me a moment to remember what we're talking about, but when I do, I can't help the teasing words that fall from my mouth.

"Are you an idiot?"

He laughs, throwing his head back and leaning further back on his arms. I watch his reaction with a smile, and I want to run my hand through his messy hair. It would be so easy to reach up and touch the blonde locks, and the scariest part is how natural it would feel to do it. It doesn't help that his arm is now not only touching my thigh but pressing into it, too.

Still laughing, Easton pushes himself off the counter and once again takes his place in front of the stove. I fight the frown at the loss of contact. He flips the current piece of bread in the pan as he says, "Someone woke up swinging."

"Someone's gonna keep swinging."

"Easy there, tiger," he grins. The new nickname has my heart doing somersaults, and I roll with it. With the look in his obsidian eyes, I'm not the only one he should be calling tiger, though.

I laugh and hop off the counter to shake off the effect of Easton's look, my veins feeling like one long electrical current whizzing round and round. On wobbly legs, I take down two mugs to fill with the freshly brewed coffee. I grab the creamer, making sure to fill Easton's mug roughly halfway and mine an eighth.

"I'm in a good mood because it's sunny. I can finally go out and resume my tanning," I explain to him as I pour the coffee.

"I knew that."

I snort and say, "Sure," knowing full well he *did*, in fact, *know that*.

Easton gasps, and as he flips the first piece of French toast onto a plate, he says, "Just for that, I get the first piece."

I laugh and swipe another piece of bacon from the other plate, dodging his hand and bringing my mug to the table to wait. Groot follows my trail, sitting patiently at my feet as I sit down. I give him the last bite of bacon.

"So I take it hanging out with us isn't even a possibility for today?" Easton asks.

"You are absolutely correct," I nod, but I do remember how much fun I had last week. Maybe I would decide to hang out with them another time this summer, but after my lack of beach time this week, tanning is a priority. Plus, playing football or whatever they're doing would completely defy my "no friends" rule now that I've remembered it again. I already broke it once for Easton.

"Bummer. I was looking forward to tackling you again."

I scoff, "You must have hit your head on the way down, because I was clearly the one who tackled you."

Easton turns to face me, a wide smile on his face. "Someone's gonna keep swinging, indeed."

I smile sweetly as I take a sip of my coffee.

———

THE BEACH IS FAIRLY EMPTY WHEN I GET DOWN THERE at eight thirty. It's a little chilly, but when I get situated under the sun, I warm up fast. I don't bother putting in my AirPods right away, instead just playing music out of my phone's speakers. The silence, aside from my music and the natural sounds of the beach, is welcomed.

A few more people trickle down to the sand within the hour, and I slip my AirPods in so my music isn't disrupting them. I'm in my bad bitch mood, so I switch to my playlist titled exactly that.

By lunch, the beach is overflowing. I eat my peanut butter and jelly sandwich while watching little kids splash around in the surf. I take my AirPods out while I eat, screams and boat motors and other people's music filling my ears instead. There's plenty of people-watching to keep me occupied, everyone wanting to get back out on the water after days of nothing but storms. People are tubing, parasailing, skiing, kayaking, and I even see some boats out in the distance fishing.

I finish my sandwich, reapply sunscreen, and lay down on my back, putting my Airpods back in and settling on a more chill playlist for the afternoon. I know my tan will be significantly improved from today, and I smile at the thought.

I'm half asleep when something suddenly blocks the sun from me. Groggy and confused, I open my eyes to see a shirtless Easton standing between me and the light. I glare and sit up, noticing the navy and white striped towel in his hands.

He never brings a towel to the beach.

"Can I help you?" I ask, the single look of his smile already making me less angry about him disrupting my tanning nap. I take an AirPod out so I can hear his response.

"Not really," he shrugs, and he lays his towel down right next to mine. Like, *right* next to mine.

Okay, then.

Scrunching my eyebrows and fighting my smile from his mere presence, I question, "Then what exactly are you doing?"

"Well, you did cave and hang out with us last week, so I thought I could return the gesture and tan with you."

"Correction: I did not cave. I simply decided it wasn't worth my time to argue with your persistent ass."

"I don't know," he sighs, sitting down on his towel and looking at me with a teasing smirk. "Sure sounds a lot like caving to me." He's only inches away from me, a fact I cannot ignore.

Rolling my eyes, I say, "You're impossible." I lay back down and close my eyes, bending my elbows and resting my hands above my head so the sun can get the undersides of my arms. I leave the AirPod out, because with Easton here, there's bound to be a conversation.

"Like you're not," he retorts, and I hear him move. I peek an eye open and see him lying down as well, replicating my position.

I try not to stare at his bare chest for too long, or think about just *how close* he's lying to me. Did he intentionally put his towel this close to mine?

"Never said I wasn't," I respond, closing my one eye and finding comfort in the feeling of the sun on my skin again. It's something to focus on so I don't focus on the other things crowding my brain.

Easton doesn't say anything for a couple of seconds, and then he asks, "So, is this all we do? We just...lay here?"

"Um, yeah. That's kind of what tanning is."

"Okay." And a few seconds later, "Can we listen to music?"

"Sure." I pass the Airpod I'm not using to Easton, and he tucks it into his ear. "What would you like to listen to?" I ask, scrolling through my list of songs.

"What do you want to listen to?"

"I don't care," I say. "I'm not super picky with music."

"Neither am I. Why don't you shuffle your library."

I nod and click shuffle. A song I used to love comes on, bringing back nothing but good memories that now put a bad taste in my mouth. I try to play it cool as I skip it. The next one stops the wave of sadness, an upbeat song that lets me forget everything.

"Why'd you skip that? It's a great song!" Easton gasps.

"I hate that song," I mutter as I glance at him, swallowing the bad taste of the memories.

Easton's dark eyes are confused for a moment, then fill with understanding. The simple look he gives makes my chest flutter. I don't have to explain myself to him, not like I once thought. He understands me in a way that has me looking away so he doesn't see the small smile spreading on my face.

Fuck.

CHAPTER EIGHTEEN

I RUSH INTO WORK RIGHT AFTER ELEVEN ON SUNDAY morning after receiving a frantic call from Mandy. Their dog got ahold of an entire pack of chocolate muffins this morning, and Fred is rushing him to the vet. I'm scheduled to close but didn't have anything else going on today, so it was an easy yes.

"Anything I can do to help?" I ask as soon as I'm clocked in. The first hour is always slow, so I usually clean or help with what I can so I'm not just standing around. Mandy's standing in the back between shelves with a clipboard in her hand, counting and writing numbers down. At the sound of my voice, she glances at me with a smile.

"Always so eager to do something," she teases, and it makes me wish I grew up with a grandma in my life to tease me this way. "If you want to count how many packages we have of each topping, that would be amazing."

I grin, "Of course." I grab a notepad and pen to keep track of my numbers and rejoin her at the shelves. We're both silent for a moment before Mandy speaks up.

"Easton seems to be pretty fond of you."

I'm glad my back is to her so she can't see the blush that rises on my face, and I'm even more glad she can't feel how fast my heart starts beating. *Easton talks about me with his grandmother?* "Um, what do you mean?" I ask, needing to know *what* exactly makes her think he is. Sure, we hang out a lot and he's my only friend here, but being *fond* of me?

"He speaks very highly of you. Not that he doesn't speak highly of others, but especially you. You've become his favorite person to be around, I think."

Highly of me? I'm a five foot three girl with a six foot attitude eighty percent of the time, and the other twenty percent I'm nothing but a cold-hearted bitch. And his favorite person to be around? "Did he actually say that?" I ask, turning around to look at Mandy as she turns to look at me.

Her soft smile helps me relax as she explains, "He didn't have to. I know my grandson. I helped raise that boy. With how much time he's spending with you, it means one of two things: he thinks you need a friend and has declared himself as that friend, he likes spending time with you, or both." And with the look Mandy gives me, she knows it's both.

"Has he...told you anything?" I ask quietly, looking down at the floor.

Mandy's voice is so soft, my worries flow right out of me. "Not anything I shouldn't know. He said you had a really rough experience, things aren't great with your dad—" I snap my eyes up to look at her, but wait for her to finish speaking, "—and he's worried about you."

"What did he tell you about my dad?" Everyone but me seems to think *highly* of Trevor Redding, so I refuse to talk to anyone but Easton about him, and even that's pushing it.

Once again, Mandy gives me a reassuring smile. *Is this what it's like to have a grandma?* "He didn't have to tell me anything. Your dad has spoken a lot with me, and I saw your face when Fred mentioned your dad's name the night you applied. You do well at hiding it, but I didn't grow old for nothing. I notice those little things."

Maybe I've had enough of keeping it in, or maybe she's just *that good* at seeing through me, but I find myself telling Mandy about everything. Nate, Ellie, my dad. I wipe away the calm tears as I ramble on about how much my life fucking sucks.

By some miracle, no one comes into the store as I'm pouring my heart out to Mandy. It's not long into me talking that she leads us out to the dining room, sits me down in a chair, and takes a seat across from me. She listens to every word I say, and at one point grabs my hands from across the table. It stops me from fidgeting with them and reminds me that she's there and she cares.

"And I just...What am I supposed to do? I got shitty cards dealt to me, and I don't think I can handle another one."

Mandy doesn't say anything for a few seconds, then, "Aliyah, you are one of the strongest people I have ever met. You've gone through more at your age than most people do in a lifetime, and you're still here. You're still fighting, despite every single person who has tried to break you. Healing takes time. It's okay you haven't forgiven your dad yet. It's okay you haven't moved on from Nate and Ellie and your old friends. It's okay to not be okay."

I don't break her eye contact. She's gripping my hands as if she's not only saying her words but giving them to me, and it makes me cry more. Mandy stands up and pulls me into a hug. It's one of the most comforting hugs I've ever received.

This is definitely what it's like to have a grandma.

"Thank you," I whisper.

"You don't need to thank me. This is what grandmothers are for," Mandy says, and though she is wise, I don't think she realizes how much her words mean to me. How much I needed them and how much they really say: *You can always talk to me.*

THE SHOP PICKS UP AND STAYS BUSY THROUGHOUT THE day. The weekend tourists heading out are all stopping in to get ice cream before their journey home, and the flow of customers is nonstop. Easton and Fred are here now (their dog is okay and in the kennel at home), and we figure out a good routine of Mandy being at the register, Fred stocking anything we need, and Easton and I scooping like our lives depend on it.

It would be great if those muscles would kick in right about now.

The rush dies down around seven thirty, and Fred and Mandy head out after taking care of some things in the office. Easton and I remain, and with the flow of customers significantly less than it has been the last few hours, we finally have time to relax. My arm is more sore from this job than it's ever been, and I wipe away the perspiration between my brows. The temperature in the building usually isn't too bad, but with the crowded shop and a constant open door letting the cold air escape, it's hotter than ever.

I watch Easton wipe away beads of sweat from his forehead with the bottom of his shirt. His tanned abs are on display, as well as his scar from falling down the stairs, and I can't look away. With his shirt covering his face for a moment, I hope he doesn't notice my inappropriate gaze. I remember my conversation with Mandy earlier, of Easton supposedly being *fond* of me. When he drops his shirt, the strength to look away consumes me, and I snap my face to the front windows.

"That was crazy," I murmur, looking out at the almost empty beach.

"This is what Sunday nights are like once tourist season picks up. It's crazy, but look at the tip jar," Easton says, and I glance his way to see him gesturing toward the clear mason jar next to the register. The jar usually only holds a couple of dollars, but right now, it's completely packed with change, ones, and I even see some fives.

"Damn."

"Jackie and Naomi have gotten lucky with the Sunday night shifts so far. Usually it's every other week, but they wanted more hours to make up for the week they were gone," Easton explains, referring to his cousin and her friend who I have yet to meet. In my almost month of working here, I've come to learn the two of them usually work together, and Easton and I work together. Fred, Mandy, or both of them will work when none of us are working or more than two people are needed. I'm sure I'll have the pleasure of meeting the two girls at some point this summer if the schedule ever works out since they have soccer practice, but in the meantime, I don't mind always working with Easton.

"How much money do you think is in there?" I ask, gesturing my head in the direction of the tip jar.

"At least thirty or forty."

"Are you serious!"

"Dead ass."

"That's, like, an extra hour or two of pay."

"It's the best," Easton nods, leaning back against the wall next to the door heading into the back. His signature smirk tugs at his lips, his crossed arms revealing the defined muscles of his biceps. I try not to stare too hard.

Fuck. This needs to stop.

"Mhm," I mumble.

"What are we doing when we get off?" He asks the question so casually, like it's a given that we automatically hang out. I raise an eyebrow and think about me being his favorite person to hang out with. It's impossible to stop the silly grin from growing on my face.

"I didn't know we were doing anything," I muse. I grab one of the sample spoons and scoop some vanilla ice cream out of the carton. I look at Easton when I eat it off the spoon, grinning at the eye roll I get for my choice of flavor.

"It's kind of our tradition. We close together, we hang out. I'm surprised you didn't know that by now." It's my turn to roll my eyes at his offended tone for me not knowing this "obvious" information.

"My bad," I respond, holding my arms up in a weak surrender before asking, "What do you want to do?"

"I don't know. That's why I'm asking you."

"You're horrible at making decisions."

"Watch it, Redding." He points a finger at me, and I swat it away. The bell above the door chimes as two people walk in. It's Gabe and Josie, hand in hand with a backpack slung over each of their shoulders. The awkward square shaped bulge of Gabe's is a clear indicator he's hiding a case of beer.

"Hey guys," I wave, approaching the counter.

"Hey, Aliyah," Josie smiles. "How's it going?" Her long hair is in a half up-half down braid, and I have a hunch her backpack may hold some other necessities for where they're going with Gabe's case of beer. The clinking of the glass bottles gives *her* away.

I shrug and say, "Not great. I'm stuck working with him all night." I gesture my head in Easton's direction, fighting the urge to turn to see his reaction. There's no need to look, though.

Gabe lets out a laugh, and Easton says, "Li! I thought we were bonding! I thought I was your favorite coworker!"

And I'm supposedly your favorite person to hangout with, too.

"Oh...well, uh...that's embarrassing," I stutter, turning to look at him. The frown on his face doesn't match the twinkle in his dark eyes. He's looking directly at me, and it only takes a moment before he breaks out his signature grin. Not his real smile I've grown so fond of, but the one everyone else sees.

"Looks like you've got your hands full tonight," Gabe tells me, and I shrug again as Easton steps beside me.

"When do I not have my hands full with him? He's at my house everyday." I see his jaw drop out of the corner of my eye, but I just smile at Gabe and Josie and ask, "What can I get for you guys tonight?"

They're both grinning as I so obviously change the subject, and Josie hops on board. "A medium vanilla, please."

"Any toppings?" I ask over my shoulder as I grab a medium bowl, my excitement filling up in hopes she says no.

"Nope. I'm feeling very simple tonight."

I already have the ice cream scoop in my hand, and I point it at Easton and say loudly, "Ha! I'm not the only one who prefers a simple scoop of vanilla!"

"Woah, tiger. I thought we've settled this," he grins, hands already up in surrender.

Gabe laughs again as Josie says, "Seems like this has been an ongoing battle between the two of you."

"Since day one," I confirm, scooping her ice cream with more ease now that I've had a break. I hand her the packed bowl of vanilla ice cream and turn to Gabe.

"Medium cookies n' cream." Easton beats me to it, scooping it out before I even turn to grab the bowl. "We're heading down to the beach for a fire. You guys should come when you get off," he invites, motioning to their backpacks. "We've got the usual."

"We're in," Easton says, confirming the plans for both of us. I don't even bother protesting.

"Sweet," Josie grins.

Gabe pulls out his card to pay, but Easton and I both wave it away. "Nah, dude. You know how it goes," Easton says, handing over his ice cream.

"I don't want to be the one to put your grandparents out of business," Gabe fights.

"With all the tourists we had earlier, I think we're covered for the next decade," I joke.

"She speaks the truth," Easton confirms.

"Fine." The little argument seems like it happens every time Gabe and Josie come in for ice cream, a conversation that comes so naturally to all of them.

Would making some friends here really be that bad?

I mean, I've already spent a day on the beach with them, and now I'm going to a bonfire.

The bell above the door rings as Josie and Gabe wave goodbye, and as soon as the door shuts, Easton asks, "What's on your mind?"

"Huh?" I ask, refocusing on him in front of me.

"You zoned out. What are you thinking about?"

Shit.

"Spit it out, Li. You'll tell me eventually," he says, his grin turning into a smile. A real smile. The smile that gets me to tell him almost anything. It's all the convincing I need as my resolve melts.

I mumble, "Maybe...you know...it wouldn't be the worst thing in the world to make some friends this summer."

"Sorry, what was that?" Easton asks, holding his hand up to his ear in my direction.

"You know exactly what I said," I huff, wishing I could wipe the smirk right off his face.

"Of course I did. I just wanted to hear you say it again."

"Not gonna happen, King."

———

WE CLOSE UP QUICKLY ONCE NINE O'CLOCK HITS, already seeing the faint flames of the fire down the beach. The sun is almost down, the sky a mixture of dark blues with a faint stretch of pink. We're both eager to get down there and hang out with everyone.

Even me.

I take my shoes and socks off before we hit the sand and carry them in my hand. The grains are still warm under my feet as the two of us walk side by side in the direction of the light. "Do you drink?" Easton asks.

"I haven't since coming here, but yeah. I used to pretty often with my friends, though I'm really careful about it," I tell him, shutting down the memories I don't want to think about. "And I know you drink," I tease, thinking about his pre-hangover picture.

"Haha," he drawls, "But not much this summer."

"Because you've been spending so much time with me," I laugh, nudging his shoulder with my own.

"To help you get to this exact moment," he responds.

"What do you mean?"

There's a comfortable silence before he says quietly, "I know what it feels like to be broken. My friends are what got me through it. I know your old friends are the people who let you down, but that doesn't mean you can't make new friends. Even if you are going to leave at the end of the summer."

Easton's words hit me deep, a warm, bubbly feeling filling my chest. The tone of his voice is like nothing I've heard from him before, and the rawness in his voice breaks my heart. Opening up to me like that, letting me see how much he once had to rely on his friends when he's usually the one being relied on, how he's not letting himself rely on anyone now, changes something for him.

It changes something for me, too.

"Easton," I say softly, stopping in my tracks and grabbing his arm at the elbow to stop him. He turns around to face me, the moon light hitting his dark eyes just right to make them shine. "You know you can talk to me, right?"

"I do talk to you. All the time," he says, cocking his head in confusion.

"That's not what I mean. You've been there for me since day one. When will you let me be there for you?"

"I do let you be there for me," he says, though understanding dawns in his eyes.

"Easton," I sigh, looking past his shoulder at the bonfire. "You don't let anyone be there for you." I see figures moving around the fire, laughing and dancing to the faint music I hear. "When is it going to be your turn?"

Easton grabs my hand in his, and I turn my gaze back on him. The tingles that erupt from even the brush of his fingertips on mine leave me frozen as I wait for him to say something. "Li, letting people in means they know I'm still hurting. I just want everyone else to be happy and not worry about me. If everyone else is okay, that's all I care about."

I want to be there for him so bad it hurts. "I know," I say quietly, squeezing his hand. "But you need to focus on someone being there for you sometimes, too. You can't push away all your pain forever. I tried, and look where that got me."

He nods, holding onto my hand with a more secure grip. "I won't. I promise," he says, taking our conjoined hands and turning it into a pinky promise. He holds the link up in front of our faces.

"I'm holding you to this. You better not let me down, King."

"I will never let you down, Redding."

CHAPTER NINETEEN

EASTON AND I REACH THE BONFIRE AND ARE immediately greeted with waves and some hugs from everyone. Josie approaches me as Easton heads over to grab us each a beer. She's holding a red solo cup of a mystery liquid.

"You made it!" Josie cheers over the music, cheeks rosy in the firelight. Her words aren't quite slurred together, but she's for sure had at least a few drinks. She pulls me in for a one armed hug, and I awkwardly wrap my arm around her.

"I did," I smile as we pull away.

"Are you drinking? I can get you something to drink if you are," she offers, grabbing ahold of one of my hands with her free one.

"Easton's grabbing us drinks," I tell her, letting her lead me over to a group of girls. Evianna is in the group, and she waves when she sees me.

"Hey, Aliyah!" she greets, and I move to stand by her. She's holding a beer in her hand, and by the slightly crushed-in sides, it must be almost empty.

"Hey, Evianna. How have you been?" I ask, staring into the flames of the fire.

"It's summer, so, you know, living my best life," she grins. "We haven't seen you since you played football with us. You kicked Easton's ass and disappeared off the face of the earth."

I knew I beat Easton.

I almost tell her I've been busy, but the lie is so obvious that anyone within a mile radius would be able to call my bullshit. "Yeah," I shrug, my mind stumbling over what to say. "It's...been a less than ideal summer," is what I come up with.

She gives me an encouraging smile, not phased at all. "If you ever want to talk to anyone about things, you can talk to me. I know we hardly know each other, but I've been told I'm a great listener. And as awesome as Easton is, sometimes a girl just needs some girl-talk, you know?"

"Yeah, thanks," I chuckle, knowing I won't take her up on her offer.

"You're here now, so let's hang out. We'll have a great time, and you can experience your first New Haven beach bonfire," she says. I'm grateful she doesn't push it.

"Sounds like a plan."

Easton rejoins me and hands me a can of beer. It's a brand I've never had, and I pray it doesn't taste like shit. My expectations are low since it's probably one of the cheapest ones they can get their hands on.

I go to crack open the top, but Easton smacks my hand away. "Absolutely not. We're shotgunning," he grins, pulling out his keys.

I sigh and give him a pointed look, eyebrows up and chin down, but hold out my hand nonetheless for one of the keys. He slips a key off the ring with ease and places it in my hand.

Josie slips her hand into mine and squeezes. "You got this, Aliyah." I grin at her, return Evianna's smirk, raise a challenging eyebrow in Gabe and another guy's direction, and finally turn my gaze to Easton.

"Let's do this," I say.

"Ev, wanna count us down?"

"On it," she grins, moving to stand right in front of us. "On go. One. Two. Three." She speaks loudly, letting the suspense build up as other people join the crowd to watch this. When Evianna says, "Go," I slightly crack the top of the can, dig the key into the side of it with as little force as possible, and bring the cut to my mouth.

The beer does indeed taste like shit, but I swallow more and more as I crush the can. I'm no amateur at shotgunning nasty beer, and I'm determined to beat Easton. Letting him win this is signing up for at least a week's worth of bragging from him.

When I empty the can only seconds later, I tear it away from my mouth and hold up the crushed aluminum in what I hope is victory, beer dripping down my chin. Cheers erupt with my name. I look at Easton as he takes his own can away from his mouth. In the light of the fire, I see how much beer has soaked his white Scoops T-shirt. There's some beer dribbling down his chin, and I fight the urge to wipe it away with my thumb.

I'm screwed.

"Damn it, Li," he swears, shaking his head and not bothering to hide his wide smile.

I regain my composure and say, "Half of your beer ended up on your shirt and I *still* beat you, King." I shake my head in mock disappointment.

A course of "damn's" and whistles follow my retort. Gabe approaches and pats Easton on the back while grinning at me. Easton looks defeated, but he looks even more surprised at the fact that I won.

"Damn, Aliyah. Where'd you learn how to shotgun like that?" Gabe asks in amazement.

I shrug like it's no big deal, "My brother. He made sure I would win any shotgun competition I took part in, so I've had a lot of practice." Not a lie. Andy and I have been shotgunning cans of lemonade and Sprite since I was six years old.

"That was awesome, girl!" Josie cheers, wrapping an arm around my shoulders again.

Evianna grins across from us, and she holds up her hand for a fist bump. "You gotta show me how to do that so I can take these dumbasses down," she tells me, gesturing to Easton, Gabe, and the other guy who's name I don't remember. I'm patiently waiting for someone to say it so I don't have to ask.

"Give me another one," I grin back.

A course of "ohhhs" erupt around me and Evianna as we're each handed a beer. I hand my empty one to Easton and say, "I don't really know how to help you aside from practice. For me, the more I did it, the better I got at it and the easier it became to chug the entire can." Evianna hangs on to my every word, and I can't help but grin at her eagerness. "Let the beer go straight down your throat, don't sip or slurp on it."

"Wise words," Easton says, cracking open a beer for himself and taking a sip.

"They are indeed," I agree, meeting his eyes. It's just a second, but it feels like the moment lasts a lifetime. There's a new look on his face, one I haven't seen before. It's not his signature grin, but it's not the real, true smile that meets his eyes, either. His smile is small, but I have no doubt it's real. His eyes are what throw me off. In the light of the fire, they're a deep amber, and they hold a spark that makes my toes curl.

I feel that smoldering amber gaze down to my core.

Tearing my gaze away from him is harder than I would like it to be. "Ready?" I ask Evianna, positioning the can and key in my hands so I'm ready to go. Evianna copies my moves, so I take a moment before we start to show her specifically how I hold them.

Friends or not, when I leave at the end of the summer, one of these girls can carry on my legacy, and who better than Evianna with her platinum blonde hair and faded blue tips?

Easton makes a big show of announcing our start. "One. Two. Three. Go!" I repeat my actions with the key and quickly bring the can to my mouth once again, squeezing the can and letting the disgusting beer run down my throat. I finish a few seconds before Evianna, but, unlike when Easton lost to me, people wait to cheer until both of us are holding our empty and crushed cans in the air.

"Good game, partner," Evianna laughs, wiping the beer from her chin before holding out her hand. I grab it and give it a solid shake.

With two beers in me now, I take it easy. I take both of my crushed cans to the black garbage bag to throw them away, then slip a full one out of the case to sip on. I am in no way a light weight, but I'm not planning to get plastered tonight.

I grab another can for Evianna and rejoin her by the fire, bumping shoulders with her as I pass her the beer. "Oh, thank you," she smiles, cracking it open and taking a sip.

"It tastes like shit," I say, but I take a sip anyway.

"It does indeed, but it's cheap and does the job."

"It does indeed," I mock with a grin, the alcohol starting to take effect on my body. It's not much, but a lazy smile becomes permanent on my face.

"Easton said you're here for the summer," Evianna says.

"Yeah. Some shit went down back home and this was my only getaway option. Not ideal, but it hasn't been all bad," I respond. The growing effects of the alcohol are opening up that can of worms.

"Well, despite whatever shit went down, we're all glad you're here," Evianna says. "Hopefully we'll see you at the King's Fourth of July party next weekend. Most of us and our families will be there."

I meet her navy eyes, the fire lighting up the blue and making them look endless. "Easton hasn't mentioned it to me yet, but I'm sure it has something to do with me being against a social life this summer," I laugh, the alcohol spilling the words out.

They make Evianna laugh, too. "So that's why you haven't

been around," she teases, and I shrug my shoulders as if to say *You caught me.* "Whether Easton's told you or not yet, you know you're invited."

"I'm sure I am," I reply.

"Speaking of Easton, you two seem like you're getting pretty close."

I find Easton from across the fire, watching as he laughs with a few guys whose names I don't remember. "Yeah. He weaseled his way into my life and didn't take no for an answer," I tell Evianna. "I'm glad he didn't, though. I would be in a far worse place if I didn't have him as a friend." I'm still watching him through the flames, noticing the smile he's wearing. It's a real smile, but when he glances at me and sees me staring, the smile changes. It's *my* smile. I smile back, unable to look away until Evianna's voice breaks me out of the trance.

"Just as a friend?" Evianna teases, and I break my gaze with Easton as she nudges my shoulder. I lock eyes with her navy ones again. Her question throws me off guard, but we're only staring at each other for a moment before we burst out laughing.

"Yes, just as a friend," I lie. "Nothing more."

It can't be anything more, even if any part of me wanted it to be.

If someone else sees what's going on, I'm in deep shit.

"Well, I need another beer," Evianna says, tipping over the can in her hand to further prove her point that it's empty. I shake mine and hear sloshing towards the bottom. I tip it back and finish the contents.

"Bring me one?"

"Already planning on it," she grins, taking the empty can out of my hands and walking away.

A song comes on that has everyone cheering, and right as the beat drops, a warm hand grabs my own. I'm spun around and find myself face to face with Easton, a wide smile on his face.

"Hi," I giggle, laughing even more as he starts to sway to the music with my hand still in his. "What are you doing?"

"Dancing with you," he tells me. His eyes are still smoldering in the firelight. I don't look away.

"Okay," I say quietly, and I start dancing with him. We join the crowd of teenagers around us and start singing the lyrics as we dance. I let loose, laughing as Easton does some weird move with his hands up in the air. I copy his actions, basking in the laugh that escapes his own mouth.

We keep coming up with crazy dance moves, linking our hands and trying to keep in step with each other but inevitably failing. I'm not saying I haven't had fun with Easton this summer, but I haven't had *this* much fun in a long, long time. Being this high on life is something I didn't even know I was craving.

The song ends, and I stumble into Easton's body, out of breath and unable to catch it due to my laughing. He catches me with an arm around my waist and holds me steady until I can stand on both feet. No skin touches, but being wrapped in his embrace feels like home. The permanent smell of sunscreen lingers on him.

Instead of fighting the hug, I lean into it, resting my head right below his shoulder. I calm down and finally catch my breath, but I don't step out of his hold. His arm relaxes and remains, keeping me there but not holding me up.

I'm in some deep, deep shit.

I can't find it in me to care right now, though.

Every reason I was clinging onto before slips my mind for the night, and the smile doesn't leave my face once. I shotgun another beer with Gabe, we have a cartwheel contest that Evianna turns into a round off back hand spring, and Easton and I win a game of chicken against Josie and Gabe in the water.

I'm still smiling when I stumble through the backdoor at four in the morning, and not even the sight of my dad reading in his chair at this ungodly hour changes that.

CHAPTER TWENTY

THE NEXT DAY, I WAKE UP IN MY BED WITH GROOT'S body pushed up against me. My mouth is dry and I'm desperately craving ice water. I pat Groot's body twice before throwing the covers back and slowly crawling out of bed. I feel tired, but there's no headache or nausea. I didn't drink enough last night to be hungover, but it's been a while since I've drank at all, so who knows what could have happened. I grab my phone from my nightstand and check the time. It's almost two. I have a few texts from numerous people I don't read yet.

I drag my feet across the wood floors to my bedroom door. It's cracked open, so I know Easton must have come in to get Groot earlier this morning for their run. I don't know what planet he's from if he still went on his run this morning.

Groot hops off the bed and stops right beside me, looking up at me as if to say, "I'm ready when you are." We head downstairs, and the first thing I do is grab the biggest cup I find and fill it to the brim with ice water. I look out the kitchen window to the beach as I chug the glass, the pitter-patter of rain hitting the house finally registering. I wonder if it was raining this morning when Easton went on his run.

I finish my water and refill the glass, sitting down at the table and pulling out my phone. There's one text from Easton, one from a random number, one from my dad, and one from Andy.

Easton: *You were out cold when I got back from my run. Lmk if you want to hang out later*

I almost type back that I'm awake and he can come over whenever, but flashes of last night run through my mind. Our absurd dancing and the way I stayed in his arms for much too long after that are both bright red warning signs now that I'm sober. Leaving him at the end of the summer is already going to hurt like a bitch, so I can't let myself get more attached to him than I already am.

I make the decision and quickly type it out, hitting send before I read too much into it.

Me: *i need a day to recharge. i'll see you tomorrow?*

I check the next text from the random number.

Random number: *hey its eviamma! we shoulf hangoit soon*

I smile at her drunken misspellings, creating a contact for her.

Me: *definitely!*

I'm not sure if I mean it or not, but I don't think I'll regret it if we do. I check the texts from Andy and my dad next.

Andy: *Call me when you're up*

Dad: *I'm going to pick up Thai food on the way home from work. Here's the link to their menu. Let me know what you want.*

I smile at the smiley face emoji at the end of my dad's text. I click on the link to check the menu of the restaurant, quickly deciding on chicken fried rice and a side of egg rolls. I text him my order before calling Andy. It rings once before he picks up.

"She's alive," he says dramatically through the phone.

"Not funny," I grin.

"Sure sounds like you think it is. I hear you grinning from across the country."

"Yeah yeah, whatever," I laugh. "What's up?"

"Same old, same old. Work, eat, sleep, repeat. What have you been up to?" I hear bustling from his end of the call, and I know he's getting ready for work.

"Work. Tanning. More tanning," I tease, feeling bad my summer is significantly more fun than his.

"Sounds like a blast."

"Oh, it is. I went to my first beach bonfire last night," I tell him.

"That sounds like even more of a blast. How was it?"

"A lot of fun, actually. I blew everyone away with my shotgunning skills."

"Taught by yours truly. My baby's all grown up," Andy says dramatically, and the image of him wiping away a fake tear is so clear, he could be standing right in front of me.

I laugh, and Andy continues on.

"They grow up so fast. Before you know it they're out of the house and you're all alone."

"Oh, you poor thing. Being an empty nester is clearly messing up your routine."

"It is." His tone does a fast one eighty, from lighthearted and joking to sad and longing. "I miss you Ali. Pancake Saturday isn't the same without you."

"I miss you, too. Two more months. I'll be back before you know it."

"Will you?"

Andy's question throws me off guard, and I quickly ask, "What is that supposed to mean?"

"Will you actually be back in two months?"

"Wha—yeah. Why would I not come back?" I don't like where Andy's taking this conversation.

"Because you might not want to leave."

"Andy—"

"Aliyah. I'm just saying." The sound of my full name has me shutting my mouth. "You're spending three months on the beach with Dad. I know you're still working on the forgiveness part, but you've slowly been building a life for yourself there. I mean, you went to a bonfire last night. You wouldn't have gone if you didn't have at least one person you were becoming friends with."

It's exactly what I wanted to avoid by coming here this summer. It was supposed to be work and the beach. No friends, no dad, no Groot.

No Easton.

"I'm not wrong, am I." It's a statement, not a question.

"No," I say softly. "You're not. But I am coming home. I just needed to get away for the summer."

"But why? It's been a month and you still haven't told me what happened. What was so bad that staying with Dad for a summer was the better option?"

"I don't want to talk about it, and you know that."

A frustrated sigh comes from his end, and I know he's running a hand through his hair. It's the same light blonde as mine, though nowhere near as long. He likes to keep it shoulder length.

Andy changes the subject, but it's just as frustrating. "How are things with Dad?"

I don't understand why Andy keeps asking about our dad like things are going to change overnight. The question only angers me this time, and my response is short.

"Still avoid him at almost all costs. I didn't come to New Haven to hang out with him."

Andy sighs again. "Ali, please give him a chance. And before you cut me off," he starts, and I close my mouth instead of spitting out my defensive words. "I know you didn't go to New Haven to hang out with him, but you're there. Dad knows he fucked up, and I think the fact that he's letting you live with him when you hardly talk to him is enough of an indication he wants to start over and be part of our lives."

"You say our, but where the hell are you?" I snap, regretting it immediately.

"You know damn well why I can't be there. I have to be here to work to make sure we don't become homeless."

The tone Andy uses on me is a tone I've never heard from him before. He's always been patient and kind with me, taking my shouts and mood swings with ease and being there for me when I apologize. He's never turned my harsh tones back on me until now, and I hate the empty feeling growing in the pit of my stomach.

Now I know what it feels like.

"I'm sorry," I whisper, hoping he can't hear the quiver of my voice or know there's a tear running down my cheek.

"Ali," he says softly, regret pronounced loud and clear. "I'm sorry. I didn't mean for it to come out that way."

"I'll give Dad a chance." And I mean it this time.

———————

MY DAD GETS HOME FROM WORK TWO HOURS LATER, Thai food in hand. I've showered and cleaned the kitchen and living room, wiping down the counters and vacuuming up the sand I've tracked in from the beach each day.

When he walks in, I'm waiting in the living room watching *Friends* with Groot. The smell of Thai food hits my nose. It smells amazing, and apparently Groot thinks so, too. He ditches me on the couch to sniff the contents of the plastic bag in my dad's hand.

"Hey," I say awkwardly, looking into the kitchen as he sets our food on the table. The word sounds weird coming out of my mouth. I run my fingers down the baby hairs framing my face, trying to style them enough so they're not flying all over the place.

My dad looks in my direction, hiding the brief surprise that takes over his features. "Hey," he smiles. He pulls out one of the chairs to sit down, the legs scraping against the wood floor.

"How was work?" A little less awkward, but still forced. We're getting somewhere.

"Pretty good. The cabinets for the house we're building came in today, so those got placed. How was your day?" His question is tentative. Confused, almost.

I gesture to the TV, "I've only been up since two, so this is all I've been doing. I talked to Andy for a little bit." It's starting to sound like a normal conversation. Andy would be proud of me.

"You got back late last night."

"There was a bonfire Easton and I went to when we got off work," I shrug, pausing my *Friends* episode and heading into the kitchen to grab my dinner. Since I woke up later and knew my dad would be home with food within a few hours, I've only eaten a banana and some Oreos. I'm starving.

"That sounds like fun." I wait for him to start questioning or lecturing me about drinking, knowing it would ruin the cautious conversation we are having, but he never does.

I may drink underage, but I'm careful about it. I've never blacked out. I've only puked once. I've never lost control. After watching my dad do all of these things for my entire life, I vowed to make sure I would never be in the same position. I would sooner not drink at all.

He pulls out food from the plastic bag and sets it down on the table. I grab two forks and sit down across from him. I cross my feet, then uncross them.

"It was." I grab my rice and egg roll, and my dad grabs a fork. I cross one leg over the other and still feel awkward. I uncross my legs and settle.

"I'm glad you got out and got to meet some others your age," he nods, opening his food and taking a bite. Some of the rice falls off the fork and onto the table between the container and the edge. He scoops the grains into his hand and tips them back into the container.

"Everyone seems pretty nice," I say, taking my first bite. It's delicious, and I become ten times hungrier at the mere taste of the food. My stomach grumbles loudly right before I swallow, and I shove another bite into my mouth. Some of the rice falls onto the floor, and Groot is quick to snatch it up.

My dad nods again as he takes another bite of his food, moving his head over the container so the rice that falls only falls back into it. "Do you have any plans for tonight?" I shake my head at his question. "I'm surprised you're not hanging out with Easton."

More warning signs. "I just needed a day to myself," I shrug, busying myself by pulling one of the egg rolls out of the bag they came in. I take a bite and let the wide array of flavors take over my taste buds. I meet his eyes. "We could watch a movie later, if you want."

It would be an easy way for us to spend time together without having to continue forcing this awkward conversation.

The smile that breaks out on my dad's face relaxes me. "Yeah, let's do that," he agrees. "I'll shower after dinner and you can find one for us to watch."

What feels like hundreds of movies race through my mind, all romantic comedies or teen dramas. I doubt he would want to watch *The Notebook* with me, although I wouldn't mind rewatching it again.

"Okay," I say, shoveling more rice into my mouth.

CHAPTER TWENTY-ONE

I HAVEN'T SEEN OR HEARD FROM EASTON SINCE yesterday after I told him I needed a day to recharge, and by the time two o'clock hits, I can't shake the idea he might be upset with me and, therefore, avoiding me. Since the day he's gotten my number, we've had a constant flow of conversations and memes going back and forth without fail, so this isn't like him. *Did I do something without even realizing it?*

The sun hides behind a thick layer of clouds, but there's no rain in the forecast. The air is just hot and humid, and since I can't tan, I'm staying inside with the air conditioning. I'm anxious, though, so I clip Groot's leash onto his collar, check my phone one more time in case I missed a text from Easton, and then head out the front door.

My gaze falls on the King's home, the siding a faded yellow. It looks the same as it always does, yet something still feels off. I think about walking up the porch steps and knocking on the door, but I don't know what I would even say to Easton if he answered. So, I keep walking.

There's no logical reason for why I thought I could leave my hair hanging all over my neck and shoulders other than I didn't know what true humidity was until today. I don't even make it to the end of the block before I pause to gather all of it into a messy bun on top of my head. Groot's just happy to be out here, and he sniffs at the grass while he waits for me to be done with my hair.

"C'mon boy," I say, and we keep going.

I walk around the block twice with Groot, stopping in front of the pale yellow house once again when I pass. The urge to knock on the door and find out what's going on is even stronger, and when I set off for another lap around the block, I know I have to do it.

What will I even say? It's only been a day of not hearing from him. In any other situation, this would be normal and I wouldn't even realize it, but my gut is telling me *something* is happening.

Something isn't right.

Groot bounds up the driveway when we finish our second lap, panting from the heat. I let him in the door, chug some water as he splashes his all over the floor in his haste to hydrate, and then I make the journey next door, cutting through the yards out front.

The porch steps creak as I walk up them, and then I knock on the door. I take a step back and wait, growing more nervous by the second. What if Easton really doesn't want to talk to me?

No. If I did something to upset him, we're going to talk about it. I refuse to believe he would let me down this easily after knowing how my summer started and promising he wouldn't let me down.

I knock again.

Maybe I should go back home.

I wait. Knock again. Ring the doorbell. Knock a fourth time.

There's finally the sounds of movement inside, and then the door swings open. Easton stands there, and I fight the urge to gasp at his appearance. His hair is a mess (like, more than it usually is), he's got dark circles under his eyes, and his white breast cancer T-shirt is wrinkled like he's been laying in bed all day.

His dark expression barely changes at the sight of me, but he steps aside to let me in. I step over the threshold and Easton closes the door behind me. He walks into the kitchen without a word, and I follow him. "Are you okay?" I ask softly, but there's no response.

He grabs a glass and fills it with water from the fridge, sipping from it without looking my way. "Hey, what's going on?" I try again, but there's still no response. It hurts to have him ignore me like this. I want more than anything to help him, but if I can't even get him to say one word, how much help would I really be?

I take a deep breath and try one more time. "East, did I...do something to upset you?" I ask quietly.

"This has nothing to do with you, Li," he says harshly, a tone he's never used on me before. The only relief in finally hearing his voice comes from his use of my nickname. It's not enough to push away the tears that form in the corners of my eyes.

I don't like how his tone makes me feel, but I believe his words. *This has nothing to do with me.* God knows East has put up with my cruel words and harsh tones more times than I can count this summer, and isn't this what I wanted? I wanted to show Easton the same friendship he's shown me. I now realize how heartbreaking it is to have wanted something like that, because it means he's hurting so much he can't even try to hide it.

Easton needs me, and I won't let his harsh tone push me away.

"East," I whisper, a lump forming in my throat as I approach him one step at a time. He doesn't move away, and that gives me the courage I didn't have before. When I'm standing in front of him, his head down so he can't look me in the eyes, I cup his cheeks in the palms of my hands and gently make him look at me.

I'm shocked to see tears in his eyes, and the broken look on his face causes my own to start falling.

Whatever is causing him to feel like this, I will destroy it with every fire I possess in my body.

I wipe away the one tear that rolls down his cheek, then whisper, "Talk to me, East."

He doesn't talk. Not yet, at least. He does, however, wrap his arms around me and pull me tightly to him. My arms slip around his neck, and as he buries his face in my neck, his hair tickling my bare skin, his shoulders start to tremble.

My heart wars between breaking into a million pieces for him and wanting to protect him at all costs. It's a protectiveness I didn't know I was capable of, something only the boy who is clutching onto me like his life depends on it can bring out of me.

I rub his back, humming a soft, "Shh, I'm here," into his ear every so often. One hand crawls to the base of his hair and just holds him there. His tears land on my shoulders and soak into my tank top.

When Easton is ready, he pulls his head away from my neck, and my hands fall to rest on his chest. I don't have much of a choice, since his arms are still clasped around me. "I want to show you something," Easton whispers, and I nod.

I follow him out the garage, and into his truck. I don't let any of my confusion show.

Easton drives and I sit in the passenger seat, and I don't make a move to turn on any music. Easton rolls the windows down to let a humid breeze into the car, and that's enough for both of us. I risk reaching my hand across the center console and clasping his in mine, and he doesn't pull away. He holds on tight, and it makes me feel needed and a whole lot of other things I ignore.

Twenty minutes later, Easton pulls into the last place I would have thought of but should have seen coming.

A cemetery.

Pieces start connecting in my head faster than I can keep track. Easton pulls his hand out of mine, a feeling I instantly miss, and hops out of the truck. I let him guide the way through the grave stones, knowing exactly where he's going. He stops in front of one toward the back, wilting white flowers in a stand next to it, and I read the engraving.

Michelle King
A loving wife, mother, and member
of our community. A person
we all aspire to be.
March 1, 1980-June 29, 2022

Today is June twenty ninth.

Easton lost his mom three years ago today.

Images of a fourteen year old boy hunched over a hospital bed, crying as his mother takes her last breath flood my mind, and all I say is, "Oh, East."

He falls to his knees in front of the grave, and I fall next to him, wrapping my arms around his shoulders. He doesn't start crying again, but my arms stay wrapped around his hunched shoulders for a long while before he speaks.

"Today's the one day I always need for myself," he whispers, and I can't stop myself from cradling his head to my chest at his vulnerable tone. I do wonder if he doesn't want me here, if he truly wants to be alone, if I should go back to the truck, but he invited me. He didn't have to do that if he didn't want me here.

Plus, I think about all the times I was falling apart this summer, when I thought I didn't want anyone around but Easton didn't listen and stayed and I ended up being grateful for it.

I'm going to do the same for him.

I press my cheek to the top of his head, and he seems to let himself finally go limp in my arms. "I've got you," I whisper.

Never again will I wish for someone to be vulnerable with me just so I can return a favor, because this sucks.

"Thank you for being here," Easton whispers.

"Thank you for letting me be here," I whisper back, feeling no greater honor.

"Usually my dad takes the day off work and we bring fresh flowers together, but he couldn't get today off. We're coming here together when he gets off work to do it, then going to her favorite restaurant for dinner."

"I don't think there's any better way you could honor her," I say. I finally pull away so I can sit next to him. I sit cross legged and Easton joins me, sitting close enough for his leg to overlap mine.

Easton murmurs quietly, "I'm sorry I was ignoring you."

I shake my head. "Don't be. Today is not about me at all. I'm sorry I thought you ignoring me meant I did something wrong."

"You've had a lot going on this summer—" Easton starts.

"—but that doesn't give me any right to put my feelings before anyone else's. I'm sorry I've been so caught up in my own issues to not think about yours. It's been incredibly selfish of me."

"Li," he starts again, and I'm overjoyed to hear the hint of a smile in his voice. "I want people to be so caught up in their emotions they don't think about mine. I've mastered how to make that happen."

"Yeah, but—"

Easton cuts me off, "No buts. Your wounds are much fresher than mine."

"It's not a competition, East."

"I'm not saying it is. We are both allowed to feel our own pain without comparing it to each other. I've had three years to feel my pain, though, and you've only had a month. Letting others talk about their pain helps me with my own." And then, so quiet I have to lean closer to hear him, "It's what my mom always did. During all of her treatment, all she wanted was to help others. It was never about her."

I don't know how to respond to his words. It gives me so much insight as to why Easton tries as hard as he does to be the friend he is, and it's making me speechless. Words don't need to be spoken anymore, though, as a peaceful silence settles over us.

We sit in front of his mother's grave, the air still just as hot and humid as earlier, our legs overlapping, and I know our friendship has reached a new level. Deep in my bones, though everyone in town may know where Michelle's grave is and be free to visit her at any time, I just know Easton has never taken another soul here in the way he took me here today.

And that says more than any amount of words ever could.

CHAPTER TWENTY-TWO

TAP TAP.

Tap tap.

The noise sounds like it's coming from the back of my mind, so although it wakes me up for a brief moment, I fall right back asleep.

The tapping wakes me up again, and this time, I know it's not just a dream. The tapping has gotten louder and more insistent. I sit up in bed, and Groot lays at my feet staring straight at the curtains, ears perked up at full height. At my movement, he whips his head to look at me before returning his gaze to the curtains.

No need to find out where the noise is coming from, then.

I throw the quilt back and slip out of bed. My cracked phone screen lights up on the nightstand, revealing it's almost two in the morning. I'm cautious about what's tapping against the glass at this time of night, but I'm more irritated than anything.

Groot follows me at the same groggy pace to the other side of the room. His nails click quietly against the floor, his ears remaining perked as the tapping sound continues. I reach for the left curtain and pull it away from the balcony door.

Easton stands on the other side in all black, and he has what looks like a blanket thrown over his shoulder. The hood of his sweatshirt is pulled up, but the clear night sky illuminates his face enough for me to know exactly who it is.

Plus, I don't know a single other person who would show up at my balcony doors at two in the morning.

When the curtain is pulled back and my eyes meet Easton's, a smile breaks his face. I unlock the door and slide it open, crossing my arms over my chest. "How the hell did you get up here?" I hiss, stepping aside to let him in. He drops the blanket on the floor and pulls his hood back. His hair sticks up in all directions like he just woke up, and I'm once again reminded of how attractive he is. His messy bedhead is clearly one of my weaknesses.

"The tree," he points out, and I glance at the oak tree that does happen to stand very close to the edge of my balcony. "I climbed." He bends down to pet Groot, and the dog doesn't waste a second in devouring Easton's face with kisses. I notice he's not wearing any shoes or socks. *He climbed the tree barefoot?*

"Well no shit, Troy Bolton. What are you doing here? It's the middle of the night."

"Oops, I forgot. You're not a morning person." The glint in his dark eyes says he definitely did *not* forget.

"Not in the slightest," I reply, my tone a deadened monotone. "So let me ask you again. Why are you here?"

"As you can see," he gestures to the balcony door, "The sky is clear. You have now been here for a month and have yet to go stargazing on the beach, so I decided it was about time you did."

"We're going stargazing at two in the morning?" I ask slowly, raising a single eyebrow at his unwavering grin.

"It's prime time, Li. Grab a sweatshirt and let's go," he says, waving his arm in the direction of the balcony doors. I don't make a move for my closet, so Easton takes it upon himself to cross the room, open the door, and pull out a black one with my school logo on it. He throws it in my direction and it hits me in the face before landing in my arms. I pull it over my head and keep the hood up, waiting for Easton to make the next move.

He rejoins me by the balcony door and steps around me to open it. His finger barely grazes the skin of my thigh as he swoops down to pick up the blanket from the ground on his way out. A shiver runs through my body, and it's not from the temperature change as I follow him out the door into the chilly night air. The balcony floor is cold on my bare feet, but there's no point in grabbing a pair of shoes when we're going down to the beach.

I guess I'm going to find out how to climb a tree barefoot.

As if he were a ninja in a past life, Easton hops over the balcony railing and steps onto the tree with ease. He does it so quickly, I forget to watch and learn. He turns back to me from the tree with a grin, like he's waiting for me to need his help in crawling down, and I'm desperate to prove him wrong. "You can head down, you know," I grin back as I approach the edge of the balcony.

"I know," Easton says, and I get a flash of his smile before he disappears from sight.

Maybe I was wrong about him assuming I would need help.

I grip the white railing in my hands, swinging one leg over the railing so I'm straddling it and then the other. Being on the opposite side of the railing with just my hands holding me on has my heart racing, so I take a deep breath before focusing on the tree. There's a thicker branch a foot below the edge of the balcony that would be perfect for my feet, and if I slide my hands down the poles of the railing, I can safely make it before transferring my hands to the tree as well.

My movements are stiff and awkward, my mind constantly focused on the fact that I could fall to my probable death if I make one wrong move. I go slowly, making sure I feel secure with each foot being on the branch before removing even one hand from the railing. I sit down to straddle the branch, planning to inch my way to the center of the tree and make my way down from there.

What feels like hours later, my bare feet finally hit the cold, damp grass. It's relieving after the rough bark of the tree. I hop down from the last branch, stumbling a bit before using the tree to steady myself. Easton leans against the trunk, arms crossed and a smile on his face. "Eh, I'll give it a seven out of ten," he shrugs, pushing himself off and starting the trek down to the water.

I gasp and rush to close the few feet between us. "Only a seven!" I keep my voice low, the window to my dad's bedroom only feet away from us. For all I know, though, he could be up reading.

"One point off for taking five times as long as me, one point off for holding on for dear life, and one for the clumsy landing. Amateur moves," he teases, holding up a finger for each point he took off of my descent. I gasp playfully, pushing his fingers away from my face.

"Unfair. I think I did pretty good for my first time!"

"I didn't say it wasn't good. It just wasn't ten out of ten good." I nudge him as we fall into step beside each other. We reach the sand, and I let Easton lead the way to the spot where we'll be stargazing. The cold sand is a stark contrast to how it feels under the sun most afternoons.

It's easier to keep up with Easton on the uneven ground than it was a month ago. Just like my scooping skills, my sand walking skills have greatly improved.

"I think you're just jealous of my mad parkour skills."

Easton snorts, and he's the one nudging me this time. "Yeah. That's it."

I scoff, rolling my eyes as I say, "Of course it is. Your eyes say it all."

This makes Easton laugh, and then a comfortable silence settles between us, the waves crashing onto the shore the only sound filling the air. They're tiny, nothing like the waves I've seen from my balcony during the violent thunderstorms we've had. I follow him to a spot on the beach not far from our homes, and he lays the blanket down for both of us. It's a fleece tie blanket, a blue checkered pattern facing up and tied to a dark grey on the other side.

Easton sits down on the blanket, and I don't hesitate to sit down next to him. It's not a huge blanket, but there's enough room for both of us if we don't leave space between. The blanket is soft against the backs of my legs, the pilling making it clear this blanket has been loved.

I'm the first one to lay down on my back, and Easton's quick to follow suit. I look up at the sky, realizing how many stars I can see here. I'm struck with amazement at how they fill up every inch and corner of the deep blue, the light of them never ending.

"Wow," I whisper, tearing my gaze from the sky to look at Easton. Our arms are lined up with one another, my skin feeling like it's having a malfunction with all the sparks and tingles from the contact. If I move my left foot not even a centimeter to the left, I would be able to touch the skin of his ankle, too.

Easton's staring back at me, and a small smile lifts his lips. It may be small, but there's no doubt it's one of the realest. In the glowing light of the night, his eyes look almost black, and I curl my toes from the intense look in them.

I snap my gaze back to the sky, blinking away the images I was conjuring of Easton and I. A shiver runs through my body. I pray he doesn't feel it.

I search for the only constellation I know. When I find it, I raise my arm that was pressed against Easton's to point and say, "There's the Big Dipper." I try to find the Little Dipper by following the line from the handle of the Big Dipper to the corner of the Little Dipper, but it's something I've never been able to do.

"And there's the Little Dipper," Easton says, moving his own arm up to point. He points, but I see nothing.

"I can't see it. I've never been able to find it," I admit.

"Never?" His tone isn't judging at all, and my body relaxes at the sound of it.

"Never," I confirm. "I can always find the Big Dipper, but when I follow the handle to try and find the little one, I get nothing."

A laugh escapes his mouth, and he quickly muffles the sound with the same hand he was using to point. I look at him, briefly forgetting what happened only seconds ago. "What?" I ask, more annoyed than hurt that he's laughing now. A moment ago, I thought he was accepting of my constant defeat. His laugh proves me wrong.

"Li, you don't follow the handle to the corner. You follow the corner to the handle," Easton says through his quiet laughter, looking back at me. The look that was turning me inside out is nowhere to be found; it's only his signature smirk and playful eyes I see.

"Are you serious?" I ask, turning back to the sky so there's no chance he'll see the blush heating up my cheeks. I'm too embarrassed to even try to search for it now, so I continue to stare at the Big Dipper.

"Here, I'll help you," Easton says, grabbing my hand in his and pointing my finger at the sky. The sudden touch from him makes it hard to focus on anything else, and I'm glad his next words remind me of what I'm supposed to be doing. "You see the Big Dipper, right?" I nod as I trace the stars that make up the only constellation I know, hoping the concentration will take my mind off how much Easton's hand wrapped around my own affects me.

These damn tingles are going to be the death of me.

"Here's the edge, and you want to follow the way it's pointing to the handle of the Little Dipper." He guides my hand along the best he can to show me what I'm looking for. I try my best to only focus on the stars so I can finally know and find a second constellation. I look at the Big Dipper again, tracing the pattern of it to clear my head, and then I follow the edge of two stars to try and find the handle of the Little Dipper.

And I finally find it. I see the three stars that make up the handle and the four that make up the bowl. I grin, returning my eyes to the Big Dipper so I can feel the joy of finding it for a second time. Easton's hand still holds onto mine. Somehow, I know he doesn't want to let go just as much as I don't.

But I let my hand fall, resting both of my hands on my stomach so I'm less tempted. Easton brings his arm back down to his side. I fight the urge to rest my arm against his again, for our hands to be close enough to intertwine.

I turn to look at him, saying into the night, "Now I know two constellations."

He turns to look at me, his dark eyes completely focused, and replies, "Only two? We gotta fix that."

"Okay," I say quietly, letting myself get lost in the look he's giving me. It's dangerous to let myself do it, and it scares me how easily I do, but I can't seem to find a reason why I shouldn't tonight.

CHAPTER TWENTY-THREE

I don't get nightmares often, and even less often do they really spook me. Being wide awake for open heart surgery performed by Nate and Ellie, both with grins so wide their faces were splitting up to their ears, and having to watch them tear my heart apart piece by piece takes the cake, though. I bolt up in my bed, gasping for breath and grabbing at my chest, still feeling the ghost of a knife carving out my heart as it pounds against my palm.

Deep breath, Aliyah.

Groot is on high alert, and I remember something about dogs being able to sense people's emotions. His ears are perked up and he's sitting up straight, eyes trained on me in the faint glow of the night. As my breathing calms and my heart rate slows, Groot inches his way toward me, scooting closer and closer until he lays his chin in my lap. I run my hands through his fur, unable to forget about the dream as it replays again and again.

It will be a little while before I fall back asleep, and I don't feel like laying in bed until that happens, so I throw on a sweatshirt and head downstairs. Groot is on my tail, hopping down from the bed the moment my feet hit the floor and letting me lead the way.

My dad is awake when I round the corner to the kitchen, something I knew the moment I opened my door and saw the glow of the light. "Hey," I murmur, already moving to help myself to a glass of water. I wonder again why he's up, if it's by choice or not.

"Hey," he responds. "Can't sleep?"

"Oh...Um, nightmare," I admit, not looking over at him. I stare into my water, at one of the ice cubes floating at the top, and decide to go for it. "Why are you up?"

He doesn't answer the question right away, and I turn toward him to see if he actually heard me. He's looking at me, eyebrows scrunched as he thinks. The lamp beside him provides enough light for me to see the bags and age creases under his eyes, the yellow light making the features appear ghastly. I don't know if him thinking this hard should scare me or not, but, regardless, I go sit down on one end of the couch and set my cup on the coffee table. He slides a bookmark into his book and closes it, his full attention on the conversation.

"I..." My dad starts, and my ears perk up at his quiet tone. "I haven't had a drop of alcohol since the night before I left Denver." *Since he left Andy and I.* "Some nights, though, especially when I have a lot on my mind, the urge to have even one drink makes it impossible to sleep. I've taken to reading on those nights, until the urge has passed. It helps." He holds up the book he's reading, some self help book I can't quite read the title of.

His words are a confession, one I wasn't expecting to hear. I think that's why I blurt out, "If it makes you feel any better, I just had to watch my ex-boyfriend and ex-best friend carve out my heart and cut it into a million pieces." My dad winces at my bluntness, but there's a ghost of a smile at the sarcastic tone I use.

"Doesn't sound too far off," he says, and I almost can't believe it. *Did my dad make a joke?*

"Yeah," I snort, then remember he doesn't actually know the full story, or really anything that happened at all. I wasn't planning on telling him any of it, of opening up to him like we have a normal father-daughter relationship, but things are always easier to say at night.

"You know how when I first got here, I told you I had just broken up with my boyfriend and had a falling out with all of my friends?"

"Yeah," he says slowly, like if he speaks too fast it'll stop me from saying anything more.

I twine my fingers together, "I found out the night before I came here that he cheated on me with one of my friends on the spring break trip I wasn't able to go on, and everyone in our friend group knew about it. Even my best friend, Ellie." I swallow, the words hurting to speak aloud. "The girl, Sierra, posted some screenshots of the text messages between the two of them on social media, and that's how I found out. I made the split second decision to come here for the summer, and I was on a plane the next day." I find myself struggling to breathe calmly as I recount the story, the words spilling out of me. It's harder to say it like this than it was to say it with anger, like when I told Easton my first day here.

"I'm really sorry that happened to you," my dad murmurs. I shrug, because what more can I say? "If you want me to go bash his car with a bat, I will, but I don't think that will help the situation."

I snort again, not understanding how I'm even having this kind of conversation with him.

My *dad*, of all people.

"I'd be right there with you with my own bat," I respond, grabbing my water and taking a long sip. "It's weird now, though, being on the other side and realizing he wasn't as great as I thought he was. Not just because he cheated, but with other things, too."

"Sometimes, that's what it takes. Removing yourself from the situation makes it that much clearer for you to see what was actually happening," he says, his voice so quiet it's almost a whisper. His words sound like they're not only referencing what I think about Nate, but like he has personal experience with them.

Is that what happened after he left?

And even though this conversation feels really nice to have, getting too close to talking about why my dad left suddenly hits my truth-telling quota for the night. I stand up, finish my water, and ask, "What time are we heading over to the King's tomorrow?"

He doesn't falter at the abrupt change of topic and responds, "We can head over there whenever. I know they would love some help with food prep before everyone else starts showing up."

"Maybe after breakfast, then?" I ask, thinking about the blueberries, raspberries, and whipped cream we got at the grocery store for our morning.

"That sounds perfect," my dad smiles, and right before I round the corner, I see him pick up his book and reopen it, the smile still on his face.

There's one on mine too as I fall back asleep, the nightmare forgotten.

————

THE FIRST THING I DO IN THE MORNING (AFTER cuddling Groot, of course) is open the white curtains to let the sunlight in, and the clear sky does not disappoint. It may not be a beach day (I was heavily warned by Easton we *do not*, under any circumstances, go to the beach on the Fourth), but that doesn't mean I won't be taking advantage of the nice weather. It's barely past ten, but I see the beach is already packed with tourists in red, white, and blue apparel. As much as I would love to be down there today, I don't want to be caught in the mass chaos.

I grab my phone, put my new slippers on , and head downstairs to make some breakfast. Groot hops down from the bed and follows close behind me, nails clicking on the wood the entire time.

My dad sits at the kitchen table with a cup of coffee and the paper laid out in front of him, the crossword front and center. He's twiddling a black pen back and forth between his thumb and pointer finger. He's already looking up when I come into view, Groot's nails on the wood giving the two of us away.

"Morning," he says, nodding his head once in my direction before taking a sip of his coffee. There's no awkwardness after our heart to heart last night.

"Good morning," I reply, maneuvering around the kitchen to get coffee for myself. I pour what's left in the coffee pot into a pale yellow mug, pull the creamer out of the fridge, and empty the carton as well. I start a new grocery list on the blue note pad hanging on the fridge with a New Haven clip magnet, cursing myself for not picking more creamer up yesterday when we were at the store.

I take the first sip of my coffee. With less creamer than I prefer, the bitter taste of the coffee is strong, but it'll do for today. I may have to break my Bean Hut virginity and try it out this week in the meantime.

"Do you want to make the pancakes or should I?" my dad asks. "And what's a five letter word for 'We were on a *blank*'?"

"*Break*," I say immediately, turning to him with an incredulous look. I watch as he writes in the word on the paper before his gaze turns to me. "Have you not seen *Friends*?" I gasp. He shakes his head back and forth. "Dad!" I gasp again.

His eyebrows raise at my word, and my own facial features morph into the smallest look of shock. It's the first time I've addressed him all summer. We blink once at each other, and then I start pulling out ingredients to make the pancakes like nothing happened.

"Not really. I've seen small clips on TV, but never from beginning to end."

"'We were on a break' is such a popular saying, though. You really haven't heard that?" I glance at him to see he's shaking his head, watching me move around the kitchen. I see the still-hesitant look on his face, his thoughts so clear they could be popping up in little cartoon bubbles above his head. He doesn't want to mess things up with me now that I've actually started giving him a chance. I break the brief silence by saying, "We should start watching it."

I know I'm committing to something with my dad, but maybe bonding over a TV show will give us the option to spend time together without having to force awkward conversations like we've been doing for the last few days.

"Okay," he nods in agreement. I offer a smile before turning back to our breakfast. I estimate the measurements, feeling confident after making pancakes multiple times a week for the last however many years. I don't need a measuring cup to tell me how much to put in the bowl.

"When we're done with breakfast, I have to make the brownies and pasta salad and get ready, then we can head next door," I say. I start mixing the batter, realizing I forgot to put a frying pan on the stove to heat up. I pull one out from the cabinet and place it on the stove, turning the heat up to just below medium. While I'm waiting, I start pulling out the ingredients for the brownies first.

"That sounds like a plan. How's work going?" my dad asks.

"Really good. It's a lot of fun, and Mandy and Fred are really awesome bosses. Easton's been a huge help in showing me the ropes. And I don't have a complaint about the free ice cream," I ramble. Most teens hate their jobs, but I can't help but love mine.

He smiles at my words, setting his pen down and taking another sip of his coffee. "I'm glad you're liking it so much. Mandy and Fred are some of the nicest people I've met in my life. They helped me out a lot when I first moved out here."

"I've heard a little about it," I say softly. I pour pancake batter into the frying pan and turn back to face him, leaning back against the counter.

"I had just moved here and was looking for a job. I was looking for one on the boardwalk and ended up in Scoops. They said their son owned a construction firm and they could try and get me a job. I had the job within the week."

"That was really nice of them," I say softly, but I can't help but wonder where my dad would be now if he didn't have such a great support system when he first arrived in New Haven.

He nods, taking another sip of his coffee before saying, "They helped me with anything I needed. Dave quickly became part of that. I owe everything to their family."

Hearing him talk so fondly of the King family brings tears to my eyes, and I quickly turn away to watch the pancake cook. The brownie ingredients are sitting in the corner of my eye, and I pull out another bowl to start making them. "Knowing them, they won't accept anything in return."

"I'll get around them somehow."

"They deserve all of it," I say.

My dad nods, and then he says, "Oh, I finished fixing your chair this morning. I didn't want to wake you by bringing it up, but it's ready whenever."

I almost forgot about the chair he showed me a few weeks ago, and I let a smile grow on my face. "I can't wait to see it. I'm sure you did a great job." I'm tempted to run out and see it now, but part of me wants him to move it to my room first so I can be surprised. I wonder if he ever went back to bed after our talk or if he's been up since I last saw him.

"I think it's going to look great in your room," he responds. "I'll bring it up after breakfast."

"That'd be awesome. Thank you again," I say, glancing at him from across the room.

"Of course. It's the least I could do."

The pancakes are done, and I scoop them off the pan with a

spatula and onto an awaiting plate. I pour more batter onto the frying pan for the next round. Groot has moved from my dad's feet to mine now that I have food, and I smile at his patient sitting and perked ears.

"No buddy, these aren't for you," I coo, leaning to kiss his forehead before bringing the plate of pancakes to the table for us. The whipped cream and fruit are at the table, so he can load them up as much as he wants. Groot stands up and follows me to the table, sitting down at both of our feet as I peer over my dad's shoulder to look at the crossword. None of the unfound answers have clues that make sense to me, so I walk back to the stove to flip my pancakes.

We fall into a comfortable silence as I work around the kitchen, making the pancakes and brownies and pasta salad as he works on his crossword and tears off little pieces of his pancake for Groot.

It feels normal. It's the kind of morning I wouldn't mind getting used to.

CHAPTER TWENTY-FOUR

THE BOWL OF PASTA SALAD BALANCES ON THE PAN OF brownies in my arms as my dad and I cross the yard to the King's. Groot trots beside us, but when Easton comes into sight in his backyard, the dog takes off to say hi. A smile breaks onto my face at the sight of him, my heart just as excited as it jumps in my chest.

"Hey, buddy," I hear Easton say as he gets down to Groot's level and lets the dog give as many kisses as he wants. A couple seconds pass before he stands up and sees the food piled in my hands. My dad sets the lawn chairs he was carrying down next to the fire pit and heads inside as Easton takes my food containers.

"Thank you," I grin, pretending to wipe sweat from my brow. "What would I do without you?"

"You would do nothing without me," he teases, setting the food down on one of the tables set up. There's red, white, and blue banners hung throughout the backyard, and the tablecloths are patterned with American flags.

"Ouch. You don't know that," I throw back, taking the bowl of pasta salad and heading inside. Easton and Groot follow me in, and I squeeze around my dad to put the pasta salad in the fridge until everyone else gets here later.

"Hey, Aliyah," Dave smiles, his hands wrist-deep in a bowl of raw beef.

"Hey, Mr. King. How have you been?" I ask, looking around the kitchen for something to help with. There's a large watermelon sitting on the island, so I start hunting down a large enough knife to cut it.

"Ready to relax today, that's for sure," he responds. "What have you been up to lately?"

I find a knife in one of the drawers, and Easton hands me a worn white cutting board. It seems our kitchen routine has upgraded to include tasks other than making breakfast without needing to be choreographed. "Work and hanging out at the beach. Sticking to the same routine," I tell him. "Easton's been pretty annoying, though."

"Hey!"

"Knock him upside the head. Does the trick every time."

"Dad!"

Knowing Dave can't do it with his raw-meat-covered hands, I playfully smack the side of Easton's head. He whips his head to look at me and gasps, and I casually turn back to the watermelon and set it on the cutting board. "It really does do the trick," I smirk.

"Low blow, Li."

"Oops." I place the blade of the knife on top of the watermelon and start cutting, the sound of our dads laughing at our banter filling the kitchen. I manage to safely cut through the watermelon and realize I need something to put it in. "East, can you get me a bowl please?"

"Yeah," he says, and he pulls out a large blue one.

I nod in approval. "Very festive. Do we want cubes or slices?" I know my answer, and I'm testing Easton to see if his answer means we can continue being friends or not.

"Slices, obviously."

"Right answer. Who's all coming later?"

"My grandparents. Jackie and her family, Naomi, Gabe, Josie, Ev, their families, and some others. Some guys our dads work with. It's a whole party."

"Sounds like it."

"There are fireworks at the beach at ten, but we have the luxury of being able to watch them from our backyards. I'm thinking some of us can go up to your balcony or the roof and watch from there."

"You're on," I grin, focusing on the watermelon in front of me. When I cut the first official slice, I take a bite of it instead of putting it in the bowl. "Mmmm. I haven't had watermelon in so long." I cut another slice and hand it to an awaiting Easton.

He takes a bite and says, "There might not be any left for anyone else."

"Don't you dare, King."

"I would never, Redding."

I snort, "Yes you would."

"She's right, kid. You definitely would."

"You two keep ganging up on me!"

"You make it so easy," I tease, poking his side with my free hand. He grumbles something incomprehensible under his breath. I laugh along with our dads, only making him grumble more.

The next couple of hours are spent bustling around the kitchen preparing food and rushing in and out of the house. We bring out Cornhole, Kubb, and Spikeball from the garage and set them up around the yard. We even set up a Pong table, the red solo cups filled with water. I fill a cooler with cans of beer and seltzers, and another one with water bottles, lemonade, Sprite, and root beer.

People start showing up around two, and Easton and I get a game of Kubb going with Evianna, Josie, Gabe, and another guy named Logan. It's a game I have lots of experience with, mostly because I was so stubborn to get good at it after I played it for the first time at Nate's cabin and accidentally hit the king on my first throw.

We decide on boys versus girls, a decision that takes five minutes to make after people declare Easton and Evianna can't be on the same team because they'll automatically win, Gabe and Josie can't be together because they're always together, and Logan and Evianna end up trash talking a little *too* aggressively when they're on the same team.

"How are your Kubb skills?" Josie asks me in our girl huddle. "Because Ev and I are pretty damn good, but so are the boys. You're the only unknown factor here."

"I think we'll be just fine," I smirk. "Also, Ev, I love the hair." The tips are dyed again, but only half are dark blue this time. The other half is a bright red, and, although I know she did it for the Fourth, she's a dead ringer for Harley Quinn. The half up half down pigtails only help this case.

"Thanks!" she says happily, her navy eyes lighting up. As always, her eyeliner matches them. "I think the dyed tips are growing on my mom, but I don't think she's too fond of the half and half yet."

"Well, I think it looks great."

"Courtesy of yours truly," Josie says. Her smirk reveals a playful mood Ev and I are quick to match.

And the game begins. We throw two rods first ("Ladies first" Gabe had said with a smirk, winking at his girlfriend), and Josie and Ev each knock a block down.

"Off to a good start," Ev murmurs, dialed in as the boys get into stance to take their turn. They throw the two blocks first, one close to the middle line and the other about half way onto our side. Logan throws his rod first, and though it hits the closest block and causes it to teeter, the block stays upright.

"Yes!" Ev and Josie cheer, and I grin.

"Damn it," he curses.

"Maybe a little more force next time?" Ev says to him sweetly, and he rolls his eyes at the trash talk already beginning.

Easton and Gabe both throw a rod, knocking down the two blocks they threw at the beginning of their turn, and they play Rock, Paper, Scissors to decide who will throw the fourth and final rod. Gabe wins, and he successfully knocks down another block.

"Suck on that, ladies!" he says, pumping a fist in the air.

Ev grabs the three blocks the boys knocked down and gives one each to Josie and I. Ev throws hers first, and her block lands perfectly right behind the middle line. Josie throws hers next, and it hits Ev's block. "That's what I'm talking about!" Ev says, high fiving Josie.

I move to stand in line with the two of their blocks, getting into position to throw my block and hopefully hit theirs.

"Alright, Aliyah," Easton grins. It's weird to hear my full name from his lips, and I wonder why he used it. "Show us what you got!" His words make this task that much more daunting, and I know the girls are counting on me to get the triple stack. I take a deep breath, focus in on the two blocks I'm aiming for, and toss my own block into the air.

It makes a *clink* sound as it hits one of the blocks.

I can't help but smirk at Easton, cocking my head to the side.

"Not bad," he smirks back as he goes to stack the three blocks. It's a tedious task, but he manages to stack them without them falling over on the third try.

"You should do the honors, Aliyah," Josie says, gesturing to the tower.

"Oh, God, the pressure," I laugh, but I take one of my rods and prepare to throw it. Despite the pressure, it's an easy target; it's as close as it can get, and knocking over a tower is a lot easier than knocking over a single block. I hit it with ease, emitting another round of cheers from Ev and Josie.

"Take that, bitches!" Ev says to the boys, and Logan sticks his tongue out at her.

"Oh, take a breather," he taunts. "We haven't even had a full round yet."

Ev shakes her head, her hair swishing with the movement. "Just trying to help you understand what it feels like to lose so it doesn't hurt as bad when you do."

Logan sticks his tongue out again.

I see what the others meant about the trash talking getting a little too aggressive between the two of them. I'm sure when they're on the same team, it's relentless. And hilarious.

As Ev and Josie each throw their two rods, I end up in a staring contest with Easton, and when I throw my second and the final rod of the round, I miss. Granted, Ev missed one and Josie missed both, but I was trying to keep up my reputation I've built this summer between football and shotgunning.

"Uh oh, they're already at it!" I hear a girl say from somewhere else in the backyard, and I turn to see who it is. Her curly dark hair is wild around her face, barely contained by a red headband, and she has the same green eyes as Mandy and Dave. I assume it's Jackie, Easton's cousin, and the dark skinned girl with the long black braids next to her is Naomi. The two of them are approaching us, grinning from ear to ear.

Other people are also starting to wander into the backyard as well, chatting with the people they know and helping themselves to food and drinks. A speaker next to the back door plays a summer playlist Easton and I created this week for the occasion.

"Jack, Naomi, this is Aliyah. Aliyah, this is Jackie and Naomi," Easton introduces, the game and the trash talk pausing for a few seconds. The full name throws me off again, despite it being an introduction.

I smile, "It's nice to finally meet you guys. Easton complains a lot about you."

"What! I do not!"

Jackie and Naomi both start to laugh, and it's a good feeling to know right away I don't have to watch my sarcasm with them.

"So, who do we think is going to win?" Naomi asks, pulling up a lawn chair and sitting down.

"My bet is on the guys, but I don't know how good Aliyah is," Jackie responds, pulling up a chair for herself.

"Not that good," Logan calls, and Ev flips him off.

"The girls dominated last time, though," Naomi counters.

"Five bucks?"

"You're on."

———

UNFORTUNATELY FOR NAOMI, THE GIRLS LOSE THE hour-long game by one block, and she reluctantly slaps a five dollar bill into Jackie's awaiting palm. It was the funnest game of Kubb I've ever played, but all the trash talking and focus has left us hungry.

Easton and I stand at the table together, and I ask him, "Why didn't you call me Li earlier?"

"It's my nickname for you," he shrugs, heaping a big spoon of the pasta salad I made onto his plate. "If I start calling you Li in front of everyone else, they might start calling you that, too."

I can't help but smile at his response, my stomach trying to compete with Simone Biles at the Olympics. I probably shouldn't be smiling this much at Easton being overprotective of his nickname for me, but it's Easton. How could I not?

I fill my plate with a little bit of everything, eager to try the dishes everyone brought for the potluck along with the handful of things Dave, Easton, my dad, and I prepared this morning. There's my pasta salad, Dave's burgers, homemade whipped cream and a fruit tray Jackie's parents brought, some kind of red jello dish from Logan and his family, to name a few. I snag one of my brownies, too.

Easton seems to do the same, and we sit down in a patch of grass in the corner of the yard to eat with our friends. I find my dad in the small crowd, and when I see a can in his hand, it triggers a surge of anger that almost has me snapping my plastic fork in half.

I thought he didn't drink. I thought he truly was better. In control. Easton's done so much to convince me of this, but—

"Woah, tiger," Easton murmurs, cupping my hand in his and slowly easing my grip.

His gaze follows my line of sight, and then he turns back to me. "Li," he says softly, loud enough that only I hear it over the chatter of our friends. "It's just a root beer."

It's just a root beer.

At Easton's touch and words, I look more closely at the can wrapped in my dad's hand, and even though I can't see all of it, the parts of the can I do see are identical to the root beer cans. I let out the breath I didn't realize I was holding through my anger and look at Easton, tears welling in my eyes.

"Hey, it's okay," he murmurs, his smokey eyes not leaving mine as my anger quickly fades at my false assumption.

"I—The can—It—"

"I understand. I get it. It's okay," Easton tells me, nodding with his words. I nod back, feeling it in my very soul that he understands every single word I'm struggling to get out. "It's okay," he whispers again.

A few more deep breaths, and I feel calmed down as I whisper, "Thank you." Easton nods one last time, offering me my favorite smile, and that's all I need to feel completely better.

"So, how about a rematch after we eat?" Ev asks the group of us.

There are some groans at the thought of another hour long game of Kubb, and Gabe says, "Can't. Jos and I are playing Cornhole against Logan and Naomi."

Ev huffs, but the smile on her face gives her faux anger away.

Easton turns to me, smirking, and asks, "Do your Pong skills compare with your shotgunning skills?"

I smirk right back. "Guess you'll have to find out. Ev, wanna be my partner?" I fail at hiding my laugh as Easton's jaw drops.

"Of course," Ev responds, laughing right along with me.

"Aliyah!" My full name has my stomach doing more somersaults and flips, especially knowing why he's using it. "I thought I implied we could be partners! Who am I supposed to play with now?"

"Hey, partner," Jackie laughs, nudging him in the ribs. "Guess you're stuck with me."

———

Gabe, Josie, Evianna, Logan, Naomi, Jackie, Easton, and I crowd onto my balcony for the fireworks, armed with blankets to lay out and the remaining pan of sugar cookies Josie and her mom made for the party. I sit shoulder to shoulder with Easton against the door, our legs spread out on the same blanket we went stargazing with last week and Groot sprawled out with his head resting on my shins.

It's a spectacular show. I didn't even know there could be a firework that exploded in the shape of a smiley face until tonight, and I can't tear my gaze away. Groot handles the fireworks surprisingly well, only jumping when the first one goes off.

The beach clears out as soon as the show is over, faster than I've ever seen it clear out. The group of us head back to Easton's backyard to sit at the fire and warm up, the night cooling down now that the sun has set. The music is still playing and people are still lingering, but Easton's backyard also starts to clear out.

Long after midnight, it's only the six of us who played Kubb left sitting around the fire. We've all had enough s'mores to make our stomachs hurt, but when Easton passes me the marshmallow roasting stick, I don't say no. The sound of the fire crackling is one of the only sounds filling the air around us as I take another marshmallow and slide it onto the prongs at the end of the stick. I hold it just above the fire, slowly rotating it for a few minutes to get the perfect golden brown toast.

"You know," Josie says quietly, breaking the silence, "The beach is cleared out." The mention of the beach has me focusing on the sound of the waves in the distance. I've become so accustomed to always hearing them, they have become part of what I associate with silence.

"I thought it was basically treason for a local to go to the beach on the Fourth," I joke, glancing at Easton.

Josie laughs, and Ev says, "It is, but technically, it's the fifth."

"You got me," I say, holding up a single hand in defeat; I'm holding my s'more in my other hand, and I fear if I move it, the entire thing will drip and fall apart.

"Let's do it. I gotta put the fire out and then we can go," Easton says, standing up from his lawn chair beside me. He reaches his arms above his head to stretch, his shirt rising up to reveal the toned lines of his stomach. In the light of the fire, I see the scar above his hip bone.

"Are we going to swim?" I ask, and everyone nods. Despite knowing we weren't supposed to go down to the beach today, I still wore my red swimsuit under my denim shorts and white tank, so I won't have to go home and change.

"A middle of the night swim is a right of passage when you live on the beach," Ev smiles as she stands up from her own chair. She stretches her arms above her head and leans back to stretch her back, a popping sound echoing into the night. "Ouch. Too much," she says, and she circles her left arm a few times while rubbing her shoulder.

I laugh softly, standing up and stretching out my own body. Easton smiles at my movements, a smile hidden from everyone else, and therefore, a smile just for me. I smile back, feeling it meet my eyes in the dark.

The rest of our group stands up too, stretching out their backs and limbs as Easton rounds the side of the house to grab the hose. He comes back holding the end of it, directs it at the fire, and presses down on the lever. Sizzling and popping fills the air as he douses the fire, making sure every ember goes out. Logan and I start cleaning up the s'mores ingredients, and I step inside the house to set them on the kitchen counter.

"Everyone ready?" Josie asks once Easton and I are back from our respective tasks, and everyone nods.

Gabe grabs her hand in his, and the two of them start leading the way, talking quietly with each other. Their linked hands make me smile, and I find myself instinctively looking at Easton. He's already looking at me with another small smile, and I let him see my smile for a moment before turning and following Gabe and Josie.

Silence settles over our group as we navigate the sand, and it's just as peaceful on the beach as it was when Easton and I went stargazing. There's not a soul in sight other than us, the waves peacefully dancing with the shore.

"Do you guys go swimming this late often?" I ask softly. It feels disrespectful to the environment to speak any louder.

"A couple times a summer," Gabe responds, just as softly.

"Yeah. Usually we're all asleep, watching a movie, or calming down for the night at this point," Ev nods in agreement.

"Sometimes the best waves come at night, so we'll occasionally plan for a night surf," Logan adds.

"It sounds like a blast to grow up so close to the beach," I sigh.

"But we don't get any snow. It must have been a blast to grow up so close to the mountains," Josie says. "I've always wanted to go skiing."

I used to love skiing. Every winter break for the last three years, I've gone up to Montana with Nate and his family on a ski trip for a week. Some of my favorite memories of the two of us have been from those trips. Racing down the slopes, getting one hot chocolate after another at the lodge, cuddling in front of the fireplace each night after an exhausting day.

Now, all of it brings a bad taste to my mouth. Even the thought of skiing reminds me of Nate.

"It's fun, but I would take the warmth over the cold any day." Easton's walking right beside me, and out of the corner of my eye I see him turn and stare at me for a few seconds. I glance up at him, acknowledge I know he heard the change of tone in my voice with a small smile and a shrug of the shoulders, and turn back to the group. They're debating whether it would be worse to live where it's below freezing in the winters or here in August when the temperatures and humidity are over one hundred.

We all know what my choice is.

CHAPTER TWENTY-FIVE

"WAS IT JUST ME OR WAS IT WAY BUSIER THAN USUAL tonight?" I ask Easton once the last customer leaves and the door is locked behind them. There's an actual pile of sand by the door, drops of melted ice cream are all over the floor on both sides of the counter, and the toppings are littering every possible surface. I've never seen the shop in rougher shape than it is now.

"Yeah. It's the weekend of the Fourth. Busiest weekend of the summer," Easton tells me.

"I forgot about that," I laugh. "Makes sense."

"Amateur."

"Hey!"

"Am I wrong?"

"I mean...no. But still!"

Easton laughs as I grab the broom and start sweeping the sand toward the door, planning to sweep it all out onto the boardwalk before sweeping any remaining grains into the dustpan. Easton grabs the ice cream scoops and the topping spoons, heading through the swinging back door to wash them.

We're out within a half hour, the dishes washed, floor swept and mopped, counters wiped clean, and everything stocked for tomorrow morning. I've closed with Easton so many times now that we have our routine set in stone, down to who does what tasks and in what order to blasting One Direction through the speakers once the last customer leaves.

The boardwalk is empty as the two of us walk down it. There are a few stragglers on the beach, both locals and tourists packing up for the day, but it doesn't have anywhere near the same buzz it has in the afternoons.

"Movie tonight?" I ask Easton as my feet hit the sand. I sit down on the edge of the boardwalk to take my Converse and socks off, not wanting the sand to pour into the little ringed holes in the sides of my shoes. Easton slips his own shoes and socks off, too.

"As much as I would love to, I'm helping our dads tomorrow morning at work. They're putting the hardwood floors into the house, and they're down a pair of hands. Gotta be there bright and early at six."

"Disgusting," I say, scrunching my nose to hide my disappointed frown as I stand up. The sand is still warm between my toes even though the sun has mostly set.

"Sometimes it's nice to get up when the sun comes up," Easton shrugs.

I shake my head in mock disgust, "You are from another planet."

"I know, I know. Waking up before ten A.M. is a crime," Easton says, the tone of his voice relaxed yet confident in his words. I smile at it. I like that Easton knows something about me so well to feel confident in teasing me about it.

"You are correct," I agree.

"I'll probably be done around eleven or twelve. I'll come over and we can make lunch and find something to do before work."

"I'll make mac and cheese for us. I've been craving it for days now."

"That sounds amazing right now."

"Right!"

"It's the only thing that's going to get me through the morning. I can't wait."

"Me neither," I say. I don't add that it's not just the mac and cheese I'm looking forward to.

We reach our backyards, and Easton keeps walking with me up to my porch. "Have fun tomorrow morning."

"You know I will. Have fun sleeping."

"You know I will. See you tomorrow," I wave, sliding the back door open and stepping inside. I slide it shut and lock it, Groot quick to meet me with kisses and a wagging tail. "Hey, buddy," I coo, bending down into a squat at his level. I scratch behind his ears as he licks my face, the excited force pushing me back and onto my butt. I laugh, burying my face into his neck.

He smells like he needs a bath.

"Alright," I say quietly so as not to wake my dad, "Let's go, boy." I stand up, and Groot follows me through the kitchen and down the hall to the stairs. The door to his bedroom is open enough for Groot to have squeezed through when I got home, and I hold my breath as we pass to be safe.

Once in my bedroom with the door closed, I flop down on my bed and pull my phone out of the back pocket of my shorts. I switch my ringer on now that I'm not at work, already seeing a text from Easton.

Easton: *Do you have hotdogs? Sometimes I cut them up and put them in my mac and cheese*

My response is immediate.

Me: *what are you, 12?*

I throw the phone down on the bed beside me and force myself up to get ready for bed. I don't feel like sleeping in my sweaty T-shirt and denim shorts.

I change into pajama shorts and a graphic T-shirt, pulling my hair out of its French braid so the waves hang loose for the night.

My phone dings with another text from Easton, and I grab it off the bed as I head into the bathroom.

Easton: *Ouch. Taste doesn't have an age you know*

Me: *but a recipe does*

I brush my teeth and wash the makeup and sweat off my face within a few minutes, and I don't waste another second before crawling into bed with my laptop to find something to watch. I keep my phone in my hand to continue the conversation with Easton.

Easton: *You're one to talk miss-i-eat-my-whip-cream-with-a-side-of-pancake*

I snort out loud as I type my response.

Me: *like you don't do the same thing*

I scroll through Netflix and quickly settle on *New Girl*, picking up wherever I left off.

It's not long before my phone dings with another text, and I think it's Easton teasing me even more about my choice of food. With a smile on my face, I pause *New Girl* and pick up my phone.

My phone unlocks before I have the chance to see the random number the text is from, and then the image is all I see. I see it clearly even through my shattered screen. I want to look away, pretend I never saw the horrible image, but I can't.

Looking at it hurts, but trying to look away has me frozen in place. I blink to push back the tears, but there's nothing that can stop the fat drops rolling down my cheeks. I sit up and shove my laptop to the side.

She's wearing a light pink bikini, the pale color a gorgeous contrast against her tan skin. Her dark hair is pulled back into a messy and sexy ponytail, and her fingernails are painted to match her bikini. Fancy white sunglasses sit at the top of her head. His hair is usually darker than hers, but it's lightened from the sun in the picture. He's wearing the navy and white wave patterned swim trunks I got him for this trip, and the black sunglasses I got him for his birthday two years ago cover his eyes. I don't need to see them to be reminded of how those green eyes used to look at me like there was nothing else more important in this world.

His hands grip her ass as she straddles him on the seat of the boat, her perfectly manicured nails holding the side of his face. Their lips are pressed together with so much force I feel nauseous.

I quickly turn my phone off and throw it to the other side of my bed. I want to throw it across the room, but if I put it through any more torture, it will break. I don't have the money to buy a new one, so I fight the urge to pick it up again and throw it as hard as I can against the wall.

Silent cries escape me as my body starts to shake with shock.

I want to scream. How the hell did she—

Her number is blocked, so how—

She must have used a different phone to send the picture.

Blinking through my tears, I throw the sheets back and crawl out of bed. My body is jittery, anger surging through every possible corner without an escape. I start pacing the floor, the wood lightly creaking beneath my feet.

Groot tracks my movement from the bed, ears perked up and eyes clearly anxious about what's going on.

Pink walls surround me. The same pink as her swimsuit in the picture. I can't find another breath. I place a hand on my heart as I struggle to take in air.

I need to get out of here.

I'm on autopilot as I slip around the curtains, unlock and open my balcony door, climb over the railing, and scale down the tree. The rough bark scrapes at my feet, the pain grounding me in a way that makes it a little easier to breathe. I land safely in the grass with ease.

With the nerves running through my body, I think I'd give myself a solid nine out of ten.

I take off down the grassy path to the beach, needing to be anywhere else but *here*.

Unfortunately, everywhere feels like *here*.

When my feet hit the sand, I don't stop. I'm kicking the grains up behind me and feel it on the backs of my legs, but I keep going. I go a little farther than the boardwalk and shops until I'm away from human civilization, but I'm still not far enough.

The anger is building, and with it the scream I need to let out. She has already put me through enough, backstabbing me and taunting me with her TikTok before I came to New Haven. I did everything I could to rid myself of both of them, and yet she still feels the need to rub it in.

No one should be expected to control themselves in a situation like that.

I realize there's nowhere far enough away to let out this anger without being heard. I stop running, staring out at the sea. Breathing is easier, and I take deep, gasping breaths, both from running and from the anger consuming me.

An idea comes to mind as a wave crashes onto the shore.

I don't think. With my pajamas on, I wade into the darkness up to my thighs. No further, because I know what I'm doing is reckless and I don't need to get caught in a rip current or pulled under by a wave.

The water is cold, but it's exactly what I need. It grounds me, and my breathing slowly but surely falls back to normal. The waves slowly rush past me, floating between my shins and my belly button. My pajamas are soaked through, sticking to my body like a second skin.

Though the cold water helps pull me back from the ledge of anger, I still feel it flowing freely through me. It needs to be released.

I put my head underwater and finally let out the scream, and it feels better than I ever could have imagined.

CHAPTER TWENTY-SIX

THE PINK WALLS OF MY ROOM WILL *NOT* DO ANYMORE. They're a constant, painful reminder, so even with my puffy eyes and pounding head and raw throat, I wake up on a mission. I throw the salty strands of my hair into a pile on top of my head so it's not in my way, and even though part of me wants to curl up in my bed and cry until I have absolutely no tears left, the anger to fucking *get rid of it all* drives me.

I Google necessary paint supplies, compile a list of what I'll need, and head out to the garage to find it all. I don't think I've ever been more grateful for my dad and his construction job, therefore his endless supply of tools, than I am right now. I easily find everything I need on a shelf labeled "Painting."

There's a few cans of paint on the shelves, a key factor I was counting on, and I pray at least one of them isn't pink. Even if it's some hideous poopy brown, I would gladly take it over the color on my walls right now. I find a screwdriver from the toolbox to pop the lids off the paint cans.

The first one I take down is almost empty, and of course it happens to be pink. I quickly use the other side of the screwdriver like a hammer to secure the lid and all but throw it back onto the shelf, an ugly *clang* echoing through the garage.

My other choices are the light blue in the kitchen or a light gray. I go with the light blue. I grab the can and the supplies I'm able to carry and lug it all up to my bedroom. I make a second trip and carry the rest.

I get my music going on my speaker, blasting my summer playlist. My mood may not match the happy and upbeat songs, but I'm hoping they'll rub off on me. I push all my furniture away from the walls and into the middle of the room, including the freshly refurbished chair I absolutely love.

I don't know if we have any old blankets or sheets to lay out on the floor in case I drip paint, and I almost start crying again.

The door slamming from downstairs stops my quivering lip, and Groot bolts out my bedroom door. "Li!" I hear Easton call, and I quickly wipe away the single tear that manages to fall and turn down the music. I glance at the time on my phone for the first time today. It's past noon.

"Up here!" I call back loud enough to be heard over the music, brainstorming how I should go about this. Part of me doesn't want to tell Easton what happened simply because I don't want to even think about it, but how? I've got paint supplies everywhere and all my furniture is in the middle of the room. It's not like I can hide it and pretend I'm okay.

Plus, it's Easton. He'll be able to see through my facade the moment he lays his beautiful eyes on me.

The clicking of Groot's footsteps on the wood, followed by heavier but not quite as loud footsteps, lets me know Easton is coming up. There's no way to conceal something terrible has happened since he last saw me, so I remain standing where I am next to my balcony doors.

Easton appears in the doorway of my room, and the sight of him with the backwards white cap and his mom's cancer T-shirt has all of my defenses crumbling.

"Woah, what's going—Li, are you okay?" He cuts himself off mid sentence when his eyes land on me standing with my arms hanging limp by my side. The concern in his voice has my bottom lip quivering again, and I shake my head no.

Easton crosses the room in two large steps and pulls me into his arms.

I bury my face in his chest to muffle the sounds of my sobs, the smell of sunscreen grounding me. My arms wrap around his lower back and pull him closer.

This hug is everything I need. It calms me, it comforts me, and it makes me feel better again. I let my sobs out without an ounce of hesitation, knowing some of these tears have been waiting since the beginning. Easton holds me the entire time, cradling my head against his chest and his other arm wrapped around the curve in my back.

He doesn't say anything.

When I know I'm done crying (for now) and loosen my arms from Easton, he lets me go. I meet his dark eyes, not missing the shadow hanging over them, and I can't tell if he's more angry or worried.

"What happened?" he asks, and I instantly know it's both. The tone of his voice is so soft yet so protective.

I skirt around Easton and grab my phone from my dresser. I go into my messages and click on the thread, quickly turning the phone in his direction so I don't see it. I get a flash of the light pink swimsuit and want to hurl the non-existent breakfast in my stomach.

Easton's eyes turn dark when he sees the picture. He takes the phone from my hands to get a better look through the cracked screen. "That's your ex."

He has no idea what Nate looks like, but there's no question in his voice of who it is. The dark haired boy could only be Nate with the reaction it extracted from me.

"And that's Sierra, the girl he cheated on me with. When he

cheated on me. She texted it to me last night from someone else's phone."

"Why?" Easton sounds just as hurt as me. It's only one word, but it conveys more emotion than a thousand words could. It sends my heart into a frenzy. A frenzy that's starting to become more and more familiar.

"To hurt me. To remind me of it. To taunt me."

"I don't want to call her a bitch..." he trails off, and I finish for him.

"...But I do. She's a fucking coldhearted, lying, snaky bitch." I don't know how I say it as calmly as I do.

"Li, you don't mean that."

"Yeah, I do," I say sternly. *There's the anger.* "She was one of my best friends, and she's the fucking bitch my boyfriend of three years cheated on me with!" My voice grows heated, and I'm yelling by the end. *That's more like it.* "I hate her!"

Easton pulls me back into his arms, and my attempts to push him away are useless. I fall limp in his hold and once again start bawling. *So much for not having anything left.* His white T-shirt is already soaked, so what's a few more tears? He holds me with one arm around my lower back and one hand cupping my head into the crook of his neck again. My own arms snake around his abdomen, hands connecting in the back to hold me there.

It's impossible to tell how much time has passed when I'm wrapped up in Easton's arms. When my cries become hiccups and I really have no tears left to cry, Easton slowly peels my body away from his. My arms fall to my sides, and he gently holds onto each bicep. I stare down at the hardwood floor beneath us.

"Li, look at me," Easton says softly, and when I don't, he removes a hand from one of my arms and uses two fingers to lift my chin until I'm looking at him. There's a look in his eyes I've never seen in anyone before, and all I know is I want more of it. *Need* more of it.

"What?" I hiccup, my voice hoarse.

"Take a deep breath with me, okay?" I nod once. His fingers tingle against my chin, and I crave the feeling when he removes them. He starts breathing in through his nose, his shoulders rising and chest expanding. I follow his lead, the air filling my lungs until there's no room left. I hold his gaze for three seconds, and then we both slowly blow the air out of our mouths. "One more." We repeat our actions, and I already feel my body regulating itself. Whether it be because of the deep breaths or Easton's touch, I'll never know.

"Better?" he asks. I nod. He's still holding my phone, the picture still pulled up. Without me needing to ask, he taps the screen a few times before passing it back to me. "There. Number's blocked and the picture doesn't exist."

I set my phone on the bed and murmur, "Thank you."

"Of course. Now, what can I do to help you, Li?" His voice remains calm and soft the entire time, and there's no way I'll ever be able to convey how thankful I am for him.

"Help me paint my room. I hate this color."

"I hate it, too. It was never your color anyway," he responds, the smallest of grins appearing on his face.

I laugh.

———

EASTON LEAVES FOR WORK AROUND THREE AND TELLS me I don't need to come in tonight because it will be so slow. I know he's lying, but I also saw him texting Mandy to come in and work with him so I could have the night off. *That scoundrel.*

I start the second coat of paint after Easton leaves, feeling like a pro after the last three hours. After grabbing some spare sheets from his house, he taught me everything I need to know about painting a room.

It's only been on the wall for a few hours, but I already love the change. I'm sure most of that love is because it's anything other than that horrendous pink.

Groot keeps me company the entire time, laying on my bed with his head propped right on the edge. When I finish the first wall, my arm tired from moving the roller up and down, I pause and take some time to cuddle with him. He curls up on my stomach, and I gently stroke the space between his ears, looking around my room and once again thinking about how much I love the color.

When Groot suddenly bounds off the bed, using my stomach as a launch pad and forcing an, "Oof," out of my mouth, I know my dad is home from work. I don't move from my spot on the bed, knowing he showers right after work and I can meet him downstairs when he's done so we can figure out what we want for dinner.

What I don't expect is for him to appear in the doorway to my bedroom. He never comes up to my room, other than when he moved my chair up here. I sit up on my bed and pause the music playing quietly from the speaker. Groot hops back onto the bed, and I resume my petting as I stare at my dad. He's looking at the walls of my room, his head cocked to the side.

He meets my eyes and smiles. "Hey. How was your day?"

"Not great," I shrug, my legs dangling over the side of my bed. "How was yours?"

"Busy. Did you paint your room today?"

I want to laugh at the question. The answer is so fucking obvious, but I see the glint of amusement in my dad's eyes as he attempts to bring some humor into my shitty day.

"No. It was like this when I woke up." A small grin spreads on his face, and I say, "Easton came over and helped."

"I'm guessing you guys didn't paint it for fun?" It comes out as a question, and his cautious tone makes me want to tell him why.

So I do.

I meet his blue eyes and pat the spot on the bed next to me not occupied by Groot. He hesitates for a moment before closing the distance and sitting down. He leaves a good foot of space between us, still taking things slow.

This is a big moment for us.

I pause to catch my breath, using the same technique I used with Easton earlier. "Last night," I begin, my voice cracking as the horrendous picture pops into my mind. My dad hears it, and he places a delicate, comforting hand on my shoulder.

He murmurs, "Aliyah, you don't have to tell me if you don't want to."

I shake my head, wiping away the single tear that has already escaped. It certainly won't be the last if I keep talking about this, but I push forward anyway. "Last night. Um. The girl Nate cheated on me with." Saying his name creates a large lump in my throat that makes it hard to speak. "She texted me a picture of them on the trip." I swallow, the motion hurting the back of my throat. "Kissing." I can't make myself say the word in anything louder than a whisper.

More tears leak out of the corners of my eyes, and I wipe them away with my fingers. I stumble over my next words, wanting to get them out as soon as possible. "Her swimsuit was the same color as the walls. The first thing I did this morning was grab painting supplies from the garage. I...I couldn't be surrounded by the color."

My dad moves his hand from my shoulder to wrap his entire arm around me, scooting closer so there's not a gap between us. I willingly let my head fall onto his shoulder so I don't have to hold it up anymore. "Aliyah, I am so sorry that happened. No one deserves to be treated like this," he says, his voice quiet.

A silence settles in the room after his words, and there's not an ounce of uncomfortable tension in the air. He rubs a soothing hand up and down my arm as I softly cry, wiping my tears before they soak my T-shirt again.

Being wrapped in my dad's arms brings me back to being a little girl, before his drinking turned into a daily occurance. On his good days, when he didn't drink at all, we would curl up on the couch together and watch my favorite Barbie movies with a package of Fudge Stripes in front of us. I would get up to sing and dance to the songs when they came on, and when they were over, I would crawl right back into his lap.

"Is there anything I can do to help?" he asks. I shake my head and keep it resting on his shoulder. He lets me stay there for as long as I need, remaining quiet and continuing to rub a soothing hand up and down my arm. When I finally stop crying, I lift my head and wipe my eyes with the heels of my hand.

"I'm sorry for breaking down," I apologize, standing up and feeling the wood floor on my bare feet. There's a few grains of sand that stick. I haven't vacuumed my room once since I arrived here.

Shaking his head, my dad tells me, "You have nothing to say sorry for, Aliyah." I only shrug, looking around at the empty blue walls of my room. There's a few moments of silence, and then he surprises me and says, "Let's head into town and get some things to decorate your room."

I turn my gaze to his as he stands up from my bed, eyebrows shooting skyward. "Really?" I ask.

He nods, "Yeah. There's a few home decor stores we can check out. We'll grab dinner, too. It'll help get your mind off of things."

I smile as I grab my phone and follow him down the stairs, slipping my feet into my sandals before heading out to the car. Groot tags along, hopping into the back seat and sticking his head out the window the moment my dad rolls it down. As always, the classic rock station plays, and I turn the volume up for *Don't Stop Me Now*.

"When are you planning to head back to Colorado?" he asks as he turns off our street.

"I don't know. I haven't booked my flight yet, but probably sometime the week before school starts. Why?"

He shrugs, glancing at me and saying, "Just wondering." There's a silence Queen fills for a brief moment before my dad says, "I hate this, but I'm going to be out of town over your birthday. We have a job in Charleston we've had booked for months, and I can't get out of it. Believe me, I've tried."

"That's fine," I shrug, the new information not having any effect on me. My birthday was never a huge deal for me since I grew up hardly celebrating it. The last few years were good when I had people in my life who put the effort in to make it good, but I've been fully expecting to wake up this year on August fifteenth and not even realize it is my birthday.

"We can celebrate before or after, whichever you want. I'll order a cake from the bakery in town."

"Dad, you really don't have to do that. It's not a big deal," I tell him, and add quietly without thinking, "My birthday was never a big deal."

I regret the words as soon as they slip out of my mouth. There's no reason for why I said them. I glance at my dad, seeing the relaxed look he was wearing morph into one of hurt at my words.

"I'm sorry. I shouldn't have said that," I say, the pink in my cheeks reflecting my regret.

"No," he shakes his head, glancing at me again. "You're right. You didn't get a proper childhood, birthdays included. That's my fault, and I'm the one who should be saying sorry. You have nothing to apologize for."

I can't think of anything to say in response, but he beats me to it. "I'm going to do everything I can to change things. I can't change the past, as much as I wish I could, but I can make sure the future isn't the same."

For the first time ever, I fully believe what my dad says. Since arriving in New Haven, he has done nothing but prove he has done everything he can to be a better father, and though my past self is surely calling me every foolish and bad name in the book, the determination in his voice to live up to his words can't be ignored.

"Okay," I smile.

I hope I don't regret that.

CHAPTER TWENTY-SEVEN

It's five minutes to close, the last customer finally leaves, and I start to go down the checklist of closing procedures. Easton leans against the wall with a bowl of ice cream in his hands. With his mouth full, he says, "We're going over to Gabe's to watch a movie with everyone tonight." I have no idea how I understand him.

"Okay," I say, my back to him as I put the covers on the ice cream tubs. I've gotten used to Easton declaring our plans like we made them months ago. "What time?"

"When we get off."

"Do I have time to shower? I smell like B.O. and sweet cream."

"How long will this shower take? Because I know people who will literally be in there for an hour."

"Like, five minutes," I snort, turning to meet his gaze.

Easton snorts right back, "Bet."

"What, you don't believe me?" I taunt, grabbing the ice cream scoops and heading into the back.

Easton follows me through the swinging door, throwing away his empty bowl as he responds, "A five minute shower is almost impossible for me. I can't imagine you can do it with all that extra hair."

"Bet," I mock, knowing he's setting himself up for failure. Easton starts grabbing paper bowls and plastic spoons to restock the front, and I wash and rinse the scoops in the sink. When I'm done, I say, "Time me."

"I will," he responds with no hesitation. I follow him back through the door and, as he starts stocking supplies for tomorrow, I start counting the till.

"Be prepared to lose," I cackle.

"Good self preparation."

I scoff, "Those words weren't for me, dumb ass."

"Ouch," Easton says, and I turn to glance at him right as his face contorts to a look of pain.

"Do you need a bandaid for that booboo?" I tease, turning back to the cash drawer.

"No."

I laugh but don't respond as I start counting the money. Easton starts sweeping the store, and when I'm done counting the money and bringing the drawer to the safe in the back, I start mopping in his tracks. We skip the One Direction tonight as our banter fills the silence, and we're out by nine fifteen. We exit the shop, Easton locks the door, and the two of us start walking back to my house.

"Who's all going to be at Gabe's?" I ask, slipping my shoes off when we hit the end of the boardwalk. The sand is still warm under my feet from the sunny day we had.

"Us, Gabe, Josie, Evianna, Logan, and probably a few others." I nod, kicking some sand so it blows out in front of us. Some grains get stuck between my toes, but the urge to wipe them away has long since disappeared. I'm becoming more of a beach girl at heart every day. Going back to Denver in August will be a culture shock.

A comfortable silence settles over us, and half way home, I

break it by ramming into Easton with my shoulder. Not expecting the impact, he trips and lands in the sand. I take off running, and a loud cackle escapes my mouth.

"LI!" Easton yells, and I urge my legs to go faster. The uneven sand is an easy terrain, and I make it to my house before Easton does. I throw my shoes down at the door, and I don't wait for him to come in before heading upstairs and locking myself in the bathroom. I'm still laughing when I hear him bang once on the door. Groot barks. "I'm so getting you back for that!"

"Try me," I taunt, starting the shower and slipping out of my clothes. I silently hope Easton has indeed started a timer, because I will never pass up the opportunity to prove him wrong. I'm so intent on proving him wrong that I hop in the shower before the water has even warmed up, the cold water an unwelcome shock to my skin. I push through and immediately squeeze some shampoo into my hand, furiously scrubbing it into my scalp.

I think I set a new shower record for myself, and I know I do when I turn the shower off and Easton yells from my bedroom, "Damn, Li! I'm impressed! Three minutes and forty seven seconds. I don't even think I could shower that fast!"

"Ha!" I reply. I step out of the shower, ring out my hair, and wrap the white towel around my body. I showered so fast there's hardly any moisture clinging to the mirror, and the usual haze that hangs in the top half of the room from the hot water doesn't exist. I pull my brush out of the cabinet and start running it through my hair.

Once my hair is detangled, I realize the dilemma I have put myself in. I was in such a hurry to get away from Easton, I forgot to bring a pair of clothes into the bathroom to change into. Now, I have two options. One, put my dirty work clothes back on to grab fresh clothes, or two, walk into my room with only a towel covering my body, knowing Easton is probably laying on my bed scrolling through TikTok.

I stare at myself in the mirror for only seconds before making a hasty decision. I swipe my dirty clothes from the floor and unlock the bathroom door, gripping the towel at my chest until my knuckles turn white. Walking in front of a boy with only a towel on doesn't feel like it should be that big of a deal, but this isn't just any boy.

It's Easton.

I walk through my open bedroom door and say, "Hey, sorry. Forgot to grab clothes. Was trying to run away from you and everything." I meet his gaze right away from where he's lying on my bed, and his eyes widen at the sight of me. I scurry into the closet and close the door behind me, sitting in darkness for a moment before my hand finds the light switch. Heat floods my cheeks, and I don't have to look into a mirror to know they're flaming.

Picking out a sweatshirt and athletic shorts is easy, but then I remember my sports bras and underwear are in a drawer in the dresser. Outside my closet. In my bedroom. I sigh and prepare to be in front of Easton yet again with only my towel.

I make it quick, shooting an embarrassed smile in his direction as I grab what I need and dart back into the closet. I quickly slip into my clothes and accept the permanent blush on my cheeks. Easton is still lying on my bed, one arm behind his head and one arm propping his phone against his chest. Groot has his head resting on Easton's abdomen.

Easton glances at me when I step out, and on instinct, I throw my wet towel at him and ask, "Ready to go?" He catches the towel with ease and whips it back to me, his signature grin on his face as he sits up. Just like that, the awkwardness of me scampering around in my towel is gone.

"I have to run home and change first," he says, gesturing to his blue Scoops T-shirt with a chocolate stain down the front. I nod, leading the way out of my room and making a quick stop to hang the towel on a drying hook in the bathroom. Groot trots after us, nails clicking on the wood floor as always. At the back door, I grab my sandals but don't put them on quite yet. Easton picks up his own shoes, and the two of us head over to his place through our backyards.

Easton goes upstairs to change quickly, and I raid the kitchen for something to eat. There's a bag of kettle corn in the pantry, and I help myself while I wait. I jump up and sit on the counter, my head leaning back against the wooden cabinets. I hear Easton's footsteps from above, moving around his bedroom as he changes out of his work clothes. I realize I've never been in his room before, never even seen it from the doorway, but he's running back downstairs before I dwell on the thought.

"Now I'm ready," Easton grins, sporting the same black sweatshirt he wore when we were stargazing and light gray sweat shorts. His gaze lands on the bag of kettle corn in my hands, and I freeze with a handful halfway to my mouth. "Are you eating my kettle corn?"

I quickly shove the handful in my mouth and aggressively shake my head back and forth, ignoring the few pieces that fall out of my grasp and onto the ground. Easton makes a grab for the bag, but I yank it above my head so he can't reach it with his initial grab. He moves in closer to me and easily grabs it, the extra foot he has on me not making the job hard for him at all.

The close proximity is all I can think about. With me sitting on the counter, we're at eye level, and Easton standing in between my legs leaves the two of us in a *very* intimate position. In his grab for the kettle corn, his other hand lands on my bare thigh, something he makes no move to change as our eyes meet.

The air shifts. The playful smile falls from his face, replaced with an intensity in his eyes that makes my toes curl. It's not the first time I've seen him look at me like this, like I'm simultaneously the most precious and terrifying thing he's ever laid eyes on. There are glances from across the ice cream shop, when we're watching a movie on the couch, even when I'm tanning and he's a hundred yards away hanging out with his friends.

It's never been this intense, though. "Um," I breathe. "We should probably get going." The words come out with their own breaths, a pause situating itself in between each one.

Easton blinks. Blinks again. "Right. Yeah." His hand leaves my leg and he takes a big step back, the bag of kettle corn still in his hand. I slip down from the counter, stumbling a bit as my feet hit the ground. Easton reaches out his arms to steady me, and I offer a weak smile in thanks. My mind still whizzes from the close proximity.

He puts the kettle corn back in the pantry as I pick up both of our shoes from the back door. Easton says something about going to the bathroom really quick, but I don't register his words until after he's disappeared from the room. I still don't bother putting my shoes on as I head into the garage and slip into the passenger seat of his truck. Our shoes land on the floor next to my bare feet.

Leaning my head back on the seat to wait, the shock of what just happened hits me. I'm aware of how quick my heart rate goes up as I replay the moment in my mind. Nothing actually happened, but everything happened in that nothing. That look Easton gave me is coming with me to the grave.

Leaving at the end of the summer is going to be a lot harder than I had planned.

Easton exits the house and slides into the driver's seat as the garage door opens. Not even a moment passes before he says, "So, there's usually a two sided debate to movie night, horror or comedy. Depending on who's all there determines what side wins, but then there's the debate of what movie to watch." His tone is normal as he backs out of the garage, like nothing happened between us five minutes ago in his kitchen.

Am I reading into what just happened?

"Li?"

"Wha—Huh?"

"I asked if you're team horror or team comedy," Easton laughs, turning off our street. "You zoned out."

"Team horror. Definitely," I say, attempting a smile. Even I know it doesn't reach my eyes, but it's dark enough outside where I don't think Easton notices. If he does, he doesn't say anything. I reach for the aux cord and plug my phone in. "What's the mood?"

"Something upbeat."

"2000's hits? Taylor Swift? Rap? You gotta be more specific," I urge, scrolling through Spotify.

"Taylor Swift."

I burst out laughing, not expecting him to actually pick one of the random choices I pulled out of my ass. "T Swift it is," I grin, queuing well known and upbeat songs in her discography. *Love Story* is the first song I play. When Easton belts out the first lyrics with me with no shame and continues to belt out the rest of the lyrics, I don't know whether to be amazed or tease him relentlessly.

Gabe doesn't live far away, so we only have time for *Love Story* and *Cruel Summer*, another classic Easton doesn't fail to scream the lyrics of with me, including the bridge.

"So you're a Swiftie?" I tease as the ending notes of *Cruel Summer* are replaced with the beginning of *Blank Space* right as Easton pulls onto Gabe's street. Evianna is getting out of her car, and she watches us with an amused grin as Easton parks on the curb.

"Some would say that," Easton smirks, and he starts singing the opening lines to *Blank Space*. I join him, and as Evianna approaches the car, we roll down the windows and resume our screaming. Easton waits for the first chorus to be over before turning the car off, and, still barefoot with our shoes in my hand, we join a waiting Ev on the street.

"You two were destined to be best friends. You know that?" she grins.

I shrug and say, "We try," as if it's a joke that has no effect on me, and I hope Easton can't see me panicking. He's the best friend I've ever had, but who am I to him?

Grinning, Easton and I fist bump. Even the split second of direct contact of our knuckles touching brings me back to the brief moment in the kitchen we had. I quickly step away and start toward Gabe's house, but Easton catches up in two strides. He leans down as we walk and whispers in my ear, "You have nothing to worry about. You *are* my best friend, you know."

I turn to face him, my smile splitting my face. I have no idea how he knew, but I wear that smile all the way inside.

There are five people in the living room. I only recognize Gabe, Josie, and Logan. There are two guys whose names I can't remember, one with very light blonde hair and the other with dark skin and black hair cropped close to his scalp, but I recognize them both from when I played football with everyone. Josie spots the three of us first and grins at the sight. "Aliyah! I didn't know you were coming!"

"I didn't either until an hour ago," I laugh, setting Easton's and my shoes down next to the front door.

"Come join us," Gabe says, gesturing to the couch. He's standing in the open concept kitchen, dumping a bag of popcorn into a large bowl.

Easton, Ev, and I make ourselves comfortable with everyone else on the U-shaped sectional. Gabe joins Josie in one corner, and Easton takes the other one with ease, setting his arms out on the top of the couch. I sit next to him with his arm behind me, squishing to make room for Ev on the other side of me. The entire left side of my body is in line with and pressed against Easton, and I stop thinking clearly.

I still can't remember the names of the two other guys here, so I lean even closer to Easton to whisper in his ear and ask. I pull away after whispering my question just for Easton to lean back in. "The blonde is Hayden, and the other is Carter." I turn to look at him and smile in thanks, not realizing his face is still right there. I quickly turn back, and I'm able to play off my surprise by turning my attention to Gabe.

"So, what's the mood tonight, fellas?" he grins.

"*Endgame*," Logan says. It doesn't fall into the horror or comedy sides Easton was talking about, but then again, he did say *usually*. It doesn't seem like there's going to be a vote, either, as everyone immediately agrees and starts talking about how long it's been since they last saw it.

Ev turns to me and says, "We all went and saw *Endgame* in the theater on opening night when we were in middle school, and the energy in there was unbeatable. Everyone was dressed up as a character or wearing some kind of MCU apparel, and when Cap summoned *Mjolnir*, the entire theater erupted into cheers."

"That sounds amazing," I laugh. "What did you guys dress up as?"

"Black Widow, obviously," she grins, pointing to her hair. "Easton dressed up as Cap and Gabe dressed up as Thor, so we made him give Easton his hammer when it happened."

"Easton dressing up as Cap is very fitting," I say, and Ev nods in agreement as Gabe shushes us all. The movie starts, and I lean back at the same time Easton moves his arm forward a little, resting it right under the back of my head.

I don't move. I tell myself I should, that this is not something that can happen, that I'm only digging myself into a deeper hole, but none of those words seem to matter.

Nothing but the boy beside me matters.

CHAPTER TWENTY-EIGHT

I MANAGE TO CREEP DOWN THE STAIRS WITHOUT making a sound, and I take advantage of that. Just like I knew he would be, Easton stands at the stove in a black T-shirt and light gray sweats when I peek around the corner to the kitchen. He's flipping pancakes in one frying pan and sizzling bacon in another. Groot sits at his feet, eyes wide as he waits for a piece of bacon.

His back is to me, and I stare. His dirty blonde hair is still ruffled from sleep, a style I have become incredibly fond of. He moves effortlessly at the stove, and something about that ease has a smile forming on my lips. As if he can sense my smile, Easton turns to me and offers one right back.

Goosebumps form on my skin. It's the smile I've grown to love. The smile that makes my heart jump and fingers tingle and toes curl.

"Morning, sleepyhead," he says through his smile, meeting my gaze with his own dark eyes.

"Good morning," I smile, sitting down at the table. I pull my knees into my chest and rest my chin on top of them. Groot comes over to say hi, wagging his tail and forgetting about the bacon for a brief moment. I grab his face between my hands and say to Easton, "I take it no run this morning."

"Are you kidding me? Have you seen the weather outside?"

"Heard. Not seen." I glance out the back door and notice how powerful the wind is. The bushes in the backyard are all slanted at an angle, the leaves each having a bizarre mind of their own. "What are you talking about? It looks like perfect running weather."

Easton snorts, flipping a pancake onto a plate. "I'd like to see you try."

"Oh no. Not my thing," I rush out, shaking my head as I stand up to grab the pancake he just finished.

"Exactly," he laughs. I roll my eyes and nudge my shoulder against his. His loose stance isn't expecting it, and he has to grab the edge of the counter to stop himself from falling over. It's my turn to laugh, and I duck out of arm's reach with a pancake dangling from my mouth before Easton can grab me. I swipe a piece of bacon on my way back to the table and reach for the whipped cream already sitting out.

"What's the plan for the day?" I ask, sprinkling the chocolate chips over the already-melting whipped cream. I eat a small handful of them.

"Well, for starters, a bonfire on the beach."

"Haha, very funny," I say sarcastically, taking a bite of my breakfast.

"I'm not kidding! The storm is supposed to clear up by one, and the chilly weather is the perfect time to have a fire."

"You're kidding?"

"Nope," he says, shaking his head from the stove. He flips a pancake onto his plate and starts a new one. "And we're on s'mores duty, so a trip to the grocery store later is also on the itinerary."

"How did I get placed on s'mores duty?" I snort. I get up and grab a yellow New Haven mug from the cabinet, pouring myself my coffee. "The only other numbers I have are Ev's and Josie's."

"I signed us both up in the big group chat. I can add you if you want, but I know you're planning to leave at the end of the summer, so I didn't know if you'd want me to or not."

He says it so simply, like me leaving at the end of the summer won't have any effect on either of us. Like we'll be able to go about our lives like this summer never happened. I grow nauseous at the thought. Will he be able to go about his life in New Haven like we never met?

Like I was just the random girl next door this summer?

"Aliyah?"

My full name breaks me out of my mind. Easton's sitting across from me now, the extra bacon and pancakes on the table between us. He hasn't even touched his food yet, his eyes focused solely on me. If it wasn't for the fact that he used my full name, I would have known he was worried from his wide eyes alone.

"Sorry. Zoned out," I say, pretending I'm okay when I'm very much not. I shove a massive bite of pancake and whipped cream into my mouth so I don't have to explain further. If Easton doesn't see our friendship the same way as I do, there's no way in *hell* I want to tell him how much it's going to hurt me when I leave.

"What's wrong?" He still doesn't touch his food, waiting for my answer.

"Nothing's wrong," I lie. "Just thinking about how I was so adamant to not be doing any of this at the beginning of the summer."

His lips pinch at my words, but even that isn't enough to get me to open up.

I change the topic, taking a sip of my coffee before saying, "So, s'mores. Bonfire. What else?"

Easton grins, and it's not his signature cheesy one. It's cynical and challenging. "I believe you owe me a rematch at Monopoly."

"I do not! I won fair and square last week!" I defend.

"You hogged all the houses so I couldn't get any!"

"It's in the rules! Would you like me to read them for you? Again!"

"No, once was plenty. Still seems a little sus, if you ask me," Easton pokes.

"You should have saved up the money to buy straight through for your hotels. Not my fault you can't budget properly," I throw back.

"How can I budget anything when I'm landing on Boardwalk with four houses every single lap?"

"Don't land on Boardwalk," I shrug innocently.

"I don't until it's out of my price range!"

"Seems like a you problem."

Our food has been laying forgotten between us up until this point. Easton moves to throw his hands up in the air, his elbow slamming into his coffee cup in the process. The drink goes flying across his food and the table, straight into his lap.

"Shit, hot!" he gasps, shooting up from his seat and pulling the now-soaked fabric of his sweats away from his thighs. I jump up and grab the paper towels from beside the sink. I tear a bunch off and pass them to Easton to wipe himself off, and then tear another large bunch off to wipe up the spilled coffee on the table, chair, and floor.

The dark liquid quickly soaks through the paper towels, and I use what's left of the roll to clean it all up. The mug thankfully didn't shatter when it hit the floor, and I pick it up from near Groot's feet. Through the chaotic fifteen seconds, he stayed at the edge of the kitchen where the mug was, tail wagging at the sight of us moving around.

"Damn it. These are my favorite," Easton groans, looking down at the stained sweats after throwing his paper towels in the garbage.

They're mine too, but I keep that bit of information to myself.

"Go run home and grab another pair of pants. If we throw them in the wash now, they might be okay," I say, setting the coffee mug in the sink.

"Good idea," Easton nods, "I'll be right back."

He doesn't bother shoving his bare feet into his sandals before sliding out the back door, opting to go barefoot instead. The sound of the storm slips through the crack for the second it's open, and the powerful wind is frightening with nothing to shield us.

Groot barks at the sound and continues to bark at Easton not being here, standing guard at the door he ran out of. He looks back at me, whimpering, and his eyes are wide with worry about Easton running out into the storm.

He's not the only one.

I finish my pancake in the time it takes Easton to come back wearing a fresh pair of sweats (these ones black) and the coffee-stained gray ones in his arms. He puts them in the washing machine down the hall and starts the load. I drink my coffee, listening to the sound of the water being dumped into the machine as Easton comes back to the kitchen.

"The wind is insane. It almost blew me over on my way back," he says, helping himself to another cup of coffee before joining me at the table. He takes extra care in putting the mug out of elbow's reach.

"Wish it would have."

"You definitely owe me a rematch after that!"

I smirk and say, "I have a better idea."

"Let's hear it, then," Easton says, cocking his head to the side as if there's no possible idea that could be better than a Monopoly rematch.

"Minecraft."

My Xbox controller dies around four. I stand up to dig more batteries out of the hall closet, but Easton stands up with me. I raise a questioning eyebrow. "Store time," he explains, making sure our game saves before turning off the console. He reaches his hands above his head and stretches out his back, and it's so tempting to sit and stare at the sight of his beautiful, toned abs. I fight the temptation and repeat his actions, my back aching from hunching over on the couch for the last four hours. We managed to build a pretty sweet looking fortress, explore the Nether, and start the journey of defeating the Ender dragon.

I didn't even know that was an objective until today. I just like building cool houses and killing the bad guys.

We put our shoes on, I grab my rain jacket, and I glance at Groot sitting near the back door with his wide eyes. "Let's go, boy," I grin, and the three of us head out back. The storm has let up, but the humidity is unbelievable. It's the worst it's been all summer, and I already feel my armpits sweating on the short walk to Easton's. We walk through the house so he can grab his keys, Groot following us with a wagging tail.

Once in the truck, I plug my phone in for music as Easton backs out of the driveway. "Requests?"

"Not today. What do we want for dinner?" I didn't realize we were getting dinner, but my response is immediate.

"Burgers."

"Burgers it is."

I play my beach playlist to match the vibes of the sun finally coming out from behind the clouds. We don't talk on the ride, both of us opting to sing along to the music playing instead. It slowly turns into a contest of who can sing the lyrics worse.

We pull up at the grocery store too soon, and Easton finishes a horrendous edition of a new pop song that came out last week. How he already knows the words, I do not know. When the torture finally ends, I almost launch myself into the car parked next to us from how eager I am to escape the truck. Easton half rolls down all the windows for Groot since we can't bring him in. He barks once as we walk away, sticking his head out the window and staring at us.

"What else do we need besides stuff for s'mores?" I ask as we enter, Easton grabbing the handle of a cart to push along with us.

He shrugs, "I don't know."

I roll my eyes and grin. "You are hopeless."

We're in and out of the store in twenty minutes, taking our time as we stroll through the aisles. We end up with a package of chocolate chip cookies from the bakery aisle we dig into once back in the car. Groot sticks his head between the front seats, and I break off a piece of my cookie with no chocolate and give it to him.

A few minutes later, Easton pulls up at one of the local restaurants. It's busy, and I thankfully see patio seating behind the building. The humidity is still terrible, but the slight chill in the air helps. "I'll go get us a table. I'll be right back," Easton says, rolling the windows down before hopping out of the car. I watch him walk inside, finding it impossible to tear my eyes away until he disappears inside.

Groot rests his chin on my shoulder, his breath warm on my neck. "Hey, buddy," I coo, turning to him and holding his face between my hands. He licks my face, and I quickly close my eyes and mouth. I bury my face in his neck to stop anymore face kisses, running my hands through his fur.

I realize I only have Groot for a little longer than a month. I freeze at the thought and let my arms slip around his body to hold him. He rests against my body, his chin still on my shoulder.

Easton comes back to the car to me still hugging my dog, and all it takes is a glance at him to know he knows what I'm thinking as well.

Damn him and his stupid intuitiveness.

He offers me a smile, opens the passenger door, and steps out of the way so I can hop out. Groot jumps to the front and lands on the pavement beside me, and we head through the fence to the patio. Easton leads the way to our table, and we make ourselves comfortable. Groot lays down at my feet.

The waitress arrives right away to give us our menus and take our drink orders. We place our food orders too since we both know we want a burger, and I ask for a bowl of water for Groot. The waitress leaves after giving Groot some love, and I reach down to pet his head.

"Do you know when you're leaving to go back yet?" Easton asks. A pit forms in my stomach, something unavoidable at this point.

I meet his gaze and shake my head back and forth. "I haven't booked my flight yet." I take a deep breath and add, "It's kind of hard to commit to a day when I know exactly what I'll be going back to." I don't add *and what I'll be leaving.*

Easton nods. "You know..." he trails off, not finishing his sentence. *That's a first.*

"Know what?" I ask softly.

A hopeful look appears in his dark eyes as he says, "You don't have to go back. You could...stay."

His words confirm what I've been worrying about all day: I'm not just the random girl next door this summer.

Leaving just got that much harder.

I swallow, hoping the action will ground me so I don't cave. "East, my brother's there. I have to."

His face falls, and I look back at Groot so I don't have to see. I also don't want Easton to see the small smile growing on my face. Leaving him is going to suck, but at least now I know I'm not the only one who's going to be affected by it.

Our food arrives shortly, and our usual antics start up as we dig in. We ignore the thoughts of me leaving at the end of the summer. My burger and lemonade are a delicious combo, and

Groot seems to enjoy the last bite of my burger just as much as I enjoyed the rest of it.

After we pay, the three of us load back into Easton's truck. The sun barely starts to set, and the slight chill in the air still remains. As soon as Easton pulls out of the restaurant parking lot, I roll down the windows and blast my summer playlist again.

Easton pulls onto the freeway, both of us screaming the lyrics to every song like we have front row seats to a concert. I look over at Easton as a song ends, and he's looking at me with shining eyes and my favorite smile, and suddenly every nerve in my body is aware of what is happening.

What *has* been happening.

And knowing Easton wants me to stay just as much as I don't want to go is the last piece to click into place.

A shiver runs through my body, and it's not from the chilly air blowing into the car. My heart thumps in my chest, my mind focused only on the dark eyed boy in front of me.

I should've known I was a goner the first time I saw his secret smile. Shit.

Shit.

I am in love with Easton King.

CHAPTER TWENTY-NINE

THE RAIN STARTS UP AGAIN IN THE MIDDLE OF THE night, quickly killing the crowd at the fire. Easton and I part ways at our backyards, and I get ready for bed right away. I'm still not over my realization, and every time I looked at him tonight, I was reminded of it. Of already being head over heels in love with someone barely two months after my heart was thrown into a meat grinder.

I'm shocked at how fast it happened, at how easily I let my guard down, but it's hard to resist the smile only I get to see, the way he looks at me with so much promise in his eyes. There's no way it couldn't have happened—it was inevitable.

It doesn't help that I still feel buzzed from the handful of drinks I consumed at the bonfire, and it was harder and harder to keep my gaze off Easton with every drink I had. When he met my eyes from across the fire after I shotgunned a beer with Ev, eyes smoldering through the light, I'm surprised I didn't melt into the sand.

I toss and turn in bed, but Easton's smoldering eyes keep me awake. Around three, I finally give up. I throw my covers away from my body and sit up, running a hand through my hair to push it away from my face. It's coarse from the salty air and the sea.

Groot barely opens his eyes when I slip out of bed. I pull open the curtains in front of the balcony door, a strike of lightning illuminating the air in purples and blues a moment after. I smile as the crack of thunder is thrown across the sky. I sit down on the floor and cross my legs, staring out the window and waiting for the next strike of lightning like a child waiting for her parents to come home from work.

The wind is as violent as ever, and a small branch from the tree next to my balcony joins the collection of branches already scattered across the surface. I can't look at the tree without being reminded of the night Easton and I went stargazing—I still feel the tingles running through my left arm.

How am I going to leave him? How does one leave someone whose life has become so intertwined with their own? How am I supposed to leave that all behind and go on with my life like it never mattered?

I watch the sky until the sun rises. The world gets slightly-less-dark in shades of gray, and the last of the alcohol wears off. By five thirty, I'm sober and exhausted. I hear my dad moving around quietly downstairs getting ready for work. I debate going downstairs to say hi, but I think sleep might finally find me.

I push myself up from the floor, close the curtains to block out the light, and crawl back under the covers. I'm out like a light, the still-raging storm the only lullaby I need.

———

EASTON WORKS UNTIL FIVE TODAY, SO I SPEND MY afternoon laying out on the beach. The tourist crowds have gotten even thicker in the August heat, and I end up next to a family with more kids than I can count. They're constantly coming and going to the green and white checkered beach blanket their parents have laid out, the one in pigtails complaining about having to pee and the little boy wanting his lunch and an even younger boy throwing a tantrum over nothing.

I turn my music up as loud as my Airpods will allow.

At four thirty, I pack up my stuff and make the trek back home, weaving between the chaos of everyone else packing up their belongings as well. If this is how crazy the beach is on Friday, I don't even want to think about how busy it will be tomorrow and Sunday. Spending time at the beach between my shifts at Scoops probably won't be in the cards this weekend.

As I get closer to my backyard, Groot runs around from the front of the house to greet me. My dad must be out in the garage. I let myself in the back door, and Groot bounds in behind me and goes straight to his water bowl. I grab a cup and fill it with water for myself, chugging it as relief floods through me.

The mail is sitting on the counter, and the only reason it catches my eye is because of the envelope on the top of the pile. The handwriting is as familiar to me as my own; I've seen it scribbled on grocery lists, post-it notes tacked onto leftovers, notes for school. The return address in Colorado confirms exactly what I assumed, and I grab the envelope with a shaky hand.

I rip it open and unfold the white paper, and there's a page full of my brother's scraggly handwriting.

DEAR DAD,

I'm glad to hear things are going well with Ali. I've been worried about her since she left Colorado, especially before she started making amends with you. She still won't tell me what happened. I don't know if she's shared any of it with you, but if she has, please do whatever you can to be there for her. She puts up a tough front, but she needs someone right now.

Things have been good with work. I'm still hoping I'll get the manager promotion at the end of the summer. If I get it, I can cut back on hours and have more time to spend with Ali before she leaves for college next year. This promotion would be a life saver for both of us.

I was thinking we could come visit you in the fall, for Thanksgiving, or maybe you can come visit us in Colorado. I've been thinking about it for a couple of weeks now, but I wanted to see how Ali felt about her relationship with you before making the suggestion. I think, with where she stands right now, she'd be open to it. It could be a really good step in the right direction.

Love, Andy

FRESH, HOT TEARS ROLL DOWN MY CHEEKS AND BLUR my sight as I read, landing on the paper. When I finish and see the words 'Love, Andy', I tighten my grip on the letter. I don't care if I'm wrinkling it. I don't care if my dad will know I read it. It's not like they cared to tell me they were talking to each other, and obviously have been for a while.

How come Andy never told me?

I shoot to my feet, scaring Groot, and storm to the door to the garage. I kick it open, startling my dad as he sands down a wooden dresser. "How long have you and Andy been talking?" I ask, my voice low and shaking as I hold up the letter. Groot trots up to him to say hello.

He's wide eyed as he sets the sandpaper block down, a deer caught in the headlights. "Aliyah—" He cuts himself off, and I wait for a response. I don't look away as he struggles to find the right words to say, his eyes darting back and forth. My blue eyes pierce his, dominating this conversation. Eventually, with a sigh of defeat, he says, "A year."

A year.

One whole fucking year.

Three hundred and sixty five days.

My brother, the one person who has never let me down, has

spent the last year lying to me. He betrayed me. He betrayed me just like everyone else in my life.

Does the betrayal ever stop?

I wipe the uncontrollable tears from my face, but it's useless. I throw the letter in the general direction of my dad and storm back into the house, slamming the garage door behind me with as much force as I can muster. I don't want to be in this house, though.

Anywhere is better than this fucking house.

I barely make it past my backyard before the weight of everything hits.

My lungs can't seem to fill with enough air, so I settle for gasping breaths that double as sobs.

The waves sound louder in my head than they should.

I'm slipping, spiraling, losing control.

I bring my hands up to cover my ears, trying to block out the noise. I crumple into the sand, bowing low and closing my eyes. I block out as many senses as I can, my body struggling in every way.

Does the bullshit ever stop?

A hand touches my back, and I jump at the sudden contact. I know exactly who it is, and I turn to face him.

Easton looks terrified.

"Li—"

He stops talking once he sees my face. His terrified expression morphs into anger.

Easton pulls me to my feet and wraps me in a bone crushing hug. The weight of the hug, his arms circled around my back, my face buried in his chest, the smell of sunscreen that has become so familiar, calms me down. He tucks the top of my head under his chin, a simple gesture that makes everything else disappear.

I never want to leave this.

"It's okay," Easton breathes into my ear, and I feel a feather-light kiss pressed to the top of my head. "It's okay."

Breathing becomes easier, and the noise around us falls back to normal. I start to hiccup, each one causing my head to bump against Easton's chin. I don't need to see it to know there's a soft smile pulling at the corner of his lips.

When my breathing is under control and the world around me settles back into place, I pull my head away from Easton's chest and look up at him. He's looking down at me with the smile I knew he would be wearing, and he moves his hands from my back to my face to wipe away the last of my tears. His fingers leave a trail of sparks along my skin. I close my eyes as a very noticeable shiver racks down my spine. When I open my eyes, his smile has turned into the smallest, most endearing of smirks, and I know he knows how his touch affects me. The smirk doesn't last long at all, and the anger and worry return in the shape of a hard frown.

"Come on," he says softly, grabbing my hand in his and leading me into his backyard. I follow him into his house, slip my feet out of my sandals at the door, and let Easton lead the way upstairs. I wonder where his dad is for a moment, but once I'm through the bedroom door, everything else disappears.

Easton closes the door behind us. I look around his room, smiling at the football trophies and pictures of him with his friends and the signed football sitting on his bookshelf. There's a framed and signed black, white, and light blue jersey on the wall next to the window, whoever player ninety five is on the Panthers. All of it, down to the navy walls and gray bedding of any teenage boy, is exactly what I would imagine for Easton.

I crawl onto Easton's bed, curling up under the tie blanket from stargazing and looking up at him. "Thank you," I murmur as he sits down beside me, pulling his phone out of his pocket and setting it on the nightstand. He wastes no time in leaning back against the headboard and pulling me into his side. I accept the comfort, not even needing to readjust because Easton's arm around me makes anything comfortable.

"Li," he says softly, his lips moving against my hair, "You don't have to thank me."

"But I want to. It means a lot."

"You know I would do anything for you, Li." His words bring tears to my eyes, the love I feel for him overflowing into every crevice it can reach. "What happened?"

I think about the letter, and I shake my head. My bottom lip quivers, and I'm not surprised Easton sees this. He wraps his other arm around me, and in a move to hug me, he pulls me into his lap. His arms curl me into his chest, and he tucks my head under his chin again.

"Do you want to talk about what happened?" Easton asks, and I nod my head from its spot under his chin. Tears roll off my cheeks and land on his T-shirt. "Was it Nate?"

I wish.

I feel numb as I shake my head back and forth.

"My brother," I whisper.

"Andy?" Easton says, his body tensing underneath me. He tightens his arms around me and asks, "Li, what happened?" His voice is soft as he asks again, his lips moving right against my ear and creating goosebumps along my skin. It takes me a moment to process his words, and another moment to figure out the words I need to respond.

"He's been talking to my dad for a year. I found a letter in the mail. He never told me. He pretended like he hadn't heard from him since he left us."

"I'm sure he had a good reason," Easton murmurs, his lips still moving against my ear. His grip tightens even more. The pressure is like my own personal security blanket.

"There's no good reason to keep something like that from me." I start to move my arm to wipe away some tears, but Easton beats me to it. One arm stays secured around me, and he uses his other to wipe them away. I lean my head deeper into his chest, his hand on my bare cheek all I can think about.

"No, you're right," Easton says, cupping my chin between his fingers so our eyes meet. I can't help but glance down at his lips for a split second, only centimeters away from mine. When I meet Easton's gaze, his eyes are on the same path up from looking at my own lips. *Glad I'm not the only one.*

I could bask in that sparkle he has in his eyes all day.

Easton must have more self control than I, because he finishes what he was saying. "Up until a month ago, you hated your dad, Li."

Looking away from those dark eyes, I huff, "For good reason." Easton brings my face back to where it was so I have no choice but to look at him.

"Maybe he had no idea how to tell you."

More tears well in my eyes. "I'm so fucking tired of people not telling me things."

"I know," he whispers, pulling me into him.

Easton holds me and rocks me, and my love for him only grows. I cling to his wet and snotty T-shirt from my crying, and I can't help but laugh.

"What?" he asks, the smallest of smiles on his face when I look up. I can't help but match the smile, taking a picture in my mind so I can remember this moment after I leave. No one has ever looked at me with such a soft fierceness before. There's not a single hard line on his perfect face, but he would, without a doubt, move universes for me if I asked him to.

Nate *never* looked at me like this.

"You have snot all over your shirt," I say, and then the giggle comes. "I'm so sorry." He laughs, his whole body moving with the sound.

"Are you planning to cry any more tonight?" he teases. No meanness, no judgment, no disgust.

"Planning to, no. Could it happen? Likely," I respond. Easton ponders this for a few seconds. I wait for the verdict.

He lifts me up like I weigh nothing, sets me down on the bed right beside him, and says, "Don't move." I freeze, watching him like a hawk as he gets up, pulls a fresh navy blue graphic T-shirt out of one of his dresser drawers (second one down from the top), and switches it out for the gray one he had been wearing. He walks back to the bed as he pulls the new one down over his head, and I stare at the tanned six pack on display. I know he knows exactly what he's doing, yet I still blush when I meet his gaze.

Easton flicks the light off, and we're enveloped in darkness before the TV screen flickers on. It illuminates the room, and Easton crawls back into the bed next to me. He works his way under the comforter and sheets, but I don't move a muscle.

He told me not to.

Easton grins at me, a twinkle of understanding flashing in his eyes. "Smartass. You can move now."

"Oh thank God. My foot was starting to fall asleep."

He laughs, holding out his arms as he says, "Come here."

And I do. It's so natural, like we've done this a million times. I slip under the covers with him, moving into his arms and molding my body against his. I rest my head in the crook of his neck as he tightens his arm around my body, resting his hand on my hip bone.

I can't breathe again for very different reasons. Our legs have minds of their own as they twine together, the most skin-to-skin contact we've ever had. Easton's legs have a light layer of hair over lean muscles from running.

When he leans his cheek against my forehead, I think I may pass out. "What do you want to watch?" he asks, his voice barely above a whisper. The sound makes my heart jump in my chest.

"Anything." *Because I'm with you right now and even the worst movie in the world couldn't ruin this moment.*

He puts on *New Girl*.

"I'm assuming you haven't eaten dinner?" he asks, his voice the same low volume. My heart jumps again. I shake my head against his cheek. "Pizza sound good?" I nod.

I don't want to talk. I'm scared my voice will crack and not match his perfect volume and ruin this moment.

Not letting his grip around me loosen, he removes one arm and reaches to grab his phone from the nightstand. He pulls up the Dominoes app and places the order in thirty seconds: it's saved as his go-to. One large pizza, extra cheese, pepperoni, sausage, half with bacon, the other half black olives and green peppers.

And then his other arm is back around me.

Easton pulls my body closer, and an unconcealable shiver takes over my body. He squeezes, a silent way of telling me he feels exactly what this does to me. I smile, burrowing myself closer to his body.

When the pizza gets here, I frown when he gets up. He sees my expression and responds with a teasing yet sad smile. I know he hates it just as much as I do. "I'll be right back," he says. He runs downstairs to grab the pizza, and he's back within sixty seconds. The smell of the pizza fills the room.

He crawls back into his bed, but I know we can't exactly resume the position we were in and eat dinner at the same time. I regretfully sit up as Easton opens the box, and we dig in. We use the box as a plate.

"How are you feeling?" he asks me in between bites, his voice still low.

"Better," I say. "Still mad."

"You have every right to be mad, I know I would be." The validation feels like all I need, especially coming from Easton.

"I'm just...so sick and tired of not being told the truth. Of things being kept from me. Especially when it's Andy. Him not telling me he's been talking to our dad for a year...what am I supposed to make of that?"

"Have you asked him about it at all? Maybe his reasoning will make sense."

I shake my head in response to Easton's initial question. "I don't want to talk to him right now." I take another slice of pizza. "He's just another person who's been lying to me, and it's even worse because he's my *brother*." Easton frowns, and I shake my head. "Please, don't. I know I should talk to him, and eventually I will, but not now. Too much shit has happened in the last two months. Just let me be stubborn for once." My last words come out as a joke, and they succeed in lightening the mood.

Easton smiles, rolling his eyes as he grabs another slice.

We finish the entire pizza, and Easton gets up once more to throw the box away. When he returns, he's back in bed and I'm back in his arms before my mind can process what's happening. Our legs entwine, my head rests perfectly in the crook of his neck so his cheek lays against my forehead, and his arms circle and tighten around me like letting go is the biggest sin in the bible.

There's just Easton, and we have officially crossed the point of no return.

CHAPTER THIRTY

I SPEND THE REST OF THE WEEKEND DODGING MY DAD and holing up in my bedroom or Easton's. I know I can't avoid him forever, but I want to let myself be mad for a couple days.

On Monday morning, I wake up with Groot still in my bed. With a four week countdown until school starts in New Haven (and five weeks in Colorado), football practice has begun. Easton is occupied from seven A.M. to noon Monday through Thursday, which means our mornings together have gone down to one day a week.

Since Groot's usual morning routine has also been disrupted, I decide to take him on a walk down the boardwalk. The fresh air and exercise will be good for both of us. And, after two months, I finally go to Bean Hut.

The boardwalk is almost empty, the weekend rush of tourists gone and only a few visiting for more than the weekend lingering around. The sun has already come out at full force, and the August heat is not something to mess with. I wonder how Easton is handling it with practice, and a smile comes to my face. It felt weird to wake up alone this morning when I've woken up beside him each day since I found the letter. Dave either didn't notice or didn't care there was a girl sleeping in his son's bed, and I don't particularly care to find out.

There are two young teenage girls sitting outside of Bean Hut, and I ask them to keep an eye on Groot while I'm inside. They both happily oblige, gushing over how cute he is.

The smell of coffee beans invades my nostrils the second I open the door, and I welcome it with a smile. The floors look like the exact same shade of beige wood we have at Scoops, and the colors throughout the rest of the shop are light wood, black, and white. The big-leafed plants add a beachy touch, and I love it.

There's a short line for the register, and it gives me time to examine the menu to decide what I want. My usual go-to coffee order is an iced caramel macchiato with oat milk from Starbucks, but just like everything else this summer, I change it up. I order an iced mocha, still opting for oat milk because I like the flavor it adds to my coffee.

Once my drink is in my hand, I head back outside and rejoin Groot. He sees me and stands up, wagging his tail as I approach. "Hey, buddy," I say, scratching between his ears with my free hand. "Thank you both for watching him," I tell the girls.

"He's such a sweetie," one of them smiles, holding out her hand for him to sniff again.

"He is," I smile.

I walk Groot to the end of the boardwalk, and instead of turning around, I keep going and take a path through the downtown area of New Haven. The colorful buildings are just as they were when I drove in this summer.

My phone rings, and I pull it out of the back pocket of my shorts. Josie's calling. "Hey, what's up?" I ask, moving my coffee to the hand I'm also holding Groot's leash in. I really hope he doesn't try to yank right now.

"Hey girly! Ev and I are going to get our nails done. Want to join?" she asks.

"Like, right now?"

"Yeah, we're leaving in ten or twenty minutes."

"I'm out walking Groot right now. If you can wait thirty, I'm in."

"Deal. I'll text you when we're on our way." She hangs up, and I immediately set off on the route for home with Groot. It's a twenty minute walk from wherever I had wandered to, so I have enough time to make myself a sandwich to-go. I sneak Groot a few little pieces of ham, something I know I shouldn't do but can't help when he looks at me with his wide eyes. He's too cute for his own good.

I slip my sandals on, say goodbye to Groot, and head outside right as Ev and Josie pull up. I hop into the back seat behind Josie in the driver's seat. "Hey girly," she grins, glancing at me in the rearview mirror. She backs out of my driveway and heads down the street. Music plays through the speakers at the perfect volume for us to still be able to talk.

"Hey!" I say, pulling down the cupholder in the middle seat so I can set my coffee down.

"Oh, you got Bean Hut! What did you get?" Ev asks, turning in the passenger seat so she's facing me. The tips of her hair are a bright purple, looking like they were freshly dyed in her high pony. It might be my favorite color I've seen from her so far.

"I love the high pony, Ev!" I say. "And I didn't get anything special. Just an oat milk mocha. This is my first time getting it."

"Thank you, thank you," she flaunts, flipping the ends up. "My go-to from the hut is an iced white mocha with almond milk and a half shot of raspberry."

Josie grimaces, "I don't know how you can stand that. It's way too sweet."

"What do you usually get?" I ask her.

"An iced latte. One pump of vanilla if I'm feeling spicy."

"Bor-ing," Ev teases, and Josie rolls her eyes. Still facing me, Ev turns her blue eyes on me, and I don't know what to expect from the glint in them. "So, I have a question."

Oh no. "I don't know whether to be curious or scared," I say, and Ev laughs, throwing her head back.

"She just wants to know what's going on between you and Easton," Josie snickers.

"I'm not the only one who wants to know! You're just as curious!" Ev defends.

"Fine. We *both* want to know," Josie admits, glancing in the rearview mirror to smile at me.

Heat rises in my cheeks at the mention of Easton after spending the weekend curled up in the same bed as him, and both girls see it right away.

It's the only answer Ev needs. "I knew it!" she exclaims, turning to Josie and then turning back to me.

"We called it," Josie laughs.

"What do you mean, you called it?" I ask. I know exactly what they're referring to, but not having any friends to talk to about what's going on between Easton and me has me latching on to even the slightest mention of it.

Ev says, "The chemistry between the two of you has had us in a major choke hold since the first time you hung out with all of us. We haven't had a chance to ask you about it until now, though!"

"And lunch at the party on the Fourth!" Josie adds, fanning her face with her free hand. "I don't know what you two were talking about, but that eye contact was *intense.*"

"Speaking of eye contact, the fire last week! Aliyah, you *have* to tell us what's going on. We're dying over here."

I can't help but smile so wide my cheeks hurt as they mention all these moments of Easton and I. It's always felt like Easton and I are in our own little world and these moments are just for us, but I guess not. "You've noticed something for that long?"

"Yes, *that long*! Aliyah, I haven't seen that boy look at anyone like he looks at you, and I've known him since we were all in diapers," Josie says, glancing at me in the mirror again with a smile. "I don't know what magic you possess to have grabbed the attention of Easton fucking King, but whatever it is, do not ever let him go. Easton hasn't even glanced at a girl since Ellie cheated on him."

I freeze. Through the mirror, I see the smile drop from Josie's face, and Ev, still facing me, looks confused. "Has Easton not... talked to you about Ellie?" she asks. I shake my head, still too stunned to speak.

"Shit. I wouldn't have said anything if I had known. Y'all are attached at the hip, so I assumed he already told you."

Both girls mistake my shock for finding out Easton was cheated on. They're not wrong, but they're not entirely right. I'm almost more shocked at hearing her name: *Ellie.*

We were both wronged by an Ellie. His girlfriend, my best friend.

And we were both cheated on.

Why didn't he tell me?

"Aliyah, are you okay?" Ev asks.

"I didn't mean to cause an issue, I promise," Josie says, giving me a quick glance in the rearview mirror that's full of regret.

I shake my head, clearing out enough thoughts to speak. "No, not at all. Just shocked." Adding more shock to my own plate, I find myself not only telling them but *wanting* to do so. "I'm not mad he didn't tell me. The reason I came to New Haven for the summer is because I was cheated on. All my friends knew and didn't say anything, even my best friend. Her name was Ellie."

Josie and Ev listen, and both of their eyes widen at my words. "Damn," Ev murmurs. "I can't even imagine." She turns to Josie, and as if she's trying to lighten the mood, she says, "Jos, if you ever do that to me, I'm telling Gabe you peed the bed after the fire last week."

I can't help but laugh, thankful for the joke, and Josie's gasp turns into a laugh. She looks at me in the rearview mirror again and defends, "I chugged a Gatorade before I went to bed so I wouldn't be hungover. Ev and I were up until, like, three in the morning, and I was so exhausted the electrolytes went right through me."

"Hey, I'm not judging," I laugh, and I find myself aching for the long, giggle-filled nights of a sleepover. Ellie and I used to talk about everything and nothing in the wee hours of the morning, darkness surrounding us until we dozed off in the middle of a conversation.

Ev and Josie must see the quick drop of my face, and Josie says, "Really, though. Losing all of your friends and your boyfriend at the same time is brutal. How long were you together?"

"Three years," I murmur, feeling that twinge of anger as I think about what Nate did.

"The time makes it even worse," Ev says, disgust filling her features. I nod in agreement, and it feels really good to have someone backing me up. Not that any sane person wouldn't, but knowing I have Ev and Josie in my corner still helps me feel better.

"Now *I'm* shocked Easton didn't tell you anything," Josie says as she pulls into the parking lot at the nail salon.

"Whatever his reasoning is, it's a good one," Ev tells me as the three of us get out of the car. "Easton is the best person in this town, hands down. *None of us* deserve him."

"I know," I smile softly.

"Are you going to make a move?" Ev asks me as she opens the door for us. Josie grins at the question, and I know I'm not on the same page as them. There's no one at the front desk to check us in, so we wait right inside the door.

I hesitate in answering before shaking my head. Both girls frown at my response, and Josie asks, "Why not? The two of you are head over heels for each other." My stomach starts doing somersaults.

"I'm not staying in New Haven," I say. "I'm only here for the summer. I'm going back to Colorado in less than a month."

"Why wouldn't you stay?" Ev asks.

"Why would you go back?" Josie asks at the same time.

I take a deep breath. It's nice to have Ev and Josie to hang out with and talk to about some things, but we're not close enough for me to talk about everything behind those seemingly simple questions.

Thankfully, a woman approaches us at the desk and checks us in, and the topic is dropped. While we're waiting for them to set up stations for us, I sit down in the little waiting area. Josie and Ev follow me.

"I haven't gotten my nails done in so long," I say, looking through the basket with all of the color samples. I'm drawn to a mint green shade.

"When was the last time?" Ev asks, looking through some of the colors as well.

"Eighth grade, I think. I went with Ellie and her mom for Ellie's birthday," I admit. I'm hit with the memory of that day; the two of us giggling over the endless options of colors, getting frozen yogurt afterwards and piling our cups as high as we could, and finishing the day off with a sleepover and watching as many of the *Twilight* movies as we could. It was a really good day, one of the first after my dad had left.

Josie gasps, "You didn't get your nails done for prom?"

I shake my head, "I got a stick on French manicure from Walgreens." I don't add it was all I could afford and I had to miss out when all my girlfriends went the Friday night before. I told everyone my request off form didn't get approved and I had to work. I did have to work, but I never submitted a request. I didn't want anyone to feel bad about me not being able to go because of money and offer to pay for me.

My words sound pathetic, but Josie and Ev show no sign of judgment. "Saving some money," Ev grins. "No one can complain about that. I think I used two weeks worth of pay to get my nails done for prom. They looked great, but damn did it hurt the bank."

I laugh, relief flooding through my veins at how easily the conversation didn't turn into a pity party. "What do you think about this color?" I ask the two of them, showing them the mint green I'm looking at.

"I love!" Josie says.

"I'm doing purple," Ev says, showing us the swatch she's picked. It's identical to the tips of her hair, and I tell her I love that they'll match.

"For another day or two," she laughs, "Before the color starts to fade. Who knows, maybe I'll keep the purple up."

"I think you should," Josie says.

"At least for the rest of the summer. Then it's back to red for football season."

"I think I'm going to do red for my nails. Thoughts?" Josie asks.

"Yes," Ev approves.

"Absolutely," I grin.

Hanging out with them and deciding what color we want our nails painted makes me feel normal, and it's refreshing. I *almost* let myself imagine what it would be like if I stayed.

I can't, though.

So I don't.

CHAPTER THIRTY-ONE

"Did you see it's supposed to storm tonight?"

"Of course I did," Easton says matter-of-factly.

"So what's the plan once we get off?" I ask, scooping little bits of ice cream off the edges in the freezer and back into their proper cartons, my back to him. "Or do you want to go to bed early for practice?"

"Why? Did you have something in mind?" he replies, his tone making my toes curl in my Converse. *Damn him and his stupid, silky voice.*

"A movie night?"

"I think I could pencil in a movie tonight." I don't have to see him to know he's smirking, and it makes me smile. "Any particular movie in mind?"

"I'm not sure. Maybe a horror movie?"

"You just want to cuddle with me during the scary parts."

I gasp, turning away from the freezer of ice cream to face him, the scoop still in my hand. "Who says you aren't the one who wants to cuddle with me!"

Never mind the fact that he so casually dropped the invitation to *cuddle* during our movie night. It sends my body down a roller coaster with as many loops and twists and turns as possible.

Trying to figure out how to bring up his ex-girlfriend fits right in, just another dip that has my stomach dropping.

"Easy there, tiger. I never said I didn't."

That has me zipping my mouth shut because what am I supposed to say? Easton continues to smirk in triumph, only leaving me further speechless.

"You got your nails done today," he points out, completely changing the topic.

"I did," I grin, holding out my hand to show off the mint green color. I'm surprised it took him until almost close to mention them. I wiggle my fingers, and Easton laughs.

"I like the color. It suits you," he says.

"Thanks," I laugh, pulling my hand back. I put the scoop back and grab the lids. "I went with Josie and Ev." It's the perfect opening, and I don't even take a breath before continuing, "Speaking of them...they mentioned Ellie today."

Easton doesn't say anything, and when I turn to face him, his back is tense underneath his blue Scoops shirt. "East..." I say softly, putting the lids on the counter and approaching him. "They thought I already knew. They didn't tell me anything, and I don't want to hear it from anyone but you." I put a hand on his shoulder, but he shrugs me off. I pull my arm close to me, doing everything I can to fight off the hurt.

"I don't want to talk about it," Easton shrugs, his voice empty. *That's a first.*

"Okay," I say, stepping away. I'm not going to push; Lord knows Easton has been more than patient with me this summer. I grab the lids I was holding and start putting them on the ice cream cartons in the display freezer.

Moments later, Easton says quietly, "Did you have fun hanging out with Josie and Ev today?"

"I did," I smile, risking a glance in his direction.

"I'm glad you broke your no-friends rule for them," he teases. There's a little bit of tension hanging in the air between us, but if we keep acting like our normal selves, it should dissipate. Any tension or awkwardness we've had this summer has never lasted long.

"Yeah, well, I blame you for starting that trend," I joke.

Easton gives me a knowing look, and I realize where he's trying to take this. After he shut me down, no way am I letting him talk to me about making friends here after all. My guard goes up, and quietly, I say, "Please don't."

"Li—"

"Easton. I asked you not to," I snap. His full name sounds foreign on my tongue, and the silence after tells me everything I need to know about how he feels about hearing it.

This tension is not going anywhere any time soon.

For the first time ever, we close down the shop in silence. We don't even have music blaring, making the silence all the louder. The entire time, I feel him stewing over whatever he's going to say next. All I want to do is think of something to say to break through the tension, to make things go back to the way they have been.

Our routine is messed up from the silence, and it's fifteen minutes later than it usually is when we finally step outside. The storm clouds look menacing, thunder already rolling in from the Atlantic and making sure we know it's not planning to play nice. I take off my Converse as I wait for Easton to lock the door, and we set off down the boardwalk together. "Are we okay?" I ask quietly.

East takes a deep breath, avoiding my gaze as I glance at him. "Aliyah..."

The sound of my full name has me gulping, a lump forming in the back of my throat and my walls flying up.

"You have spent all summer running from everything. From Nate, Ellie, your dad, Andy. Making close friends here. Having anything tie you down here." *Asshole. I am already tied down here. You should know that better than anyone.* I don't think he's going to say anything else, but then, under his breath but loud enough I know I'm supposed to hear, he says, "Me."

A deep, angry breath rumbles through my body as we step onto the sand. It's still warm from the day, and the grains slip between my toes and only fuel the fire inside me.

"I don't want you to keep running from everything," he continues, getting louder and more out of control with each word. "Sure, the easy things you get out of the way right away, but anything bigger than that and you dip. I get life sucks sometimes, but it's going to keep sucking if you don't face it! You can't avoid everything forever!"

"Like you avoid everything that sucks in your life?" I fire back, no control of the words coming out of my mouth.

"What is that supposed to mean?" Easton asks while running a hand through his already-messy hair, and I hear the shake of anger in his voice. I've never seen him this angry before.

I huff, my words laced with rage, "All you do is pretend you're fine when you're not. At least not all the time. You have no right to tell me to stop running and face my problems when you can't even face your own!"

"What the *fuck*, Li?" Not even the sound of my nickname is enough to stop the course of rage.

"NO! You don't get to 'Li' me, Easton." Hot, angry tears start to form, pushing out of the corners of my eyes. "You never even told me about Ellie, much less what happened with her! And I know losing your mom so quickly was some of the worst pain you ever felt, but you don't let anyone see you're still hurting! I know I'm a mess right now, but that gives you no right to tell me how I should handle my own shit." I hate the words spilling out of me, hate that I want them to hurt Easton just as much as he hurt me. Rain starts sprinkling down.

Easton is silent until we reach the split of our yards. "No right, huh?" he asks quietly, the saddest smile on his lips as raindrops wet his hair and run down his face. *God, I'm so in love with him.* He turns and walks toward his house, and I don't watch him leave. I storm up the back porch to my own house and slam the door closed, locking it to make sure Easton doesn't try to come in and keep telling me everything I'm doing wrong. I wipe away the tears still streaming down my face, catching some snot on my wrist as well.

I guess we're not watching a horror movie and cuddling tonight.

My dad sits in his chair reading, and his head pops up at the sound of the door slamming. I don't want to talk to him, and I must give that away because he doesn't even nod in my direction. I head straight upstairs, Groot on my heels, and slam my door. For good measure, I make sure my balcony doors are locked. The rain starts pouring as I do this, and the first big clap of thunder and flash of lightning makes it known the storm has arrived. It's the only reason I don't close the curtains.

I pace the floor of my room, the words Easton and I exchanged in our fight replaying in my mind over and over.

The storm is a fitting soundtrack for the warring emotions in my body, every crack of thunder matching a wave of anger and every flash of lightning fueling the hurt.

My tears don't stop, and the angry huffs turn into quick, uneven gasps. I can't catch my breath, and I keel over with my hands on my knees. I read somewhere once that you need to put your head below your heart when you can't catch your breath, but it doesn't seem to be helping.

What did I do?

My anger at Easton doesn't go anywhere, but my anger at myself grows.

I fucked everything up between us. There's no way he will ever forgive me for the words I said to him.

A wet nose nudges my face, Groot right in front of me. His eyes are wide, clearly worried, as he starts to lick the salty tears off my cheeks. I fall into a pile on the floor, and Groot nuzzles me until he can see my face again.

I wish I could take him back to Colorado with me.

Colorado.

My phone is still in the back pocket of my shorts, and I scramble to pull it out. The cracked screen lights up, and there are no texts from anyone. I swipe up to unlock it, type a few things in on Safari, and then flights to Colorado are popping up for tomorrow.

They're even more expensive than what I paid to get to New Haven, and I don't have enough money. I sigh, though it comes out more of a garbled sob, and I bury my face in Groot's fur again.

So much for getting out of here so I would never have to face Easton after saying the most hurtful words I could to him.

The storm rumbles on outside, each crack of lightning illuminating my bedroom. A bedroom that was barren two months ago and now is filled with a comfy chair in the corner, canvas paintings on the wall, glow in the dark stars on the ceiling, and a framed photo on the dresser, the very first picture Easton and I took together.

A bedroom I have made into my home. A home I really, really don't want to leave.

I can't believe Easton said all of that to me. I can't believe he thinks all I do is run from my problems. Sure, I came to New Haven for the summer so I wouldn't have to deal with Nate and Ellie and Sierra and everything else until I was ready, but I had every intention of going back and telling them just where exactly they can shove it.

At least, I think I had every intention to do that.

Groot's looking at me with wide, tired eyes. He still looks a bit worried for me, but more than anything, he looks like he wants to curl into bed. I put him out of his misery and pick myself up off the floor, falling into the same pile on my mattress. Groot is eager to jump up beside me and wastes no time circling himself thrice before plopping down in his usual spot at the foot of the bed.

I curl under the covers, wishing I could wake up and this was all some terrible dream. I simmer over the words Easton said to me, the sinking feeling in my stomach reaching the very pits only meaning one thing. Something I refuse to admit.

My phone lights up as I shift in my bed, and my heart soars at the first thought of it being because Easton sent me a text. If he sent me a text we can fix this and everything will be okay.

But it's not Easton. It's someone texting in the big group chat, and it's not long before others are texting back. With every ding, I check to see if Easton has said anything, either to me or in the group chat, but his name never flashes across my phone. I think about responding in the chat, wondering if Easton is staring at his phone and waiting for my name to pop up, but I don't want to be the first to give in.

I don't hear a peep from Easton for the rest of the night, and he doesn't hear a peep from me. I may regret the words I said to him more than I've ever regretted anything in my entire life, but he still basically told me to stop being a chicken and grow a pair. No way am I reaching out to him first.

If he wants to call me out for avoiding my problems, then that's exactly what I'm going to do.

CHAPTER THIRTY-TWO

THIS IS EXACTLY WHY I DIDN'T WANT TO GET CLOSE with anyone this summer. If I had stuck with that plan, I wouldn't be stewing over my fight with Easton as much as I am.

It wouldn't feel like someone was carving out every vessel of my heart with a knife, one at a time. The dream I had about Nate and Ellie doing open heart surgery on me is nothing compared to this.

By day three, I think I've gone mad. If not, then I'm for sure only one step away.

I've stayed in the house, not even wanting to brave the beach in fear of running into Easton. I've switched all my closing shifts with him to day shifts, trading with Jackie or Naomi. When I text them, they both ask if everything is okay, and I lie. I don't think they believe me, but neither of them pushes.

The Notebook has been playing on repeat, and I zone out playing mindless games on my phone. I even start reading one of my dad's books, a World War II novel that has some romance in the storyline. I enjoy it more than I thought I would.

I haven't spoken with Easton since he walked away from me

the other night. Not that I blame him for walking away. I was a bitch to him, and not the kind of bad bitch I like being.

Day three is when I finally decide it's safe to go down to the beach. If Easton hasn't reached out to me yet, I don't think he'll approach me at the beach. Anyway, he's at football practice until noon, so I have at least two hours until there's a chance of running into him.

So I make myself breakfast, change into a swimsuit, grab my beach bag, and walk the familiar path down to the water. I'm one of the first people there, and I lay my towel out near the water but not so close I'll get splashed every other second. There's a mom here with two young boys, and I make sure to stay far enough away to be out of their splash zone, too.

I also make sure to sit far, far away from where Easton and his friends usually hang out. He may not approach me, but I'm not taking any chances.

The sun quickly warms my skin, and for the first time in three days, I forget. It's just me and my music and the beach. *Exactly how this summer was supposed to go.*

Hours later, my tanning is rudely interrupted when I'm bombarded with sand, the grains landing on my back, in my hair, up my nose. My eyes fly open, and I see a little boy no older than seven running away. It doesn't look like he even realized he kicked sand all over me, but the sand flying up behind him is all the evidence I need to know he's the culprit.

It feels wrong to be irritated at a little kid that means no harm, but as I sit up to blow the sand out of my nose and try to brush it out of my hair, I can't help it. My phone starts ringing, and I reach behind me to answer it, seeing my boss's name on my phone. After a quick check to make sure my phone is still connected to my AirPods, I say, "Hey, Mandy. What's up?"

"Hey sweetie. How are you?"

"Trying to get sand out of my nose, but otherwise fine. How are you?" I ask, and Mandy laughs on the other line.

"Oh darn, I'm interrupting your afternoon. I'm sorry," she sighs, and I laugh as I continue to run my hands over my messy bun to get rid of the sand.

"I'm just at the beach, nothing special. Is something wrong?"

Mandy sighs, "Naomi's been puking all day, and she's scheduled to close tonight. Is there any way you want to close with Jackie tonight? Fred or I have no issues closing if you don't want to, I don't want to pull you away from the beach. I figured I'd reach out to see if you wanted the hours. I know you've been trying to pick up as much as you can."

"Yeah, I can absolutely come in," I tell her, thinking about the extra money on my paycheck. Any money I make is more than needed. *And she said nothing about Easton being there.*

Mandy lets out a sigh of relief. "Are you sure? I really don't want to pull you away from the beach."

I laugh, "Seriously, Mandy, don't worry about me at all. The hours are more than welcome, I promise. I hope Naomi's okay."

"Me too. I'm sure she'll be feeling fine within the next day or two," Mandy says.

I nod in agreement, pulling the classic non-verbal response before realizing she can't see me. "Me too. What time do you need me to come in?"

"It's three to close, but if you need to push it back, I can stay later."

"No, three works for me!"

"See you then! And thank you again for being willing to come in," Mandy says.

"No need to thank me. I'm glad I can help out," I say.

After hanging up, I set a timer on my phone for two in case I start dozing in and out. It leaves me enough time to run home and wash the sunscreen, sweat, and sun off my body, grab something to eat, and get back to the boardwalk by three.

In between the pause of hanging up and my music starting up again, I hear laughter coming from the spot I've been trying to avoid looking over at, and it's too tempting to fight for a moment. I look, and right away I know the person I'm looking for isn't here.

I worry that he's not hanging out with his friends; it's not like him. He's either with me, them, or at work every afternoon, but right now none of those are accurate. *Where is he, then?*

I try not to care. I lay back down and turn my music up as loud as it can go as if it will drown out the thoughts of whether or not Easton is okay. My heart hurts from how much I want to know, but it's too late. What's done is done.

My timer goes off all too soon, and I gather my belongings and start the short walk back home. The sand is hot beneath my bare feet, a feeling I welcome since I won't have it for much longer. I don't even wear shoes when I come down to the sand anymore because there's no point. They either dangle from my fingers or are stuffed to the bottom of my bag the entire time.

My eyes go to Easton's bedroom window, like maybe I'll catch a glimpse of him, but the blinds are drawn. I keep walking, ignoring every increasing worry about how Easton is doing.

I let Groot out to go potty when I get inside, refilling my water bottle and chugging a third of it while I wait for him to do his business. I let him back in and head upstairs to get ready for work.

After my quick shower, the hair goes up in a claw clip and a swipe of mascara goes over my lashes. I slap together a sandwich in the kitchen, fill my water bottle again, say goodbye to Groot, and head out the back door, this time wearing shoes.

Easton haunts my mind the entire time.

A bittersweet feeling sinks in as I take it all in on my walk. The water, the boardwalk up ahead, the neighborhood behind me. I can't help it. I only get so many more walks to work with this view.

I walk into Scoops and head directly for the back, throwing a quick greeting out to Mandy and Jackie. Fred is in the back sitting at the computer, and I greet him as I put my stuff in my cubby.

"Oh, Aliyah," Fred says, catching me midway to the doors leading out to the counter.

I keep tying the apron around my back as I say, "Yeah, what's up?"

"Are you sticking around for the school year?" he asks. "Easton said you weren't sure yet when I asked him yesterday."

Yesterday?

I stutter, "Um, no, I'm not. I'll be heading back to Colorado in a couple weeks. My last day is probably August twenty-ninth." Fred nods, and I keep walking through the swinging doors.

A deep breath shutters through me. *Yesterday?*

Easton told his grandpa I might not go home YESTERDAY? Why would he say that? We're not even on speaking terms right now.

My mind whirls with why Easton would lie about me staying. He knows I'm not staying, whether we're on speaking terms or not. *Why would he say I don't know yet? Why would he say that when—*

I know why.

Of course I know why.

I hop right into the flow of things at work, scooping ice cream and sprinkling toppings and thinking about Easton and how much I love that smug little bastard. Mandy and Fred head out within the hour, leaving Jackie and I to man the shop.

By the end of our shift, I'm cursing myself for not getting to know Jackie more this summer. Her sense of humor is hilarious, and she makes me forget about my dad and Andy and Easton for the whole five hours we're working. I hear all about the drama on the girl's soccer team and Naomi and Logan have been flirting all summer and finally went out on a date last week (that's top secret and the only other people who know are obviously Naomi and Logan and I'm not supposed to tell anyone, not even Easton).

We split paths at the door, her to the parking lot and me on the path to my house.

All of my thoughts catch up to me before I even step off the boardwalk, and I end up sitting down on the wood with my feet in the sand and chin resting in my hands.

I finally let myself admit Easton was right.

I've been running from *everything* that matters.

Not anymore. That's not who I want to be.

And most important, I don't want to lose Easton. I won't lose him.

I just have to figure out how to get him to forgive me.

———

WHEN I GET HOME, I'M SURPRISED TO SEE MY DAD STILL up and sitting at the kitchen table. He glances up when he hears me walk in the door. I wasn't expecting him to still be up, but since he is, I'm going to take advantage of it.

No more running.

I take a deep, shaky breath, swallow the nausea, and take a seat across from him. His eyebrows raise in surprise at the abruptness, but he manages to keep his jaw closed. Groot trots up to me and lays his head on my thigh. I give him some head scratches, hoping he'll help with the anxious feelings flowing through every single vein in my body.

Looking my dad directly in the eye, hating the identical shade to mine, I say, "Talk. You know exactly why I'm mad, and you know I have every right to be."

He nods, managing to hide his surprise at my bluntness a little better.

"I reached out to Andy a year ago. I was back on my feet, and I didn't feel like I'd be a burden in your lives anymore. I knew it was a long shot, given how I'd left, but the only thing worse than trying was not trying. I was surprised when I got a letter back from Andy two weeks later.

"We've slowly been building our relationship, and I did ask about you. All the time. He told me you were a lot angrier at me than he was, and a letter wouldn't do anything at this point in time. So I didn't. I trusted that Andy knew what was best for you. He's taken care of you more than I ever have."

I resist the urge to snort and say *ain't that the truth*. I don't need to make him feel any worse. Instead, I say, "You're right."

"We decided it would be best to break the news to you slowly. Or maybe me coming into town for a week and you could have the option to see me. It took us both by surprise when you up and decided to spend the summer in New Haven for what appeared to be no reason. I was surprised, but I felt like it would be the best chance to repair what I broke between us.

"And I feel like it was. You were opening up to me, hanging out with me. We were starting to build the father-daughter relationship you should have had the moment your mother and I found out we were pregnant with you."

As hard as I try, I can't fight the tears starting to roll down my cheeks. He looks heartbroken at every word he says, and even the dumbest person in the world would be able to see how much he's trying to make up for his wrongs. I'm grasping for all the hate I've attached to him for almost seventeen years, hopeless as it flees the scene. I shouldn't feel a need to hold onto it so tight, but I've held onto anger for my dad for a long time. I'm terrified that losing the anger will also mean losing a part of myself.

"Aliyah, neither of us meant to hurt you by not telling you. You have every right to be mad, and I take all the responsibility. Don't be mad at your brother for trying to respect how you were feeling the way he thought was best."

"I know," I nod, wiping my palms across my cheeks to wipe away the tears. "I know." And I can't say anything more because the break down finally happens. I stand up to hug him, and he meets me halfway. He holds me as I cry, the way he should have held me when I was six years old and scraped my knees after falling off my bicycle.

It's comforting, something I never thought I would say about hugging my dad. And that makes me cry even more. The tears wash all the hate away, cleansing the hurt and the pain and the feelings I've been trying so hard to hold onto.

Nate, Ellie, and Sierra can still go fuck themselves, but see if I care anymore. If they hadn't all screwed me over, I never would have met Easton, and that would have been the biggest tragedy of all.

When the tears are manageable, only sniffles left in me, I pull away from him and wipe my face with the palms of my hands again.

"Aliyah, when I found out you were coming to stay with me for the whole summer, that's the best news I've gotten since you were born." *Since my mom died.* "I swear to you, I'm going to do any and everything I can to make things right with you and your brother."

I look up at him through my tears, nod, and whisper, "I know, Dad."

CHAPTER THIRTY-THREE

My heart thumps so loudly in my chest as I slide the spare key into the lock, I think I might go into cardiac arrest. What I'm about to do is either the best idea I've ever had or will be my ultimate demise.

I ever so slowly turn the key in the lock and turn the knob, hoping and praying to whatever higher power the door *does not squeak*. It's never something I thought to focus on when I walked through it. Why would it have been?

There's a small squeak as soon as the door moves, but no other sound emits as I inch the door open. I step inside, thankful for the open curtains letting the light shine into the house so I don't have to scramble around for a light switch. Easton might know my house like the back of his hand, but I've only been in his house a handful of times.

I close the door behind me, cringing at the squeak that sounds again and hoping Easton isn't a light sleeper. The only thing I truly know about his sleeping habits (other than the fact that he's a great cuddler) is he wakes up when someone steps on him.

Who wouldn't?

I head to the kitchen and set my backpack on the counter to

pull out all of my ingredients. I didn't want to steal the King's food, so I brought my own ingredients to make pancakes as well as a package of bacon, a can of whipped cream, and a bag of chocolate chips.

Everything I need to make the perfect "I'm sorry" breakfast.

Thankfully, I know my way around the kitchen enough to find a bowl, a frying pan, utensils, and a couple of plates. I start whipping up the pancake batter, wanting to get started on the pancakes right away since they'll take the longest. Every second I waste is another second I risk of Easton waking up and coming downstairs before I'm ready.

I move carefully, setting things on the counter with care to not create too much noise and making sure I'm not moving too fast. It's pointless. I catch the handle of the frying pan with my hip before I'm even done mixing the batter.

Every hope of Easton staying asleep goes right down the drain as the frying pan clatters to the ground with a series of *clang*s. I jump out of the way before it lands on my bare toes, grateful I didn't have it heated on the stove yet, and let out a sigh of defeat as I hear footsteps creaking upstairs.

Easton finds me staring at the frying pan on the floor with my shoulders slumped and a frown on my face. I meet his gaze, the first time I have in almost a week, and it's the easiest breath of air I've taken since I saw him last. The sight of his dark eyes alone would be enough to cure my worst day ever. Even better than his eyes, I see him fighting against the raising corner of his lips, not wanting me to see him smile.

I've missed him so much.

"That wasn't supposed to happen," I say quietly, pointing at the frying pan on the ground. "You weren't supposed to come down until breakfast was ready."

"Why are you in my house making breakfast in the first place?" He stays by the stairs, not making a move toward me. He at least had the thought to put on a shirt, and it's the only time I won't complain about it so I'm not drooling through my apology. I want to run up and wrap my arms around him and tell him how much I missed him and that I love him.

I love him so much it hurts, but I don't think I'm ready to take things *that* far.

There's no beating around the bush. I don't want him to think I'm running or trying to dodge anything, so I try and say the only words that will prove to him how serious I am. Unfortunately, they're also the hardest words I've ever had to say, and they get stuck in my throat.

"I...I..."

Swallow your damn pride, Aliyah.

I take a deep breath. "I'm sorry. For everything. You...You were right." Easton doesn't say anything, which makes this apology that much harder. I deserve it, though. He leans back against the banister of the stairs and crosses his arms over his chest. That pose and his straight-out-of-bed messy hair make my knees go weak and my stomach turn into jelly. *Why was I ever trying to fight my feelings for him?* How *did I ever fight my feelings for him?*

I keep talking, "I am a runner. Theoretically. You'll probably never see me running actually unless we're racing. But that's besides the point. I...I don't like when things make me feel real emotions, I guess. I like when I'm in control and things don't bother me. And when they do bother me, I run away so I can pretend they don't exist."

I pick up the frying pan after scrambling for something, anything to do with my body, and I set it back on the counter. I don't look back at Easton as I continue, "Life does suck, and I've had enough of it, but you were right. Life will keep sucking if I don't do anything about it."

The bastard still doesn't say anything, and I look up to meet his gaze again. He's making no move to say anything in response to my words, and even that corner of his mouth that was threatening to pull up no longer exists. It's almost as if he's saying *and?*

"I'm sorry for what I said to you about your mom and Ellie. It was really shitty of me to use your own pain against you, and that's not the kind of the person I want to be. And I'm sorry for saying you have no right. You were trying to help, and I should have let you. You have every right. More than anyone else."

He remains silent and emotionless, and I don't know how much longer I can grovel for his forgiveness. The seconds feel like hours. Days, even. And still, Easton stands at the bottom of the staircase doing nothing.

Oh, fuck it.

"East, you gotta give me something," I beg. Actually beg. I don't think that's something I've ever done in my entire life.

And as I stare at Easton, feeling heartbroken and desperate and wanting any show of emotion from him so I can figure out what's going through his mind, that bastard has the audacity to smile, and I realize he's been playing me this whole time.

I gasp, "You—I cannot believe—"

Easton bursts out laughing, the most beautiful sound I've ever heard, and he uncrosses his arms and holds them out wide for me. Despite being pissed that he got me to beg on purpose, I rush toward him, and when his arms settle around my body, I know I'm never giving it up. I'm never giving *him* up.

Ever.

"That was so mean," I mumble into his chest, and I feel his body start shaking with laughter. He starts running his hands up and down my back, pressing me tighter into him.

"That wasn't my plan, I swear. I didn't know you would take an apology this far, though, trying to surprise me with breakfast. It was too good of an opportunity to pass up," he chuckles, his lips moving softly against my ear. I shiver.

"Well, I don't apologize to just anyone, so you must be special."

"I sure hope I am."

My cheeks start to hurt from how big my smile is, but I don't care. I have Easton back, and he's not mad at me, and we can have breakfast together like we always do. "I missed you," I find myself whispering, and he presses me even tighter into his body, every one of our crevices lining up perfectly.

"I missed you too, Li," Easton whispers back.

His familiar scent fills my nose, sunscreen and salty air. I take a deep breath of it before finally letting him go. I've got a breakfast to make, and I'm not going to stop because we're okay now. I resume my spot in the kitchen, taking time to move the handle of the frying pan toward the green tiled backsplash of the kitchen. Easton tries to help me, but I bump my hip with his enough to knock him off balance.

"Hey—"

"No way. You're not helping with breakfast this morning. It's not much of an apology if you're helping with your own apology."

"I want to say what you said makes no sense, but unfortunately it does," Easton grins, and he takes a seat at one of the island stools.

I shrug my shoulders, "I'm kind of a genius."

Easton snorts, "Only when you want to be."

I gasp. "Rude!" He mocks my shrug, and I turn away to pour batter into the frying pan for the first pancake.

Being back around Easton and having everything about us fall right back into place is like waking up on Christmas morning. There's no hope of hiding the wide smile on my face, and nothing will be able to chase it away.

Nothing except what Easton brings up.

Even with my back to Easton, I feel the air around us change from ecstatic to serious in a matter of moments. I turn to face him, and though he still holds a smile on his face, I know exactly what that look in his eye means. I'm reminded of my words from our fight, of Easton's words last week after I found the letter from Andy, and I know he's finally going to tell me about Ellie.

"You really want to know what happened?" he asks softly, and I pause making breakfast and face him head on.

"East, of course I want to know what happened. Why did you think I wouldn't?"

He shrugs, avoiding my gaze for a moment. "You've had a lot going on this summer. I didn't want to add to your plate."

Could this boy get any more perfect?

"East," I breathe, resting a hand over his from across the counter, all thoughts of breakfast forgotten. He doesn't pull away from me like he did last week, and my skin tingles where it meets his. "You can't force yourself to be my friend and not let me be yours. You've been there for me through *everything* this summer. Especially last week. When are you going to let me be there for you?"

"It was a while ago. I'm ov—."

"Bullshit."

A pained smile plays on his lips, his eyes dulling as he thinks about whatever Ellie did to break his heart. He looks down at our hands as he starts talking, but I keep my eyes focused on him. "We started dating freshman year of high school. We fell in love. We thought we would be together forever. We talked about our wedding and kids and future house. You name it, we had it planned out, just like every other couple in love for the first time. She moved to Florida in the middle of sophomore year. We were doing the long distance thing." His voice cracks, and I squeeze his hand from across the table. He looks up and meets my eyes, and he doesn't look away. "Four months later, she called to tell me she was pregnant and the baby wasn't mine. I haven't spoken to her since."

I whisper, "East, I am so sorry." I walk around the counter to his side, wrapping my arms around his shoulders. For once, we're at the same height with him sitting on a stool. His arms snake around my back, and in one fluid motion, he pulls me into his lap.

Not being in the midst of a mental breakdown, my body reacts to the proximity in a plethora of ways, more than it did when I hugged him. My heart and stomach skyrocket, exploding like a star on its deathbed. Every nerve in my body is jumping on a different trampoline, and it takes every ounce of self control I have to not shiver in Easton's arms. I adjust my position in his lap so I'm comfortable, and he rests his head in the crook of my neck. The skin-to-skin contact is too much for my body to handle, but I make no move to get out of the position we're in. Instead, I lean my cheek against the top of his head, focusing on the light smell of sunscreen I associate with Easton now.

With a shaking hand, I start running my fingers through his hair at his neckline. I hope it's coming off as comforting to him, but all I can think about is how soft his hair is and how much I love feeling it in between my fingers.

"I'm so sorry," I murmur. It's all I can say. When you've been cheated on by someone you're in love with, no words are going to make you feel better. You have to take the time and heal from it.

"I'm okay now. It happened over a year ago," he whispers into my neck, his breath warm against my skin and creating goose-bumps down to my collarbone. "I was terrified to be with someone new."

I hear the implication in his words, but I want to hear him say it. "Was?" I whisper, my question a mere breath.

"Yeah. Not anymore."

Even if I wanted to respond, I don't think I could. I stay exactly where I am, arms around Easton and my hand running through his hair and my mind all too aware of our synced breathing. One of his arms wraps securely around my back, and his other drapes over my legs, a solid hand resting on my thigh.

I want to capture this moment in a snow globe so I never lose it.

Minutes or hours later (my internal clock was stolen by East-on's touch), he finally pulls his head away from my neck. Our faces are close, only centimeters apart. I can't help but glance down at his lips, pink and slightly parted, waiting for me to take the bait. I bring my gaze back up to his eyes, and he's a second behind me. His eyes raise from my own lips. They're so, so dark this close, and I fight every urge to cup his face in my hands and do the thing we both so desperately want.

I want to know what it feels like, to know, just like our bodies, our souls, if our lips fit together perfectly like everything else has. If every part of us being together feels like fate.

Not yet.

I still have an apology breakfast to make, and I know, all the way down to my core, even one kiss will distract us for the rest of the day.

So instead, I break his gaze and plant a feather kiss to his cheek. My lips buzz and tingle from the contact with his skin, like they can't believe it just happened.

If this is what it feels like to kiss his cheek, I *really* need to know what it would feel like to kiss his lips. And soon.

I remove myself from his lap, his arms sliding away from my body and having me crave a drug I didn't know I was addicted to. I resume my position at the stove, pouring batter into the frying pan and starting a pot of coffee. Only then do I look up from across the island. Easton is smiling at me, the most adorable cross between a smirk and a million-watt grin.

"What?" I ask, pausing in my movement.

Just barely, he shakes his head back and forth, the smile staying right where it is. "One day, Redding. One day."

I gulp.

CHAPTER THIRTY-FOUR

"I'VE COME PREPARED WITH COFFEE AND DONUTS,"
Easton grins, passing me a large plastic cup with a dark, milky
liquid in it and a Long John donut with chocolate frosting and
blue and green sprinkles. I take them both wordlessly and take a
sip of the iced mocha, sitting down on the kitchen floor with my
back against the cabinets. My floral sundress flutters around my
legs.

Who the fuck decided we needed to get up this early today?

"Wow, you really are *not* a morning person," Easton has the
nerve to point out, and I don't bother looking at him as I shake
my head. It's too early for words.

While I sit numbly, sipping on my coffee and chowing down
on my donut, Easton stocks a cooler and a tote bag for our big
day. The coffee and donut help me wake up, and by the time
someone honks the horn from my driveway, I have a smile on my
face.

As soon as we're out the front door, Gabe yells, "Dudes, let's
go!" from the driver's side window of his truck. Easton flips him
off as we hurry as much as we can down my driveway, the cooler
between us filled with beer, seltzers, water bottles, and ice. I have

the tote bag thrown over my other shoulder with towels, our phones, wallets, and sunscreen.

"Don't 'let's go' us until you're the one carrying this damn thing!" I yell back, gesturing to the cooler with my chin. It's heavy as hell.

Gabe takes that as a challenge and hops out of the truck, running over to us, and taking my side of the cooler. I gladly step aside, more than happy to not have it weighing me down anymore.

I skip across the lawn to hop in the truck, grinning back at the two boys as Gabe finally understands what we were dealing with. But, being almost the same height as Easton and stronger than me, the two of them move a lot faster than we were.

Still no complaints.

After throwing the tote bag in the back of the truck, I squeeze into the back next to Ev, her blonde and purple hair in two French braids. There's no blue eyeliner today, but her navy eyes still pop out. She's wearing a crochet white crop top with blue and purple flowers on it. "I love your shirt, Ev. Where did you get it?" I ask.

"Thank you! I made it, actually," she grins, looking down at it.

"Of course you did! That makes it a million times better!"

Ev laughs. "I can make one for you, if you want."

"Definitely want," I smile.

She's sitting next to Josie, and Logan's in the passenger seat, grinning at the two other boys as they haul the cooler the rest of the way to the truck. They lift it into the back of the pickup, almost spilling the contents all over the yard. Gabe returns to the driver's seat, and Easton squeezes in next to me.

When he puts his right arm around me to make things a little comfier for both of us, I don't protest at all; instead, I lean into his side like it's the most natural thing in the world.

"Finally!" Gabe exclaims, pulling off the curb and heading down the street. Logan turns the music up. All the windows are down, and the breeze feels nice as we start driving down the road.

The speedboat rattles behind us, the cover aggressively flapping and trying to come off.

Ten minutes later, we pull up to the boat launch. Logan and Easton hop out of the car to help direct Gabe as he backs the boat into the water. My eyes are glued to Easton, and my heart falls a little more in love with him at the wide grin on his face. He's cracking jokes with Logan and Gabe, and every couple of seconds he catches my gaze. His eyes soften and the corner of his lips turn up a little bit more.

It's a look meant just for me.

When the boat is in the water, I turn back to Ev and Josie. They're both smirking, and Ev raises her eyebrows up and down in a suggestive manner.

"What?" I ask defensively.

"You know what," Ev taunts.

"Girl," Josie says, her eyes screaming *are you for real*? "You are *so* whipped!"

"Am not!" I gasp, to which they both laugh because all three of us know I totally am.

I start laughing with them, and it hurts just as much as it helps. It reminds me of Ellie and Sierra and what it's like to have friends.

I have friends again, and I'm about to leave it all behind.

But you don't have to leave, a voice deep in the back of my brain whispers, and it's the first time I let myself believe in the possibility of staying. It doesn't surprise me that I'm only considering it because I'm the one who finally thought about it, being as stubborn as I am.

I get Easton. And my dad. And Easton. And Ev and Josie. And Easton. And a whole group of friends. And Easton. And a fun senior year.

And Easton.

There will be none of that if I go back to Colorado. All I'll have is Andy.

So what if I do stay?

The thought takes control of my brain as Easton drives the truck to the parking lot, Gabe drives the boat to the dock, and we load it up with our things. A blown up tube was sitting in the boat, and once they take the cover off, they throw it in the water behind the boat. A smile grows on my face at the sight of it. Tubing is one of my favorite summer activities, though I only did it a handful of times with Ellie's family.

I'm excited to do it again and make some new memories to associate with the activity.

We wait at the dock for Jackie, Naomi, Hayden, and Carter to show up. When they do, I don't miss the sly smile Logan gives Naomi and the kiss she blows to him in return. I meet Jackie's eyes, and we grin.

The ten of us scramble into the boat, and Gabe pulls away from the dock as Easton still straddles the side of the boat, one foot on the seat and one foot on the dock. He stumbles as the dock is removed from under his foot, and I grab his outstretched hand to help steady him. He grips mine tight, meeting my eyes and grinning. I grin back.

He doesn't let go of my hand. Instead, he sits down on the seat and pulls me to sit down next to him, placing an arm along the side of the boat behind me like he did in the car. Once again, I don't protest.

"Jos, here," Gabe says, passing her his phone as he navigates the boat through the no-wake zone. There are a few other boats around, but given it's Friday morning, the big throng of tourists hasn't arrived yet. I'm sure the water will be packed this afternoon.

"What do we want to listen to?" Josie asks the group, unlocking Gabe's phone. She sits down in his lap, and he easily adjusts to make room for her. I yearn to have that kind of ease with someone, to be in a relationship with someone I'm that in tune with.

Well, not just someone. *Easton.*

We already have that ease, though. We just don't have the relationship part.

Yet.

"Play the summer playlist on my profile," Naomi says, breaking me out of my dreamland.

"That sounds perfect," Logan calls from the back of the boat, and I don't miss the wink he throws at her when she smiles at him. He starts to untie the rope from where it's holding the tube right behind the boat, keeping a tight hold on it as Gabe drives through the no-wake zone, but the second we pass the buoys, it's game time.

"Who's up first?" Logan asks, turning back to the crowd.

"Us!" Ev says immediately, turning to Josie and I. She beckons her head to the back of the boat where she's sitting. I stand up, Easton holding out his hand to help me balance without any kind of communication needing to pass between us, and it makes me smile as I think about my thoughts from a moment ago. I hold onto him for as long as I can, until I'm able to reach Ev's outstretched hand. She pulls me to sit down on the back bench beside her, and then she helps Josie. Life jackets are handed to the three of us.

"Just a heads up," Ev mutters to me as we strap our life jackets on, "Gabe is pure evil when he's driving the boat. All of them are."

"I can't wait," I grin.

Gabe slows the boat to a stop, and Logan holds the tube in place while the three of us girls crawl onto the back deck of the boat and onto the tube. We lay on our stomachs, Josie in the middle with Ev and me on either side of her. The water isn't too bad, the perfect temperature to help us cool off under the baking sun. Our arms all cross in the front as we hold onto the handles. "Have fun," Logan smirks, gently pushing us away from the boat before Gabe starts moving again.

"You better not kill us, Gabe!" Josie hollers over the sound of the motor.

"Baby, I would never!" he hollers back, glancing back at us for a second with a smirk more evil than Logan's.

"Oh shit," I hear Ev mutter, and Josie risks taking a hand of the handle to flip Gabe off. I grip my handles tighter, excited for what's to happen and also a little scared.

I meet Easton's gaze a moment before the tube is pulled by the boat, and he looks like he's barely keeping his laughter in check. Josie has to grasp for the handle, barely grabbing it in time before the rope goes taught and the tube is yanked across the waves.

Gabe whips the boat around like a pro, sending us flying over the wake created by the boat as well as the waves from the ocean. I keep my face against the tube to avoid face and mouth fulls of salt water. I cling on for dear life, keeping my body tight to lessen the chance of me falling off. There are shrieks from the three of us when the tube seems like it's out of control, but there's no way to tell who they come from.

With my face hidden against the tube, I don't realize it's happening until it's happening. We fly over a huge wave and into the air, and the tube flips. Josie, Ev, and I all fly off, hitting the water with a painful *smack*. I'm under for no more than three seconds before my life jacket brings me to the surface, and water floods into my nose.

I cough and blow my nose, a mixture of salt water and snot flying out. *Gross.* My left thigh burns from where it hit the water.

Ev and Josie are only a few feet away from me. I swim to them, we all exchange a look, and then burst out laughing. One of Ev's braids has come out, the wavy curls that would be there flattened from the water.

The boat pulls up beside us, and its passengers are still laughing. The three of us swim to the back of the boat and hoist ourselves up. Logan and Easton are right there to greet us. I roll my eyes at their antics, accepting the towel Easton hands to me and wrapping it around my body after taking the life jacket off.

"All laughing aside, are you okay?" he asks softly as the two of us make our way back to our seats at the front of the boat. Laughter still trickles out of him, but I can't even pretend to be mad when he looks so concerned for my well being.

We sit down, and I move the towel to look at my thigh. The skin is red, but the pain is quickly retreating. "Nothing I can't handle," I reply. Easton brushes his fingers along the red skin. A shiver runs through my entire body, goosebumps spread along my thigh, and Easton looks up and smirks, silently saying *I know* exactly *what effect I have on you.*

Nervous, I let a small smile grow on my face, hoping it doesn't give away too much. I bring my legs up to my chest and pull the towel around my skin, the goosebumps creating a chill. And like a choreographed dance we didn't have to learn because our bodies just know, Easton wraps an arm around my body and closes the few centimeters between us. My thighs fall into his lap, and I'm curled into his abdomen. More shivers and goosebumps, but I don't move. The familiar scent of Easton fills my nose, a touch of the salty sea water mixed in with it.

I relax my body into his, laying my head on his bare shoulder. Like everything else between Easton and I, it feels natural. His shoulder was made to fit my head perfectly.

And when the forehead kiss comes, I know I'm a goner.

CHAPTER THIRTY-FIVE

On August fifteenth, I wake up to breakfast in bed from Easton, a white tray holding all of my favorites in his hands. Groot hops onto the bed and circles a few times, laying down next to me and staring at the food.

I sit up at the commotion, smiling wide at the sight of Easton. "What's this?" I ask him as he sets it down in my lap. He opens my balcony curtains before sitting down on the other side of the tray, right on top of my feet. Out the doors of the balcony, I see dark storm clouds in the distance, and when I say dark, I mean *dark*. I grow excited at the prospect of such a good storm hitting on my birthday, but I quickly turn my attention back to Easton as he grabs my foot through the blankets.

"Happy birthday, Li," he says, a smile as wide as mine on his face.

I look at my breakfast: a stack of waffles, bacon, my coffee in my favorite purple mug, the color just the way I like it, and a can of whipped cream. I look back at Easton, smiling wider at the gesture but also confused. "How did you know it was my birthday?"

He shrugs his shoulders, grinning like it's his greatest scheme of the summer. "Your dad told me. He was worried with him being gone, you would act like it was any normal day, and neither of us could let that happen."

"Of course he did," I say, rolling my eyes with a grin. I look back at the food. "Are you going to help me eat all this? As wonderful and delicious as it looks, this is enough food for me for a week."

"I was hoping you would ask," Easton grins. I laugh, reaching for my coffee first.

I take the first sip, and it truly is made to perfection. I go for the waffles next, skipping the fork and knife Easton so graciously added to the tray. Instead of slathering in my usual topping, I rip a small piece off and eat it plain. Though plain, there's a perfection to the simple taste.

Once I swallow, I say, "You didn't have to do all of this, you know. I love it, don't get me wrong, but—"

"Don't you dare say it's not a big deal. It's your birthday. I'm going to make it a big deal." His words make him so happy and determined, and I can't fight any of that. Unknowingly, my bottom lip juts out in a semi-pout as I try to fight how big my smile wants to become. I only realize when Easton's gaze immediately drops to my lips. His eyes are smoldering, and *oh my* is it working for me.

My cheeks heat up, and that's only the beginning.

This tension building between us isn't going to last much longer. He and I both know it. My resolve is cracking, each layer I've worked so hard to keep up this summer disappearing as if it were nothing. The list of valid reasons I had at the beginning of the summer don't seem so valid anymore.

I can't handle Easton staring at me with that look anymore, like he's about to forget about the food in front of us and devour me instead, so I shove the rest of the waffle I was holding into my mouth. Easton bursts into laughter as I struggle to chew and swallow. I pick up my phone, expecting to see a bombardment of "happy birthday" texts like I have every other year.

There's nothing, though, and I remember why. Not even from Andy, and that's the only absence that hurts.

My face falls, and when Easton asks, I offer a tight smile and tell him I don't want to talk about it. Nothing feels worse right now than my own brother forgetting my birthday. He was always the first one to tell me happy birthday, right at midnight.

Easton and I move on with the rest of the morning and pretend like nothing happened, and the mere presence of him uplifts my mood almost immediately. There's still a smolder lingering in his eyes through it all. It's barely there, but I notice it when I catch him staring at me on our walk with Groot, our short lived game of Monopoly, and the trip to the grocery store to buy ingredients for cupcakes. It has me heating up each time all over again.

When we run back into the house, we're soaking wet from the rain despite the short crossing from where Easton parked his truck in my driveway to the front door. "I'm going to go change," I say, slipping off my sandals. "I'll be right back." Easton nods in response, slipping his sandals off as well.

Upstairs, I change out of my T-shirt and denim shorts into black leggings and an oversized crewneck sweatshirt. The rain has caused the temperature to drop, and there's no reason to dress like I'll be spending the day in the sun. I still haven't heard a peep from Andy, and the pit of hurt and anger in my stomach is growing the longer it goes.

I still have Easton's gray sweats from when he spilled coffee on them a few weeks ago, and there's a hoodie he left here one night after we were watching a movie. I bring them down to him, and he quickly changes in the bathroom. I take the time to officially say hi to Groot, getting down on my knees and taking the attack of kisses. It brings me a little comfort at the fact that my brother forgot my birthday. Groot's fur is wet, so I take it Easton let him out while I was upstairs.

"Alright, birthday girl, let's get started," Easton says, clapping his hands together as he comes up behind me. The sound of his voice and the clap spooks me, and I jump a little.

"Don't scare me like that," I grin, giving Groot a good scratch between the ears before standing up. Easton looks sexy as hell in his black hoodie, and the gray joggers are certainly not hurting his look. *Happy birthday to me, indeed.*

Easton grins back, "Too easy. Can't let any opportunity pass."

I shake my head back and forth and try to give him a light shove as we head into the kitchen. After two and half months, though, he anticipates me doing exactly this, and he dodges the shove by delaying a step and then throwing an arm out to catch me before I lose my balance. I end with my back flush against his chest, our sweatshirts doing nothing to conceal the heat we're both radiating for each other. He holds me there for a moment and lets me go all too soon. When I spin to glare at him for dodging my shove, trying not to think about the feel of his chest on my back, he's got a smug grin on his face.

He knew exactly what he just did, and he knows that I know exactly what he just did, and I can't be mad at him for that.

Real smooth, King.

I grab the cupcake mix from the counter and look at the ingredients. Eggs, butter, milk, and the mix. Seems simple enough. I pull the other three ingredients out of the fridge and find a bowl in one of the cabinets. Just like making breakfast almost every morning, Easton and I fall into an unspoken rhythm. He preheats the oven and starts melting the butter. I crack the eggs and measure the milk while he dumps the mix into the bowl.

While the cupcakes are in the oven and then cooling, we resume our game of Monopoly. We're seated on opposite sides of the coffee table. My legs are crossed in front of me, and Easton has his legs spread out under the table and resting on either side of me.

He's finally started to warm up to my method of playing, and, not surprisingly, he's holding his own a lot better now. "See. I told you it works," I gloat.

"Don't brag," he warns, rolling the dice.

"But it's my birthday. I have bragging rights," I grin, tickling the bottom of his foot. He reacts accordingly, yanking his leg toward him and hitting his knee on the underside of the table. He hits it harder than I expected, and our houses scatter across the board. "East!" I gasp, knowing full well it's my fault.

"Li!" he mocks, maneuvering his leg out from under the table and rubbing his knee where he hit it. "I can't believe you would sabotage the game like this just because I'm winning!"

I gasp again, this time with much more surprise. "You were *not* winning. We were keeping up with each other perfectly!"

Easton shakes his head back and forth, grinning ear to ear. "Were not, but I'll make a deal with you, since it's your birthday and all."

I roll my eyes, but Easton knows the slight raise of my eyebrow means I'm interested in whatever deal he's about to offer.

"Who can frost the best cupcake? Winner takes the game. Including bragging rights."

"You're on."

We hop up and rush into the kitchen, forgetting about the destroyed game of Monopoly. We have purple and blue frosting to work with, and I pull out a Ziploc bag to use as a makeshift frosting bag. Somehow, by the birthday gods themselves, I manage to get purple frosting in one half of the bag and blue on the other. When I squeeze it onto the first cupcake, the combination looks just as I had hoped. It also reminds me of Sully from Monsters Inc.

Easton jumped right in, grabbing a knife and slathering purple frosting on his cupcake. I don't know what his plan is, but

I don't judge. He's bouncing on his toes, an uncharacteristic trait for him, and I have no clue why. When I point it out to him and ask, he shrugs and responds, "I'm just really excited it's your birthday."

"You're acting like there's some surprise party I don't know about," I joke.

"It wouldn't be a surprise if you knew about it," Easton says, trying to be all cryptic, focusing on his cupcake.

"So there is a surprise party?" I look at him with a raised eyebrow.

He laughs, his eyes shining with an almost unbearable amount of passion as he finally looks at me. How am I supposed to pretend that look doesn't exist?

"Whether there is or isn't, I'm not going to tell you."

"Now you're being sus," I say, crossing my arms and making sure to not squeeze the bag of frosting under my arm. I pout, forgetting the little pout I gave him this morning and the effect it's had on both of us all day.

Easton's eyes zero in on my lips once again, and I freeze. The playfulness from a second ago is gone. He's so focused, his smolder only leaving my lips to look me in the eyes. His are dark, and though I've seen a similar look from him before, it has never hit this intensity. "Li, if you keep pouting like that, you know exactly what's going to happen, and I'm not going to keep holding back."

I gulp, the tone of his voice and his chosen words igniting a fire in me Nate never had the capability of producing. With a plan forming in my mind, I find the courage to say, "So don't." It comes out in a raspy whisper, but Easton hears me loud and clear.

And boy, does he not waste any time. He takes a single step toward me, and I uncross my arms so they don't become trapped between us. It would ruin my plan.

Easton moves his hands to cup either side of my face. The

look in his eyes only increases in intensity, the only fuel I need to keep the fire burning and growing inside of me.

I hide the grin that so desperately wants to break free. Easton's eyes ask me once if this is okay, and I almost forget about my plan at the gesture. Even after all the tension that's built up between us this summer, he's still asking moments before if I'm okay with it.

Instead of giving him a look back, I raise the hand holding my bag of frosting and squeeze it directly onto his face.

Now, don't get me wrong. I want to kiss Easton *bad*. Now more than ever. I'm done fighting it. But, in the wise words he spoke earlier, *I can't let any opportunity pass.*

Easton freezes, and I muffle my laughter. "I win," I say, insinuating he is the best decorated. Without a question, he is. Despite his insanely good looks, he's got blue and purple frosting about to fall from his face, leaving a smear of it on his cheek. How could he not be?

"Li," he says, a certain warning in his tone, and I realize a second too late what's coming. I turn to run, but his arm moves too quickly. He snatches me around the waist, grabs a spoon from the first frosting container he can get his hands on, and smears blue frosting all over my cheek. I squeal, but I'm not trying hard to get out of his firm grip. With my back pressed firmly against his chest again, I'm surprised I even try at all.

His lips move against my ear as he says, "That is only the beginning of my revenge."

I'm losing my resolve, both at his arm being so firm around my waist and his lips being against my skin in any capacity. In a swift motion, he wraps his other arm around my waist and starts spinning me in a circle. I shriek out a laugh, and Easton loses his composure at the sound that escapes me.

In some distant land in my brain, I hear the front door swing open, multiple sets of feet pounding into the house and the force of the wind and rain for a moment. My first thought is Easton really did plan a surprise party with all our friends, only they're coming to us instead of us to them.

But then a voice I never wanted to hear again says, "Ali." It's full of hurt and shock, and how dare he sound like that.

How dare he have the nerve to show up here.

My mind starts whirling at a million miles a minute, the confrontation I thought I was in control of coming out of left field. All my anger from this summer comes running back to me, building up faster than it did the first time.

Easton feels me stiffen and quickly stops spinning me around, setting me down so we're both facing the direction of the front door. I miss his touch and the elated feeling moments before. If my happiness was a balloon, someone just took a butcher knife to it. There wasn't even time for it to fly around the room as it deflated.

There are three people standing in the entryway, dripping wet from the rain and jaws on the ground. At the sight of all of them, the anger takes over.

"What the *fuck* are you doing here?"

CHAPTER THIRTY-SIX

Nate, Ellie, and Andy stand in the front entryway. Groot bounds over to greet them, his tail wagging. Andy's the only one to pay him any attention, but he keeps his eyes on me as he runs a hand through Groot's thick fur. I glare at him, but at least I now know why he hasn't acknowledged my birthday.

Nate's leading the group, and I watch the last evidence of hope in his green eyes disappear at the sight of Easton twirling me around my kitchen. I get a sick feeling of satisfaction from watching it, but the look on his face quickly turns menacing. My anger erupts. What kind of audacity does he have to fly across the country to find me and think he has any chance at winning me back?

Also, how the hell did he even *get* across the country?

Ellie and Andy both looked shocked, but Ellie's quicker to hide it than Andy is. I wouldn't be surprised if Andy still has no idea what has happened since June. I wouldn't put it past Nate and Ellie to twist the story to their advantage to get here. Not after all the other scheming they've been part of. It creates a whole new level of anger I have no control over.

Ellie's the first one to speak up in response to my harsh question. "Ali, are you serious?" she asks, her face full of hurt and bright green eyes welling with tears. I'm not surprised. She was always the more emotional one between the two of us.

The rage I feel is past the boiling point, exploding out in bursts as my body starts to shake in anger. I don't think I've ever been this angry in my life.

"It's not like I'm joking. What the fuck are you doing here?" I spit out. I still feel Easton's chest against my back, standing protectively in case I need him but letting me lead the way. In normal circumstances, I would be over the moon at his actions, but the abrupt arrival of my ex-boyfriend and ex-best friend has thrown me off. I feel like a computer system going haywire.

"Ali—" Andy starts to say, but Nate cuts him off without realizing it.

"What the fuck, Ali? Are you cheating on me?"

It takes a moment for the words to process in my mind, and when they do, there's no holding back.

"Am I cheating on *you*? Are you kidding me?"

"No, I'm not kidding," Nate says. Did he always sound that whiny? "You just left. You didn't even give me a chance to explain myself!"

"Explain what?" I rage, seeing bright red. "That you fucked Sierra on spring break and then convinced everyone to lie to me about it?"

Nate hesitates at my words, and I wonder how I never before saw the calculating wheels moving in his mind to figure out how he can manipulate his words and the situation to his benefit.

"Well, you're clearly fucking him," Nate shoots back, gesturing to Easton standing behind me, "So we're even. Now, can we please talk about this?"

The bright red turns to a dark, burning, no-remorse red, and I'm so mad I don't even know what comes out of my mouth next, my whole body shaking with rage. "So we're *even*? That is not how that works, asshole! And even if I had been fucking him all summer, me and you were still way over before that happened. He's just a friend, though, so even if in your delusional world that makes us even, we're still not fucking even!"

I don't realize what I've said until the heat from Easton's body behind me goes cold. He'd been standing so close, so when he takes a step back at my words like they were a physical punch to the gut, I feel it all. I whip around to face him, wild tears finally escaping my eyes. I immediately try to reel the words back in, try to erase the damage I know they've done.

The damage is done, though. "East—"

I don't know if it's the heartbroken look on his face or his next words that stop me from saying anything. I want to tell him I didn't mean it and he is so much more to me than just a friend, but the words get stuck in my throat. The only thing I manage is blubbering.

Easton's dark, dark eyes, the ones that feel like home, bore into me. There's no smolder in them, no sparkle. *No home.* "I'm going to go, Li. I'll see you later." He turns away from me without hesitation and heads out the back door, barely needing to stop to slip his feet into his sandals. Then he's gone, escaping into the pouring rain. Groot bounds for the door, whimpering at the retreating figure.

I broke more than just mine and Easton's hearts.

Hot tears fall down my face, and there's no stopping the anger. Anger at everyone still standing in the house, including myself. I hate myself for what I caused. Easton just walked out, and who knows if he'll ever come back. If he feels anything close to what I feel right now, his heart ripping into two like sharks playing tug-o-war, then I wouldn't blame him.

And I had just accepted what I had spent all summer trying to deny.

Talk about bad timing.

I whip back toward Nate, Ellie, and Andy. "Actually, he's so much more than just a friend," I spit out, seeing fire as I direct my words to Nate. "*You* are the one who cheated on me. You fucked one of my friends behind my back and then lied to me for months. So we are over, Nate. You should've realized we were over as soon as you even thought about putting your hands on her. Not that I owe you *any* kind of explanation." I turn to include Ellie in my address. "Either of you. You have no right to come here and act like I'm the one who's in the wrong. You both chose where your loyalties lie in March. Now get the fuck out of my house. You can wait for your Uber in the rain." There's a loud crack of thunder as I finish speaking, the storm clearly on my side and rooting for me.

Nate and Ellie look more than taken aback at my cruel words; I've never in my life spoken to anyone like that, much less two of the people who used to be some of the most important people in my life.

Andy looks like a deer caught in the headlights. My earlier guess was definitely correct: Andy still has no idea what happened. I watch his calculating eyes put the pieces together, and when he realizes not only what Nate and Ellie did, but what he has done by bringing them here, rage consumes him.

My brother is many things, but cruel has never, ever been one of them. The meanest I've ever seen him is when he was defending me against our drunken dad the second he was old enough to realize what was going on. I was never scared of Andy then. The look on his face now, though, the tense jaw and fire from hell in his eyes, is enough to send a shiver down my spine.

"You heard her, you piece of shit," Andy growls to Nate. He's so mad, I wouldn't be surprised if he grabbed Nate by the collar of his shirt and slammed him up against the wall. It's a sight I would pay to see, but I can't be in this room a second later. I trust Andy to take the trash out.

I pivot on my foot and run upstairs, Groot right on my tail. I close and lock the door of my bedroom, lean my back against it, and slide down to the floor. The sobs make their appearance, and I do nothing to try and compose myself. After what happened downstairs, I deserve every second of this breakdown.

It's mine.

Groot cuddles up next to me, pressing his body into mine and laying his head in my lap. As always, the pressure of him is my personal weighted blanket, and I take it. I wrap my arms around him and bury my face in the soft fur. He doesn't seem to care that my tears and snot are ending up in his neck; all he's focusing on is me and if I'm okay.

A few minutes later, or maybe an hour for all I know, there's a soft knock on my door. I've transitioned to the floor, using Groot as a pillow. "Ali, it's me," Andy says. I lift my head, and Groot licks my cheek. He probably loves the taste of the salt.

"Go away."

"Ali."

I don't respond, concealing my sobs enough so he won't hear them through the door. Groot continues to lick my cheek, so I rebury my face in his body. I know I need to talk to Andy, the letter to my dad still looming between us, but it's not happening now.

A minute later, his footsteps retreat, and I hear him go back downstairs.

With the peak of the breakdown over, I finally stand up, using the door for support as my legs regain feeling. It doesn't get any better from there as I drag my feet to my bed. I crawl under all the blankets, burying myself and Groot in the darkness. He curls up right next to me again, licking more tears off my cheeks.

I start crying all over again, only mourning Easton this time.

How mad at me is he? Or is there a chance he's not even mad, just confused? It's foolish to think this, to think there's any chance of reconciliation. The look on his face, the lack of any emotion in his beautiful eyes, tells me all I need to know.

I've ruined everything.

The knife continues twisting in my chest, a pain like none I've known before.

It's finding out Nate cheated on me all over again, only ten times worse because it's my fault.

The knife twists again and again. I don't doubt I loved Nate, but the love I have for Easton is so much more than what I ever felt for my ex.

My stomach protests at the loss, empty yet no room for anything. My mind can't grasp how much the last hour has changed everything in my life, but I know how severely I fucked up.

The mere thought of having to go about my life without Easton is unbearable. It feels like someone adds a second knife to the wound in my chest.

I wouldn't wish this on my worst enemy. Nate and Ellie have no idea how much they've been spared by that.

For the first time ever, Easton's face is what haunts me as I fall asleep. That look in his eyes cut so deep, and I don't know if I'll ever recover.

CHAPTER THIRTY-SEVEN

HOURS LATER, I WAKE UP WITH PUFFY EYES, A DRY throat, and unable to remember if I had a terrible dream or if Nate and Ellie really did show up here. It's not night yet, but the sky is starting to darken in the distance even more than it already was from the storm. I don't hear any rain or thunder, but it doesn't look like it's over yet.

I left my phone downstairs earlier, so I have no way to check what time it is. I'd guess it's around seven.

Groot is still curled up next to me, and when he notices I'm awake, he starts plastering my face with slobbery kisses. Despite feeling like a train wreck, a small smile pulls at my lips.

And everything from earlier comes rushing back to me. East's face. Ellie's tears. Nate's voice. Andy's shock. And back to East's face. It's the most prominent image, the one I can't stop thinking about. I have it memorized. I slip into another round of crying, once again burying my face in Groot's fur to muffle the sobs.

Easton's face keeps coming back, another twist of the knives and another jolt of pain.

I ruined everything.

When I pull my face away from Groot, I use the bottom of

my T-shirt to wipe away the snot on my face and the snot on his fur. He licks my face again. I sigh and close my eyes, and I let my dog love on me. The hiccups start, and Groot gives me a weird look after the first one before burying his head in my neck.

There's a soft *tap tap*, a noise I dismiss as the pounding in my head from all the crying. I hear it again, though, and when I still don't move, it comes back stronger the third time. I lift my head from my pillows, and Easton is standing on my balcony.

I gasp, almost tripping over my sheets as I jump out of bed and run over to unlock the door and let him in. Every emotion of grief and hatred I've been feeling since he walked away is replaced with shock and confusion and hope. I try not to get my hopes up, but it's damn near impossible when he's standing right there.

The second he's through the door and sees my tear stained face, he drops the backpack he was wearing and wraps me in a bone crushing hug. Groot circles us, tongue out and tail wagging back and forth. He's just as happy to see Easton as I am.

I burst into tears again, wrapping my arms around his midsection and burrowing into his body as much as I can. He holds me close, one hand stroking my hair and the other tracing the length of my spine. The trail feels like the red stone we laid out when rigging an explosion on Minecraft a few days ago.

There's so much I want to say to him, so much I want him to know before anything else happens that could ruin it all again. I'm sobbing too hard to even think about getting a word out. I can't stop gasping for breath, the hiccups not making it any easier as I lose control faster than I can attempt to regain an ounce of it.

I'm so relieved Easton is here, I can't find it in me to care.

He's here.

Easton came back, and he's here.

He doesn't release his hold of me until I'm finally under control. He peels me away from his embrace and holds my biceps at arm's length, and I laugh through the remainder of my tears at how soaked his T-shirt is now. He's changed into his breast cancer awareness one from the fundraiser for his mom. He grins, knowing exactly what I'm laughing at, and says, "I never liked this shirt anyways."

"Yes you do. It's your favorite," I say, still smiling. I wipe my face with my palms, tears and snot and everything.

"Well, I wouldn't want to have anyone else's fluids on it."

"Gross!" I laugh again, tears still falling. I think they're happy tears. "You say fluids like I peed or something." This has him laughing, and then he's pulling me back into his chest. I don't resist.

He brings his lips right to my ear, and there's no way his hands don't feel the shiver running down the length of my spine. I feel his lips turn up into a smile at the feeling. He knows exactly what he's doing to me. "I'm sorry your birthday turned into a shit show," he murmurs. "Andy coming was the surprise I was so excited about. I had no idea he was bringing Nate and Ellie." It takes a moment for his words to process in my mind, too focused on his lips moving against my skin. When I do realize what he said, though, I plant my hands on his chest and push him away. His hands slip to my lower back, arms still hanging loosely around me.

"East, you have nothing to be sorry for. If it had just been Andy, it's the only thing that would have made my birthday better than it already was," I say. The rain starts up again, splattering against the balcony doors and windows with no warm up. I add, in a voice barely above a whisper, "I'm the one who's sorry. When Nate accused me of cheating, I—I saw red and my mind went blank." I can't drag up the words my apology refers to.

He looks into my eyes, tilting his head to the side. I recognize the look on his face, and I patiently wait for him to say whatever he's thinking about. One hand comes up to my face and wipes away some of the lone tears, and I can't help but lean into his palm. It's instinct, a motion I can't control.

"Am I really just a friend?" he asks quietly, his lips barely moving. I almost have to ask him to repeat his question, but then I make out what he asked and feel my heart break. I hate myself for putting him in a position where he even has to ask.

Shaking my head, I say just as softly, "Even on the first day we met, we were always more than just friends."

His lips turn up, the corners pulling until the biggest smile I've ever seen breaks onto his face. His eyes crinkle in the corners, and every emotion is written clear as day on his face. Joy, happiness, excitement, love.

I can't put it off any longer, and the boom of thunder outside agrees.

My hands snake up from his chest to either side of his face, pulling him to me as I rise up on my toes to meet him halfway. Our lips collide with a powerful force, strong enough to break through all the tension that has built up between us this summer in anticipation for this moment right here.

Easton's lips mold to mine as he tightens his arms around my back, crushing every part of our bodies together. I move my fingers to tangle themselves in the hair at the base of his neck and tug, an urge I'm done fighting as I try to bring myself even closer to him.

His tongue swipes across my bottom lip, emitting a gasp from me and giving him perfect access to my mouth. I can't help but smile as he deepens the kiss, responding with just as much force as he is.

The realization of what is happening hits me like a freight train.

I am kissing Easton King.

And he is kissing me back like his every survival instinct depends on it.

Easton seems to come to the realization of what is happening at the same time I do, because we both become increasingly more desperate to have more of the other person. Our hands are everywhere, and the moment Easton's hands slip past my waist to cup my ass, the entire moment shifts.

Aside from pulling our lips away a mere millimeter, neither of us moves a muscle. Our foreheads press together, my chest smooshed against his, and I feel how turned on he is against my stomach. I can't think straight with his hands on my ass, but there's only a few other places I would rather they be. We're both gasping for breath, sounding raspy and like we just had the kiss of our lifetimes.

Quite frankly, I did. I don't know how Easton could say no to that, either. His next words only confirm this.

"If I had known kissing you would be like that," he whispers, his lips close enough to brush against mine as he speaks in a deep voice, "I would have kissed you the very first moment I saw you."

My mind flashes back to that moment, when I first saw him standing in my kitchen with our dads. The look he had in his dark eyes, though incredibly intense then, not even comparing to any of the looks I've received from him recently. The memory of it still has my toes tingling.

"You probably would have gotten slapped across the face," I murmur, my lips now the ones brushing against his. Lightning strikes outside, and a boom of thunder comes only a second after.

"Would have been worth it," he murmurs. My lips turn upwards. I desperately want to kiss him again and lose myself in whatever he has to offer, but when I go to do just that, he stops me with a question. I know his self control is wavering just like mine, but he wouldn't be Easton if he wasn't a gentleman.

"Is this okay?" he asks, gently squeezing my butt in case I didn't get the hint to what he was asking. His lips move against my own, and I ache for whatever comes next. The heat and anticipation is like nothing I've ever felt, filling my bloodstream and reaching the very tips of my fingers and toes.

I wrap a hand around his neck and peck his lips, not having the control to hold it off any longer. A smirk grows on his lips as he kisses me right back. He's clearly enjoying his effect on my self control, or lack thereof. In between kisses, I say, "Easton, the only right answer is yes. It will always be yes."

That's all he needs to hear. As he presses his lips firmly against mine, he lifts me up so I can wrap my legs around his waist. In this new position, there's not a foot of height separating us, and I'm able to deepen our kiss on my own terms.

Easton walks over to the bed, laying me down and breaking the kiss. "Wha—" I say as he walks away from the bed, leaning up on my forearms to see what's going on. I feel like I just had a bucket of water dumped on me, but replace the water with all the emotions I've been bottling away. Now that I've had a little taste of Easton (figuratively and literally), there's no way I can't *not* have him.

I watch him circle my bed and lead Groot to the bedroom door. He unlocks it, opens it, and Groot races downstairs, like he wants no part of what happens next. Easton closes and re-locks the door.

He turns around, smiles at the sight of me smiling, and races for the bed. He lunges onto it, and I fall back so I can use my arms to stop him from completely crushing me. We're both laughing as he collides with my body, and our lips are quick to find each other again.

Our bodies adjust so Easton is on top of me and my legs are circled around his waist, and then it's all roaming hands and sloppy kisses and the release of a summer's worth of tension. I slip my hands under Easton's T-shirt, grazing his abdomen with my fingertips. His entire body shudders, and I grin into his lips. It's the first time, as far as I know, that I've done that to him.

I take my time exploring his stomach, loving what my teasing is doing to him but also wanting to feel the outline of each defined muscle. His skin is warm and smooth, except where the scar is above his waist on the left. There, the skin loses its smoothness and becomes tight, rising slightly. Easton shudders again as I trace it.

I continue my exploring, enjoying the teasing way too much. "Fuck, Li," Easton says into my lips, the words coming out in a whispered moan. It's my turn to shudder, and I slowly crawl my fingers past his abs and to his chest. More shudders from him as I touch new skin, trace more muscles. "You're killing me."

"Good," I rasp, resting my entire hand on his pecs instead of just my fingertips.

I take my time, but I finally do pull his shirt over his head. Our kiss breaks, and when the shirt is removed, I meet his eyes. Goosebumps and shivers rack through my body, and I know Easton feels it all as a soft smile forms on his lips. His blonde hair is a mess from me running my hands through it, and I push some of it out of the way of his eyes.

"Can I tell you something?" I ask softly, but we both know it's not an actual question. I'm going to say what I'm about to say no matter what.

"Of course," Easton says, moving his face closer to mine and kissing the tip of my nose. He nuzzles his nose against mine. I close my eyes for a second and ingrain this moment into my mind.

I open my eyes and tell him, "I love you."

They're big words, but I'm not scared to say them. On the contrary, they feel like a fresh gulp of air after holding your breath for as long as you can underwater.

Easton smiles, staring into my eyes as he replies, "I sure hope so."

"Hey!" I giggle, swatting gently at his chest. Mostly because I want to touch it again. I've seen him shirtless plenty of times this summer, but it's a far different experience to see it this way.

He presses a kiss to my lips, pulls away, and says, "I love you too, Li." My heart sores at the words, everything that happened this afternoon forgotten. I move a hand to the back of his neck and kiss him again, pouring every emotion I feel into it and making sure he knows just how much I love him.

———

Easton's fingers trace random patterns on my back, a peaceful touch that has been putting me to sleep for the last hour. "I have to tell you something," Easton whispers in my ear, his lips brushing against the skin before nipping at it. I don't fight the shudder that runs through my body as I turn in his arms to face him.

"What do you have to tell me," I smile.

"Remember at the beginning of the summer when you asked why I was always here for breakfast, and I told you it was more fun than being alone?" I nod, not able to tear my gaze away from the dark eyes staring back at me. "I lied."

I gasp, playfully swatting Easton's bare chest. He laughs, grabbing my hand and entwining our fingers. "What was the real reason?" I smile, not at all mad.

"I had to be around you."

All I can do is smile.

Easton leans forward to kiss the smile on my lips, then says, "I have a present for you."

"You do?" I ask, forgetting for a moment it's my birthday as I lean away from him. He laughs, leaning toward me to kiss my lips once more.

"Yes," he answers. He starts to move away from me, but I grab his wrist and pull him back.

"No," I say, burrowing my head into his chest.

He laughs again, but he maneuvers his arms around my body and squeezes me tight. "Fifteen seconds tops. Don't you want your gift?"

I grumble, and he takes that as a yes. With a kiss to the top of my head, he pulls away again and crawls out of the bed. The only light in the room comes from outside, and it's completely dark now. I see every outline of Easton's naked body, though, and I take it all in as he crosses the room to his backpack. I push up to my forearms, my bedsheets falling down to my stomach. I don't even think about covering up or feeling self conscious when Easton turns around and grins, clearly liking what he sees.

He has a small wrapped box in his hand. He comes back over to the bed and sets it down on the nightstand. He leans down and kisses my lips, and I happily tilt my head back to the right angle. He pulls away all too soon, meets my gaze, and says, "You are so beautiful, Li." I smile. I've been doing a lot of that tonight.

Easton finds his boxers on the floor and slips into them, and I pout. He laughs when he sees me, handing me his T-shirt. I don't miss the way his eyes zone in on the pout, and his next words confirm my thoughts. "Trust me, Li, this is only the beginning." I huff at his words but sit up and begrudgingly take the T-shirt, pulling it over my head. It smells like him.

"I hope you know I'm keeping this."

"I wouldn't expect anything less."

"And I want a sweatshirt."

"You have full access to anything you want from my closet."

I can't help but giggle at his words and fall back onto my pillows.

Easton turns the lamp on the night stand on, grabs the gift, and slides back into the bed next to me. "Here," he says softly, passing me the gift. I take it, smiling at the silver paper and light blue bow. For the most part, it's wrapped better than I would have expected from a teenage boy.

"Did you wrap this?" I tease. Easton grins and kisses me in response. I sigh through my smile. I will never, ever get bored of his kisses. I turn to the gift and gently pull the bow off before tearing the paper. It's a plain white box. I take the top off and gasp, sitting up once again. "East, it's beautiful."

It's a silver necklace with a small pendant, and there are waves and a sun etched into the pendant in a beach scene. I lift it out of the box, careful with touching it. I feel like I'm going to ruin its beauty.

Easton pulls me into his lap and says, "Turn it over." He rests his chin on my shoulder as I do, and I gasp again. There are tiny letters etched into the back of the pendant, and I move it closer to my face to read it.

I'll never let you down, Redding. - E

"East," I whisper, turning to look at him. His face is right there, and I move the hand that's not holding the necklace to cup his cheek. "I love it."

"You do?" he asks, and it may be the first time I've ever seen him look unsure of something.

I nod, pecking his lips. "I do. I really do. You could not have knocked it further out of the park."

In the unchoreographed dance we've perfected, I unclasp the necklace and hold either end of it up so Easton can grab them and clasp it behind my neck. He kisses the skin above where the clasp sits, and I shudder as he wraps his arms around me and pulls me into him, falling back onto the bed. We adjust, and I turn over in his arms, tangling our legs together.

I meet Easton's gaze, and I smile at the sight of his dark eyes staring back at me.

I smile because he's all mine.

CHAPTER THIRTY-EIGHT

THE NEXT MORNING, AFTER A VERY LONG SHOWER WITH Easton, he gives me a very long kiss goodbye, tells me he'll be over in a little bit, and sneaks out the balcony. On my way downstairs, the closer I get to Andy, the more it feels like two magnets rejecting each other.

Groot meets me at the bottom of the stairs, and I give him some extra love since he got kicked out of my room last night. Andy appears in the hallway with a mug in his hands. I stare at him without smiling. I'm still not happy with him. I stand up and walk down the hall, glancing through the open door of the guest room and seeing Andy's things.

I don't say a word as I make my coffee. Andy stands awkwardly next to the island. Neither of us knows how to start this conversation.

Coffee in hand, I walk into the living room. I grab a blanket from the basket and sit down in the corner of the couch, pulling the blanket over my legs. Andy sits on the opposite side of the couch, and Groot hops up between us and rests his head on my legs.

There's so much to talk about between Nate, Ellie, and the

letters to my dad, and I have no idea what to even start with. I take a sip of my coffee to buy some time, and Andy speaks up before I figure it out.

"I'm sorry I didn't tell you about the letters. That I was talking to Dad," he apologizes. I wait for him to continue, staring into my coffee. "I knew how you felt about him. I didn't know how you would react if you found out I was in contact with him and he was back in my life. And I didn't want you to feel like it was Dad and I versus you. No one is versus anyone. I thought I was doing the best thing I could to respect how you felt about Dad. I never intended to hurt you by not telling you."

"I know. I just wish you would have told me," I say quietly, glancing up at him.

Andy sighs, running a hand through his hair before he speaks. "Aliyah, you hated Dad. You would have blown up if you knew I was in contact with him."

"Maybe so," I agree. "But it would have felt better than being lied to for a year."

"I know. I'm sorry."

Neither of us says anything for a few minutes. We sip our coffee in silence, and I scratch Groot's head between his ears.

"Are we okay now?" Andy asks. I look up at him, see the remorse in his blue eyes, and know if he could go back and tell me right away, he would. So yeah, we're okay.

I have one more bone I want to pick with him though before he knows that.

"No. You never wished me a happy birthday."

Andy facepalms. "I didn't text you because I wanted to wish you a happy birthday in person. I still did, and I was hoping I would get the chance." I knew that's exactly what his response would be, and when he follows it with, "Happy birthday, Ali," I smile.

"We're good now," I say, and Andy realizes I played him a little bit but smiles nonetheless.

"Good. Now what the fuck happened this summer? You can't lie anymore; we both know where that gets us." We both chuckle at his lame attempt to joke about the situation.

I explain everything, the story not hurting like it used to. "I figured if I didn't have any friends, I might as well not have any friends at the beach. And staying in Denver seemed like the worst possible thing I could ever do." Andy's facial expressions appropriately match the news I'm finally telling him, and even though it was my choice to not tell him, it feels good he finally knows everything.

"Ali, why didn't you say anything to me?"

I shrug, looking back at my coffee. "My reasons all seem stupid now. I was embarrassed. Humiliated. I didn't want you to know how shitty they all were. I didn't want you to hurt because I was hurting." And then, "You know how stubborn I am."

"Fuck all of that except the part about you being stubborn because it's one of my favorite things about you." It makes me smile as he continues, "You and I have been through more together than most siblings go through in a lifetime. You know I would have stood by your side and backed you up." There's a build up in his voice, similar to how he talked to Nate yesterday but not nearly with the same anger.

"Andy, I know. That's not why I kept it from you. I just...I don't know. I didn't want you to see me all butt hurt about my entire life imploding like it did. I know you would have done anything to help me through that, and don't think for a second I don't know that."

"I would have egged that bastard's house if you asked me to. Actually, maybe I still will." This gets me laughing, and Andy starts laughing too. A thought must cross his mind, though, because he sobers up within seconds. "Shit. I brought them right to your doorstep yesterday." I sober up at the memory of an emotional Ellie and an angry Nate.

"Why did you bring them with?" I ask.

"I had no idea what was going on. Nate's been coming to the house every once and a while this summer to see if you were back. He said he fucked up and he wanted to apologize, but you weren't speaking to him. After I made the plans with Dad to surprise you on your birthday, I asked if he wanted to come and surprise you, too, to make things right. I knew things were rocky with you two, but I had no idea he cheated on you. I thought it was fixable and you just needed some space. If I had known, I would have slammed the door in his face the first time he showed up. And Ellie was a no brainer. I had no idea you weren't talking with her anymore either."

It all makes perfect sense. Nate had always seemed like a good boyfriend; before this summer, neither Andy nor I would have believed he would ever cheat on me. After finding out he cheated on me and lied about it for two months, I'm not surprised he lied about what happened to Andy to make it seem like it wasn't as bad as it was.

My heart does mourn for my friendship with Ellie, though. If I had been confident Nate would never cheat on me, then I was even more confident Ellie would have been there to trash his car right beside me if he did. Not know it happened and not say a word to me about it.

"Well, it is what it is," I shrug, finishing my coffee. I lean forward and set the empty mug down on the coffee table.

"You miss her," Andy observes, and I don't do or say anything. It feels wrong to miss someone who lied to me about something like this. "Have you thought about reaching out to her? Not to make amends, but to get closure?"

I shake my head. I hadn't thought about that, and in the seconds that follow, it sounds like it might actually help me a lot. If Ellie is still in New Haven, I could meet her on the boardwalk, say my piece, listen to her side if I'm in a good mood, and leave. "That's not a bad idea," I respond, and Andy nods before moving on.

"I can't believe he was still trying to get you back," Andy says. His words hold a tiny bit of the anger I saw yesterday, like he can't believe the audacity of my ex.

I snort, "He should have thought about that on spring break," I say. I know I should probably feel some kind of emotion about my ex-boyfriend trying so hard to win me back, but I feel nothing.

He means nothing to me anymore.

"I take it you have absolutely no sympathy for him?" Andy asks.

I scoff, "That's an understatement."

A corner of Andy's mouth lifts up in a teasing smirk, and I know exactly what's coming. "Would it have anything to do with the boy you were *very* close to when we got here yesterday? And I'm assuming the same one who spent the night?"

My cheeks heat up, and I bury my face in my hands as Andy starts laughing. "Oh God," I mutter, thinking about last night. Easton and I weren't loud, but we also had no idea Andy was here. I didn't even think Andy would be staying in the guest room, though putting the pieces together now makes it the obvious answer. I didn't even put it together when I saw his stuff in the guest room on my way down.

How mortifying.

"Don't worry," Andy says through his laughter. "My head-phones and I became well acquainted."

I start laughing with him, still hiding my flaming face beneath my hands. "This is mortifying," I giggle, wiping a tear that escapes my eyes. I lift my face, and Andy's wide, knowing smirk sends me into another fit of laughter.

"So tell me about him," Andy says through his own laughter.

"His name is Easton. He's my best friend. He's the kindest human you will ever meet in your life. And I am head over heels in love with him."

"Well, that's a relief to hear," a new voice says from across the room. Easton's walking in the back door with a big smile on his face. He slides the door shut behind him and kicks off his shoes. At the sight of him and remembering Andy knows exactly what went down between us last night, my cheeks grow red again.

"Oh, God," I say again, laughing into my hands as I rebury my face in them. Groot jumps off the couch to greet Easton, and Easton repays him by stealing his spot on the couch, sitting close enough to me where our legs are touching.

"East, this is Andy," I say, moving my hands to my cheeks so I can look at the two of them but still hide their bright color. "Andy, this is Easton."

In typical Easton fashion, he holds out his hand and says, "It's nice to finally meet you, man. I've heard a lot of things about you. All good, of course."

Andy laughs and shakes his hand in return. "I wish I could say the same, but I first heard about you thirty seconds ago."

Easton makes a joke about that being classic Aliyah, then turns to me, pokes my cheek between two of my fingers, and asks, "What did I miss?"

I debate saying it's nothing now and then telling him later, but I want him to feel the same embarrassment I feel. Plus, I know Andy won't be mad. He looks like a kid on Christmas morning at the sight of me and my bright red face. He'll just poke fun at us until something better comes along.

"Andy stayed at the house last night," I say, hoping it's enough for Easton to get the hint. It takes him a few seconds, but when he realizes what it means, his cheeks become redder than mine. Andy and I burst out laughing as Easton leans over me and buries his face in my shoulder. I remove my hands from my cheeks and wrap them around his shoulders, patting his back as he playfully groans.

I bask in the fact that we can do this now. That we can touch each other as much as we want. *That Easton is mine.*

Andy stands up and grabs both of our empty coffee mugs, walking into the kitchen and setting them in the sink. "Don't worry, kiddos. Your secret's safe with me. Though I would be careful about making sure dad isn't home next time it happens. He may not be as forgiving as I am."

His words are met with another groan from Easton and a middle finger from me. We're all laughing within seconds, though, and I can't help but feel like a large part of my life was put back together.

CHAPTER THIRTY-NINE

THE AIR AROUND ME IS HUMID FROM THE STORM yesterday, and I'm glad I chose to wear a loose sundress to meet Ellie at the boardwalk. I lean against the railing, forearms against the wood as I look out at the ocean.

A view I'm not giving up.

The boardwalk is packed, the throng of tourists not wasting their chance to be at the beach after yesterday's storm. I'm in front of Scoops, and I'm pretty sure the door hasn't closed in the last fifteen minutes due to the steady stream of customers going in and out. Through the window, I see Naomi, Jackie, Fred, and Mandy scooping and sprinkling and handing over bowls and cones like their lives depend on it.

Footsteps approach me, and I'm only able to pinpoint they belong to Ellie because of how cautious they are. She approaches the railing next to me and quietly says, "Hey."

I had no idea if she would still be in town when I unblocked her number and told her to meet me here at three. The text was immediately read, and ten seconds later she responded with *I'll be there.*

"Hey," I say, continuing to stare out at the water.

"Ali...I'm so sorry," Ellie starts, and I look over to see tears already welling in her eyes. "I never meant for things to get this far out of hand."

"How could they not?" I ask.

"I know," Ellie nods, more tears escaping. "I know. I should have told you as soon as it happened. Actually, I should have smacked Nate upside the head first, then called you."

I nod, "You should have."

Ellie nods again, wiping away hoards of tears. "I just...I knew it would absolutely break you, and I didn't want to tell you when we were all still on the trip because I knew how bummed you were about not being able to go. And I wanted to be there to comfort you. But that gave me time to think about it and I knew it would ruin the dynamic of our group and Nate and Sierra should have been the ones to tell you, not me, and I was just—"

"You were just what, Ellie? Stop making excuses."

She pauses for a moment, then says quietly, "I was scared."

"You didn't tell me because you were *scared*? How do you think I felt?"

"Ali, I know!" Ellie sobs. "I know I should have told you, but the longer I didn't, the harder it was to bring it up because I knew you would be mad at me for hiding it from you."

I take a deep breath, because I don't want this to turn into another rage fest like yesterday. I came here for closure. "You threw fourteen years of friendship down the drain because you were scared to tell me my boyfriend cheated on me."

She gulps, and then says again, "I know. I should have told you, but then you blocked all of us and I had no way—"

I shake my head, getting angry that Ellie keeps trying to grasp for excuses, and say, "No. I blocked everyone after I found out. You knew for two months before that, so you had *plenty* of time to tell me."

Ellie takes a deep breath, almost in defeat, and says one more time, "I know."

The world around us comes back into my attention, and I have no idea how I completely tuned out the noise once Ellie got here. It's *loud*. I turn my attention back to the beach and the water, then glance all the way to my house. I want to get back. I want to get back to Easton.

"I know you were hoping I would forgive you," I say quietly, turning my attention back to Ellie as she nods at my words. "And I do. I understand it was hard to say anything. But we will never be friends again." Her face starts to rise at the flicker of hope before falling again. She swallows, I'm sure with a lump in her throat, and nods.

This is probably the last time I will ever see Ellie, and that brings a lump to my throat as well. I have no second guesses about my words, but she was still my best friend for fourteen years, since that very first day of preschool when she found me in tears.

I wipe away one single tear, say, "Thanks for sharing your mom with me," and walk away.

———

I GET A TEXT FROM MY DAD THAT AFTERNOON THAT he's leaving Charleston and we can order take out for dinner. I tell him Andy and I have dinner covered. I have something to tell him, and a home cooked meal feels better for the occasion than a take out pizza.

"So, what are we making for dinner?" I ask Andy and East, putting my phone down next to me on the couch. I'm practically laying on top of Easton, and Andy sits on one of the chairs. The beach was so packed with tourists that none of us felt like braving it, so we've been playing Minecraft all afternoon, trying to see who can build the coolest base.

Well, I am. The boys keep blowing the other one's house up with TNT.

"Spaghetti? Tacos?" Andy suggests.

"Fajitas?" I toss out. "I haven't had them all summer."

"Fajitas," Andy agrees with a nod of his head.

"Let's go," Easton says, moving me to a sitting position so he can get off the couch. He holds out a hand for me and I take it. He puts way too much force into the pull, and I crash into his chest. When he puts his arms around me for a hug, I know he did it on purpose.

This boy.

"You two are insufferable," Andy groans, fake gagging as he gets up from the chair.

"You just wait until it's your turn," I fire back as I slip my sandals on, and that shuts him up about Easton and I.

"Where are we going?" he asks, joining us at the front door.

"Target," Easton and I say at the same time. We look at each other and smile, and I want to kiss him but don't for Andy's sake. I can tell he's thinking the same thing.

After locking the door, the three of us cross the front yards to Easton's truck. Easton opens the passenger door for me and I hop in. Andy slides into the back, buckling into the middle seat. Easton's sitting in the driver's seat, and then we're off.

I start playing music, and Easton and Andy start talking about football. I don't add much to the conversation, but I hang on to every word they say. They've known each other for a matter of hours, but anyone who didn't know they just met would assume they've been friends for years. A warm, bubbly feeling rises in my throat at the two most important people in my life welding together so easily, and I quickly look out the window to hide the lone, happy tear that escapes.

When Dave and my dad walk through the garage door a few hours later, I don't think the house has ever smelled more appetizing. My mouth has been watering for the chicken since it started sizzling on the stove, the combination of spices an addiction I forgot I had. I've forgotten how much I love fajitas.

"Something smells good," Dave grins, sitting down at the

kitchen table. Andy, Easton, and I are all moving around the kitchen working on different tasks. Adding one more person to the mix would only create chaos.

"It tastes even better," Easton replies from his position at the stove, sneaking a piece of chicken. I'm the only one to catch him in the act, and he winks at me. Andy sets the knife he was using to cut the onion and peppers down on the counter to greet my dad. I take over. There's one pepper left and the onion.

My dad has a smile on his face as he sets his duffle down next to the door, and Andy doesn't hesitate to greet him. "Hey, Dad," he says, and they give each other a long hug. I start slicing the pepper, trying and failing to keep the seeds under control.

"How was your flight yesterday?" he asks as they separate.

"Not bad. Accidentally brought along two stowaways," Andy responds, coming back to the kitchen. My dad raises an eyebrow in confusion, and I'm the one to break it.

"I never told Andy about Nate and Ellie. They didn't tell him either and came along to 'surprise me'," I say, handing the knife back to Andy. He resumes cutting the last pepper, avoiding the explosion of seeds.

He frowns, but not at us. "That couldn't have gone well."

"Our little badass handled it like a champ," Andy grins, putting his hands on my shoulders (thankfully the knife is on the counter) and shaking me a little. I smile, removing myself from his grasp to pull the cheese out of the fridge.

"When you have pent up anger for almost three months, it's not that hard," I shrug, finding a bowl to crumble the cheese in. Dave looks lost but doesn't question anything, but I change the subject anyway. "How was Charleston?"

As both dads start talking about the trip and how well the contract went, I crumble the cheese and fight a wide smile as Easton finds every possible excuse to touch me. Leaning over me to grab a paper towel. "Accidentally" leaning against the counter with his body pressed against mine. Brief, secret touches on my waist or any other part of my body. He doesn't waste a single opportunity.

I'm not complaining. Every touch sends me to the moon, and I can't stop staring at his lips and how soon until I can kiss them again.

I zone out as thoughts of last night replay in my mind, and I don't realize I'm past done crumbling the cheese until Easton puts his hands over mine, my fingers still miming the motion. "Easy there, tiger," he murmurs in my ear, his lips brushing against the skin. He's so good at finding the perfect distance away when his words are only for me to hear. It drives me crazy. "Keep zoning out like that and we won't make it through dinner."

A blush rises on my cheeks, a sight that has Easton grinning in satisfaction.

We sit down for dinner a few minutes later, and there's hardly any extra room at the table. Everyone's reaching over everyone to make their plate, so I lean back in my chair and wait for the chaos to die down. It gives me a minute to think about how I want to bring up the conversation with my dad, but thinking about it also brings on a bout of nerves I didn't have before.

When the guys all have their food and are digging in, I make my plate. Easton waits for me to take my first bite before he starts to eat. When I smile across at him, he captures my ankles between his under the table. The skin to skin contact is a relief to the nerves about the conversation, but they create a whole new set that have nothing to do with my dad and everything to do with crawling into a bed with Easton as soon as possible. To distract myself from the warmth tingling between my legs, I turn to my dad sitting next to me.

"I'm going to stay in New Haven," I blurt out, watching his face for any reaction. He stares at me for a few seconds, pauses chewing, and I panic. "If that's okay with you, of course." Another second goes by, and I'm terrified about what he's going to say. Easton's ankles tighten around mine, a gesture that tells me

I've got this. My dad swallows his food, and my mind comes up with a million and one worst case scenarios.

Was one summer with me enough?

Does he not want me here permanently?

Did I read into us rebuilding our relationship this summer too much?

I thought he would love nothing more than for me to move here officially, but maybe I have it all wrong. Maybe I misunderstood all of our conversations and interactions this summer. And if that's the case, it means saying goodbye to Easton right after I thought we would get to be together.

When a huge grin breaks onto my dad's face, I know all my worries are just that: worries. "Are you serious, Aliyah? Of course that's okay with me!" he says. It's the most excited I've ever heard him, and I smile. A wall of relief buries all of the worries until they don't exist anymore.

One glance around the table shows me four ear-to-ear grins, and all I can think is how much I feel at home.

This is my home.

———

AFTER DINNER AND CLEANING UP, EASTON AND DAVE go home, leaving me with a promise from Easton that he'll see me later and a suggestive wink. I know exactly what later entails.

"Well, how about an episode of *Friends*?" my dad suggests.

"Sounds good to me," I smile.

"Can you queue it up? I've got to grab something from my room," he says. I nod, and Andy and I head into the living room as my dad heads down the hall to his bedroom.

"I can't believe you're leaving me," Andy jokes, but there's sadness in his voice. He sits down on the chair, and I curl up in one corner of the couch with the remote. I turn the TV on and maneuver to *Friends*. We're on *The One Where Ross And Rachel*

Take A Break, and I grin. Finally my dad will understand the phrase.

"You know I'll miss you like crazy," I respond softly. My unspoken words of *I need to do this* hang between us. Andy nods, and I know he knows. He's the only person who would keep me in Colorado, and I don't want to spend my last year of high school working my ass off and holing up with my brother. Especially not when the person I'm pretty sure is my soulmate is across the country.

Our dad rejoins us, and he's holding a light green gift bag with white polka dots and sparkly white tissue paper. "Happy birthday, Aliyah," he says, handing the gift bag to me and sitting on the opposite side of the couch. The bag has a bit of weight to it I'm not expecting.

"Oh, thank you," I say, shocked as I set the bag down in my lap. Before this summer, I can't remember the last time my dad actually got me a gift. "You didn't have to—"

"Yes, I did," he says firmly, and more unspoken words fill the air between all of us. *I should have been doing this since you were born.*

I don't say anything as I pull the tissue paper out of the bag and reach in to grab whatever's in the box. The box is smooth to the touch, and I think I might know what it is, but there's no way he got me one. When I lift it out of the bag, though, my guess is very much correct.

My dad got me a brand new iPhone. "Dad," I gasp, whipping my gaze to his.

My mind races with how expensive a new phone is and if he can afford it and if I should even accept this gift. He starts talking before I can make it much further in my thought spiral. "I know you shattered your screen when you got here. At first, I was going to offer to fix it right away, but I knew the chances of you accepting that were zero. After you told me about what happened, I thought getting you a new phone, a fresh start, would be better."

Tears well in my eyes as my dad talks. When he finishes, I set the box and bag on the coffee table and crawl across the couch to give him a hug. I wrap my arms around his neck and say, "Thank you." It's all I need to say and all he needs to hear.

With that fresh start on my mind, I take my previous spot on the couch and press play. I unpackage the new phone as the episode starts, powering it up. The first number I program into it is Easton's, and I send him a text.

Me: *my minecraft base is cooler than yours*

Easton: *Not a chance in hell*

Me: *youre just jealous i actually finished mine instead of it being blown up*

Easton: *How can i be jealous when i get to call you mine*

Me: *i love when you say stuff like that*

Easton: *Get used to it baby*

Easton: *I love you*

Easton: *So much*

Me: *i love you too*

A pillow hits my face, and Andy says, "Are you going to keep texting lover boy or pay attention to the episode? This is a monumental moment."

"ANDY!" I gasp, glancing first at the screen right at Rachel says she needs a break from Ross and then at my dad. His eyebrows are raised with a knowing look at "lover boy."

"It's about time," he grins, and I bury my flaming face in the pillow to suppress the groan.

"Not you too," I say, my words muffled against the fabric. They both start laughing, and I decide the best course of action is to ignore it. Once I feel my face cool down from the embarrassment of my dad knowing about my romantic life, I pull the pillow away from my face and whip it back at Andy. He catches it with ease.

The three of us return our attention back to the screen, but I still sneak more texts to Easton as the episode goes on. We watch the next one too, and I find a new hatred for Ross burning in my gut. When the episode is over, I turn to my dad expectantly. "So? Were Ross and Rachel on a break? It's a very important question."

"Yes, but not the kind of break where you see other people. They clearly had a lot more to work through with their relationship."

He meets my grin with one of his own as I say, "You pass with flying colors."

CHAPTER FORTY

"EAST!" I SQUEAL, LUNGING ACROSS MY BED TO GRAB MY sundress from his grasp, but he holds it out of reach again. My body collides with his, and he effortlessly guides us to fall back on the bed with me on top of him. The dress ends up on the ground, and Easton's rolling us over so he's hovering over me.

"I like you much better like this," he says, trailing kisses from the corner of my lips, down my jawline, neck, collarbone, and finally on the curve of my breast. I close my eyes and bury my fingers in his hair, my head fully relaxing into the pillows. Easton stops his trail where my bikini begins. I open my eyes as he's popping his head up, a wicked look in his eyes.

"No," I giggle, gently pushing his head, and therefore his body, away so I can slip out from under him. I pick up my discarded dress and finally slip into it as Easton moves to sit on the edge of my bed, pulling me in between his legs. I wrap my arms loosely around his neck, my chest fluttering at the smile he's giving.

I still can't believe he's all mine.

"Did I ever tell you how much I love your eyes?" I whisper, and his dark eyes light up at my words.

"Did I ever tell you how much I love *your* eyes?" he whispers back, and I don't wait any longer.

I lean forward and press my lips to his, getting lost in him. Easton's grip tightens on my hips, and I move my hands to his jaw, fingers splayed on his cheeks and neck. His hands slide to my bare thighs and re-grip my hips, this time under my dress. "Easton," I giggle against his lips, "I already said no. We're running late as it is. Everyone is already there."

"They can wait. This is more important," is his answer.

I continue to giggle as we kiss, and Easton doesn't push things any further. He'll tease all he wants, but he never pushes, never makes me feel like we have to do anything. I find the strength in me to pull away from his mouth, stepping out of his grasp so I don't dive right back into him.

"Come on," I say, holding out my hand and laughing as he groans. He grabs my hand, and I pull him out my bedroom door.

"You look gorgeous," he says as we head downstairs.

"You always tell me I look gorgeous, even when I roll out of bed."

"Because it's true," he grins, squeezing my hand. "You're always gorgeous, even when you look like a little rat."

We burst out laughing as we walk into the kitchen, passing my dad in the living room.

"Are you two heading out?" he asks, looking up from his book.

"Yeah," I nod, not bothering with shoes at all. We're going down to the beach; shoes are absolutely pointless.

"Be safe," he says, and I smile.

"We always are, Mr. Redding," Easton says. "I promise to bring her back in one piece." He even adds a salute. My dad laughs.

"Bye Dad, love you!" I say as Easton slides open the back door, realizing how easily the words slip out.

I see his face morph into brief surprise, but a grin quickly replaces it. He holds up his hand as we leave, calling out, "Love you too," as Easton closes the door.

He doesn't waste a second in capturing my hand in his as we start the short walk down to the sand. I see the flames in the distance, as well as a crowd of people lingering. Some are splashing in the water, and the cloudless skies mean the moon shines bright over the entire scene. We're still too far to see who is who, but I realize how excited I am to go hang out with our friends.

My friends.

I still can't grasp how I came to New Haven almost three months ago adamant to not make any friends. All I wanted to do was work and hang out by myself at the beach. I had no idea how curable this place would be. I made friends, I started fixing my relationship with my dad, and I met Easton. Speaking of—

I stand up on my toes and press my lips to his cheek.

"What was that for?" he asks, turning his dark gaze to me. "Not that you ever need a reason to kiss me. Just to make that clear."

A laugh escapes my mouth, and I say, "Thank you for not letting me down this summer."

Easton doesn't say anything at first, but the hand squeeze and forehead kiss are all I need. The forehead kiss makes me weak in the knees, and I lean into Easton for support. He presses another kiss into my hair, then whispers, "I'll never let you down, Li. Never, ever, ever."

I think about the necklace he got me for my birthday, the one I've hardly taken off since last week. I reach up to touch it with my free hand, like it's proof this is all real. "I know," I say, tilting my head up so I'm looking directly up at him. His lips come to me for a third kiss, this time meeting my lips. It's short, sweet, and conveys everything he's feeling right now. We keep walking hand in hand, the images of our friends getting closer.

"Remind me to give you my jersey tomorrow if I forget,"

Easton says, smiling down at me. "I need my girl representing my number at the game." The first game of their season is tomorrow night, and I'm more than happy to go and support my boyfriend.

My boyfriend.

I can't help the wide grin that breaks across my face. I don't know if it's from the thought of wearing his jersey or hearing him call me his girl or the adoring look in his eyes. Probably from all three, if I'm being honest. "Okay," I say.

We reach the fire and find Gabe and Josie first. They're each holding a can of shitty beer and arguing about who would win in a fight: Captain Marvel or Scarlet Witch. Gabe sees us first, and with a big gesture of his hands, he says, "Thank God. More opinions. Please tell Josie she's wrong and Captain Marvel would win that fight."

"Absolutely not, man," Easton laughs, patting Gabe on the back in greeting. "Scarlet Witch is taking that win. She almost obliterated Thanos without laying a finger on him."

"Yeah, but Captain Marvel could probably take whatever power Scarlet Witch uses on her and brush it off like a speck of dust. You saw the way she flew right through the ship and brought it to the ground. Aliyah?"

I shrug and side with East and Josie, saying, "Sorry, dude, but they're right. Captain Marvel is strong, and that fight would last for days, but Scarlet Witch is walking away in the end. Thanos couldn't get close enough to throw her around like a ragdoll."

Gabe huffs, "Y'all are Captain Marvel haters."

"Looks like you're out of luck, babe," Josie teases, her words not quite slurring together but taking on a very relaxed tone. She's tipsy. She kisses Gabe on the cheek before looping her arm through mine and saying, "Let's go find Ev."

She's pulling me away and my hand falls out of Easton's. I meet his gaze and smile, puckering my lips and giving him an air kiss as Josie drags me through the sand. "Beer first," I say to her, hunting the area for where the drinks are. When I locate them, Ev happens to also be there. I turn Josie in that direction.

"So, you and Easton," she says to me as we reach Ev. She's wiggling her eyebrows up and down, and I don't think her knowing smirk has ever been more knowing. "I saw that hand holding. You can't skirt around it anymore."

"Wait a second. Hand holding?" Ev asks, handing me a beer. I crack it open and take a sip, ignoring the piss taste as it runs down my throat. The disgusting beer is part of the experience just as much as the fire is.

"Yes, hand holding," Josie leers.

"Um, spill!" Ev says excitedly. "Josie's right. There's no dodging that."

"Okay," I laugh. "Yeah, we're together now."

"How?"

"When?"

I'm not sure who asks what.

"My birthday last week." I tell them the story of Easton and I making cupcakes, Nate and Ellie surprising me with Andy, and the events that followed until Easton snuck into my room. I spare them the details of that night, but they get the gist.

"I'm happy for you," Ev says. "Both of you."

"I'm glad something was finally done about all of that tension. I was starting to suffocate," Josie says, and the three of us are laughing again.

"What happened to not wanting to make a move?" Ev asks. "You were so intent on it last time we talked about it."

I shrug, my smile giving me away. "There was no way I couldn't."

Both girls see my smiles, and Ev says, "I'm glad you finally came to your senses."

"Me too," I laugh, then remembering another thing I wanted to tell them, "Oh, also. Do you two want to go back-to-school shopping this weekend? I haven't even started."

"What do you mean?" Josie asks. "I thought you were going to be in Colorado."

I shake my head, warmth filling me as both girls realize what I'm saying and smile. "Are you staying in New Haven?" Ev gasps, and I nod.

"Of course I am," I say, searching the beach and meeting the gaze of exactly who I was looking for. I don't break the gaze as I say to the girls, "How was I supposed to leave that behind?" I don't have to see them to know they know exactly who I'm talking about. Easton smiles at me from across the fire, and my stomach bubbles with every happy emotion. He starts walking around the fire toward me.

I turn back to Ev and Josie, and they're both shaking their heads at me with wide, wide grins. "What?" I ask, but giggling because it obviously has something to do with Easton and I love that boy with my whole entire heart and then some.

"You are so whipped," Josie says.

"And you've got that boy wrapped so tight around your finger," Ev adds.

"Correct to both, ladies," Easton says, appearing beside me. Shirtless. God, that chest could shatter diamonds. "And now, if you don't mind, I've got a dare to complete to prove it."

Before I realize what's happening, Easton picks me up and holds me over his shoulder. "Easton!" I gasp, steadying myself with my hands on his bare back. The muscles react to my touch with a shudder. "What—don't you dare!" I shriek. I hear and see Ev and Josie laugh. Gabe and Logan join their side, laughing right along with them.

Looks like none of my friends are helping.

"Sorry baby," Easton says, not the least bit sorry. "Duty calls."

"What duty?" I laugh, knowing whatever it is pointless to fight against. The sound of the tide gets louder as we get closer to it.

"A dare that you're whipped. Can't back down."

"No. I suppose you can't," I sigh, but I don't plan on letting this go easily. "But don't forget, I also have you wrapped around my finger." I'm able to contort my body enough to land my lips on his neck, and he sucks in a breath of air at the touch.

"You play dirty," he says, his voice taking on a husky tone. He takes the first steps into the water.

"Must be because I'm whipped," I whisper, just loud enough for him to hear. With my hands on his back, I feel the way his muscles tense with a shiver at my words, and I smirk. It's the last thing I do before Easton's hands grip my waist, lift me off his shoulder, and toss me into the ocean.

The water is cold as it surrounds my skin, and my feet quickly find the sand so I can stand up. I break the surface and hear a laughing Easton. He's standing right in front of me, and my revenge makes me forget about the cold. I launch myself at him with no hesitation. He's not quick enough to brace himself for the fall, but he does manage to take me down with him.

I'm under water and then above water, still tight in Easton's hold. We're both laughing, and I turn away from him slightly to let the water drain out of my nose. I don't need to get snot all over his bare chest right now, whipped or not. "I'm so getting you back for that," I say once I turn back to him. "You'll never see me coming." I realize my mistake of words only after I've said them.

His dirty response has a gasp of laughter escaping my mouth, soon smothered by a kiss. I pull away still laughing. "How did I not know how dirty minded you are until *after* we got together?"

"One of my many features for your eyes only," he responds.

"Or ears."

"Smartass."

"You love me."

"That I do," Easton smiles, and then he's kissing me again as his grip on the backs of my thighs tightens. I snake my hands up his chest, intense satisfaction running through my veins at each shiver that racks through his body. He pulls away for a moment to whisper my favorite words, lips still brushing against mine the whole time.

"I love you, Aliyah Redding."

ACKNOWLEDGEMENT

And just like that, I published my first book.

This has by far been when one of coolest things I have ever experienced. I started writing this book on my phone in a hotel room in Florida, and four and a half years later, I've started my own publishing company and am a published author. Never would I have thought when I typed those first words that this is what it would become and this is where I would be, but I wouldn't have it any other way.

It took a small village to bring this story to life. Small but mighty. My mom, for reading the very first draft and immediately demanding a sequel (sorry Mom, still not happening). She's been my cheerleader since day one and never failed to ask me when she'll get to read this book again. To my friends who read this book in the beginning stages—Mara, Payton, thank you for hyping me up and making sure this story would actually be a story one day. And Mara, thank you for telling me to knock it off with the messy buns—I didn't realize until you pointed it out. You three put up with "Our Summer" in its early, messy stages, and I'm pretty thankful for that.

To my editor, Laura, words will never be able to express how much I appreciate the time, energy, and thought you put into "Our Summer". The random phone calls for me to talk through a new idea and process what needs to stay and what needs to go made all of this possible, but none of it would have been possible without you. I can't wait to return the favor.

Graicee, thank you for the unbelievably amazing cover! I am

still not over how perfect it is, and I will forever keep staring at it with a smile on my face because of that. You blew it out of the park, and I know I keep saying things like that, but you deserve to hear it.

And Jack, thank you for being my person. I love you.

www.ingramcontent.com/pod-product-compliance
Lightning Source LLC
Chambersburg PA
CBHW010532100726
47903CB00011B/2987